GUN CRAZY

A True Tale Of Murder And Justice In Texas

HAMILTON BOOKER

&

ANN GADDIS

EAKIN PRESS
AUSTIN, TEXAS

COVER DESIGN: COCO CATES

FIRST EDITION

Copyright © 1995
By Hamilton Booker & Ann Gaddis

Manufactured in the United States of America
By Eakin Press
A Division of Sunbelt Media, Inc.
Austin, Texas

ALL RIGHTS RESERVED. No part of this book may be reproduced in any form without written permission from the publisher, except for brief passages included in a review appearing in a newspaper or magazine.

ISBN 1-57168-024-1

2   3   4   5   6   7   8   9   0

Cover Design: Coco Cates

Contents

I	Shameful Murder	1
II	The Killers	23
III	Aid For Edmund	51
IV	Darwin's Dream	80
V	Texas v. Tommy and Andy	105
VI	He's Just Evil	131
VII	Hidden Serpents	159
VIII	The Defense	185
IX	The Girlfriends	208
X	The End	234
Epilogue		254
Photo Section		257
Appendix		261

Chapter I

Shameful Murder

JUST BEFORE SUNSET one day in the spring of 1992, two sheriff's patrol cars raced north on Texas State Highway 55. They crossed a bridge at Cedar Creek and pulled off the pavement. There was an ambulance parked off of the roadway, and its Emergency Medical Service crew was waiting outside. The odor of hot engines and electronic gear engulfed a crewman as he broke away from the group and walked quickly up to the lead patrol car and got in. The cruisers turned off the highway and sped down an unpaved road. The units moved almost recklessly on the dirt road as if barely under control. There was no time to waste. A murder had been reported at a nearby ranch. It was seven P.M.

The deputies turned left again onto another dirt road. There had been just enough rain to dampen the caliche roadbed so they left no telltale dust plume. Overhead the sky was still blue with waning daylight, but along the road it was dark and gloomy. The cars raced along the north side of a wide canyon covered with scrub oak and cedar trees, at its bottom ran the creek.

The deputies were not running code three. No lights flashed, no sirens blared, but they were in a hurry. The deputy in the lead car was a big man with a dark, well-trimmed mustache.

His hair was sprinkled with grey. He wore his uniform exceedingly well. His name was improbably, Buck Pruitt. He was imposing and looked every bit a Texas lawman. He drove with self-assurance, if not self-importance, down the rough back road. The insignia on the side of his patrol car identified him as a Real (pronounced as in Spanish, as Ray-all) County Deputy Sheriff. He was out of his jurisdiction here in neighboring Edwards County, but he was responding to an emergency.

Jimmy Baxter from Camp Wood directed Buck from the passenger seat. Baxter was a part-time EMS technician and undertaker. In the patrol car behind them, Edwards County Sheriff's Deputy Wayne Woods followed. He took law enforcement every bit as seriously as Buck, but without quite the same imposing presence. Woods, nonetheless, worried about what and who they would find at the ranch. He was in his proper jurisdiction. Buck just got to the turnoff first.

No cop likes the prospect of barreling onto a scene of violence. There is always the threat of a gunfight lurking in the background. It is one thing to contemplate in the abstract but another to face it for real. The vision of some half-crazed felon whipping out a pistol and pulling the trigger is disquieting. If the situation came to that, Woods knew he probably would not even think but just react. The sweating came later, after it was over, if he were lucky. Facing down determined gunmen was a rare event; still it happened. Usually lawmen just clean up the mess, take reports, make measurements, and fill out reports. They essentially react to crime. Nonetheless, a cop automatically gets the respect paid to anyone armed and the authority that comes with the badge. In return, he must confront situations like this.

They headed to the Cedar Creek Ranch, also known as the James Ranch, five miles from Highway 55. The two drivers plunged their cars with practiced ease across a low-water crossing, slicing through the inch or so of creek water. They had been doing it for years. Each car hit the water at just the right speed to cross quickly but without stalling the engine, a humiliation to be avoided right now. They scrambled up and down a series of small limestone hills, their big V-8 police special engines straining to maintain traction on the caliche roadbed. They reforded the creek, climbed the last hill, and ran down the other side toward a third creek crossing. On the other side of the water a crushed limestone driveway led up to a complex of ranch buildings just visible in the gloomy twilight. The house itself was shaded by trees and dimly lighted. Buck had been on the radio throughout the drive making arrangements and barking orders. He knew the EMS team was still waiting, and a slew of other lawmen were arriving back on the highway. Each one of them was just itching to get into the act.

Buck wanted to be first on the scene. He knew Woods should have been in the lead and in command, but Buck was used to deference. He was every bit an alpha male, the leader of any pack he came upon. Buck sought mightily to take charge of any task at hand. He radioed the ambulance crew and told them to wait at the highway.

"We didn't want to get them in a bad situation," he later explained.

Buck roared up the driveway and stopped his patrol car just at the edge of the yard. He scanned the scene and immediately spotted a body lying facedown near the ranch house's back door. He told Baxter to stay in the car as he carefully got out. Woods joined him and also spotted the body. They looked at each other. The killers could still be around. They heard voices coming from inside the house. They unsnapped their holster straps and armed themselves.

The lawmen approached the house in a loose skirmish formation, Buck in front, Woods slightly behind and to the right. Both were alert and ready for anything. The pupils of their eyes were wide open under the effects of adrenaline. It was the combat rush, and no drug in the world was quite like it. Their senses were about as fully "on" as they would ever be in their lives. As they approached the body, they realized there was something odd about the voices they heard. Canned laughter rolled across the lawn. It was a television playing in the house. The back door of a renovated log cabin, one of the main ranch buildings, was open. It was a spooky scene. The TV babbled on, yet, it was strangely quiet around the house.

There was an aura of awfulness, something police expect at murder scenes. It was not the awfulness of horror. Police encountered dead bodies all the time; rather it was the awfulness of pathos. There is very little romantic about murder. The crime usually inspires moral disgust. Untimely death is disturbing to the living. As the two lawmen approached the body, they could see a middle-aged male dressed in casual outdoor clothing lying facedown, his hands clutched underneath him.

Buck knelt down and touched the man's neck. There was no pulse, and the skin seemed ice cold. He could see clotted blood on the neck and back, but, oddly, there was not much of it. Buck noticed small holes in the man's shirt. No doubt about it. The victim had been shot many times and had been dead for quite a while. Buck relaxed slightly. It was doubtful his killers were anywhere near. He told Woods to relax but to carefully search the grounds. Buck recognized the victim but did not personally know him. The man owned the ranch.

"It's Edmund James," he announced and turned back toward the patrol car to report in.

On the last evening of his life, April 8, 1992, Edmund James had good reason to feel at peace with his world. It was a grandly pleasant Texas spring evening. Edmund cut limes in his kitchen with two Labrador retrievers and the television as his only companions. He was content. He was wealthy, loved, and lived a life of his own choosing. Edmund inspired devoted friendship from almost everyone who knew him. His accomplishments, perhaps modest by more aggressive standards, were immensely satisfying to him.

Edmund's approaching death was needless and stupid. His killers were neither hardened street punks, ruthless gang bangers, nor murderously bored rich kids. They came from a nearby small town and had apparently never committed a serious crime before. To this day, they do not have sufficient insight to explain why they did it.

Their crime had more to do with Dostoyevsky's dark vision of our times, a century of increasingly nihilistic anarchy. The young men who killed Edmund had never heard of DaDa or existentialism. They would not know a Cubist if they tripped over one. They had never even heard the word "nihilist." They did not personally hate Edmund. These killers had no political agenda. They harbored no extravagant grudge against him. They simply wanted to kill someone to see what it was like. The young men felt an urge and acted on it. They thought Edmund would be an easy target. He was.

While their crime was shabby and pointless, their trials say much about our legal system's struggle to maintain constitutional rights in a disintegrating society. The old, much ridiculed, inner restraints, once called "common decency," woven into our personalities by religion and family are fast disappearing. In their place, we have only a judicial system to formally protect us. Just how far the criminal justice system and its courts can go to fulfill this role is anyone's guess. Our legal system, encrusted with assumptions and characteristics common to another era, strains to cope with an onslaught of modern lawlessness.

Besides the crime and the subsequent trials, this is the story of an amazing man, virtually poor and ill-educated, who mobilized astonishing inner resources to save his son. It is also the story of a small town attorney who desperately defended his client against the double threat of a wealthy family's wrath and the polished skills of a famous Texas lawyer.

At forty-four, Edmund James was handsome. He was in excellent health partly because he religiously combated middle age with exercise. He was of medium height with curly brown hair. Edmund was soft-spoken and well-educated. He lived an outdoor life on his family's ranch located amid the splendid landscapes of Central Texas. "Robustly avuncular" would have been an excellent short description of him. Edmund's vices were few, if any, and no one had anything scandalous to say about him. On the contrary, friends and acquaintances routinely praised his character.

He was worth a few million dollars, but lived simply. He had never married but had plenty of lady friends. His photograph albums chronicled his occasional participation in the social life of the San Antonio elite. Edmund, although slightly eccentric and reclusive, elicited a fiercely affectionate loyalty from his family and friends. People simply loved Edmund.

He had, in a sense, renounced his birthright by choosing to live on his family's ranch. He could have had an elegant life in San Antonio high society, a very exclusive world entered only by birth. Edmund had the right stuff: old money, intelligence, and good looks. He was the grandson of C. H. Guenther, founder of Pioneer Flour Mills. Edmund was also related to the founder of a well-known regional oil company. He was a direct descendant of John James who had surveyed early Texas. In short, his family was not only rich and powerful, they were historic.

He belonged to the Order of the Alamo and The German Club, organizations impossible to just join, members had to be born into them. Edmund was an honest-to-God scion and grew up in a world cushioned by subtle privileges taken for granted by those who enjoy them: debutantes, Fiesta balls, old family ranches, and association with other "to the manor born" families. It is a polite society, still well-graced with southern charms. Personal honor is given and expected. It grants a life well-shielded from the "new" San Antonio characterized by real estate hustlers allied with young Hispanic politicians, glitzy city hall consultants, and cynical businessmen. James's family did not deal in prime real estate — they owned it. Edmund's life was the stuff of best-selling novels. It was a life journalists scrutinize in hopes of scandal, while social editors lavishly chronicled every available detail. Edmund grew up in that social stratum which produces gentlemen of the highest order, insufferable bores, and drunks galore. Edmund was a gentleman, the best of the type.

For wealthy San Antonians, having a ranch was one thing; there were plenty around. The difference in status was having a family ranch handed down through a couple of generations. Old families made careful, if not elaborate, arrangements to insure ranches were not broken up through inheritance. One level up in status was having a family ranch which one could afford to maintain. That is real class, the top of the heap. The alliance of the James family and Pioneer Flour Mills insured that the Cedar Creek Ranch was such a desirable ranch.

Edmund did not particularly want the social life in San Antonio; instead, he chose to withdraw to the ranch. His self-imposed isolation was not absolute. He "came into town" quite often, but he did not remain for long. He was not angry, rebellious, or bitter. Edmund James was a romantic. He passionately loved the ranch — and with good reason. It was simply beautiful. Hidden away in the best part of the Hill Country, it made more sense to him than the modern urban world. Cedar Creek Ranch had been in his family since the early 1900s. His attachment was such that, upon graduating from Trinity University, he had "taken it upon himself to take care of it," as his nephew put it. "He didn't like to leave it very much. He felt like it was a part of him . . . "

The ranch sits a few miles out of Barksdale, Texas, covering more than 19,600 acres. The ranch houses were built on an expanse of alluvial soil deposited on a creek bed. Back in 1876, Lafayette M. Pellen bought a block of land farther down Cedar Creek and built a house. Part of the land became the town of Barksdale. The James Ranch, farther west up the creek, is five or six miles from the town. It has two main houses, a huge garage, and a couple of outbuildings, surrounded by flourishing green lawns. The gently sloping canyon walls are thickly covered with cedar trees and scrub oak. Wild deer graze on the lawns in the cool mornings (if the dogs are in the house), and raccoons make nightly raids on any carelessly stored refuse. There are fish in the creek and birds everywhere; in short, wildlife abounds.

From a high vantage, Nueces Canyon appears to guard the southwestern approaches to the Edwards Plateau, which includes the Texas Hill Country. It is awesomely seductive land, sort of a country within a country, having a wild beauty found nowhere else in Texas and few places in the world. Compact deep valleys guide splendid rivers over limestone beds. Stubby trees cover the steep hills, and tall cypress line the rivers. The landscapes remind knowledgeable visitors of Greece, parts of Africa, or even the Holy Land as it must have been before deforestation. The land has a decidedly Mediterranean quality despite the lack of a nearby sea.

The plateau is a huge expanse of uplifted layered limestone stretching out to West Texas. The Hill Country is on its eastern side and is roughly in the shape of Australia. It sits slightly off center to the geographical heart of Texas. The Hill Country runs about 100 miles north and south and 170 miles, at its widest, from east to west. Almost due west is the town of Del Rio, the Rio Grande River, and the Mexican border. San Antonio dominates the southern flank with Uvalde to the west. Farther around, at the two o'clock position, is the state capital, Austin. Besides recreation, natural beauty and limestone for construction, the Hill Country provides water. It hides vast aquifers underneath it which supply water to the entire region. A recent study showed the Edwards Aquifer holds more water than all of the surface lakes in Texas combined.

In the ancient past, the whole area was an inland arm of the ocean. Layer upon layer of limestone slowly built up from the dead bodies of tiny sea creatures. The rocks are chocked full of fossils and even dinosaur tracks in some locations. Then a bit of geological drama lifted it up. Streams and creeks began to carve the rugged hills. Deep in its aquifers there are small blind shrimp and catfish trapped when the seas retreated, still surviving after uncounted millennia. Up top the soil is thin and supporting only scrubby trees and shrubs, but the rivers are clean and inviting. Wild deer, pigs, and other game prosper in the woods. The temperatures are usually ten to fifteen degrees cooler than the hot cities of the plains. Rainfall quickly runs off toward the Gulf of Mexico and would leave the land arid if not for aquifers. They are like huge underground stone sponges. They slowly feed water back as springs.

The Hill Country has a "place magic." Once having seen it, people fall in love and want to live there; people who live there do not want to leave. Before Anglo settlers came, American Indians used the land. That is the problem; everyone wants a piece of it. Environmental groups are constantly fighting off ravenous developers with grandiose schemes. For the most part, the developers just nibble around the edges, staying close to San Antonio and Austin. Up on the plateau, ranchers and townsfolk are more sanguine about development. They need the income.

To those who know it well, the Hill Country holds endless delights: yet, it surrenders a living only reluctantly. The soil is so thin that in some places it is just an inch thick. Cattle raising is hard on the land and supplementary feeding is usually necessary. Sheep raising only takes land owners so far because of the peculiar prejudice in Texas against lamb. When it is available in the stores, it is expensive.

Once the exclusive hunting grounds for the Comanche and Apache tribes, the Hill Country is better suited to hunting and gathering than agriculture. It is not a kind place to small land holders. The per acre productivity is low. By its very nature, the country favors large operations, mostly cattle, sheep, or goats. What is worse, these enterprises are more expensive and chancy than in the past. Many ranchers have given up and stocked their land with exotic African game for big city trophy hunters much to the outrage of animal rights groups. The imports do very well. Other ranchers now keep herds of ostriches and emus attempting to spawn a new industry (a breeding male ostrich can bring $17,000 or more at auction.) No one has quite figured out what to do with them, except make excellent cowboy boots out of their hides.

The ranchers are like medieval barons relying on Mexican manual labor for the day-to-day operations. There is little economic room for poor whites to prosper. In days gone by, many people cut cedar trees for posts and roofing to make ends meet. Even today in high schools all over the Hill Country, "cedar hacker" or "cedar chopper" are pejorative terms. The early settlers were fiercely independent freeholders, but over the years the nature of the land forced consolidation. In the northern parts of the plateau, German immigrants settled into tidy self-sufficient farms and ranches along the fertile Pedernales River valley. Proud and answering to no one, they established prosperous communities like Fredericksburg, New Braunfels, and Harper. Many refused to support the Confederacy during the Civil War and suffered retaliation. During World War I, the anti-German hysteria sparked more persecution, but they refused to Anglicize their names and gave up their language and customs slowly. To this day, there are old folks who were brought up speaking German as a first language.

In the southwestern part of the Hill Country, around Camp Wood, Barksdale and Leaky, there is an almost Appalachian flavor. The towns are smaller and poorer. The townsfolk survive by providing services for surrounding ranches, touching their caps respectfully as the ranchers glide by in their new extended cab pickups.

The James Ranch is located here. The two nearest towns, Camp Wood and Barksdale, are on State Highway 55, which runs almost due north and south. To the north is Rocksprings, county seat of Edwards County. High on the plateau, Rocksprings is flatter and dryer. It is famous for two things: wild thunderstorms which form up over it and move south, off the plateau and for generous federal subsidies on the production of mohair, the fine coat of Angora goats. The fleece was considered vital to national security in the 1940s, and the subsidies lingered on into 1990s, a legacy of President Lyndon B. Johnson. They were recently cut back.

Down to the south is Barksdale, the only other town in the county. A couple of miles away, south on 55, sits the somewhat gloomy little town of Camp Wood. It marks the border between Edwards and Real Counties.

Edmund James, although called "rancher" by the newspapers, was not really a part of the established ranching gentry. He owned forty percent of the ranch, but for years his family leased out most of the land to real cattle raisers. The only domestic animals directly in James' care were the two playful Labrador retrievers. James' life revolved around other activities, far from cattle raising or punching goats; activities peculiar to him and immensely satisfying.

He had retained his place on the board of directors of Pioneer Flour Mills but discharged those duties mostly by telephone and home computer. He even kept a pleasant house in San Antonio. His main occupation was providing what can only be described as an ecological resort for friends and family. The ranch houses were really as much for guests as for Edmund.

The most noticeable building visitors encounter when coming up the driveway from the creek is a renovated log cabin. It houses the kitchen and combination dining room and den. When facing the kitchen, the creek is to the right, below a well-kept lawn. To the left are utility buildings for storage, a wood working shop, tool sheds, an office, and a small game room. Further back to the left is a huge three-vehicle garage. Near the driveway is a place for large campfires and outdoor cooking. A covered walkway links the log cabin kitchen to a two-story main house. Upstairs is Edmund's bedroom, which looks out over the front and side yards. The creek curves around both views in the background. Downstairs there are two wings connected by a living room, a hall, and a second more formal dining room. Each wing has a sort of dormitory arrangement with about sixteen beds. Hideaway beds are available throughout the house and add extra capacity. The James Ranch could easily accommodate twenty-five to thirty people at a time. Most visitors would come out to join Edmund in his peculiar passion — paintball war games.

Acres of ranch land were set aside for mock combat. Edmund filled storerooms with the not inexpensive, but necessary equipment: helmets complete with elaborate protective visors, camouflage clothing, boots, gloves and, most impressive, paintball guns. These guns are not cheap toys but sophisticated devices using compressed gas to fire marble-sized, soft, plastic balls filled with brightly colored paint. The more expensive paintball guns feature large magazines and automatic fire. His storerooms looked like the armory for some secret army.

Actually there was nothing sinister about it; rather, it was just fun and games for big boys. The idea behind paintball war is to ambush your opponent and splatter him with a hail of paint balls. Once marked, the victim is out of the game. The various games consist of stalking individuals, team ambushes or even full-scale assaults on fortified positions. In any case, hits on players are marked by bright day-glow splotches which eliminate disputes over who was hit. The casualties get to sit around drinking Coca Cola while they watch the action.

Paintball war gaming caught on around the world mostly among the monied upper classes. It was, at first, a rich boy's game. Then desk-bound lawyers and accountants began taking to the woods stalking each other or catching opponents in elaborate ambuscades. During the 1980s, paintball wars spread. Playing paintball war is strenuous, demanding and, above all, fun. The intense concentration of mock combat, the careful application of instinct and skill, and the elaborate tactics of the hunt are addictive. It makes for immensely satisfying comradery at the end of a day's play.

Edmund loved it.

He filled his personal calendar with scheduled "paintwars," and friends from all walks of life, business, family, old college buddies and even military personnel, would come for two or three days of yahoo shoot-outs. But Edmund also had other duties including family obligations which he took very seriously.

He passionately loved the land above everything else. At his funeral, one friend told this story about Edmund. Once a guest on a scuba expedition in a local river found ancient bear claws back up in a cave. He brought the trophy to Edmund who praised the find. Later after the guest had left, Edmund backtracked and carefully returned the claws. Everyone who knew him would immediately nod when told the story saying "That was Edmund."

He knew natural balances must be maintained. He guided family friends and guest hunters through deer, wild turkey, and dove seasons on the ranch. However, he did not condone abuses. Back in the mid-1980s Edmund cancelled contracts on over 8,000 acres of deer leases in the western sections of the ranch. The hunters had provoked game wardens once too often with violations of the rules. Edmund did not tolerate that kind of behavior. Shutting down the hunting leases meant a loss of income, but Edmund scrupulously observed state regulations.

Hunting did not bother him. He believed the principles of range management were sacrosanct. Like most Central Texans, Edmund knew very well what happened to uncontrolled deer populations. During bad times, particularly drought, starving animals stumble into human habitations in a desperate quest for food. The deer die off in hundreds. Even in good times, the deer population of Texas easily exceeds the human. The herds must be culled, and Edmund managed the ranch's hunts with skill and wisdom.

In summer, James led his guests in rock climbing, fishing and scuba diving in local rivers, motorcycling, bicycle jaunts, hiking, and target shooting. When he could find a partner, Edmund would work out with fencing foils. In the evenings there were cookouts, barbecues, and long chat sessions around a campfire. Edmund stocked his shelves with games, an extensive library of history books and a collection of movie videos (including just a couple of mildly sexy ones for older guests). He was well-prepared for rainy days. He had two VCRs and a big screen TV in the dining room where guests gathered to watch sports or movies. He had stereo equipment to play music. Edmund even had an air-conditioned room chocked full of video arcade games. No wonder one nephew said kids "loved" to visit Uncle Edmund.

It was a paradise guaranteed to bring out the wide-eyed kid in anybody, a year-round summer camp, an eternal romp in the woods. It was great fun, but it sure as hell wasn't ranching. Most local ranchers who knew of him would just shake their heads at the antics of the rich.

Edmund did not keep a staff on the ranch. No foreman or servants lived nearby. Edmund lived alone. He hired teenagers to do summer jobs around the ranch. It was a long standing tradition. One of them, Michael R. McCoy flew back from across the Pacific Ocean to testify at two of the trials. He was serving as a combat pilot with the U.S. Air Force, stationed in Korea. He had known and worked for James for years.

"I was hired by Mr. James when I was fifteen years old . . . He was looking for some teenagers to hire as general laborers. I continued to work for him for seven summers. He had projects like making hunting roads, replacing water lines, fixing fences, clearing brush, chain-sawing trees, and stuff like that.

"Usually during the summertime when I worked there we had lots of visitors come out on weekends, sometimes during the week. During the winter season we always had people come to hunt during deer season. Then there would be a lull between the end of deer season and spring.

"He would work with us. He would drive the bulldozer, dump truck, whatever. He was our supervisor on all of the work we did. During the lull times when I would speak with him, he had little projects he was working on like redoing tanks or fixing up little segments of road, or surveying for roads, painting the house, et cetera."

Still, paintwars were the centerpiece, the theme of the ranch. Edmund kept meticulous records of the games. He listed the names of players, the rosters of teams, their scores, and the days guests stayed. When a party was short of the needed numbers, Edmund recruited kids from Nueces Canyon High School in nearby Barksdale. Most were from lower-income families who otherwise would never have had a chance to pit themselves against serving Air Force personnel or rub shoulders with upper-class opponents. They loved it and were fiercely loyal to Edmund, and, even today, to his memory.

He was glad to give them a chance to enjoy a sport normally out of their reach. Over the years he helped a number of young kids finish their education and go on to better things, no strings attached. McCoy, the Air Force pilot, testified in court that it was Edmund's encouragement and assistance which enabled him to get through college and join the military.

Edmund also hired a few of the local kids. He paid them five or six dollars an hour to do ranch chores. He even lent them money on occasion, no questions asked, although he kept careful records and expected repayment. He did allow them to work off the loans at reasonable wages. Edmund knew the living was hard in Barksdale and Camp Wood. Family incomes were low, and many kids had nowhere to go for summer jobs.

Dan Waters is a "Canyon Boy," as the locals proudly call themselves. He remembers James with respect and fondness, "It was the easiest money and work I ever had. He even invited me to play paintball. It was fun, a blast. There were some real sophisticated people there, way out of my league. And some really beautiful women. It was great fun, like a party. Mr. James was a really nice guy, real generous. Hell, everyone in the Canyon owed him money."

Edmund James was an intensely private man. Only a few townspeople actually knew him, and just a handful of town kids worked on the ranch. His aging father, Ted, doted upon him. He was the youngest in a family which had suffered painful blows. His middle sister and his eldest sister's husband met untimely deaths. The extended family, drawn closer after the tragedies, would all gather at the ranch once a year for a sort of ongoing family reunion.

His father had asked Edmund shortly before the murder if he could move out to the ranch. San Antonio was becoming too violent, too crime ridden. The genteel city of his youth had been wiped out by big city hustle and development schemes. The old man was tired of it. He wanted to spend his last years with Edmund in the serene beauty of the ranch. Edmund was making plans for the upcoming move.

The Cedar Creek Ranch is not conspicuous, certainly not garish, nor is it easily accessible. A visitor has to know how to get there: in fact he has to know it is even there. No sign marks it on the highway, unlike many local ranchers who install elaborate limestone entrances arched with wrought iron silhouettes of deer, wild turkey, and javelina. There was no grandly paved driveway to the James ranch houses. To get to there, a visitor must know where to turn off Highway 55, and must find an obscure dirt road. The visitor then must know which turn to take on which gravel road. There are bump gates to navigate, so called because the driver must gently "bump" the gate with his vehicle to swing them open. This was the real reason Deputy Pruitt stopped to pick up Jimmy Baxter that terrible evening. Baxter knew the way.

Therefore, Edmund had few casual visitors. During heavy rains, the ranch was isolated for days by flood waters. Edmund liked it that way. He liked the seclusion. It was his delight, his source of strength and his downfall.

That last evening of Edmund's life he had been alone for a couple of days. His recent guests had departed the previous Sunday. There was little planned until next week, the week before Easter. Later in the month he would have to make time for Fiesta, a ten-day frolic peculiar to San Antonio. The street parades and boozy blowouts were just cover for the real celebrations; a series of very exclusive parties sponsored by the Order of the Alamo and the German Club — members only, please. They were the secret heart of Fiesta.

Earlier in the day, Edmund had worked in his well-appointed carpentry shop on a couple of small projects. He puttered around the house until evening. As the final minutes of his life unwound, on the evening of April 8, 1992, he took a break from watching television to slice limes for a sundown drink. His two Labrador retrievers joined him in the kitchen and watched adoringly. It was a quiet time, a Texas spring evening, no need for heaters or air conditioning. A perfect time.

Earlier in the afternoon three kids from Camp Wood had come out to ask a couple of favors. Edmund, to accommodate one of their requests, promised them jobs if they came back Friday. The trio, apparently satisfied, drove off late in the afternoon. It was now peaceful and quiet.

In fact, the young men did not really leave the ranch but parked a mile or so away. They had pulled a shabby little white Toyota up under some trees near an abandoned log cabin. Local legend said the cabin was the site of a nineteenth century tragedy. A jealous husband killed his wife and her lover, so the story goes. Now, a hundred years later, another murder was about to happen but it would not be a crime of passion. If anything, these young killers seemed to treat the prospect with almost breathless excitement as if they were planning some prank.

"If you were going to kill him, I wish you would have done it back then," the driver said plaintively. "We should come back tomorrow and do it."

"No! We are going to turn around. Let's do it now," replied the second with chilling determination. He was medium height, well built, blond, and handsome. He was the obvious leader, very much in command.

"Let's wait," said the boy in the back seat. "Let's wait until dark. I wouldn't feel right killing someone in broad daylight."

They decided at first to wait near the log cabin. After a while, they became restless and drove back into town. Bolstered with soft drinks, they quietly came back and parked again.

One of the boys had been to the ranch before. He had been there several times to work and on one occasion to borrow money. As the last of daylight faded, they started the car and regained the dirt road to the ranch houses.

"You're not going to freak out on us are you?" the front passenger demanded of the driver. "Come on," the driver replied.

Edmund was aware of the car as it rounded the opposite side of the canyon and started down toward the creek. He put down the kitchen knife and made ready to receive his guests. He was wearing short lace up hiking boots, jeans, and a green polo shirt. When the car stopped at the back of the yard, he opened the door and flipped on the outdoor lights. A small overhead light hung over the back door, and a larger swing out light was attached to the outside wall. Edmund shushed the two labs and made them stay in the kitchen.

The three teenagers got out of the Toyota. Two of them were carrying .22 caliber rifles, and the third had a flashlight. The rifles did not alarm Edmund. The boys had brought them earlier in an attempt to trade against a $176 debt the blond boy owed Edmund. Amused, he had taken the rifles in hand and made a show of examining them. He certainly did not need them. He had plenty of rifles of much higher quality. Edmund, wisely, did not want to start any notions around town that he would take old rifles in lieu of cash for debts. He knew he would quickly become an unofficial pawn shop for the whole county. The boys' offerings, one a Winchester with crude initials carved in its stock, the other a Glenfield, were used and cheaply made. Edmund had not wanted to hurt the kids' feelings by rejecting the rifles out of hand. After a decent interval, he had politely declined the offerings. In compensation, he granted their second request for jobs. They could start the next day, Friday, at five dollars an hour doing ranch chores. The boys had seemed happy. Now they were back, and Edmund wondered what they could want now.

The blond kid, who owed Edmund the money, walked up and cheerfully greeted him. The others followed but said little. The kid was one of those charming tough guys. Handsome and charismatic he became the leader of whatever group he happened upon. He was respectful and did all of the talking for the group.

They wanted to go "coon hunting" on the ranch, which is Texas shorthand for hunting any small game from rabbits to armadillos. Since jackrabbits are a dime a dozen and armadillos a major pest, Edmund had no objections. However, he was adamant there would be no "headlighting" deer, another old Texas custom of darker intent, where a hunter used a powerful flashlight or a car's headlights to freeze deer and then shoot them. Many country boys used .22s on such illegal hunts since regulation deer rifles were loud. A .22 could bring down a deer in the hands of an expert shot. More often than not, the result was a wounded animal crashing off into the brush to die in prolonged agony.

The boy promised they would leave the deer alone. Edmund did not notice that all three had duct tape strapped to the bottom of their shoes. He did not notice they seemed nervous and distracted. As the conversation progressed the boy holding the flashlight began to back up. He switched on the light. The light spot danced around on the ground. His hands shook. He could not hold the flashlight steady. Edmund took no notice. Edmund also did not notice that the other two boys had their fingers on the triggers of the rifles. They cradled the rifles in their arms pointing them in Edmund's general direction. It was a stance which easily could have passed for youthful sloppiness. Edmund also did not see one boy quickly flipping his rifle's safety catch on and off.

There was a pause in the talk and Edmund, who was leaning on a redwood picnic table next to the back door, looked off to his left. He looked toward the creek, as if he had been granted one last moment with the land he loved so much. As he started to turn his head back, Thomas Ray Eiland, seventeen, the charismatic, blond tough guy, raised his rifle. The end of the barrel was about three inches away from Edmund. Tommy pulled the trigger, and shot Edmund James full in the face.

The bullet smashed into Edmund just below the bridge of his nose and ripped through his head beneath the brain pan. It cut through his right sinus, various tissues, and finally exited through some fat and muscle on the right side of his neck. It traveled front to back, left to right and slightly downward. Oddly enough, this was not necessarily a fatal wound. The bullet had not damaged any major organs or blood vessels. If things had stopped there, if Edmund had received prompt treatment, he probably would have survived, or so a pathologist later testified. But, the wound was bad enough. Blood poured from Edmund's sinuses, out of his nose, and filled his mouth. He tried to say something, but could only make a choking sound as he slumped alongside the picnic table.

"Get him Andy," Tommy shouted, impetuously laughing.

Andrew James Milam, seventeen, the other quiet one with a rifle, taking the cue from Tommy as always, opened up with a flurry of shots. His rounds followed Edmund's body as it fell, face down, toward the ground. There were some hits to the head inflicting decidedly fatal injuries. Two bullets entered Edmund's head almost through the same hole, passing through his skull and ripping through his brain. One lodged just under his cheek, the other under his scalp. Another bullet sliced through Edmund's right lung, his diaphragm and into his liver. Another pierced his left lung; another ripped into his kidney; another punctured his upper intestine; another went through his left arm fracturing a bone. After the first shot, Edmund probably did not know what was killing him. Most of the blood was flowing from Edmund's mouth and face. His body was on the ground, face down. Tommy got in one more shot to the head.

In his death throes, as if outraged at his fate, Edmund clenched his fists tightly to his chest. By that time, after multiple fatal gunshot wounds, he mercifully did not hear the laughter of his killers as they stood around the body. The two young men stood and stared at what they had done while thin strands of gunsmoke still lingered in the air. It was an impromptu ritual of evil. They savored this night's work, drinking in the sight and sound of murder. They smelled the scent of blood and gunpowder. As one put it, they were "gun crazy."

Like most first-time killers they could not believe it had really happened. They were somehow detached, distanced from the event and the act. They were just watching the show.

A .22 caliber bullet is small but highly destructive. It has a high muzzle velocity relative to its size. In other words, the slug is small and fast and vicious. When it enters a body, it can ricochet off bone or dense tissue many times causing extensive damage. People tend to dismiss .22 firearms, but they are deadly. It was a .22 caliber bullet which almost killed President Ronald Reagan. Israeli assassination squads, set up to kill Arab terrorists, used .22 caliber pistols because they were efficient and quiet.

The small .22 entry wound easily deceives because it usually bleeds little. The internal damage does the killing. As the bullet bounces around in the body, it leaves long paths of torn tissue. The full track of the bullet is often hard to find. While doctors work on the obvious wounds, the patient can internally bleed to death from hidden wounds.

A postmortem examination revealed ten entry wounds on Edmund's body. The wounds to the head were vicious and deadly but the wounds in the back were shameful. Nine bullets and some fragments remained in the body. Some gun shots had been so close to Edmund's body that they left tattoos of gunpowder on his skin.

Martin David Sweeten, eighteen, the third boy and driver of the car, stood frozen in place. He shook all over, a curious reaction he battled all of his life. He hated bloodshed. Edmund's death throes mesmerized him. It was a sight beyond anything he had ever experienced. The shell casings had flown out of the rifles, sparkled in the uncertain light and disappeared into black shadows. His eyes took in the unbelievable sight of Edmund's body slumping. Edmund had not flung back like the movies show it. He had just crumpled.

Martin's hearing rang from the flurry of shots. The sharp tang of gunpowder and the metallic odor of blood blended indescribably. All of this was happening in the same way memories are recalled, a series of sharply defined pictures unfolding in slow motion. Martin was in a trance of horror. Some call it "shock." Things were just happening all around him. He was like a visitor from Mars, detached and observing.

He would forever remember the two boys standing in triumph over their kill, laughing. It was the high point of Tommy's young life. Finally he had killed someone. For years he had discussed the possibility, imagined himself doing it, savored the savage thrill. Now he had finally done it. Murder was easy.

Tommy handed Martin a knife and ordered him to cut James's throat. He was certain Edmund was dead, but he wanted Martin firmly implicated. Martin refused.

"Let's get the gloves," Tommy commanded to cover his decision not to push an uncertain accomplice any further.

He went to the car, opened the trunk and dropped in his rifle. He tossed a pair of gloves to Andy as he pulled on the other pair. There were no gloves for Martin.

"Don't touch anything Martin, just stay with Andy," Tommy ordered. He walked back to the body and checked the front and back pockets for a wallet or cash. There was pathetically little: a comb, a penny, a pencil, a receipt. He led the other two as they entered the first building and made a casual inspection. Tommy had boasted earlier that he knew where a safe was and could open it. They began searching drawers and cabinets. It was an unproductive exercise.

"Ya'll go on over to the other house and look around. See if there's a gun," Tommy ordered.

It was creepy in the house as Martin closely followed Andy. He had a strong sense of invading forbidden territory. It was as if Edmund's ghost was already behind them. The tape around their shoes made walking feel funny. They quietly climbed the stairs to Edmund's bedroom. Martin stood in the door while Andy searched. Tommy had told them to look for a safe, but there was no sign of one. Andy found a Seiko wristwatch in a drawer and slipped it on. Martin stayed by the door. Finally Andy called to him from a walk-in closet. Martin walked over. It was a large closet filled with boxes and clothes. At one end was a window.

"Open your jacket," Andy ordered as he began scooping up handfuls of loose change from a window sill. Martin dutifully opened his jacket pockets while Andy stuffed in the change and some paper money. Andy left the closet to continue searching the room. On a small table he saw a .357 revolver. He picked it up in triumph. Tommy walked into the room and began to look around. He seemed distracted as if he were just going through the motions. He said he was looking for the safe, but his search was only halfhearted. Finally he grunted in satisfaction as Andy handed him the .357.

"Let's go, let's go," Martin pleaded. "Someone is going to find us." "Come on, Tommy," Andy agreed. " Let's get out of here. I don't feel right."

Tommy uttered a guttural "Okay" tinged with sarcasm. They went back downstairs and quickly searched the other rooms finding nothing of interest. The urge to flee was growing. They went back along the covered walkway to the kitchen house. As they passed through, Tommy impulsively grabbed a half gallon of liquor on the table. Andy grabbed another bottle.

The two dogs stayed in the kitchen while Edmund was gunned down. They knew immediately something terrible had happened to their master. Both dogs liked people and were used to strangers being around. They did not connect the presence of strangers with whatever bad thing happened to their master. They did, however, want out of the kitchen. The urge to be with Edmund was overwhelming. The two dogs whined and clawed at the back screen door while Tommy gloated over his victim. When the boys opened the screen door, they bounded out gratefully, searching for Edmund.

They pulled to a fast stop beside their beloved master. It was odd, something they had never seen before, the way he was lying there motionless. The dogs gingerly approached the body, whining with worry and fear. After a few moments of inspection, they laid down beside the body, their muzzles between their paws. The air was thick with blood smell. They knew their master was dead, but they would perform one last duty and guard the body against scavengers. They would guard him for a night and a day.

Edmund left this life a legacy of goodwill, affection and beneficence, while his death raised up outrage, lamentation, and a burning desire for revenge. The consequences of this night's work were just beginning. The ripples of evil were just flowing out and would lap upon dozens of unsuspecting people.

The boys stayed in the house only a few minutes, ten to twenty. It was hard for them to remember later. Time seemed to speed up and slow down all at once. When they came out, they were carrying about $65 in change and paper money, Edmund's Seiko wrist watch, his .357 magnum pistol and the two bottles of liquor: one dark rum, one American vodka.

They walked past storerooms in the outbuildings filled with thousands of dollars worth of equipment and goodies. The trio never bothered to look. They could have filled Martin's car ten times over with valuables. They never searched.

The boys got in the car instead, in the same positions as before, Martin driving, Tommy in front and Andy slouched in the back. Martin looked like he was going to be sick, his color pale, his hands trembling, reactions which merely amused Tommy.

Martin backed the car around and turned toward the creek. He compulsively looked again at the body. The two dogs were clearly visible in the dim light. They were still lying beside Edmund, whining and gently licking his wounds. It was an image which haunted him throughout all that was to come.

The car crossed the creek, climbed the hill, and disappeared into the night.

Chapter II

The Killers

There was nothing exceptional about Edmund James's murder, at least by contemporary standards. It was not the culmination of some sordid scandal. Compared to many exotic cases, Edmund's death was "routine." The press was only interested because of the family name — "James." His pedigree made for good copy. However, the ensuing trials were casually covered and with diminishing interest. It was no one's fault. There was simply too much evil in the world. The killers stated motives were apparently so ordinary, "We wanted some money to go to Mexico." The murder seemed simple and direct.

There was only minor mystery but no enigma surrounding his death. It happens; kids kill nowadays. Teenaged youths routinely murder, rape, and torture. Many of them do it with little remorse, with almost unflappable aplomb, and for the most banal reasons. When they are caught they either wonder what all the fuss is about or bask in the media coverage.

"We wanted money to go to Mexico." Of course there was outrage and shock when people read the story in their morning newspaper. It was one of those what-are-we-coming-to stories. Within a few weeks other, more horrible, stories of mayhem washed Edmund's murder to the back pages.

Most people would have relied on the official investigative and prosecutory agencies. But the James Family, having more resources than most, did not leave it there. They decided the legal system needed an extra boost to prosecute the killers to the fullest possible extent. The family members were decent people, honorable people. They were too civilized to hunt down the killers themselves, string them up on some lonely oak tree, and then stand around posing for photographs. Instead, the family opened their checkbooks, a far more effective and relentless method.

Throughout that warm April night, James's body lay where it had fallen. The dogs remained close by keeping any predators at bay. The back door was open, cut limes dried on the counter top, and the TV nattered on to an empty room. His body cooled as his blood mingled with the patch of earth he had loved so well. His fear and pain were long past, his soul having abandoned his ill-used body for a far better place. But nature crystallized the killing moment in the wounds, the drying blood and the clumsy evidence strewn about. It was as if everything awaited discovery, but no one came. Only three people knew of James' death. Two of them had pulled the triggers. The other had watched.

Tommy Eiland, Andrew Milam, and Martin Sweeten were as good as caught even as they fled toward Camp Wood. They just did not know it. Martin was the weak reed. All it would take is pressure. Just let the cops lean on him and Martin would babble everything. Tommy now knew that bringing Martin had been a big mistake. The problem was what to do about it.

For the moment, Tommy kept telling Martin how deeply he was implicated, "You're just as guilty as us, it is just the same . . . If we go down, dude, you go with us." He repeated the message in one way or another for the rest of the evening. A more permanent solution would eventually have to be found.

Meanwhile, Andy continued to explore his lack of either profound remorse or elation. There was just a nihilistic numbness broken by bouts of uncontrolled giggling. Years of television shows led him to expect something more dramatic.

"I thought I would feel something after killing him. I don't feel any different. I really thought we would feel different," he marveled.

Both kept close watch on Martin who looked "like he had a

queasy stomach. He looked kind'a sick." Tommy decided to change tack with Martin and reminded him that he and Andy "were not afraid to kill." The message was plain and Martin got it.

He had good reason to believe them. Not only had he just watched them pump round after round into Edmund, but also they had pointed one of those rifles at his head earlier. Shortly after Martin aborted their first approach to Edmund James, the trio was driving toward the highway on the ranch road. Tommy was furious at the aborted attempt. He was berating Martin. Suddenly Tommy leaned over and grabbed the steering wheel from Martin's grasp.

"What's the idea?" Martin had complained as the Toyota wavered briefly on the dusty road.

"I want to keep control of the car in case Andy decides to shoot you," Tommy had calmly explained. Martin said he felt the barrel of Andy's .22 Winchester brush against the back of his hair.

"You're not going to freak out? Huh, dude?" Tommy challenged like someone probing another's inflamed boil.

"No, No! If I do you . . . you can knock me out and put me in the car," Martin pled, according to Tommy's version of events. Martin claimed he sped up the car and threatened to wreck it. There was a tense moment of confrontation. Tommy held onto the wheel as the Toyota weaved back and forth on the dirt road. Andy tried to keep the rifle's barrel centered on Martin's neck. It was Martin's only card to play and he was running out of road.

Tommy relented, let go of the wheel and said, "Okay, but we are going back."

Thus Martin believed, with good reason, he would be the next victim if he did not shape up and play the desperado. It was dark when they arrived in Camp Wood. Fresh from murder, they stopped at the Get 'N Go for gas and something to bolster Martin. They began to assemble their agreed upon alibi. Tommy and Andy decided they would contact their girlfriends while Martin called his father, Darwin. He told Darwin that he would be spending the night with Tommy out on his "ranch." He promised to go directly to school in the morning.

Carrie Newman was working the three to eleven P.M. shift that night, "At 10:30 that evening, Martin pulled up in his little white car. He owns it; he drives it around town," she later testified.

"Martin was good friends with my little brother. Then Tommy Eiland came into the Get 'N Go. He was the only one to come in. He came in to pay for gas. They pulled up to the gas pump, and I was up front at the cash register. I took his money and he asked me about a late movie.

"He was just as calm as could be," she continued. "I have seen him in there before many times. He cashes checks. Tommy just seemed calm. Martin Sweeten was at the pay phone outside. Andrew was pumping gas. When he was finished, he didn't come into the store; he stayed out in the car. Martin was on the phone like I said. And Tommy was asking me about a late movie. I told him the movies start at eleven o'clock but it takes forty minutes to get to Uvalde, that's the closest movie house.

"And I told him, you know, it being Wednesday night, I wasn't sure on church night if they were even open. I told him it was 10:30, the late movie would be at 11:00. If he hurried, he could get there. Then he walked out."

The only odd thing Carrie noticed was that as Tommy left the store he approached Martin, who was on the phone. Tommy started to speak but Martin shushed him silently with his finger to his lips. The three boys got in the car and drove off south toward Uvalde. That was the last Carrie saw of them until she was called to testify.

While other kids were contemplating their high school graduation, Tommy had just performed his own ceremony of defiance. To him, it was delicious irony — if only the others knew what he had done. Still, it was less savory as a secret. After all the years of anger, his carefully nursed resentments had finally burst into the open. His life just this morning seemed at a dead end, but now it was changed forever. Tommy had graduated to a real man killer. He finally knew what he wanted to "do for a living."

"Let's go," he ordered.

As they drove down Highway 55, Tommy and Andy conversed about ordinary topics which seemed grotesque to Martin. He was afraid. Tommy would break conversation at odd intervals to inform Martin that he was an accomplice and just as guilty. Then Tommy would return to chatting with Andy. They kept up a stream of talk punctuated with giggles. Martin wondered what would happen to his family if he told. Tommy was perfectly capable of hurting them. Even if Martin kept his mouth shut, for that matter, Tommy could kill him. He felt scared, guilty and sick all at once.

"Pull over up here," Tommy ordered. They were halfway to Uvalde at a place called "19 mile." Martin's stomach made another precarious lunge. He stopped, waiting for God knows what to happen. But Tommy only wanted to look at the "loot" in the trunk. They all got out and opened the trunk and silently gazed at the ludicrously paltry haul.

It was hardly the thousands of dollars Tommy originally promised. Instead, the items had become more like icons; trophies which said, "Yes, you really did it." It was a bit of reassurance even Tommy needed because the whole incident kept slipping into unreality. Had it really happened? The fact that they were the only ones who knew made it even more difficult to believe. Nothing was real until others knew. Tommy had an overwhelming urge to brag, to strut. He had finally earned his spurs as a bad guy. He was now officially as tough as he always said he was.

Cars were whizzing past. All three suddenly felt conspicuous. They shut the trunk and got back in the car. Once underway, Martin froze as Tommy pointed the pistol at his head. It seemed like a cannon gleaming in the flashes of light from oncoming traffic. It was so real and just inches from Martin's temple. He could feel his pulse pounding under his scalp. Martin kept his eyes straight ahead, afraid to challenge Tommy again by speeding up and threatening to wreck the car. That seemed stupid. Martin had no doubt that if given a reason, Tommy would kill him without a moment's hesitation. Tommy was not his friend. Martin realized that he had been a king-sized dupe, Tommy's useful new pet. He was safe as long as he was useful — and not a moment longer.

"This is what it feels like to have a gun up against your head. What'ya think up about it, huh?" Tommy softly inquired.

"It's pretty scary," Martin blurted.

"Yeah, right," Tommy said lowering the pistol.

They drove up to the movie theater in Uvalde and approached the ticket office, but it was obvious the last show was well underway. Tommy thought it was a clever idea to get ticket stubs from the last movie. They could claim they were in Uvalde that evening. Besides, even if the girl at the Get 'N Go testified they were there at 10:30 P.M., who would know exactly when Edmund was killed? Who would suspect some high school kids from Camp Wood? Most likely suspicion would fall on wetbacks or transients. No one knew they had been to the ranch that day, much less visited twice. Only a couple of people knew they had .22 rifles with them that evening. Carrying rifles in a car was nothing out of the ordinary in small town Texas.

The theater's ticket booth was shut down, but the doors were still open. They parked the car and walked into the lobby. It was a big mistake, the first of many. There were two teenagers standing outside by the entrance, Van Clinton Allen and his cousin, Elmer. By fate or chance Van had once gone to school in Barksdale. He knew Tommy and Martin from a distance.

Van was waiting for his younger sister. They shared a birthday and were celebrating with an evening at the movies. Van, a precocious sixteen-year-old, remembered the incident clearly because the trio quickly came back out of the entrance. Tommy apparently did not recognize Van. He boldly approached Elmer instead and asked for his ticket stubs. Martin waited by the Toyota five feet away. Elmer refused. Tommy did not bother asking Van.

Van kept quiet during the incident, but he later testified, "I would have said 'no' but I don't know why."

Two days later Van, his sister, and some other kids were in the Pizza Hut in Uvalde. One kid told Van that Tommy, Andy, and Martin had been arrested for the murder of Edmund James. Van felt a wave of uneasiness. A tiny ripple of evil had washed up and wet his feet. He felt he was at the edge of something awful.

"It was weird because I knew them and we saw them that night," was how he expressed it to authorities later.

The next order of business for Tommy, Andy, and Martin was food. They stopped at the local What-A-Burger and used a dead man's money to buy hamburgers, shakes, and french fries. Martin wasn't hungry. He was still ashen colored and shaking. Tommy and Andy dug in with good appetites. It was just about the last bit of satisfaction they were to derive from the murder. After eating they drove around Uvalde to kill time. Andy asked them to stop by his aunt's house. They visited for a few minutes and then left.

Around midnight they headed back for Camp Wood. It had been a long day and tomorrow there was school. Tommy anticipated the next day with glee. Andy drove Martin's white Toyota while Tommy cat napped in the back. Martin said little and gazed out of the window. He ached to go home, but he was committed to spend the night at Tommy's — a prospect he did not relish.

They pulled off Highway 55 at Bruce Park, turned onto a gravel road and made a zigzag to two house trailers. The lots were grandiosely called Live Oak Trailer Park. Tommy and Andy lived about 100 yards apart. Andy parked the car at the trailer where he lived with Patricia Butts, known as Jinks, and her granddaughter. She was James Houghton's mother. James had befriended Andy while living in Uvalde and brought him back home like a stray puppy. Patricia took Andy in with no questions and gave him the back bedroom. She was that kind of woman; there was room for all in her humble dwelling. She now wanted to formally adopt Andy.

He quietly entered the trailer and tiptoed up to Jinks, who slept in the living room. Andy leaned the Winchester rifle against her bed.

"I'm back," he said quietly. Patricia liked to be informed when Andy got home. It made her sleep better knowing everyone in her household was safe. For the same reason, she liked to keep the .22 near her bed. She was single with a young granddaughter. She was afraid of prowlers.

Patricia sleepily stirred.

"Did you get anything?" she asked innocently referring to raccoons or rabbits.

"No," Andy replied. They exchanged quiet "good night's." Andy went to his room, slipped the Seiko watch under the mattress, and fell asleep.

"You're going to spend the night with me," Tommy informed Martin as they walked the few yards to Bob Whipkey's trailer.

"No, I would rather go home," Martin said with more assertiveness than he really felt.

"You don't need to do that," Tommy said coldly.

They quietly entered Whipkey's trailer, and made their way to the bedroom. Tommy's stepmother lived in town but they had parted company long ago. Tommy had gone on to live with a succession of friends. He finally settled on Bob's place because he got along well with his sons. An amazing number of kids in Camp Wood do not live with their birth parents. Adults in town are easy going and take in their children's friends while their parents sort out their troubled marriages.

Tommy replaced Bob's Glenfield .22 and directed Martin toward the back bedroom. He pulled Edmund's .357 from his waist and ordered Martin into the bed. Martin climbed in and rolled toward the wall side. Tommy flipped off the light and lay down beside him. In the dark, Martin could hear him fiddling with the pistol, cocking it and turning the cylinder. It was to be a very long night.

Andy had been born seventeen years before to an unwed young woman named Janet Crawford. When he was three, she married and he gained the last name of Milam. The family moved constantly, never in one place longer than two years, from Texas to New Mexico and back. His mother later said she may have concentrated too much attention on her four daughters. She believed they may have distracted her from Andy's upbringing. On the witness stand, she openly admitted she felt guilty because she had not paid more attention to Andy. He became a quiet and withdrawn boy. He "kept to himself," so much so, that in the ninth grade he was put into a "learning disabilities" class. By seventeen, he had grown into a tallish, lanky kid. Young girls thought he was handsome.

When he was sixteen years old Andy came to Uvalde to live with one of his sisters. He had managed to wear out his welcome at his other sister's household in only two months. Andy settled in quietly but would not go to school or work. Finally, his sister ordered him to do something or leave. He managed to land a minor job which paid for his cigarettes and candy. Although Andy had a minor scrape with the law when he was younger, he was not violent. He did not have temper tantrums, made no threats, did not use drugs or drink to excess. Andy was almost unnaturally quiet and passive. He had lived most of his life in the company of women and did not know his real father. Andy's stepfather, his namesake, never played a major role in his life and had fallen away years earlier. Andy was a drifter and the last time he had seen the inside of a school was eighth grade in Nevada. He just drifted.

Andy gradually made friends in Uvalde and began to stay with them more frequently. He met James Houghton at a house they shared with some other kids. But they were about to be evicted. Tired of Uvalde, James was heading back to Camp Wood. Andy wanted to tag along.

"Come on," James had said. "Mama will let you stay with us."

And she did, but first she extracted a solemn oath from both boys that they would not use drugs "or stuff like that." Andy swore "he did not use drugs." Jinks took him at his word. She asked little about his past or his family. She had seen her share of hard times and had taken her share of licks. Nonetheless, she took pity on the lost. This was around Christmas time, so she went to town and bought Andy gifts. She did not want him to feel left out. Within a short time he was unabashedly calling her "Mom."

"I've taken other kids into my house," Jinks said with a heavy Texas twang in her voice. "But Andy, to me, was special. I don't know how to explain this. He was just a special person. He still is."

Jinks is a short woman with stringy blonde hair, a careworn face, and a little potbelly. Her youth and beauty are long behind her. All she has left is a kind heart and a motherly concern for kids. She is given to wearing T-shirts, shorts, and thongs. Her voice raspy from too many cigarettes, Jinks is the classic struggling, blue-collar, single mother. But Jinks is fierce in her motherhood. When she took Andy into her home, she virtually adopted him as a son.

"He was a quiet boy, he . . . I don't know, was just friendly. He never hardly did anything out of the ordinary," she later told investigators.

"He hardly cussed, not around me or my granddaughter. He cleaned his room, did his clothes, he helped me with the house and everything and seldom ever went anywhere. He mainly stayed at the house until he got to running with Tommy Eiland. But Andy was basically a good boy. I mean, I never known him to be in trouble. He never flared his temper around me.

"I put him on my food stamps. Yes, Sir! Like I said, he did his own laundry, cleaned his own room, helped me around the house and helped take care of my granddaughter, and everything. I'm an asthmatic, and I can do just so much. Basically he was good. That's why it was such a shock to me when all of this happened.

"He never told me about his family. He did not, you know, sit down and discuss it with me. My son and I had talked about adopting Andy, and we wanted to. I asked him about it and Andy said that would be great. Well, I said we have to ask your mother first. 'Well,' he said, 'I don't think she would say much.' And I said, 'Well Andy, if it is all right with her and we can get the money together, maybe we can adopt you.' I said, 'You can keep your name of Milam or you can take mine, or my maiden name, my married name or my ex-married name, or James's name, whatever.' Andy said, That would be fine. I really loved him very much. I still do."

Tommy Eiland did not inspire such motherly passion. Adults were uneasy around him. It was not as if he were threatening or violent, there was just something wrong about him. Everyone knew he had a hard childhood but few knew the specifics. He had only revealed a few, brief flashes of the painful and disheartening events of his life.

Tommy was born July 27, 1974, to Rhonda and Richard Eiland in Kansas. Richard was an oilfield roughneck. He kept odd hours and uncertain schedules. He was rarely home. The family moved to Louisiana where finally Richard's absences and rough ways proved too much. Rhonda divorced Richard and took little Tommy back to Kansas.

When Tommy was six, she was diagnosed with terminal cancer. Although he was too young to fully understand, Rhonda tried to prepare him for her death. At the funeral, he did not cry. After she was buried, the family gathered for a dinner. Relatives remember Tommy running frantically around the table stuffing his mouth with ham.

Tommy was sent to Odessa, Texas, to live with his grandparents. Tommy did grieve for his mother over the years. His grandmother remembers him waking up in the night weeping and calling out for his mother. When he was fourteen, Tommy's father remarried and brought him to Camp Wood. It was not a successful marriage.

Richard traveled constantly, and he did not take Tommy along. Worse for Tommy, his stepmother was not overly affectionate to a child not of her own flesh. The only person Tommy felt close to was his paternal grandfather also named Tommy Eiland, but he lived in Odessa, 300 miles away. The boy grew up lonely and alone.

Just before his seventeenth birthday, Tommy left Camp Wood and got a job at a barbecue restaurant in San Antonio. He did not like it. After a few months, he came back to finish high school.

He had grown into a handsome young man, about as tall as Andy but stockier, with blond hair and winning ways. He had charisma, although it was rough around the edges. Tommy knew how to charm what he wanted out of others. To adults he was deferential and respectful and he rarely challenged them directly. He just worked around them if they blocked his way. To other kids, he was dominating and fascinating. Tommy enveloped himself with an aura of danger and threat. A court appointed psychologist reported that he was highly intelligent, scoring 127 on verbal IQ, 128 on performance and 132 in overall intellect. The report said Tommy was "an exhibitionist, takes risks, very self-confident, he accepts the consequences of his actions and is not given to distress."

His running pals tell darker stories about Tommy. He constantly talked about killing and had a fascination with violence. He rarely started fights but was ferocious when pushed. There were few kids in town reckless enough to pick a fight with Tommy Eiland.

He and a few selected friends liked to go on cat hunts late at night. They would stalk domestic cats and capture them. Then the torture sessions would begin. They would torment the poor beasts in horrible ways before granting the mercy of death. The animals would scream, moan, and screech.

Tommy loved it.

At the wheel of a vehicle, Tommy would try to hit any animal crossing his path, but cats always got his special attention. Tommy strangled them, hacked them with a machete or burned them. He would rig a string around a cat's neck so it slowly strangled overnight. He would come back in the morning to admire his handiwork. He enjoyed the cat's bulging eyes and the clotted blood running in crusted streams from its nostrils and eye sockets.

Friends said he watched the "Godfather" series of films repeatedly. A girlfriend remembers Tommy watching a video of "The Silence of The Lambs" over and over again. He was fascinated with the character Hannibal Lector.

For a while Tommy dabbled with the Ouija board, a pastime which after his arrest spawned elaborate rumors of devil worship. He once approached a local preacher about the dangers of playing with the board. But how much of this was serious and how much was calculated to enhance his aura of mystery is open to question. Nonetheless, a lot of local kids were afraid of him. Tommy liked to project an aura of mystery and danger.

Kids who knew Tommy said he constantly talked about killing someone. Most of them thought it was just talk. Tommy cultivated a tough guy image and made sure he reinforced it constantly. He talked about killing his stepmother or his step-grandmother to inherit some money. He speculated about killing Buck Pruitt, the local deputy sheriff. His friends just laughed and figured Tommy was on one of his brags again.

One former friend tells of a trip to Beeville, Texas. Tommy and a pal, George, were low on funds. Tommy suggested they call for a pizza and when the delivery man arrived, "I'll bash him on the head. Then we can take the money and hide the body." George thought he was kidding. They did not send out for the pizza.

Mothers in the Canyon instinctively knew something was not quite right about Tommy. They did not want their sons, much less daughters, in his company. He lived on the fringe of their society. He was nearly feral, just on the edge of reverting to the wild. He was dangerous.

In the spring of 1992, Tommy's pleasant time at Nueces Canyon High School was ending. The pressure was on to think about the next phase of his life. "What was he going to do for a living?" was a question Tommy did not want to dwell upon. College was out. He lived an almost hand-to-mouth existence. His complete wardrobe fit into a modest cardboard box. The notion of entering, much less paying for, college was a bad joke. Adult life was closing in on him. Bobby Hatley, the school counselor, offered to take him out to the nearby Gary Job Corps center, a federal program to help underprivileged kids train for jobs.

"It was amazing," Bobby recalled. "Tommy walked into the center and in about five minutes, he had figured out who the leaders were among the kids, gone over and made friends with them . . . Then he turned around figured out who were the important supervisors and charmed them. It was quite a performance."

On the way back to Camp Wood, it was obvious to Bobby that Tommy had just been putting on a show. The idea of training to operate a bulldozer just wasn't this young man's idea of a rosy future. The other choice was to join the military but Tommy had always disdained taking orders. The thought of hopping to the commands of a drill sergeant left him cold. He wanted to give orders — not take them.

Bobby tells another story about the time he gave Tommy a job digging post holes, "Tommy was cooperative and friendly. He needed money so I offered him this job. He said, 'Great.' I drove him out to the location, gave him instructions and tools. When I came back in about a hour to check on him, he was gone. I guessed he hitched a ride back into town the minute I was out of sight."

Hatley told these stories with a certain amount of amusement, but he did not think Tommy was very funny. "There was something about him. He had charisma, but it was the wrong kind. There was something evil about Tommy. You could feel it, sense it."

Always in need of money, Tommy was good at picking up a few bucks here and there. He was not afraid to approach adults and ask for a "loan." But there were two more certain sources of money in town, Jennifer Noblett and Carolyn Sue Hodge. It is not as if they were from particularly wealthy families, just solidly middle class. They were well-ensconced in a lattice of comfort and security beyond anything Tommy had ever experienced. He was fascinated and attracted to the security of their lives. Both girl's parents disapproved of, if not actually disliked, Tommy. They did not want him around their households or their daughters. So the girls saw Tommy on the sly.

In the six months prior to Edmund's death, Tommy, Jennifer, Carolyn Sue, and eventually Andy forged a bond of friendship, which is only possible among the young. They ran around together, ate together, went out together, explored the surrounding towns together, and talked on the phone with each other constantly. It was not an unusual phenomena among teenagers, except Andy and Tommy were virtually outcasts. Neither Jennifer's nor Carolyn Sue's parents were aware of the full extent of the relationships.

A close analogy of what went on would be domestic dogs unleashed and out for fun, who stumble upon a couple wild ones living at the edge of town. If the chemistry is right, the scent acceptable, they will instantly form a pack and become inseparable. Even when the domestics head for home and a full food bowl, they know the other two are around, waiting patiently for the gates to open again. As long as the domestics do not have to choose between the comforts of home and the uncertainty of living completely in the wild, they will go at every chance they get.

Jennifer and Carolyn Sue were fascinated with Tommy and Andy. An earlier generation would have instantly recognized their James Dean-like appeal. Rebels, motherless outcasts, misunderstood by adults, these were qualities irresistible to adolescent girls. They would drive around the countryside in Jennifer's family Suburban or Blazer. They would drive to Uvalde or San Antonio, go to movies, dances, share burgers and fries. Of course, the girls would pay.

They would spend the night together. The boys on the floor and the girls safely tucked away in beds. They went everywhere together and did everything together. When they were not together, they would talk on the telephone. As Jennifer explains it "they were a family" not a gang.

"If one of us was hurt, we would stick by them," she explained. "We were real close friends. Tommy was the leader, we did what Tommy said. If Tommy got something into his head we would do it. I mean real stupid things, just for something to do. But nothing drastic, nothing like killing. That's what scared me — things changed."

Classmates believe that Tommy was in love with Carolyn Sue, but she did not want to be seen in an open romantic liaison with him. Her mother feared and disliked Tommy and had forbidden Carolyn Sue to see him. The high school version of the story said Jennifer, in turn, loved Tommy but she was too overweight and therefore excluded from his romantic considerations. Jennifer claimed Tommy did make sexual demands on her, but she refused. Despite the possible subplots, they were all close friends.

After the murder Carolyn totally cut her ties with Tommy. She would not visit him or write or take his jailhouse telephone calls. Carolyn claimed she had tried to break away from Tommy for months. She said she was forced into his company, that he persistently followed her and even stalked her. Tommy could neither leave her alone nor give her up. Schoolyard accounts say anyone who looked at Carolyn Sue with a twinkle in his eye would soon have a raging Tommy Eiland in his face, up close and dangerous. Tommy would constantly threaten to kill anyone messing around with Carolyn Sue. Carolyn claims that a couple of potential beaus were driven away by Tommy and his threats of violence. There are still lots of stories about Tommy in the Canyon.

There was the time, before Andy came on the scene, when Tommy, Jennifer, Carol Sue, a young lady named Terri and a running pal of Tommy's named Jason took off for the coast. Terri wanted to run away because of trouble at home. She said her father was "abusing" her in a very loose definition of the term. (The problem was basically the normal disagreements between father and teenaged daughter.) Tommy and the gang figured it was a good excuse to hit the Texas Gulf Coast. They gassed up Jennifer's Suburban and took off. When the money ran low, Tommy impressed everyone by deftly shoplifting.

"He was good at it," Terri later admitted. "I didn't even see him put stuff up his shirt."

Eventually the law and irate parents caught up with them in Silsbee, Texas. The leashes were snapped back on their collars except for Tommy. He had no collar. Everybody was dragged back home, heads hung low except for Tommy. He was amused. Eventually the hubbub died down. Daughters were questioned closely and often, and their answers eventually accepted. The whole escapade was written off as youthful exuberance. Terri went home, and all was forgiven. Still, there was lingering parental uneasiness about Tommy Eiland. He was always too close to trouble.

In that spring of 1992, Carolyn Sue and Jennifer announced

their time with the boys was ending. The young ladies were graduating from high school. The gang would have the summer together and then the girls would be off to college.

What was an exciting prospect for the girls was a disaster for Tommy and Andy. Their pleasant world was about to collapse. Without the girls, their lives could become very drab indeed. No money, no trips, no car, it was a grim prospect. College might as well be held on the moon as far as Tommy was concerned. It is doubtful Andy even thought about college.

A sense of hopelessness descended upon them. The girls were the only meaningful relationship in either boy's life. Jennifer and Carolyn Sue were the closest either had to real friends or social stability. Within a few months those props would be gone. By the end of summer Tommy and Andy would be full outsiders if not outcasts. It was a black future. According to Carolyn Sue, Tommy begged and pleaded with her to stay. He wanted her to give up college and stay in town. When he could not sway her, he would rage at her. He scared Carolyn Sue. She is a dainty young lady, petite in size and not quite five foot five. An angry Tommy is a giant hunk of uncontrollable menace. He made Carolyn Sue cower in fear.

As a consolation, the group planned one last, grand blowout. The girls wanted Tommy and Andy to take them to Mexico. And they really meant "take." Jennifer and Carolyn Sue announced they were tired of always paying for their jaunts. Besides, Carolyn Sue's birthday was coming up soon and she wanted something special. They wanted to go to Mexico, and they demanded that Tommy and Andy pay for it. Where to get the money was a real problem. Simply tapping Tommy's usual sources would not come near to financing the trip.

Tommy had made forays into Mexico before, down to the junky honky tonks of Ciudad Acuna across from Del Rio. He even confided to close friends that he was afraid of catching AIDS. It was something of an unwritten Hill Country tradition for high school boys to tell the folks they were spending the night with friends, then pile in a car (or better yet a truck) and head for Nuevo Laredo or Ciudad Acuna. There was no age limit on drinking on the other side. Booze was cheap and plentiful, and there was even open prostitution for the adventurous. Hitting the border was a rite of passage.

"Boys Town" in Nuevo Laredo was an almost mythical place and the source of uncounted stories and legends. Its gaudy glow still lingers in small town lore. But no matter how much money a young man took with him, no matter how cheap the booze or food, in no time at all, he found himself broke and thirsty and longing for a homegrown hot shower.

Of course, taking the girls to "Boys Town" was out of the question. But the border towns had plenty of shops and restaurants. A full-scale expedition to Mexico with two demanding young ladies in tow was an expensive proposition, and Tommy knew it.

It was at this point Tommy began to drop significant remarks to selected friends. He needed money and needed a lot of it. Tommy had worked for Edmund James a couple of times. He had come highly recommended by another teenager, a trusted part-time employee. Tommy gave Edmund a full measure of work for his pay. He knew Edmund would simply never ask him back if he cut corners. Tommy knew about Edmund's wealth and his "rich" friends. He knew Edmund lived alone and that his dogs were friendly toward one and all.

There were unofficial reports from official sources, told in lowered almost whispering tones, that Tommy had spent the night at the ranch a number of times, that Tommy had, on one of those occasions, stolen Edmund's wallet, that Tommy knew where Edmund's safe was located. There were plenty of gaudy rumors after Edmund's death. It is a fact, however, that Tommy had borrowed money from Edmund, two hundred dollars to be exact. Edmund was generous toward impoverished town kids. Working for Edmund meant a kid could borrow from him in a bind. It was an open secret. Edmund was not pushy about debts but he expected to be paid back. Anyone who welshed was not invited back to the ranch, ever.

A few months back, Tommy had needed the loan desperately. School workmen had been installing new siding on outside walls. The old siding was cracking and chipping at a disheartening rate. There were rumors the new siding was exceptionally tough and durable. Tommy decided to put the claim to the test and busted out several panels. This did not endear him to the superintendent who furiously hauled Tommy into his office. He told Tommy to either pay for the damage or not graduate.

That very evening Tommy hitched a ride with a buddy, Dan Waters, and visited Edmund James. He told Edmund what had happened explaining that his school career was in jeopardy. Edmund did not even mildly reprove Tommy. He merely opened a drawer and gave him two hundred dollars in two crisp bills. Dan remembers Tommy's eyes widening in awe as the bills dropped into his hands. He was impressed and watched intently as Edmund handed them over.

The next morning, Tommy met the superintendent as he came to work, gave him the money and apologized. A few days later Tommy did four hours of ranch work at $6 per hour. Edmund carefully entered the transaction into a little book; $24 deducted from $200 left a balance of $176. That was the only entry under Tommy's name found in Edmund's notebook.

With that kind of debt on the books, the likelihood of borrowing money from James to finance the trip was nil. But Tommy could not shake the vision of Edmund pulling the crisp bills out of a drawer. If there was two hundred right at hand in the drawer, Tommy figured there had to be more, lots of it. Besides, he was contemptuous of Edmund. Even Tommy himself did not realize just how intensely he despised Edmund James.

Edmund was the mirror opposite of Tommy. He had easy wealth. He did not have to hustle up a life. Edmund did not live on society's fringe, instead he lived in paradise. He was the most "inside" person Tommy had ever met. He had everything a man could want. He had friends, even beautiful women, flocking to him. Edmund had security and certainty in his life. People did not leave Edmund. They did not abandon him; on the contrary they sought him out. Edmund dispensed his largess from on high to lesser types. Two hundred bucks was nothing to Edmund. It was incredible that Edmund even kept his money in large crisp bills. Edmund was a jolly impresario of outdoor fun and games. He was rich, kind, and soft.

It galled Tommy to his soul, the sheer unfairness of it all, the poisonous injustice of life. Edmund had all of the important cards, all of the face cards. Tommy got the deuces and treys. Edmund's way of life was what Tommy wanted. It was a hopeless and forlorn desire, and he knew it and it infuriated him.

James had everything and Tommy was about to lose what

little he had. The few dollars Tommy took after killing Edmund were nothing but minor magical tokens. The real and secret agenda was to destroy Edmund's enjoyment of his life, to spoil it, to end it. If Tommy was denied James's riches by life, then he would deny James life itself. If God blessed Edmund and cursed Tommy, then Tommy would kill God's favorite. It was Tommy's private, twisted version of the Cain and Able story.

There was another element of magical thinking to Tommy's plans. Like ancient warriors who consumed a portion of their fallen enemy to gain his strength, Tommy hoped to take Edmund's good fortune by killing him. In any case, Tommy would prove himself superior. He would bring down Edmund's house. He would partly redress the injustice of his life and strike a defiant blow against a destiny which gave all to someone like Edmund and a pittance to Tommy. He would kill Edmund and despoil his home.

There are good reasons to believe that if Tommy had been more educated and possessed more native cunning he might have gotten away with murdering Edmund. There was little to connect him with the killing. A sound argument could be made that Tommy had elements in his personality very similar to serial killers. His childhood life certainly had incidents of severe abandonment and loneliness — if not outright abuse. He reportedly liked to set fires. He liked to torture animals. He fantasized about killing constantly. He had a sociopath's ability to manipulate and deceive people. He rarely showed qualms or conscience when he did something wrong. His one flaw was his overwhelming need to brag and impress his peers. His only mistake during his first and (it is to be hoped) only murder was to take Martin along.

As he turned notions of killing Edmund over and over in his mind, Tommy could not contain his mouth. He had to try out the "Idea" on others. He barely had enough restraint to exercise some caution. He would casually drop the subject in at odd moments. A few days before the murder he talked to Jink's son, James Houghton, on the telephone. In the background Houghton could hear Jennifer, Andy, and Carolyn Sue. It was their usual after school gathering. Martin Sweeten was not invited. He was not a part of this inner circle. Tommy used him occasionally for chauffeuring when Jennifer was unavailable or inappropriate.

During the conversation Tommy popped the "Idea," to see how his contemporaries would react, just testing, "Hey, dude, guess what?" he asked Houghton.

"What?"

"I'm going to kill Ed James."

Houghton later said he thought Tommy was kidding, boasting to shock as usual. Houghton dismissed the incident. He had heard it all before. Tommy once bragged about killing some drug dealer named Trent. No one ever confirmed the story or even heard of such a murder. Nothing ever came of it. Tommy Eiland was always talking about killing someone or something. Once Tommy speculated about raiding another ranch, the Marshall Ranch. His listeners just laughed at him.

"There are armed guards out there. It would be stupid to try," a buddy observed.

Later Tommy tried the "Idea" out on Jennifer, but more indirectly. As they were cruising around one day he announced, "Someone is going to get killed soon — And I'm going to do it."

"Why?" Jennifer asked.

"For money, I'm going to do it for money," Tommy flatly announced then snickered.

Jennifer said she didn't believe him and challenged him with "You don't have the guts to do anything like that." Tommy told her he would soon show her.

Martin did not sleep that night beside Tommy in the cramped trailer bedroom. He was sick with worry and fear. He despaired. How was he ever going to get free of Tommy? Even in sleep Tommy held the pistol. Martin was aghast about what had happened. It mocked everything his parents had taught him. It challenged everything he had once believed in and revered.

His parents, Darwin and Sue, were God fearing people. They raised their kids to be the same. They were not harsh about it, just the opposite. Darwin and Sue both suffered the effects of hard upbringings. Both had experienced the blows or verbal insults of unhappy fathers. Both vowed when they married to bring their kids up differently. If anything, they were overprotective. Martin was their shining child, the eldest son. Although they did not have much money they strove mightily to give him what he wanted.

Sue worked in a local home for the elderly as a nurse and Darwin exercised his eccentric but effective talents earning a living here and there. He built their house by himself, placing it up on a hill near the river. They had a few acres which Darwin filled with old machinery and vintage nonrunning autos. He ran a used furniture business in town. He also repaired small appliances and farm machinery. Darwin was good at it. People trusted Darwin even if they viewed him with an element of condescending amusement.

While Sue was quiet and withdrawn, Darwin was someone you did not easily forget. His usual dress was cheap jeans bought at discount stores, red snap suspenders, garage sale shirts, topped off with a baseball cap. He was amiable to the point of distraction. Even in the midst of his son's trial for capital murder, he could chat in detail about antique cars as if they were the only thing on his mind.

When Martin hit seventeen years old there was trouble between him and Darwin. Martin yearned to be free of the slightly embarrassing and suffocating life his parents offered him. He was a wallflower at school, a nerd without the redemption of computer expertise. He left home for few months and lived with his best friend, Mike Pannell. Mike's father, John, was one of those exceptional men who possessed an intuitive understanding of teenagers. They liked him and were drawn to him. John had a lively personality with a playful twinkle to it and always had time for kids. He would have made a great coach or counselor.

Darwin knew John well and was reluctantly grateful the man was willing to deal with Martin's rebellion. No father likes to see his son look to another man for leadership or inspiration, but Darwin was, if nothing else, stoic. It also took the pressure off him. Martin liked John and considered him as more of a pal than a surrogate father. That friendship between Martin and John was to be the most significant and fateful relationship Martin ever forged.

School was a point of contention between Martin and Darwin. It was a source of endless pain to Martin, a sort of hell with textbooks. A few months before the murder, he and Darwin clashed over the issue. Martin wanted to quit, take his high school equivalency test and go to nursing school in San Antonio. Darwin opposed the idea. But it was hard for him to forbid Martin to do it.

When Martin turned eighteen he was filled with youthful optimism. One day he hopped on a motorcycle and roared straight into a major accident. Severely injured, he lost a full year of school to operations and recovery. Martin spent months in casts and traction. The doctors were doubtful that he would ever walk properly again. There was even talk of braces and crutches for the rest of his life. Martin was fitted with a metal hip joint and steel pins in various bones. Walking was painful. His mother began a relentless campaign of prayers for his full recovery. Lo and behold it worked. His recovery had been grueling, but Martin was able to walk normally. The experience gave him a taste for medicine. Martin doubted his ability to take on medical school, but nursing was a possibility.

The crash took more than bone from him. His confidence was deeply shaken. His parents wanted him to get back to a normal life. They wanted him to finish school. In Darwin's family getting a high school diploma was a major accomplishment. He begged Martin not to quit. He promised to give his son a car if he would stay. It wasn't much, a little, white Toyota with many miles on it and no hubcaps, but Darwin would make sure it ran.

Martin took the deal. The car changed his life. The grinding daily humiliation of riding the school bus suddenly ceased. He was provisionally promoted out of "nerd" classification and into almost a "regular guy." Kids asked him for rides to and from school. Almost magically he became sought after. His new friends would pile into his car to cruise around town. There were even trips to Uvalde for movies. It was a whole new ball game. He made new friends. Although many merely used him as a convenience, it sure beat what he had before. Martin could not say "no" to anyone asking for a ride. He was generous, if not extravagant with the car. Martin was most pleased, quite naturally, when girls asked for rides, but so far little came of it.

He vowed to set about gaining his next goal, that of getting a girlfriend. Unfortunately, lady killing charm was not a part of the package Darwin and Sue provided. Martin, although he was a year older than the other kids, was painfully shy. He walked with a slight stoop and had yet to throw off his adolescent awkwardness. He seemed much younger than he really was. It was as if the crash had taken two or three years away instead of one. His slightly pale face was still dotted with pimples, not a lot, but enough to detract from his notion of manly good looks. The end of adolescence can be a really lousy cup to drink, and Martin got a dose of bitter dregs.

On the morning of Edmund James' murder Martin set off for school in Barksdale as usual, stopping only to pick up friends. He had a couple of things on his mind, one of which was to get a part-time job. He had checked with an older friend, David Burleson, who ran a local pizza store. David said he was going to get rid of his present help and would hold a part-time job open for Martin, but he would have to wait. Martin had another possibility he wanted to check after school. He also had a dirty little secret nagging at him. His rebellion against his father had gone a little too far.

Martin's generosity with his car had drawn Tommy and Andy's attentions. He was useful secondary transportation for them when Jennifer was not available. Martin, flattered, fell in with them. He liked the aura of outlawry which clung to Tommy. He became their fall-back chauffeur. Tommy and Andy found Martin amusing and began to test him. They wanted to see what Martin was willing to do. How far was he really willing to go?

Tommy tested Martin's mettle by taking him along on a couple of minor burglaries. They hit the Double D Rental building, a closed down business. They took a TV set which did not work, a briefcase (they threw it away), a homemade baseball bat and a tape case. They next raided empty hunting cabins and took a pair of binoculars, two blankets, two fire extinguishers, a cheap pump for an inflatable raft, a machete, cordless screwdriver and drill, canned goods, an ice pick, and butcher knife. Not exactly successful criminal enterprises, these burglaries were practice runs. Tommy closely observed Martin during these forays to see if he would keep his mouth shut and obey orders. Martin seemed to pass.

At school the morning of the murder, Tommy joined up with Martin in shop class. There are, of course, three versions of what followed. All three had similar events occurring at different times, and each boy included events the others left out. However, Tommy and Andy claim Martin was far more complicious in what followed. They still contend Martin knew what was planned and agreed fully to go along.

According to Martin, Tommy began talking about working at Ed James's ranch. He told Martin how easy it was. Martin already knew, he had worked out there before with a friend named Doug Adair. It was tough labor but fun and the wages were fair. However, it was not steady work. Martin wanted a job he could rely on, yet any job possibility in Nueces Canyon was worth exploring.

Tommy told him about the loan and how easy that had been. Tommy fed him a little more, "Look if James is not there we can rob the place."

Martin nodded, "I just want a job, but okay."

Tommy slipped in the punch line, "We can just kill him and take all the money. I know where the safe is."

"Yeah, sure," Martin responded and laughed. Martin claims he did not believe this remark. Tommy was always threatening to kill someone. The other two claim Martin knew full well they were serious.

"Hey, all safes have hinges. I can break into it." Tommy contended.

After school Martin checked with Don Jackmon, who raised ostriches and could always use good help in their care and feeding. But Martin misunderstood Jackmon's offer and thought he only wanted full-time help. Martin went away disappointed but still determined to find a part-time job which would fit in with his school schedule.

By four in the afternoon, Martin was headed for home. As he turned past the trailers, Tommy waved him over. Jennifer and Andy were there. Jennifer wanted Martin to go over to Carolyn Sue's house and get a kitten for her. Martin agreed, but he first had to get some gas money from home. He and Tommy went up the road to wait for Darwin who showed up after a thirty minute wait. They put the touch on him for a fiver.

They picked up Jennifer, gassed up and got the kitten from Carolyn and then drove back to the trailers. By now it was late afternoon. Martin stayed at Andy's while Tommy went over to Whipkey's trailer. Jennifer left for home, wisely taking the kitten out of harm's way. While Martin and Andy stood around the trailer waiting, Andy popped inside to ask Jinks if he could borrow her son's Winchester .22 rifle again. He had just taken it last night, and Patricia was mildly annoyed that he wanted some more bullets. She had recently bought a new box.

"I didn't get all them bullets for you to go coon hunting all night," she complained. "I got them for protection for around the house. We've had prowlers."

"Well, just give me four copper tip bullets from the box," Andy requested. He still had nearly a dozen from an expedition last night.

"Okay, but don't leave that gun nowhere, and you come home early," she agreed, much against her better judgment. She did not like Tommy. Martin was all right, but she knew they were joining up with Tommy.

When they finally gathered at Martin's car Tommy was carrying a Glenfield .22 rifle which belonged to Whipkey's son. Martin felt uneasy. He remembered Tommy's jokes about killing that morning in shop.

"What are those for?" he asked.

"I owe James some money and I want to see if he will trade these for the $200," Tommy casually explained.

The afternoon was fast waning when they turned right on Highway 55 and set out for the Cedar Creek Ranch. On the way they saw a deer. Andy and Tommy wanted Martin to swerve and hit it. Obliging, as always, Martin turned his precious car around to go back and hit the beast. The deer wisely fled beyond reach into the woods. Martin, secretly relieved, wheeled back toward the ranch road. Andy and Tommy were working themselves up to something. Suddenly they were talking about killing, about killing Edmund James.

"We don't need to kill anyone. All I want to do is go there and get a job," Martin weakly pleaded. He said he did not really believe them at this point. The other two ignored him.

They made the turn off, drove down the dirt road slowing for the first bump gate. The car nudged the gate which slowly swung open around a central axle. The car moved forward. The feeling changed after that passage. The land around them was owned and they were intruding. Once, then twice, they crossed the winding creek, the water coming almost up to the lower edge of the door. They climbed a hill. From the top, they could see James' houses on the other side of the creek. They made the crossing and drove up the driveway to the back of his house.

On the first visit, Martin just watched saying little except to ask for a job. James seemed very kindly, and Martin was relieved when he agreed to give them work the very next day. He was even more soothed when Tommy handed the two rifles to James and asked if he were interested in trading against his debt. James handed the rifles back and Tommy passed one on to Andy. Martin tensed, he saw Andy slip the safety off the Winchester. According to Martin, this was the first time he realized they really might do it.

Without thinking, Martin walked back to the car, opened the driver's door and said loudly, "Hey guys, let's go!"

Tommy and Andy turned toward him, their resolve momentarily broken. They came over and got in. Martin later said that was the only thing which saved Edmund on the first visit.

"They were afraid I would run off and leave them," he explained.

Edmund waved goodbye as they drove off.

They crossed the creek and drove back down the ranch road. Tommy was furious, "You were going to run out on us, leave us there!"

"No, I was just getting into the car," Martin replied weakly.

This was when Tommy leaned over and grabbed the wheel.

"Hey, what are you doing!" Martin exclaimed.

Tommy said he needed to control the car because Andy was going to shoot Martin. It was a credible threat because Martin could feel Andy's rifle brush against the hairs on the back of his head. He accelerated the car and threatened, "If you don't move that gun we all are going to die."

Tommy let go. He was fascinated and disconcerted by Martin's momentary rebellion.

"Pull over here by that cabin." he ordered, reasserting his authority.

Andy was in the back still pointing the rife at Martin's neck. He was ready to do whatever Tommy wanted. He needed Tommy whose assertive personality filled in the empty spaces in his.

"We'll wait here until dark. Then we will go back and kill him," Tommy decided.

"If you were going to kill him you should have done it then," Martin wheedled. "We should come back tomorrow to kill him."

Martin was scared; he was playing for time. He had to buy respite, a chance to gracefully break away. He had no intention of killing James or ever coming back to this place, or so he later claimed.

"No let's turn around and kill him now," Tommy was adamant.

"Let's just forget it," Martin pleaded. "Maybe we can make enough money for Mexico."

"He won't pay me for at least a couple of weeks. Besides I have to pay back the money I owe him," Tommy replied.

"Let's wait until dark. I wouldn't feel right killing someone in broad daylight," Andy compromised, breaking the immediate tension. Tommy told Martin to drive into a nearby field and spin his car around making "doughnuts" until James came to investigate, "then we'll shoot him." Martin refused. So, they waited.

Tommy suggested he and Andy would sneak up to the house and shoot James. When Martin heard the shots, he could come up to the house and pick them up. Martin said nothing. Tommy waited for a reaction. Martin was afraid that this was a test. Tommy was offering him an obvious way out, a chance to betray them. If he agreed, Tommy would figure Martin was ready to chicken out. If Tommy believed that, he just might kill Martin right there.

"Head back to town," Tommy finally ordered.

Martin let out a quiet sigh of relief and drove back to the highway. On the way back Tommy took a pot shot at a deer on the roadside. The deer jumped a barbed wire fence and bounded off into the woods. Tommy ordered Martin to stop. He leaped from the car, hopped over the fence and disappeared into the woods. Within a few minutes he came back and they drove on to the Get 'N Go.

Martin said it was about 8:30 P.M. and all this occurred before they went back out to the James Ranch. The other two say this happened after the killing. The girl at the counter said she saw them at 10:30 P.M. Martin had little reason to lie. He explained the discrepancy by claiming they went to the Get 'N Go twice, once before and once after.

Tommy told Martin to call his father and say he was spending the night with Tommy. Andy called Jennifer. "Listen, I can't talk to you now because we are going to Uvalde to see a movie. I'll call you later when we get out," he explained to her.

"Well, okay, but don't call too late," she replied. Later Jennifer said it was a strange call. Andy had never called before merely to tell her he was taking in a movie.

Tommy kept up the patter and promises as they rolled back to the ranch. But to Martin it was all delivered as one long threat. He was convinced they would kill him if he backed out now. Even if he did what they said, they might kill him. He now clearly understood that Tommy and Andy were the real pals, and he was secondary. He just had a car.

When they shot Edmund, Martin was frozen by fear, and failed to keep up his part. When Tommy said the code word, "flashlight," he had not shined the light into Edmund's eyes. He expected Tommy to turn on him with a fury. Instead Tommy was laughing and swaggering around Edmund's body. The big swing out porch light seemed to throw a circle of ultra bright light. It seemed as if Tommy would never stop laughing.

Martin was still shaking when Tommy ordered him to slit Edmund's throat. He only could croak out a "no." Tommy was amused. The rest of the evening was a blur of relentless fear: fear of what they had done, fear of the consequences, and now fear of what would happen in the morning when Tommy woke up.

Chapter III

Aid for Edmund

IT HAD NOT REALLY HAPPENED. Edmund James was not really dead. He was alive and well out on the ranch. It had just been a Tommy Eiland fantasy, something he planned to do. Martin still had a chance to get out of it.

So Martin hoped when he awoke. It was the way the day should have begun. He hoped for the comfort and sweet illusions of normality. However, it was not a normal day. Murder may seem like a dream in the morning light, but this one most certainly had happened, and Martin was firmly implicated in it. His fear rushed back over him but abated as he and Tommy went through the morning rituals at the Whipkey trailer. It all seemed like a bad hangover after some drunken spree. Perhaps they could laugh about it and say, "Gee what did we do last night? Really tore up the town, huh?"

But Martin knew full well it had not been that kind of a night. First thing upon wakening, Tommy hid the .357 pistol before leaving the trailer. He seemed so calm to Martin, so self-possessed. He was in command, detached, and almost amused. Tommy warned Martin again to keep his mouth shut. By the time they were ready for school, Martin knew two things for certain;

Edmund James had been coldly murdered last night, and Martin's life was in danger.

Tommy's usual ride, Jason White, honked in the driveway. Martin walked to his own little car. He watched Tommy disappear down the road, and then looked fretfully toward his home hidden by trees and shrubs at the crest of the hill. He had to tell someone, but who? Could he tell his father? And what would happen if he did? He gave a worried glance toward Jink's trailer; Andy was probably still asleep as he did not go to school. He always joined up with Tommy in the afternoon. Martin had twelve hours grace. He figured he could work out a plan during school. He started his car and followed Jason's dust trail to the highway.

At school he encountered a big problem; virtually every class he had was with Tommy. If he bugged out to tell someone Tommy would know it instantly. His only chance for escape would be during the confusion after school let out. He had to tell. No doubt about it. His fundamentalist Protestant conscience and his constant fear demanded nothing less.

Jason remembered later Tommy was his usual self in the car that morning, cracking jokes and passing time. He asked Jason to stop by the Get 'N Go, and then "out of the blue" Tommy announced, "We robbed a hunting cabin the other night."

"You're kidding," Jason replied doubtfully.

"Yeah, and last night we robbed another place. I got a .357 pistol. It's bad, dude, chrome. You oughta see it. It belonged to Edmund James," Tommy boasted casually. He loafed back in the seat, the portrait of satisfaction. He laughed. He just could not help himself. Tommy Eiland had to brag and to tell the world.

"What else did you get?" Jason asked. He did not know whether to believe this or not. Tommy was always joking, teasing to see if his listeners were gullible.

"We got a watch and about eighty bucks. I tried to get into his safe, but I couldn't find it."

"What about the guy, Edmund James?" Jason asked.

"Ed James won't wake up for a long, long time," Tommy replied, then laughed. Jason did not ask any more questions. He was not sure he wanted the answers.

Tommy found Carolyn Sue at school. He just could not resist the chance to shock her. "Guess what I did last night?" he asked.

"What?"

"I can't tell you, it will get you into trouble, but I killed someone." She did not believe him.

During sixth period Tommy met up with his ex-girlfriend Blanca Flores. Again the overwhelming urge to brag filled him. It was irresistible. He had to impress her and shock her. He relished seeing Blanca's lovely brown eyes go wide. He apparently believed that his world, the world of high school kids, did not touch the adult world. He thought anything he said in his world would just orbit around never breaking away to the outside world of consequences and retribution.

"Hey guess what. I killed Ed James last night," he announced while he watched intently for her reaction.

"How?" Blanca challenged. She had heard this sort of thing before.

"I shot him."

"Where?" Blanca was not buying.

"Once in the face and once in the head," Tommy replied.

"Why?"

Tommy just shrugged.

"What did you do after you shot him?" Blanca was still not convinced.

"We robbed him. We took money, a gun and some liquor," Tommy said.

"Who is 'we'?" Blanca probed.

"Andy and Martin."

"I don't believe you. Come on, Tommy, Martin Sweeten?" Blanca just could not picture such an unlikely grouping resulting in anyone's death.

"God, you should have seen Martin. He was really shocked. He didn't know what to do. He just stood there and stared," Tommy continued, then swore it was the truth.

School was hell. Tommy stayed with Martin all day. If Martin had to go to the bathroom so did Tommy. If Martin joined a group of kids to talk so did Tommy. Other students, ever alert for the slightest breeze of new social groupings and quick to jump on anything out of the ordinary, noticed Tommy's unusual attentions to Martin.

Martin still felt sick; he was pale and shaking all day. People noticed, they talked. Martin felt like a rat caught out in the open at a cats' convention. Tommy seemed to pop up constantly. Toward the end of the day Tommy pulled Martin aside. He had something to tell him. Martin moaned inwardly and plunged deeper into despair.

"You are going to drive us to Uvalde tonight." Tommy quietly announced.

"No. No. I can't Tommy. I have to be at home." Martin stammered.

"You're going to drive us to Uvalde. You're in this just like us. You're going to have to stick with us because there's no backing out now, Martin."

Martin continued to writhe and prevaricate, but he knew Tommy would have his way. He always did.

"Okay, Okay." he finally conceded.

"Good, meet us right after school," Tommy ordered.

"No. I have to give Jeff (Pannell) a ride home and I have to go home to get some money," Martin pleaded.

"Okay, but you better find us when you're through or I'll find you."

Martin's mind raced. He figured he was going to be killed tonight. He would just disappear on the way to Uvalde. Tommy and Andy probably already had excuses and alibis worked up. They would take his car and abandon it somewhere. Martin could just see them wiping off fingerprints from the steering wheel, the door handles, the gear shift. It was a plausible notion.

If he were going to tell someone and get to the police he had to go right after school. But who to tell? Surely not his father — how could he face him? "Gee, Dad, got a minute? I have something to tell you. I saw a man murdered last night and just stood there." No. He would not be able to bear the expression which would appear on his father's face. He also did not believe his father could cope with such a monstrous thing.

There was only one person with whom he trusted such a tale — John Pannell. He would know what to do. But John did not get home until after five o'clock and sometimes well after. What was he going to do meanwhile? Martin worked out a quick plan. After school he had to find Mike Pannell, his best friend. Mike was finished with high school and now worked. If he could just get to Mike, he would be protected. The best way to catch up with Mike was through his younger brother, Jeff. He had to convince Jeff to keep moving until Mike showed up and then stall until John got home. That was it, the plan he desperately needed. Jeff to Mike to John, that was his path to safety. When the final school bell rang he would have to keep moving. He could not stay in one place for too long or Tommy would find him. Keep moving and pray for luck. It was his best possibility of survival.

The day dragged on and most of the time Tommy stayed close by his side. When school let out Martin took his chance, disappeared into the crowd and grabbed Jeff Pannell. They made it to Martin's car and headed for Camp Wood five miles away. Martin casually asked Jeff when his brother or his father would be home. Jeff wasn't sure. They crossed the Nueces River and drove down Camp Wood's gloomy main street.

Back in Barksdale kids were still meandering out of Nueces Canyon High. Jennifer and Carolyn Sue had teamed up, as usual, after school. They also headed for Camp Wood but on the way they pulled up to Andy's trailer. Tommy had already hitched a ride home. The girls sat in the car as Andy and Tommy walked up. Jennifer remembers she tried to strike up a conversation, usually done without effort. Andy and Tommy just looked at each other. No matter what she said they would just mumble or evade, look at each other and break out laughing. She and Carolyn Sue were bewildered. This was weird. All they got was a peculiar look, then laughter.

"It seemed like there was a secret. To me, it felt like there was something I wasn't supposed to know, so we left," she later recalled.

Meanwhile, Martin and Jeff drove around town killing time. Ordinary habits asserted themselves, and they stopped at the Get 'N Go. Jeff went in to buy some snuff, and when he came out he saw Angela, his brother's girlfriend. She was sitting in the back seat. But there was someone else with her. It was Tommy Eiland. Up front Martin looked awful, deathly pale and quiet.

When Jeff got in the car, Martin knew he could not let the slightest hint slip loose that he was looking for Mike. Tommy would know instantly what was up. God only knew what that would set in motion. Tommy chatted away with Angela and Jeff. Martin could feel his amused glances aimed his way. It was torture listening to the laughter. Tommy asked them to stop by his trailer so he could get another pair of pants. After he changed, he told them to take him back to the high school to look for Carolyn Sue.

Tommy had second thoughts about his earlier behavior toward Carolyn Sue. Snubbing her was not the way to her heart. He had to find her and make it up. The best place to start was back at school; maybe he would see Jennifer's Suburban on the way. He ordered Martin to drive back to Barksdale. When they arrived at the high school, Carolyn Sue was nowhere to be seen. Tommy figured she would show up eventually. He got out of the car with a cold glance toward Martin.

Martin let out a long sigh and gratefully drove away. He felt pure relief as Tommy walked away. The fear was still there, but the pressure was off for the moment. Tommy had just goofed. He had made a big mistake relaxing his vigil and letting the pressure drop — all for the chance to make up to Carolyn Sue. He gave Martin breathing space, precious time to think and make his move. That is the problem with terror. It only works if the victim has no way out. If he can find just the smallest bolt hole, then the policy fails.

Martin and Jeff dropped Angela at her house to wait for Mike. Martin knew Mike would pick her up after work and then head home. He had perhaps another hour or so to kill. Martin was seeing gleams of hope and a way out beckoned. He merely had to stay cool and patient. Jeff wanted to stop by "Kanyon Video" and play a couple of games of pool. Martin agreed, anything to make the time pass.

To Martin's relief Jeff finally wearied of pool and was ready to go home. They had to cross over into Uvalde County to get to the Pannell house. As they pulled into the driveway Martin could see Mike was there. Thank God, he thought. It was shortly after four o'clock. Mike was in the backyard with Angela, his mother and brothers. Too many people, Martin thought. He pulled Mike aside.

"I've got to talk to you. I'm in big trouble," he whispered.

"Okay. We have to take Angela back home. You can tell me on the way." Mike offered.

Martin drove, Mike sat up front, and Angela was in the back.

Martin turned the radio on and cranked up the volume. He began to tell Mike what had happened — and what was in his trunk. Mike was aghast. Here they were driving Angela home with evidence of a murder in the trunk. He loved Angela, and although Martin was his best friend, he was not going to put her at risk.

"Stop right here!" Mike ordered.

Martin pulled onto Cooksey Road near a cattleguard and stopped. "What's wrong?" he asked.

"We are going to get rid of this stuff right now. We're going to get it out of this car now. God! Martin are you out of your mind?" Mike hissed.

"Mike, I'm scared Tommy is going to kill me. He's probably looking for me right now. I'm supposed to drive him and Andy to Uvalde tonight. I know they'll kill me," Martin pleaded.

They got out of the car and opened the trunk.

"Get everything out," Mike demanded. They pulled out a pillow case, two bottles of liquor, some rope, an ice pick and a roll of duct tape.

"Let's hide them behind that tree and then get out of here." Mike said with some relief.

They drove Angela home to Camp Wood.

When they returned to the Pannell house John had arrived. Martin was shaking as they walked in. He was really scared. He was crossing over an invisible borderline. Once he told, there would be no going back. It was way past the time he should have joined up with Tommy and Andy. Telling John meant he would become Tommy's open enemy. He would become a snitch. For Martin there was no choice; he had to tell. He could not carry this burden around any more, he had to do something. He was not a killer. Martin had to confess. John Pannell was home, and he was going to tell everything. All of the fear and horror could pour out and be gone. His thought ordeal was just about over. Martin Sweeten could not have been more wrong.

John listened stunned as Martin burbled out the story. He could barely believe what he was hearing. He was comfortable in the role of confidant to Martin, but a tale of cold-blooded murder was too much. There were many things a kid could not tell his parents, whereas an older friend was perfectly safe. However, murder, mayhem, and burglary were well out of John's realm of experiences. He was a settled family man.

He well knew Martin was anything but a killer. Martin could barely control himself when they had gone deer hunting. All they had to do was begin to skin a deer, and Martin would empty his stomach in great heaves of vomit. As a hunter, he was a washout. How Martin had stood around while Tommy and Andy had killed a man, was a mystery to John. By this time, Martin was weeping and shaking. He was pale. He kept repeating with variations, "They're going to kill me tonight. They're probably looking for me right now."

John calmed him and began to ask questions.

"Where are Tommy and Andy? Is the body still there? Has anyone discovered it yet? What did they do with the guns?" Finally, he asked the critical question, hoping he would hear the right answer, "Okay, Martin. What do you want to do? I'll back you up no matter what, but you have to decide," John had put the emphasis on "you."

It was time to see what this kid was made of.

"I want to tell the police, but I don't trust Buck. I don't like him. Can't we tell the highway patrol or someone like that?" Martin inquired. He was referring to Buck Pruitt, the Real County Deputy Sheriff who lived in Camp Wood. Buck was not exactly beloved among the Nueces Canyon High School population.

"I know a Texas Ranger who lives nearby. Maybe we can get a hold of him. But listen, Martin, even if we can't, we still have to report this," John advised.

"Okay, let's call him," Martin agreed, and then relaxed into his last few minutes of freedom.

Until this point of the story, recreating what was said and done has been a fairly straightforward exercise. Most of the accounts agree except on a few points. Of course, there are significant differences among the accounts of Andy, Tommy, and Martin. Those vital differences were to be explored and argued later in court. However, the bewildering welter of contradictory and confusing accounts did not arise until professional law enforcement entered the picture.

It is the sort of thing which keeps defense attorneys busy playing a form of pickup sticks with slivers of alleged fact. For attorneys, it means hours of intense cross-examination of steely-eyed lawmen who are trying to synchronize their stories with reports written months ago and who, simultaneously, are slipping covert glances toward the prosecution table for a clue on their performance. Rural deputies and even sheriffs are under a lot of pressure. All it takes is one false move, an offense against the wrong person, a screw up of one important investigation and they are out. Their gleaming badges and neat Glock 9 mm pistols are taken away. Their cars loaded with electronics, firearms, and other goodies become a glorious memory.

Rural lawmen like their jobs. The pay may be low but the perks are nifty. Chief among them are the brotherhood of policemen everywhere and a sense of superiority over civilians. Lawmen can legally wear guns and arrest people. It is an addicting thing; it beats any drug on the market. If they lose this power, the withdrawal is terrible. Their only hope is to get taken on in another county.

Even for sheriffs it is tough at the top of the heap. If they lose the election, their best hope is to find a spot on the many "area task forces" which are make-work projects for out-of-office sheriffs — courtesy of local taxpayers.

Rural deputies face a more uncertain fate. Sheriffs, after all, have the political connections. Deputies constantly risk being fired and the ultimate disgrace of becoming a civilian. It is a fall from grace, a horror. It means being thrust naked back down among the other slobs. It means no more respect, no more deference, no more stopping folks and watching them squirm.

The very thought of getting stopped themselves for a traffic ticket and being unable to say, "Look buddy, I'm a cop. Off duty, you know . . ." makes them queasy with fear. No sir, a deputy will do anything to avoid such an unthinkable fate. If it means taking shortcuts in procedures during the confusion of an arrest or stretching facts for a good cause or even shading things on the witness stand, then so be it, and who's to know?

Rural lawmen look to their sheriffs, who in turn look to their local powers-that-be. One of the most powerful at the county level is the district judge. He or she is usually drawn from the ranks of prosecutors. It is harder to become a judge with a defense background. Defense attorneys just don't make the right connections. On the other hand, prosecutors give up the chance to make big bucks in corporate law or the glory of big time criminal cases. They give up precious time which could be used to build a thriving private practice. They give it up to serve the state. In compensation, they are given the edge when it comes time to choose a new judge. So, deputies, sheriffs, district attorneys, and judges look to each other with a distinctly hierarchical, yet fraternal, interdependence.

Criminal defense attorneys, on the other hand, are scum.

Defense attorneys are ready to sell themselves to anyone, especially the guilty or at least it seems that way, unless one happens to be the accused. Then things take on a much different perspective. To his client, the defense attorney is an agent of God. He is their only hope, the only source of meaningful comfort.

Despite the corruptions of television and films, all of these roles are filled in real life by real people. A whole bunch of these real people were about to get involved in the Edmund James murder. Like large groups of diverse real people do everywhere, a lot of confusion was generated.

John Pannell called his Texas Ranger friend who was not at home. He called the local DPS officer (Department of Public Safety, Texas's quaint designation for the highway patrol with oddly faint echoes of the French Revolution), who was also not available. Since he simply had no luck reaching the few lawmen he personally knew, there was only one thing to do, John told Martin.

"Martin, we have to tell someone and do it now," he explained.

Martin agreed. John told him and Mike to wait at the house and do nothing. He called his wife, Sharon, and together they drove into Camp Wood to find Elton Baxter, the local constable.

Elton is a good man, kindly and well-intentioned. He supplements a modest income by acting as constable, one of the most thankless jobs in law enforcement. Unfortunately, his appearance is anything but menacing. His is astonishingly thin with a sort of pushed in face which makes him look odd. According to locals, he is given to overreacting to situations. Behind his back they tell amusing stories and anecdotes about his adventures. He has a hand-me-down patrol car with the usual cop goodies. Despite all, Elton loves his neighbors, his town, and his work. He will do anything for someone in need.

When John Pannell drove up to his house that evening the very last thing Elton was expecting was a report of murder. In a small town like Camp Wood, tucked in the most out-of-the-way portion of Real County, murders are infrequent but not unknown. For a lawman, even a constable, a murder offers a real break from dreary routine. It is a big dose of the real thing. John did not get very far into his report before Elton hit the "Oh-My-God!" button. Within seconds he had placed a call to the Real County Sheriff's office in Leakey, about twenty miles away. Buck Pruitt came on the line.

Elton listened to Buck's instructions, then made for the door. He was heading for John's house although it was in Uvalde County and technically out of his jurisdiction. He was to pick up Martin immediately. John stayed behind in town to find Darwin. Elton agreed to stop back in Camp Wood at the city park. He would pick up Darwin and Sue there on his way out to the James Ranch.

Elton fired up his well-worn patrol car. He roared off with lights flashing and siren blaring. It was not often he got the chance to turn them on. All of Camp Wood now knew something big was on. Hands all across the town reached for telephones.

In all fairness however, small town people take the sound of a siren very seriously. It could easily mean someone dear to them was in trouble. It could mean kids were injured or dying on a highway or that the church was burning. People in small towns tend to gather when sirens go off. They follow the sound because they are immediately and personally involved.

Martin was waiting at John's house when Elton roared up. Elton put him in the front seat and announced that he was in "protective custody." Martin felt relieved. He asked Elton to stop at the park where his parents were waiting. On the way back to Camp Wood, Buck Pruitt intervened with a radio call. He ordered Elton to go directly to the murder scene. He was not to pick up anyone.

Unfortunately, a few local folks have police scanners. After all, there is not much to do in Camp Wood, and it is a source of vital information if not juicy gossip. The word was quickly spread, "Murder! Shooting ... Cedar Creek Road ... Cedar Creek Ranch ... James Ranch ... Edmund James!"

Darwin was emptying the last few pieces from a trailer full of used furniture he had bought in San Antonio. It had been a long, hard day. That morning he had risen early to drive more than one hundred miles to the city. After loading up the trailer, he made the drive back then began unloading. He was a bit put out with Martin. It would have been nice if he had been there to help after school. He noticed his wife, Sue, was out back talking to Sharon Pannell.

"Darwin," she said, when she came into the store. "We are supposed to meet Elton at the park. Martin is with him."

"What on earth for?" Darwin asked.

"Martin is in a little bit of trouble. There's been a tragedy."

Darwin and Sue closed up the store. On the way out they noticed two boys playing at the pool hall. Sue recognized one as Tommy Eiland. John Pannell drove up and took them over to the park. They waited and discussed what to do. Tommy and Andy walked past, glanced at the four adults and walked on.

It seemed like hours before they heard the faint wailing sound. Darwin and Sue expectantly moved out to the curb. It must be Elton coming to pick them up, but with a siren going? Things must be worse than they thought. Elton's car was now visible, police lights illuminating the entire main street, the siren shrieking. He was sure going awfully fast. They almost stepped off the curb in their expectation, but the car whipped past them and off into the night. Darwin and Sue just stood there. They were stunned, confused. Their ears rang with the echoes of that siren; their vision blurred with odd after-images of the bright lights. They both had noticed the dark silhouette of their son in the back seat of Elton's car. They remembered these things because from that moment on their lives forever changed. There was nothing for them to do but sheepishly follow.

"What is going on, Sharon?" Darwin pleaded with John's wife.

Sharon told him all of the details she knew.

Darwin could not believe what he was hearing. It was simply impossible. His son was a witness to murder, maybe worse. It just could not be. In seconds, every cliché, every predictable thought a parent could think tumbled through his mind, "not my kid . . . must be some mistake . . . how could it happen . . ." then cold fear hit.

"What am I going to do?" he asked, bewildered.

"Well, I think you and Sue need to get out there," Sharon responded.

"But how much trouble do you think Martin is in?" Darwin persisted.

"I'm not sure, but I think he is going to need a lawyer."

At the Get 'N Go Andy and Tommy had walked out to see what all the noise was about. They saw Elton's car sweep through the town. They calmly left the store. Martin was no where to be found. Tommy said they would get Jennifer and go to Uvalde later.

Deputy Buck Pruitt was a piece of work. He could be picked up and set down in southern Louisiana and fit right in. He looks like an archetypal Cajun. Buck is a big man with straight dark hair, a neat mustache and all of the confidence in the world that he is God's special gift to law enforcement. Buck radiated the dauntless and presumptuous self-possession usually found in FBI agents or Texas Rangers. Some would call it arrogance, others an aura of authority. Needless to say, the minute Elton's call came in, Buck took control of the case.

He told Elton to pick up Martin, but he was not to pick up Darwin and Sue. Elton was to meet Buck on the way to the ranch. He then . . . "instructed Nueces Canyon EMS to muster a team and go to the intersection of Cedar Creek Road and Highway 55 and wait for me there." The "team" consisted of Elton's brother and the Baptist preacher's son who acted as a part time EMS tech and undertaker.

"Basically it was a real busy time, responding to 10–33's and crooked roads and trying to line everyone up . . . ," Buck later testified. "By the time I got to Camp Wood, I was aware by radio traffic that EMS had an ambulance and crew on the scene at the intersection of 55 and Cedar Creek Road. I was also in communication with Constable Baxter, and was aware he had Martin Sweeten with him and was headed for the scene. I didn't stop in Camp Wood and continued on up 55 to Cedar Springs Road.

"I had ascertained by radio traffic that there was to be one of the attendants with the ambulance who knew the area and knew where the James Ranch was. We had figured out that this thing had occurred on the James Ranch, and at that point I stopped and loaded Jimmy Baxter (Elton's brother, the EMS attendant) with me and we continued on up Cedar Creek Road. I was also in radio communication with Wayne Woods, Edwards County unit. We also notified Edwards County to the effect there had supposedly been a shooting, and at that time we were of the belief that it may have just occurred and there may still be actors on the scene ... we were not exactly sure of what we were dealing with at the time. We just knew we had a bad situation and were trying to get there."

At 7:25 P.M. on Thursday, April 8, 1992, almost twenty-four hours since he had been slain, people finally came to Edmund's aid.

Buck radioed Elton to come up to the scene. He was to park his car down at the bottom of the hill and keep Martin inside. He did not want Martin to see the scene and perhaps alter his story. Buck parked at the edge of the backyard. Deputy Wayne Woods, Edwards County, parked down the hill and came up to join him.

They both approached the body, Buck in the lead, " ... Doing a quick scan of the premises. I saw a body laying close to the front door, closer to me from the front door, in the yard. I exited the vehicle, instructing Mr. Baxter; who had been — basically my guide, to remain in the vehicle. I proceeded to approach the body directly from my vehicle to the body.

... "We were being very careful, because once again, we did not know when this act had happened. We didn't know if the actors may still be on the scene, and so we were being very cautious of everything around us and what have you. Until I got to the body, I did not know what time span we were working with.

"I approached fairly slowly, tried to ascertain if there was anybody else in the area or in the house. I could hear a television going in the house ... We were just being real careful. Wayne Woods was off to my right and a bit behind ..."

They checked the body and figured out Edmund had been dead for many hours. That relaxed the tension a bit. It was doubtful the killers were still there. Buck and Wayne searched the house just to be sure. It was "basically intact ... there was food on the counter ... looked like it had been business as usual ..." Wayne went out to check the grounds, and Buck went back to his car to call in.

"I . . . advised Edwards County we did, in fact, have a shooting victim, deceased on the scene, advised them we were going to need a judge or JP down there. Also asked for more backup."

He told the rest of the EMS crew to bring the ambulance on up but to park behind his unit. Once they arrived, he sent one attendant down to Elton's car to . . . "insure Baxter did not come on up, make sure he followed my instructions." By this time more Edwards County deputies were arriving and Buck, a Real County deputy, had to turn over the immediate investigation of the scene to them. But he was still one step ahead of them. He went down the hill to chat with Martin.

Edwards County Deputy Mike Lowrie had driven down from Rocksprings. When he arrived at Cedar Creek Road, he met Edwards County Judge Nevell Smart parking his car beside the road. He offered the judge a ride to the scene. The judge was needed to officially pronounce Edmund dead.

In his official report Lowrie said, "upon arrival at the scene were Camp Wood EMS unit #4, unit #9 Real County, Constable Baxter and unit #53. Unit #53 had Martin Sweeten in his patrol car, well away from the crime scene.

"It was later learned by the reporting officer that Sweeten was the person who informed the authorities of the homicide. Upon arrival at the scene reporting officer saw there were two dogs locked inside the structure to the northwest side of the location of the body. The body was laying belly down with the head away from the kitchen/den complex. There was a moderate amount of blood around the head area and ground with both hands folded underneath the upper torso.

"The reporting officer found no signs of struggle which might have taken place inside or outside. The kitchen area had a bar counter that looked like someone had been in the process of making mixed drinks. Many liquor bottles were opened and limes were cut and laying on the counter. The television was on in the den. There were several places in the complex that had evidence that someone had been working to either repair or build. The sprinkler system was on and still spraying on the north side of the complex."

It was time for basic police work: measuring distances, triangulations, jotting down notes, taking photographs, all of the routine procedures. They roped off the area and began work. Once the body had been formally declared dead, photographed and inspected, it was turned over to a Rocksprings' funeral home and transported. A meticulous search began that evening for any physical evidence.

Meanwhile, Martin had been transferred from Elton's car to Edwards County Deputy Sheriff Wayne Wood's unit. Since they were in Edwards County, Woods was in charge of the scene until the chief deputy arrived. But there was no holding back Buck Pruitt. Buck walked over to Wood's unit and asked Martin what had happened. Martin told him, "Tommy Eiland and Andy Milam had shot Mr. James and forced him, Sweeten, to drive to Uvalde, Texas, and held him, Sweeten, at gunpoint until he got away and was able to report the crime."

That was enough for Buck. He left the ranch, along with a U.S. Border Patrol unit, and raced back to Camp Wood. Outside the little town, he gathered a diverse crew of law enforcement officers and split them into two teams. He would lead one, and Shane Holman, a game warden, would lead the other. Holman's team checked a couple of known hangouts looking for Andy. Buck came on the air and told them to meet him near the trailer park.

Holman and two Border Patrol officers were assigned Jink's trailer. There was no problem really. They walked up, asked for Andy, and when he came to the door they arrested him. They took him out to Holman's car and read him his Miranda rights. Sheriff Earl Brice of Real County arrived along with some DPS officers. They asked Jinks if they could search her trailer. She agreed.

They found one Winchester .22 semiautomatic rifle in the living room propped up against the wall. Holman unloaded it, carefully bagging the rounds. Brice wrote down the serial number of the rifle. Under the mattress of Andy's bed they found a Seiko wrist watch. They also confiscated a knife.

Jinks was in shock and anguish. Andy had seemed nervous all day, but he had been like that before, shaking and restless. He had appeared calm when he returned from his late afternoon jaunt with Tommy. Everything seemed okay until the lawmen arrived.

Later after Jinks visited them in jail she said, "I couldn't understand what happened. The only thing I learned was the next Sunday, after all of this happened. I talked to all three of them. I asked Tommy Eiland, 'Why? Tell me why.' And he said it was for the money. 'Baloney,' I said. 'Your grandmother and them send you money anytime you want it.'

"And I said, 'Why? I want to hear it out of your own mouths.' I asked, 'Who fired first? I've got to know.' And Tommy said, 'I did.' I asked again, 'Why?' They didn't answer. Andy, when I talked to him, was crying real hard. I had my granddaughter with me and she was crying. In my own heart, I don't think Andy would have done anything like this if he hadn't been running around with Tommy. I really don't.

"I asked him, 'Why did you run around with Tommy?' And that's when he told me, 'We're scared of him.' Him and Martin both were scared of that boy. If Tommy can go and shoot a man, how do we know if he wouldn't have turned around and shot them?"

Upon arriving in Camp Wood, Buck coordinated the search for Andy and Tommy, "Prior to entering the house (trailer), we met with backup units which responded from Uvalde . . . I had obtained information from someone on the street as to their whereabouts; he advised me they were preparing to leave to go to Uvalde. We had another meeting and planned our approach to the houses where they were. They were either going to be in one trailer or two. The trailers were about 100 yards apart.

"We arrived at the front of the trailer, got out of vehicles. We met Bob Whipkey at the outside and asked him if we could enter and pick up Tommy, and he said yes we could. Officer Whitaker and I entered the trailer and took custody of Tommy Eiland."

It was as simple as that. The murderers were in custody. The whole thing had turned into a cop feeding-frenzy with diverse units descending on little Camp Wood from miles around. Sheriff's deputies from three counties, game wardens, border patrol officers and poor old Elton Baxter combined to make the arrests. It was simply amazing, a massive display of screaming tires, sirens, and blinking lights. All that police power deployed to subdue two, unresisting teenagers. In fairness, they did not know what they would encounter when they went after Tommy and Andy. It is also true there is not much police work to do in the long evenings out in Real and Edwards counties.

Tommy was patted down, handcuffed, and told he was under arrest for murder. He was put in Buck's car. They then read him his Miranda rights.

The search of the Whipkey trailer yielded the Glenfield .22 semiautomatic rifle, serial number 702612318, and a .357 magnum revolver hidden under Tommy's mattress. Andy was arrested at Patricia's and the Winchester Model 100 .22 caliber rifle, serial number B1639S61, was taken into custody. Both Tommy and Andy cooperated fully, pointing out the location of each piece of evidence the lawmen might need. Officers transported Tommy and Andy to Leakey. They went before Justice of the Peace Billy Ray Chisum. He read them their Miranda rights and charged them with capital murder.

Martin was still in the back seat of Deputy Wood's car at the murder scene when Darwin finally caught up with him. He was in "protective custody" and, in his mind, cooperating with the lawmen as a "witness." He was not handcuffed, but he could not roll down the windows or open the door.

And that was how Darwin and Sue found him, sitting quietly and alone in the patrol car.

Edwards County Chief Deputy Sheriff Jay Adams saw them at the car window, and went down to find out who they were. He wanted to make sure no one messed with his prime suspect. He overheard their conversation, but has quite a different recollection of what was said.

Darwin saw Adams approaching and intercepted him. He identified himself and began to chat with the deputy. Darwin is, if nothing else, a natural expert at this sort of thing.

"I told him I was Martin Sweeten's daddy," He recalled later. "And I talked to him about it a little bit. I asked him if he didn't think I ought to get a lawyer? He said at this point I did not need a lawyer."

Adams has adamantly denied under oath ever saying this.

Regardless of what was said, Darwin was not buying Adams' alleged advice. He went back to the car.

"Son, I think you need a lawyer. I think you ought not to say anything until I can get you one," he told Martin.

"Dad, don't worry about it. I can talk my way out of any jam. I'm on the DA's side," Martin claimed.

Why Martin had fixated on this particular notion, "being on

the district attorney's side," became the focus of lengthy courtroom debate. That a naive rural boy would come to think on his own, that he was helping the district attorney was distinctly odd. But Martin adamantly claimed the lawmen told him the reason he was kept on the scene was to "help" the district attorney. All of the deputies denied this assertion time and again under oath.

Nonetheless, Darwin was worried about him, "Martin was really upset. He was nervous and about as upset as I have ever seen him in my life. He was about to throw up. He said he needed some Pepto-Bismol or something to settle his stomach. He was also hungry, but he was fix'n to throw up. He said he hadn't slept since night before last. He was just a nervous wreck. His eyes were red and he was just shaking all over. I settled him down a little bit; not a whole bunch, but I tried . . .

"I went back and talked to Deputy Adams, and he said they were going to bring him up to Rocksprings. I asked him if it would be okay if I got Martin a hamburger and some Pepto-Bismol. He said yes, and that's what we done. It was about ten-ish, and we followed them up to Rocksprings. It was probably about an hour or so, I don't know, it seems like it took forever to make those hamburgers."

Darwin is a short man and not stoutly built, while the Edwards County sheriff that year, Donnie Letsinger, was a big man and not given to judging people by their inner glow. The struggle between the two was intense. At least, it was while it lasted. Darwin sought to halt what he believed was a legal steamroller about to flatten his son.

Darwin, Sue and John, Sharon and Mike Pannell had followed the patrol car transporting Martin to Rocksprings. They parked in front of the courthouse. Darwin led the procession up to the Edwards County sheriff's office, determined to save his son. There was a bit of historic irony in this. One hundred and two years ago the founder of Rocksprings had come to this very place. His name was Roberts Sweeten, one of three Irish brothers who immigrated to Texas. The brothers had a falling-out and separated their families and their flocks. Ever since then Sweetens have lived in the area, but no one is exactly sure how all of the various families are related to the each other. As Darwin puts it, "the Sweetens are not a hugging family."

The others followed Darwin into the sheriff's office. It was open, but strangely quiet. There was no one in the front office. The place seemed empty. Darwin was from Real County and did not know Letsinger. He walked into the back room. He saw a deputy and asked, "Who is in charge?"

Darwin was hard of hearing and tended to speak loudly. For anyone who did not know him, it was annoying, a little guy with a big mouth.

In response, Letsinger came out and said, "I'm in charge."

This was not shaping up as a friendly encounter. But Darwin persisted, "Don't I have the right to stop you from questioning Martin anymore until either I get him a lawyer or I'm at least present with him?"

Letsinger looked him over with the contempt lawmen reserve for the relatives of obviously guilty felons, "Mister, he's eighteen years old, isn't he?"

"Yes, Sir. He is."

With an air of triumph Letsinger lowered the boom, "You don't have any rights."

Darwin was taken aback by the baldness of Letsinger's interpretation of the law, not to mention, the implied threat big men with guns reserve for pushy little guys. Darwin blinked owlishly. His latent twitch rippled up his arm to his shoulder. The problem was that Letsinger was right. Darwin knew Martin was in serious trouble and headed deeper.

"You get in the office up front," Letsinger ordered, "and you sit there until I call for you."

Darwin persisted, "I think I have a right to a lawyer."

"You want me to lock you up too?" Letsinger countered and walked out.

They waited.

Darwin got the hamburgers and Pepto-Bismol and handed them to Letsinger. Sometime in the early morning, apparently shortly after three A.M., the sheriff let them talk to Martin. He was sitting forlornly in a back office. He had been under interrogation since before midnight. They let him talk to his parents for a while and then took him back for another session. At 3:30 A.M., Martin began another statement which was more damning, this was well after Tommy and Andy had been brought in. By 6:10 A.M., the interrogators were finally through with him.

When Darwin had visited with Martin, he had waded into him, "Son, you have said enough and then some already. For God's sake! Don't say anymore. Let me get you a lawyer."

Martin rose up and comforted him, "Don't worry about it," he said, as he hugged Darwin. "I'm on the DA's side. I ain't got nothing to worry about. I'm just a witness."

"Son, don't tell no lies, but just don't say anymore," Darwin pleaded. His distrust of law officers was profound. He knew Martin was tired, nervous, and scared. At that point, Darwin did not know for sure how deeply Martin was entangled in the whole mess. He did not yet know exactly what Martin had or had not done. He simply figured Letsinger would happily hang Martin as he would the other two. No matter what Martin had done, Darwin was going to stand by him.

"Dad, I told you. There's nothing to worry about, I'm a good talker. I'm on the DA's side. He needs me." Martin continued. The conversation was sounding like a catechism recitation. In a way, it was. Martin's belief in the DA was almost touching. Darwin could tell.

"Son, the DA ain't in here," Darwin sagaciously pointed out.

"I know, Dad, but they are on the phone with him constantly," Martin explained. There was that slight condescension in his voice young men reserve for their father's protests. He did not tell his father he had already been read his Miranda rights, made a statement, and signed it. His father just did not understand such things.

By this time, Tommy and Andy had been transported from Leakey to Rocksprings. They were informed of their rights for the second time. Andy was put in Jay Adams's office. The fearsome company of Tommy, at once scary and comforting, was gone. Instead he was surrounded by lawmen. He was surely scared. They read him his rights, again. Andy volunteered to make a statement.

"I figured it was the best thing to do," he later explained.

Tommy was in another room also making a statement and signing it.

Martin had arrived at the sheriff's office long before the other two. He had been quickly plunked down in front of Letsinger, Deputy Wayne Woods and Deputy Mike Lowrie. Letsinger read him his rights and asked Martin if he understood. Martin said, yes. Letsinger asked him what had happened. Martin began his tale, as the sheriff pecked out his account on the elderly office typewriter. It was not a job befitting a high sheriff, so Letsinger soon tired of it. He turned the job over to Deputy Lowrie who transferred the typewritten pages to a computer. He threw away the original typewritten pages, or so he claims. It was 11:55 P.M.

When Martin finished Lowrie let him read the statement on the screen. He asked if Martin wanted to change or omit anything. Martin agreed, it was okay. Lowrie printed it out. Woods and Letsinger came back into the office to witness the signing. Lowrie offered Martin some coffee, which he gratefully accepted. According to Lowrie, Martin had never asked for an attorney. Shortly afterward, he was allowed to visit with his family. There was a disagreement about the time of the visit.

Most ordinary people, plunked down into the middle of a major crime, want to tell everything, to purge themselves of the experience. Martin especially had been looking forward to the opportunity. He had not pulled the triggers, had not wanted to kill James and had no criminal ambitions.

Cops know this phenomena well. It is what solves most cases. People need to talk after such a horrible experience. The usual technique is to appear really concerned about the person: make him feel as if you really like him, really care about him and deeply understand his plight. Then the idea is to sit back and wait. Nine times out of ten the suspect or witness will babble away. It is an old technique, probably used by cops in ancient Rome, and it still works — but usually on first time offenders — an experienced criminal (or lawyer) just laughs. At any rate, it worked like magic that night. Everybody spilled their guts: Martin, Tommy, Andy. All willingly told their particular versions of Edmund James's murder. Martin got to tell it twice.

Tommy and Andy knew Martin had ratted on them. They were not happy about it. They were scared, but the lawmen were pleasant enough and what else was there to do?

Martin was not the only one with family trying to intervene on his behalf. Patsy Rae Eiland, Tommy's grandmother in Odessa, Texas, had heard about his arrest from friends. She immediately called Bob Whipkey's house to find out where Tommy was. She made careful note of the time. It was 8:30 P.M. Bob said

Tommy was in a sheriff's car outside. She asked to speak with him, but instead Buck Pruitt came on the line. Patsy told him she wanted to speak with Tommy and make arrangements for an attorney. Buck said there was no way. He told her she would have to wait. He was taking Tommy to the Real County sheriff's office in Leakey, and she could talk to him in a couple of hours.

Patsy Eiland waited. She finally got through to Buck again in Leakey at 11:52 P.M. She still wanted to get her grandson a lawyer. Buck said Tommy had already been before a judge and been magistrated. Tommy had been clearly told he could have a lawyer if he wanted one — besides, he wasn't even in Leakey anymore. He had been taken to Rocksprings. She would have to call Jay Adams there.

At 11:59 P.M. Patsy called the jail in Rocksprings. She was switched to dispatch, but they had no information. She called again at 12:02 A.M., at 1:07 A.M., again at 1:13 A.M., finally, at 1:25 A.M. she reached Jay Adams. Patsy asked once more to speak with Tommy and to get him an attorney.

"He told me Tommy had already signed a 'waiver.' I became real upset. I asked if Tommy even knew what a 'waiver' was? I again requested that he have a lawyer. He told me I could not talk to Tommy.

"I called back and talked to someone for about ten minutes. I don't remember who. I wanted to speak to Tommy. They told me he had waived his rights. At 1:25 A.M., they told me he was giving a statement; at 2:08, they told me he was going to give a statement. Finally, they told me not to call back. I could talk to him in the morning. They told me no plea had been entered. I didn't quite understand what that meant. So, I didn't talk to anyone until I finally got Tommy at 9:27 A.M. at the 'detention center.'

"I told him not to sign anything, but he said he already had. So I turned around and called Sheriff Letsinger. I begged him to let Tommy have an attorney. He told me Tommy had waived all rights, bond was to be set as high as possible and he would be magistrated again in the morning. He said Tommy was charged with capital murder."

Sometime after four A.M., Martin finally ate his hamburger, drank his Pepto-Bismol and coffee. After chatting with his dad, he felt much better. The lawmen repeatedly told him he was "just a witness." He was in protective custody so Tommy and Andy could not hurt him. Everything seemed to be going well. Martin felt safer than he had in days.

At the pretrial hearing Deputy Lowrie said that, while Martin visited with his parents, the deputies had a meeting, "I went and talked with Deputy Adams about the statements he had taken from the other two individuals. I took one of the statements and I circled a few key items which I wanted to ask Martin about again.

"I was convinced there was more to it all than the statement covered. So I brought Martin back in and sat him down. We sat down with him, and after a short conversation he admitted — he said, yeah, there was more to it. He said, 'but we are going to be here another two or three hours.' He asked me if I wanted to go ahead and take the second statement then or wait until later on?

"I said, 'Well, we might as well do it now, because it's fixing to be a busy day as soon as the sun comes up.' So we went at it again. And I took the second statement . . .

"He wanted to make a pseudo deal, I'm sure it was something he picked up somewhere on TV. I assured him I was in no position ever, ever at any time to make any kind of a deal . . . Now as soon as I walked into the room and I had Martin in front of me we had a very unique rapport. Everything was agreeable and cooperative."

It was fish-in-a-barrel, classic police work; just set back and let 'em come to Poppa. Lowrie's "might as well do it now . . . fixing to be a busy day" remark would bring chortles of cynical amusement from any cop in the world, and eye-rolling horror from any defense attorney. What he really meant was "this kid is stupid and I'm fixin' to nail him cold."

Cops have a standard repertoire. They bluff, "con," prompt, threaten, hint, plead, remind, hector, deal, and promise. They do all of those things to get a suspect to talk. In the old days, they would also lay on a few blows. It is the nature of police work. The first thing most crooks do is lie. It is always a fine line law enforcement officers walk. If they get a serial killer or child molester to confess, then they are heroes. If they keep a scared kid up for over twenty-four hours without food or drink, make some long promises and take a statement, then a defense attorney jumps all over them.

There were just a couple of "small details" Lowrie had "forgotten" in his testimony. Martin's attorney laid into him during a pretrial hearing.

The attorney asked, "Martin had been under 'investigative detention' since 8:30 P.M. And this was 11:55 P.M., midnight, when the statement was started. So he was still under investigative detention, is that your testimony?"

"Yes," replied Lowrie.

"When was Mr. Sweeten advised he was under arrest?"

"After the second statement."

"Could it have been at the end of the first statement?" the attorney questioned.

"No," Lowrie replied.

"After taking the first statement, but prior to taking the second statement, didn't you say you felt there was some inconsistencies between Martin's first statement and the statements of the other boys? Is that not so?" the attorney asked.

"True," Lowrie replied.

"And then you had some further conversation with Martin about coming clean and explaining the discrepancies. Is that correct?"

"Yes, sir," Lowrie admitted.

"Did you say something to the effect that, 'Martin, you are charged with murder' and that you believed part of his statement but not all?"

"I do recall that . . . those — but at what time frame?" Lowrie stumbled.

"This would be after the first statement but while you were still talking?" the attorney asked.

"Yes, sir; that's probably correct. It's hard to fit it all in, but it was about that time."

"Okay, so you advised him he was under arrest for murder at that time. Is that not correct?" the attorney asked.

The attorney's point was that Lowrie had told Martin, in so many words, he was about to be charged with murder. But, Lowrie had informed Martin in a casual, off-hand manner. What is more, Lowrie had done it before he began taking the second statement from Martin. It had been an easy point for Martin to miss. He was still laboring under the curious delusion he was "on the DA's side." (Exactly who put this pathetic notion into his head has never been determined, but it was devastatingly effective.) In other words, while Martin thought he was still a witness helping the district attorney, he was actually incriminating himself, big time. Lowrie merely had to record each word.

Lowrie had neither made the implications of what was happening crystal clear, nor had he reread Martin his Miranda rights. In theory, this was a legal no-no. Lowrie should have clearly notified Martin that his status was changing, that he had just made the jump from material witness to alleged felon. In many courts, these cute games would have raised grave procedural and constitutional questions.

There were some more inconsistencies in Lowrie's account.

"After Martin had talked to his father, do you recall he told you he would like to terminate the questioning for a period of time?" Martin's attorney asked.

"That he would like . . . ?" Lowrie replayed the question.

"Yes, that he would like to terminate the questions until he was in the presence of a lawyer?" the defense persisted.

"Not — well, I do believe there was something like that mentioned, but not to that effect." Lowrie explained. "Deputy Jay Adams had come into the room and admonished Martin that 'if he had any respect for me, he would tell the truth.' I believe Jay also said something like he thought Martin was lying.

"Jay went away, and then Martin went ahead and said . . . I think, something like — this is not verbatim, this is something very close — he said, 'I would like — to have my parents advised.' But as far as any part about wanting a lawyer, I don't remember anything about that," Lowrie continued.

Lowrie explained he had been somewhat sleepy at the time, but he would have remembered if Martin had asked for an attorney. Martin's attorney was unimpressed. He pointed out that Martin had been awake for over twenty-four hours with only a hamburger and Pepto-Bismol for food and was in worse shape than the deputy. So, he persisted, was Lowrie certain nothing was said about a lawyer?

"I think he had mentioned something about it," Lowrie then conceded. "But I asked him — I gave him the opportunity — if he wanted to terminate the questioning at any time as indicated in any Miranda warning. But he declined. He wanted to go ahead and get it over with."

In other words, the defense alleged the deputies had ignored Martin's request for an attorney and persisted in their demands for a new statement. That would have been a real big legal no-no. Lowrie had clumsily tried to dance around the question.

There was one more little problem — the TV inspired 'deal' Lowrie mentioned. That incident came after he and Jay Adams had played "good cop — bad cop" with Martin. It was another ancient cop game, and it had worked. Martin, naively intimidated by Adams, had wanted to talk only to his "pal," Lowrie.

Martin's attorney continued to cross-examine, "And then you were nicer, and said Martin could talk — could talk to you alone. You would get Adams out of the room and let Martin just talk to you. Is that it?"

"Well, I don't know if I was nicer or not, but I had started to take the statement from him and I did want to finish the job . . . ," Lowrie explained.

"Okay. At some point . . . you told Martin you couldn't promise him anything?"

"That's true."

"You did tell him that you couldn't promise anything, but it's just possible he might only have to spend a few days in a boot camp. Is that correct?"

"Well, no, if it was correct — I wouldn't have said it for a few days because no one spends a 'few days' in boot camp," Lowrie answered.

"What was said about 'boot camp?'"

"I said, well, — We were talking about penalties, and I really had no idea what the penalties would be — and, I said . . . well . . . you know, some guys go to prison, some guys get probation, some guys get this boot camp. It is this new thing they have. I said I really don't know what the deal will be because, in fact, at that time I had no idea what the official charges would be. That was not my concern at the time, only taking the statement," Lowrie explained.

They went back to fencing over Martin's request to stop taking the statement, and get him an attorney.

"Was the statement made to Martin that if he did not continue his statement, the district attorney would have to be advised that he had stopped cooperating?" the attorney asked.

"Not to my knowledge, no."

Martin had been so sure he was cooperating with the shadowy DA. He had not listened to his father's warnings, clinging instead to the notion he was "just a witness." In his mind, he was helping his friends, the police. He actually believed, even if he faced trouble, it was just minor trouble. It was pretty clear from the testimony the deputies never bothered to disabuse him of these illusions. Instead, they kept him awake for over twenty-four hours with very little to eat, ignored his request for an attorney and promised him "boot camp."

It did not take much to break Martin Sweeten. By four A.M., he was ready to sign anything.

After seeing Martin, Darwin, Sue and the Pannell family walked out of the sheriff's office to go home. Darwin was burdened with a bad feeling about the situation. Letsinger had told him he was going to take Martin over to the jail and lock him up for the night. It was still "protective custody." Darwin did not like it and had said so. The sheriff had ignored him. As they got in the car, Sheriff Letsinger called to them and walked over. He asked them to come back in for a few minutes. His tone was friendly.

"Let me think about this for a while?" he asked the family.

"Sure," Darwin gratefully allowed.

They waited for a half an hour. Letsinger finally came out to the front office.

"Look, people will think badly of me, if I let Martin go home right now," he explained. "I'm going to put him in jail and keep him in custody for tonight. You can probably come and get him in the morning."

This was, at best, sheer manipulation. Letsinger, by that time, knew Martin was in his office implicating himself into a murder charge. He apparently just wanted to placate bothersome family members. He wanted this obnoxious little man calmed down and quiet. Sugar was the easiest way to do it.

"Well, if that's what you have to do, sir. I'll understand," Darwin replied. "I sure wish you would let him go home."

"Can't do it. I'm sorry."

Darwin went home. It was nearly dawn. In the morning he

called Letsinger. He was told the sheriff had gone home to sleep and would not be back until two P.M. Darwin had a real bad feeling. He called Buck Pruitt.

"Darwin, your boy needs a lawyer, and he needed one last night," Buck told him bluntly. "Your boy is under arrest for murder."

Darwin did not hesitate. John Pannell had recommended he call the best criminal defense lawyer in San Antonio. Darwin dialed the number of Roy Barrera, Sr., of Nicolas and Barrera.

CHAPTER IV

DARWIN'S DREAM

AS OFFICERS COMBED Edmund's house and grounds searching for clues, there were still two minor mysteries nagging them. They had applied the standard operating procedures, and most of the facts had come clear. Their intense initial search had dropped off by the next morning to a more leisurely pace. The suspects were magistrated and in custody. Their statements, virtually confessions, were on record.

The spring morning was cool and pleasant. The automatic sprinklers sputtered on to water the front lawn. Except for the deputies on their knees carefully scanning the area where the body had been found, everything seemed normal. The deputies were looking for shell casings, the brass casings which held the actual bullets fired into Edmund's body.

During manufacture, lead bullets are squeezed into the shell casings which also contain a powder charge and a percussion cap. It is a relatively simple technology, refined over the last 600 years. When the trigger is pulled, the rifle's firing pin strikes the cap. The cap, a tiny bit of explosive, sensitive to pressure, explodes when struck and ignites the powder. The expanding gases blast the bullet out of the casing and down the barrel (hence the police slang for firing a gun, "to pop a cap"). It is a technology so perfected that the bullets which killed Edmund cost less than a penny each.

Tommy and Andy used two semiautomatic .22 caliber rifles. Each rifle held about fifteen shots. The bullets, or rounds, were loaded down a tube underneath the barrel and put under tension by a spring. As a round was fired, the gases which propelled the bullet also forced back the rifle's bolt. This opened the firing chamber, and the magazine's spring pushed up another round. Then another spring pushed the bolt forward closing the firing chamber and loaded the waiting round into the barrel. When a round was fired, the backward motion of the bolt would also toss out the empty shell casing, or hull. Since the rifles were semiautomatic, these events occurred each time the trigger was pulled. A more accurate term for the action is "self-loading."

Two young men, in their late teens, can fire semiautomatic rifles with astonishing speed. The effect almost approaches fully automatic rates. In a few seconds, they can empty the rifles' magazines.

Pow — P'-P'-P'- Pow! The reports from each round ran together. With each discharge, a glittering brass shell casing flew out of the rifles landing a couple of feet away.

Tommy and Andy had pumped ten rounds into Edmund's body at close range. In their frenzy, they had probably fired rounds which missed — but not many. Neither was exactly sure later just how many rounds they had loaded into their rifles. There could have been ten to fifteen shots fired, very probably more, all in rapid succession. There should have been at least a dozen shell casings strewn around the body. Yet trained professional law enforcement officers, searching for two days, could only come up with one lone shell casing. It was weird.

Worse, it was embarrassing. It had some disturbing implications because, in their lengthy interrogations, none of the young men mentioned spending time picking up a dozen shell casings. In fact, they denied doing any such thing. That is why the search around the grounds continued with uniformed deputies on their hands and knees. It should have been easy. Instead it looked like some goofy, fruitless search for a lost contact lens.

What had happened? Something was very wrong. Brass casings are easily spotted, especially with a strong police-issue flashlight. Sure, they might miss a couple, but that ten or fifteen casings were just swallowed up by the earth was hard to accept. What had happened to them?

The other mystery concerned Edmund's dogs. Like Sherlock Holmes's famous observation, it was the absence of a barking dog which was the mystery. All three boys had said the dogs were out when they left the scene. Martin especially remembered the poignant tableau of the two Labs nuzzling their fallen master. Neither Tommy, Andy nor Martin had any obvious reasons to lie about this; after all they had confessed to murder. What did the disposition of the dogs matter? All three consistently maintained the dogs were out when they left.

Yet, when Deputy Buck Pruitt, who was first on the scene, approached the house he was struck by the absence of dogs. He clearly remembered the eerie atmosphere as he approached the house. He was curious why no ranch dogs ran out to greet or challenge him.

"I approached the house fairly slowly," he later testified. "I tried to ascertain if there was anyone else in the area or in the house. I could hear a television going in the house. There were no dogs, which I found very strange. You go to a ranch house anywhere in our part of the country, and you expect dogs. We were just being careful . . . We were being very, very careful."

Later the dogs were found locked in the storeroom to the left of the kitchen. It did not make sense. The body had not been moved or molested, the TV was still on, the door unlocked. Why would someone come out to the ranch, pick up shell casings, put up the dogs and just leave? If the boys had not done it, who did? Who could have known about the murder hours before Martin had turned in the alarm? It could not have been a family member or neighbor because they would have immediately called the sheriff. If it had been transients or illegal aliens, why had they not helped themselves to the useful goodies in the unlocked house? If it had been a friend of the boys, why did they just pick up the shell casings? Why not close the door, turn off the TV, wipe away fingerprints, etc.? Who would take the chance of disturbing the murder scene and perhaps being sighted on the ranch road?

The deputies had no answers to these questions. They eventually had little choice but to shrug off the doubts. Every murder scene has some unanswered problems. If they are minor, it is just too bad if the answers are not found. The deputies had their suspects, they had their statements, they had their case. Anything else was just a minor loose end.

Martin languished. He had given up hope. He was held in the Edwards County Jail, a dismaying experience in itself. Nearby, Tommy and Andy were securely locked up. Martin got an earful. It seemed as if from the time Tommy would rise in the morning until he lay down his head at night he cursed Martin. He would threaten, promise and vow vengeance. His former friend reviled Martin hourly. Andy agreed.

But this was not the greasy bottom of Martin's despair. In the space of about forty-eight hours he went from being a free roaming teenager burdened only with adolescent concerns to an accused murderer. The full import of what he had done was constantly unfolding. Not only had he stood by while a perfectly decent man was dealt a shabby death; he had driven the damn car. To compound the mess, he had almost casually dismissed his father's pleas. He babbled to the cops, thinking they were his friends. He told them anything and everything they wanted to hear. Perhaps, it was slowly dawning on him, he had told way too much.

The often heard phrase "anything you say can and will be used against you in a court of law" took on an awful and immense reality. These words, which he had heard a thousand times on television and in the movies, now became fresh with dreadful meaning. They were not just a rote little speech every cop learned nor some expected ritual wrapping up another television case. The words meant exactly what they said. That phrase would probably doom him. Those words might just lead to a clean little room with a medical gurney and rubber tubes connected to lethal drugs. How very stupid he had been to take those words for granted. Those frightful words could take him straight to his death.

His notion of "being on the DA's side" seemed silly and naive. All of the talk about "boot camp" seemed a horrible practical joke. "Boot camp" indeed. He was charged with a murder rap. The death penalty was alive and well in Texas. Martin was eighteen years old, and he could perhaps count the remaining days of his life.

Martin was having those thoughts which come to all of us when we awaken at four A.M. and feel a dreadful reality settling over us. It is a moment when our lives and actions seem foolish and wasteful. In Martin's case the feeling did not go away with the dawn. That feeling was now his constant companion.

He realized everything he had done, from the time he drove the other two up to the ranch until the last piece of paper had been signed in the sheriff's office, was sheer folly. He still had enough of his father's religion to believe he would finally meet Jesus and be forgiven, maybe. Or maybe reality was a big black hole of nothing, a last few moments of clinging desperately to life's sensations, then blackness. These were cold-blooded thoughts, terrible and frightening. Martin had been to church enough to know how to pray and he certainly did during those first dark days. It was one thing to have faith the Lord would come to your aid as an innocent man falsely accused. It was something else again to have such faith if you were sort of guilty, not quite spotless, not as guilty as your accusers say, but then not totally innocent either. That was a lot of faith to ask from a teenager whose biggest problem a few days before was how to get a part-time job. Such cold-sweat thoughts made Tommy's anger seem secondary.

The day after his son's arrest, Thursday morning, Darwin's long wait for business hours finally ended. It had seemed like forever. John Pannell had recommended he call Barrera Senior.

"If you can get him, he is the best, Darwin," he had advised. "Roy Barrera is one of the best defense lawyers around, and I think Martin is going to need him."

"I don't know if I can afford him, John," Darwin had complained.

"Look if you want to save your boy, you better get someone like him. Because, if you sit back and let the court pick your attorney, Martin is not going to have much of a chance. It can't hurt to call. Barrera sometimes defends folks without much money," John replied.

So Darwin waited out that long night until nine A.M. arrived. He dialed the San Antonio number for Roy R. Barrera, Senior. He got Roy R. Barrera, Junior, also known as Judge Barrera because he had served on the state bench. Darwin asked for the elder Barrera, but he was not in the office. Junior asked what the problem was. Darwin plunged into his story. He told Junior everything he knew, including the rumors.

"I told him about what had happened that night," Darwin later recounted. "How the arrest went down, all about it . . . I told him I didn't think Elton had the right to pick him up when he did because Elton is only a constable. He picked Martin up in Uvalde County and hauled him through two more counties. I told him that Martin did not have his rights read to him at the time they showed up on the scene out there — and . . . I told him Martin said he was innocent of murder.

"I told him that Martin said, he didn't come out and say it, but he implied, that he might be guilty of some robberies . . . Like I said, I told him everything that Martin had a chance to tell me that night. I told him Martin definitely was an eyewitness, and he was there when it happened. I said Martin fully believed he was working with the DA the whole time — and that . . . Let's see, I told him I was with Martin until 4:30 in the morning; and that Sheriff Letsinger said, promised me very faithfully, that he was going to get him to the cell because he was too tired to talk anymore. At that point Martin was supposed to be held, to my understanding, as a witness in protective custody."

Darwin claims Roy Jr. advised him to get Martin out of jail as quickly as possible, "make bond for him, get him out, and he definitely needs a lawyer." Roy Jr. also told Darwin that he had to confer with his father. Darwin later said, "He said — he made it very clear to me — if I hired one of them, I hired both of them. They was a team . . . he wouldn't do anything without his daddy's permission."

Roy Jr. told Darwin to wait and let him contact his father. Roy Jr. promised to call back as soon as this was accomplished. Darwin waited fretfully. The day dragged on, hour after hour with no call. Darwin picked up the telephone and redialed the number.

"I think I had four or five conversations with him that day," he said, "because he kept telling me, 'I'll call you back in an hour or two when I get a chance to talk to my dad.' He never did call me. It took the better part of Thursday or Friday, and I never could get together on anything. I'm not positive it was both days, but it seems like it was two. It was long enough to be two days.

"He finally told me he had found out that Martin was being

held as an accessory to murder. See, at that time, I hadn't made connections to the sheriff to find out what the charges were. I just knew Martin was charged with something because things weren't going right.

"Judge Barrera finally told me that my son redone a statement, but I don't know whether he went into all of the details of it or not, but he said the statement was how come they decided to hold Martin, the statement that he had redone.

"Judge Barrera said he needed $15,000 for a retainer fee and five thousand for bail money . . . He said he needed to see the titles to any property I had. I told him my brother was going to try to help me get the money together, and along about then me and my wife had a — we went into quite a nervous shock. You know, it all hit us and our nerves went to pieces, couldn't sleep or nothing. My brothers took over. Doctor Todd gave us some pills to sleep and stuff . . . I finally talked to Roy Senior the next morning.

"We had a nice talk. He just asked me if I was going to make my retainer. I told him, no, I wasn't going to make it. I just couldn't do it. I told him my brother was supposed to have called him the day before and told him. He said nobody had called him."

Roy Barrera, Sr. is nothing if not kindly in manner and courtly in his demeanor. He is a dark complexioned man with straight black hair, slightly protruding front teeth which gives him a toothy but engaging smile. The general effect is decidedly avuncular, a deadly characteristic in a trial lawyer. Barrera speaks with careful clarity which betrays a hard-won education. He was born in 1927 to the dreary hardships of a poor Mexican-American family. With tenacity and determination he entered St. Mary's Law School in San Antonio and was admitted to the bar in 1951. He rose to the top of his profession as a skillful attorney. Under Governor John Connally he served as Secretary of State of Texas. He belongs to an almost bewildering list of legal associations.

Barrera's less than average stature and mild manners are deceiving. Many prosecutors have underestimated him, to their regret. Roy Barrera ate well-crafted prosecution cases for breakfast, and he did it with relish. He destroyed skillful opposition arguments with relentless precision. He won over juries with charm and swayed opinions with smooth oratory. In short, he was one hell of a defense attorney, the kind of man Darwin needed.

Darwin admitted he did not have the retainer and probably could not raise it soon. He told Barrera he was going to have to retain another attorney. It was just as well because Barrera had some hard news for Darwin. While Darwin had negotiated with Roy Junior, the elder Barrera had been approached to take on another case. A prominent San Antonio family asked him to represent their interests. They wanted him to use all of his forensic powers to insure justice was done by the Texas judicial system. Roy Barrera, Sr. was going to assist the Val Verde County District Attorney in prosecuting the killers of Edmund James.

It seemed out of character for Barrera. The links of friendship and obligations which must have led him to take on this unlikely role are not clear. The James family was determined to make sure Edmund's killers did not hide behind their youth, or wiggle free through some chink in the law. They wanted the little bastards nailed good and hard. It was difficult to blame them. They knew retaining someone like Barrera just added heft to the hammer.

The Val Verde district attorney was named Tom Lee. He also graduated from St. Mary's Law School. Tall with thinning hair, Lee was soft-spoken and friendly. He wore a tasteful western hat above his dark suit and Oxford shoes. At first glance, he did not seem formidable until he stood before a jury. Then he was coolly professional. He could lay down a minefield of reasoned arguments. Tom Lee was the ideal prosecutor, friendly but stern, an upright man who upheld the cause of the state. If he had any weakness at all, it was losing. He did not like it. Lee was given to making cracks about the defense if he lost a case. But, in fairness, he held an elective office, and any loss was ammunition for his opposition.

Lee had been in office for almost ten years, so obviously he had not lost many cases. Although he evidenced no burning ambition for higher office, like any DA worth his salt Lee knew you did not turn down the request of a powerful family without good reasons. The family had no illusions about "taking over" the case, wrenching control away from Lee. They just figured he would be agreeable to some high powered "help." Sharing the burden with someone of Barrera's stature was no shame. From Lee's standpoint he had little to lose. Partnering up with Barrera could bear fruit in the future. The gratitude of the James family was nothing to ignore. Finally, there was one basic fact of prosecution, the district attorney represented not the victim or his family but the State of Texas. Roy Barrera on the other hand would stand before the bar on behalf of Edmund and his family.

Barrera and Lee quickly came to a friendly working agreement. Roy Barrera, a prime defense attorney in Texas, would temporarily step over the line. Defense attorneys are a special breed. They see themselves as bound in a sort of Masonic fraternity. Criminal defense is more than a job. Most have spent their lives defending clients against the well armed assaults of prosecutors. Since judges tend to be former prosecutors and many courtroom procedures subtly favor the state, criminal trials can easily become the prosecution's sandbox. Most people think the famous "presumption of innocence" weights the balance of a trial in favor of the accused, but the view from the defense side is significantly different.

Defense attorneys always wait for the moment when the cold light of reality dawns on their client. It is the moment when a defendant realizes just how much trouble he or she is in, how deep the well really is. It is the moment when the client figuratively (or sometimes literally) clutches at the attorney's lapels, with a look of horror and panic. It is the "My God! You are my only hope," look. Experiences like that binds defense attorneys to their chosen profession. So, when one of their own steps over to the other side, it is rather like a family member converting to a rival religion. A collective shudder runs through the profession.

On the other hand, the arrangement is not in itself unusual. Interested parties routinely retain attorneys to watch over their interests during a trial. It is a more common practice in civil disputes. One of Edmund's grieving friends hired Martin Underwood to monitor the murder trials. Underwood practices law out of Comstock, Texas, in Val Verde County. He had faced Judge Thurmond many times. At Martin's trial Underwood was about as unprepossessing in appearance as possible. He wore a full bushy beard and dressed in boots, faded jeans and matching jacket. He looked like a demented prospector in town for an extended toot. But Underwood is one of the most respected leading criminal defense attorneys in the state. He specializes in capital murder cases.

During Martin's trial he took notes and passed suggestions and citations on relevant cases up to the prosecution table. He had been a personal friend of Edmund's. This case was the first time he had crossed over to help the prosecution. He did it out of friendship.

During the three trials, Barrera was, of course, also working on other cases. One was notorious and "high profile." While he quietly prosecuted Tommy and Andy, he defended the Reverend Walker Railey, the prominent minister of the wealthy First United Methodist Church in Dallas. In 1987 Railey was accused of the attempted murder of his wife, Margaret. She was found choked nearly to death in their home. She slipped into a deep permanent coma, and remains so to this day. It was assuredly a high profile case, a delicious criminal scandal which Texas seems to produce regularly.

Suspicion locked on Railey, who, it was found, had salted away large sums of money. Worse, he had a yummy looking mistress waiting in the wings. Public anger got so heated before he stepped down from the ministry that Railey had to give sermons wearing a bulletproof vest.

The state alleged Railey planned and carried out the attack, clumsily covering his tracks with a phony call to his home answering machine. The DA further alleged Railey botched the murder and coldly left his wife in a vegetative state. The case was sensational. It reminded murder fans of the famous Sam Shepherd case and Claus Von Buelow's trial. Naturally, the media flew into a frothing frenzy.

The case dragged on from 1987 until 1993 when it finally came to trial. While Barrera was defending the notorious minister with full media attention, he was more inconspicuously prosecuting Edmund's killers.

Barrera's decision to side with the James family devastated Darwin. An inky cloud of despair closed about him. Martin's situation was degenerating. Darwin's family had fallen into disaster. The very components of his life were loosening, threatening to spin free leaving him in a life of endless sorrow. On the one hand, it did not seem real. On the other it seemed too very real. He needed pills to sleep, but he still wakened to fretful thoughts. He was free falling into a black pit with no bottom. Every day was worse.

Darwin was used to the kicks life dealt out; he had been kicked before. It is not as if he expected life to be unfair. He simply was not surprised when it was. Darwin always managed to keep going. He wept privately, swallowed his pride and set about doing something. Darwin was not a willing, passive victim.

In fact, he is a living representative of a genuine American minority, the southern, blue-collar male. He is the sort of man to which the comfortable middle class used to extend the titles like "less fortunate" and "deserving poor." Darwin and his kind are the direct descendants of the backwoods boys who astonished Northern armies during the Civil War with their capacity to suffer and survive. But this thing with Martin was almost too much. He had already been through Martin's motorcycle accident, watching his son fight his way back from crippling injuries.

But this time life had pushed him too far. The only thing he and Sue had left was their religion. Was he, like Job, being tested to his limit by a stern God? Did God reserve his harshest test for little guys like Darwin and his family? Had he been abandoned by God to become a plaything of Satan's whims? Those were hard, dark questions for Darwin Sweeten to ponder.

Darwin prayed. Sue prayed. Even Darwin's brothers, Lee and John, who were not known for excessive piety, bent their knees. The moment the preachers always warned about had arrived. It was time to put their faith on the line.

Back in 1989, when Martin lay badly injured, Sue, sought help from prayer groups and churches all over the county. And, Praise The Lord, it had worked. The doctors thought Martin would be a cripple for life but instead, he made a full recovery. All of that biblical talk about "The Lord as a refuge and shield" was taken very seriously by the Sweeten family and with good reasons. Sue had no doubts about answered prayers.

Darwin and Sue attended one of those off-brand Pentecostal churches that dot the Texas landscape. Neither of them spoke in tongues or anything like that, and both took some Sundays off for other things. Like most Americans they were believers, but neither excessively pious nor merely Easter Sunday Christians. They believed and had faith. Intellectuals and academics may mock Darwin's kind of religion, but then they have other resources with which to console themselves in times of strife. For

Darwin and Sue, God Almighty was their last chance, and in his shadow they would make their final stand.

There is no doubt that something came to their aid. Darwin Sweeten, the funny little guy in red suspenders and a baseball hat, the odd fellow everyone looked upon with sympathetic amusement, drew forth astonishing powers in the fight to save his son. In another place and time he would have been called a shaman, a medicine man or a wizard. Through Darwin things began to happen, extraordinary things.

What mysterious internal event turned things around for him can never be known. It is something which comes from the deepest levels of a person's being, something which can never be put into words. It is a transformation of the sort which makes a defeated army turn around and fight or a mother lift a car to save her child. This extraordinary power comes from within and beyond, and it works wonders.

Darwin wrestled with a decision. Should he let the natural course of events proceed or intervene somehow. If he chose the former, he would let the judge pick an attorney to defend Martin and hope for the best. He could call it "God's will" and sit back. It was the easy way and very tempting. Martin was an adult and certainly had no money or assets. There was no doubt the court would appoint counsel for him. His experience with Barrera brought home what retaining a big-time attorney really entailed. Barrera Junior had requested that Darwin turn over titles to every piece of property he owned — cars, land, houses, whatever. It had shocked him profoundly. Defending Martin with big time legal help would wipe away what little Darwin had accumulated and put him in debt for the rest of his life. It was tempting to say, "If I can't have the best then I'll just put it into the hands of God and the court."

Something about that notion did not sit well with Darwin Sweeten. He trusted in the Lord sure enough, but his faith in the legal system had grown very tenuous. There was enough fight left in him to wonder why God would require him to leave his son's defense in the hands of some unknown lawyer of doubtful loyalty.

Throughout Real, Uvalde and Edwards counties there was a rising level of outrage over Edmund's death. Things were becoming unpleasant for the Sweetens. Many area residents had only the vaguest notion of Camp Wood and Barksdale. Camp Wood was tucked obscurely into a corner of Real County. Barksdale was considered the backyard of Edwards County. Few in Edwards County had known Edmund James personally. What most county residents heard loudly and clearly was that a rancher had been foully murdered at his residence. "Rancher" was the operative word. It was enough.

City dwellers have a difficult time realizing just how threatening such an event can be out west. They are used to, if even unconsciously, the close presence of others, quick communication and quick responses. But to ranchers, their property and ranch houses are sacrosanct. The very thought of murderous thugs invading isolated and pacific homesteads rouses fury. Most of the ranches are miles off main roads; they are little outposts of civilization. Any threat to them touches deep chords of fear and anger.

The fear had been growing long before Edmund was killed. The violence in the cities was a constant source of dismay. Illegal Mexican aliens often cut through ranch lands taking the back way to San Antonio or points north. Many came up to work on the ranches, and traditionally they were welcome. Many ranchers still keep humble shacks tucked away in obscure corners as way stations for "wets." The shacks are stocked with beans, rice and other basic necessities.

The wets are a source of inexpensive labor. As long as they are kept out of sight, the immigration service will not usually raid prosperous Anglo ranchers. But lately things had begun to change. The old friendly agreements were breaking down. In the old days, illegals would come up to work and then return to Mexico to be with their families in the off-season. Now a new breed of illegals were coming up. They did not want ranch work; they were seeking permanent asylum in the U.S. They were bound for the big cities and some carried drugs. Smugglers used isolated areas of ranches for their operations. Even cattle rustling was increasing. Stories of mutilated cattle and devil worship did not help keep things in perspective.

These newer and more ambitious illegals revived old fears of invasion. Just before the United States entered World War I, when the Zimmerman telegram scandal broke, similar fears caused huge troop movements to the border. Nowadays drug smuggling and the attendant violence fueled the anxiety. The old images of silent figures invading hapless, isolated ranch houses began to surface. Modern ranch houses now sported electronic alarms, security lights, well-oiled firearms, and alert guard dogs.

These fears were bad enough, but that Anglo kids from a local small town coldly gunned down a rancher caused frothing outrage. It was the fury of betrayal. The very thought drove out temperance and rationality. This was big city crime come to God's county; the national rot was spreading. This was vicious and evil, and the good folks of Edwards County would have none of it. They wanted the nasty little punks done away with, legally of course, but with finality.

This sentiment along with the money and power of the James family put the heat on Edwards County officials. Tommy, Andy, and Martin were not mistreated in jail, but they knew very little compassion was available to them. In Camp Wood, the general reaction was something like, "I can understand Tommy doing it, but Martin Sweeten? No way!" It seemed so unlikely. Few actually knew Andy, so they could believe just about anything regarding him. Tommy they knew all too well. His name was virtually married to the exclamatory phrases, "I knew it!" and "I told you something like this would happen!"

Martin, on the other hand, as a cold-blooded killer just did not sell.

So there was actually some sympathy in Camp Wood for the Sweetens. Nevertheless it was a painful time for them. Like most working class folk, the Sweetens were very sensitive about their reputation in the community. Having a son accused of murder was not only frightening, it was also humiliating. It forced the Sweetens to the defensive.

"Martin did not do it. He was taken in by those other two," they constantly explained.

Most folks in Camp Wood understood and believed it. In Rocksprings, Uvalde, and San Antonio, however, there was growing hostility. Even normally genteel San Antonio society ladies would go frosty when the case was mentioned and voice hopes the little "bastards" would be executed. Edmund was loved while his killers were not. It was perfectly understandable.

Darwin finally decided that if he were going to put up a fight for Martin, he must find a competent lawyer to take his case. Lawyers of Barrera's fame were out. Darwin was too poor and the case was not exotic enough to entice them. It promised no glory. That was the question, the appeal Darwin put to Heaven in his prayers.

Darwin's answer came as a dream, well, not exactly a dream. After Barrera broke the bad news to him, he had trouble falling asleep. He fretted and worried until finally he passed into sleep late in the night. He had no dream or saw no images, but he heard a clear voice. Darwin said it was a familiar voice but he could not place it. The voice told him to be not afraid and to have faith.

"The voice said that God was in my corner," Darwin recalls. "It told me I would find another lawyer soon and I would know he was the right lawyer by his attitude. The voice promised me that I would not have to give up everything I owned to defend my son."

The next morning Darwin asked John Pannell if he knew of another attorney. A few months back, some relatives of John's had some legal problems. They had been forced to sue. An attorney from Kerrville represented them and won the case along with a handsomely plump judgment. John suggested that Darwin should go see this lawyer. Darwin and his brothers got in a car and drove seventy miles to Kerrville. When Darwin met the attorney he knew this was the man the voice had told him to expect.

Scott Stehling was not exactly a typical small-town lawyer. Although he had been born and raised in Kerrville, he could have carved out a major law career in Houston or Dallas. There had been offers but Scott, after a number of career adventures, decided to settle in Kerrville. There were a lot of personal reasons for doing so, not the least of which was the town itself.

Kerrville sits about seventy miles northwest of San Antonio, in the Hill Country. It sprawls along part of the Guadalupe River valley. It is something of a retirement village and resort rolled into one. Kerrville is perhaps the most sophisticated and prosperous small city on the plateau. Slightly to the west, along the upper reaches of the Guadalupe, well-heeled Houstonians have summer homes, some of which approach Californian splendor.

In the fall and winter, hunters invade the town in search of doves and trophy bucks; in the summer, riverside camps fill up with city kids. Once a year there is a well known Bluegrass and Folk music festival. Residents love it. There is a sort of a comfortable magic about the place. It is easy to develop a strong attachment to the town.

Kerrville is high enough to escape some of the grinding

Texas summer heat. The average temperature is about ten degrees cooler than San Antonio. The pace of living is pleasant and stresses are few. It appears the all-American small town, but there is a peculiar streak of darkness haunting the town.

The infamous Genene Jones, a murderous nurse who coldly killed young children in her care, once practiced her black craft in the local hospital. She eventually moved back to San Antonio and is suspected of killing more than thirty children. One of her victims was a fifteen-month-old girl from Comfort, Texas, a town twenty miles from Kerrville. Her sad death roused the authorities' suspicions and set them on Jones' trail. She was eventually caught, tried and convicted of two murders.

In 1987 Kerrville made sensational national headlines during the famous "Slave Ranch" trial. More recently, Kerrville was the site of a bitter tragedy when buses from a religious summer camp were swept away during a summer storm. The drivers misjudged the flooding river water and the buses overturned. Several kids were lost. Many others were saved in heroic rescues by helicopter crews and citizens along the bank. It was a bittersweet tale and put the town into national news. But, these grievous moments stand out mostly because everyday life in Kerrville is so pleasant.

Scott grew up there. He was a town boy, not a "goat roper." The cowboy culture of Central Texas did not particularly interest him. His goals were always beyond the bounds of a small town. His tastes were more urbane and intellectual. He pulled it off without seeming snobbish or aloof. He excelled at Tivy High School, masking his ambitions with ironic wit and boisterous good will. Scott was not a trouble maker, but neither was he reclusive. Scott did his share of youthful hell raising, high school romancing, and blow out beer busts. But, he always kept a part of himself in reserve. He kept his own counsel, as one of his teachers put it. He took to debate with enthusiasm and a fierce determination to win, which he frequently did. When he left for the university there was only one career for him, the law.

Scott graduated from the University of Texas at Austin Law School in 1970 with a respectable academic record. He had been editor of the *Law Review* and Southwestern Debate Champion. When he graduated, he had offers from Houston law firms waiting. Scott had a streak of independence and the lure of glory in a big city law firm was balanced against the thought of slogging his way up the corporate ladder. Instead, he set up practice in Austin. Some hard lean years followed spiced with successes.

Scott was appointed a Hearings Examiner on the Texas Railroad Commission, that peculiar institution which governs the state's oil industry. (It is such an effective governing body that a group of Venezuelan exchange students studied its workings and structure, returned to their country and created OPEC, The Organization of Petroleum Exporting Countries.) As an examiner, Scott virtually had a judge's powers. It was a useful experience, but he longed to practice law.

He returned to Kerrville and served as an assistant DA from 1981 to 1984. By this time he was married with a young daughter. In 1982 Scott caught the political bug and decided to make a run for State Representative. It was a grueling ordeal and a close run campaign. He lost.

He also lost his wife. She announced enough was enough. She was sick of Kerrville, politics and Scott. She pined for the more exotic pleasures of Austin. She was just not cut out to be a small town lawyer's wife. She wanted out of the marriage and town as soon as possible.

This was something Scott had neither sought nor encouraged. It was a devastating blow. They had a seven-year-old daughter, Blake, and each parent was devoted to her. The usual painful arrangements for visitation rights had to be negotiated. Scott bowed to the inevitable, but it hurt. It hit him hard, and pressing demands to cultivate his practice did not make things easier. The word got around town. Scott was down, drinking a little too much, but, nonetheless, still a damn good lawyer.

He struggled along until his mother suggested he ask a former high school friend out for a date. Scott and Julia Wendel had known each other since kindergarten. In high school, they dated off and on. They lost track of each other during the college years. Julia married and settled in Dallas where her husband worked for Braniff Airlines. He left before it went under. They moved back to Kerrville to start over. Soon after they settled in, he was killed in a motorcycle accident. Julia was left to raise their two daughters, Ingrid and Heather.

Thus through traditional village matchmaking, Scott met

Julia again. A modest but elegant woman, Julia radiated an aura of kindness firmly backed with intelligence. Intensely feminine, she asked for little, so it was difficult to deny her anything. They fell into each other's arms and married within a few months. It was the kind of story which was the staple of 1940s movies and thought to be only available in fiction these days. Julia took over as Scott's office manager and legal secretary. Scott turned to developing his practice with renewed vigor.

In 1987 the "Slave Ranch" case broke. Wesley Ellebracht, Senior ran a family ranch northwest of Kerrville. He, his son Wesley Jr., and a twenty-year-old foreman, named Carlton Caldwell, were accused of conspiracy to torture and kill a homeless, one-eyed drifter named Anthony Bates. The Ellebrachts and Carlton were accused of recruiting homeless transients from San Antonio work centers and from the highways. They would take them to the ranch and keep them as "slaves" in appalling conditions of squalor. The state alleged that they would torture the victims then dispatch them when through.

The media fell upon the case like ravenous jackals, snarling and rending. They descended upon Kerrville like the Golden Horde. Trucks, vans and rented cars filled the parking spaces around the courthouse. A baroque forest of antennae and satellite dishes rose up around the plaza.

Scott was court appointed counsel for Carlton. Ellebracht Sr. retained Richard "Racehorse" Haynes as defense counsel. The media collectively hit the "on" button and the air was crisscrossed with magnetic fields from hundreds of video cameras, recorders and microphones. Reporters from *Time*, *Newsweek*, *The New York Times* and even *Pravda* hounded the lawyers for quotes and juicy bits. Scott remembers commenting to a *Newsweek* reporter about the prosecution, "I'll sure be surprised if they prove conspiracy against anyone." It was an unfortunate remark.

The details of the trial still make for bizarre reading. The physical proof of murder consisted of tiny burned fragments of bone found near a barn. Disastrously, the proof of torture was on audio tapes thoughtfully made by Wesley Ellebracht, Jr., and Carlton. They both had an odd passion for taping everything from the most banal of domestic conversations to ghastly torture sessions with electric cattle prods.

In one tape Wesley complained his wife did not keep jam for his bread in the house. Naturally, this became known as "The Bread and Jam Tape." The media just loved to contrast it with the most gruesome torture sessions one of which began with a DJ-like introduction, " Live from the bunkhouse, it's Shock Time." It was as if some monstrous children's fable had come to life, not to mention a defense attorney's nightmare. Once the jury heard the tapes, any explanations would seem feeble.

Scott conceded there had been torture but claimed there had been no murder. In fact, the prosecution's bones were animal. The state brought in an expert who testified that the bones were definitely human. It was a questionable theory because the bones had been burned to a carbonized state, and most were no larger than little pebbles. However, there is nothing like a paid professional for absolute certainty. Scott fought back with a copy of Gray's Anatomy and a few shrewd questions. After extensive cross-examination, he got the expert to admit there was just as much probability the bones were from a horse.

The trial dragged on for weeks. It would have been an easily defensible case but for those horrible tapes. It was impossible to deny the screams of the victims. Scott used the same tactic the defense lawyers defending the Los Angles police officers in the Rodney King case later employed. He played the tapes over and over again for the jury. He played them with any serviceable excuse. Scott would play them while asking the witnesses questions like, "Is this your voice?" or " What is going on here?" The idea was to desensitize the jurors to the sounds. Once that was accomplished he could introduce reasoned arguments and proofs in defense of his client. It is the sort of "trick" or tactic which makes people cynical about lawyers — unless they happen to be the accused.

Again and again he played the tapes, asking ever more detailed questions. It got to where everyone in the courtroom was ready to scream along with the tapes. Later Racehorse Haynes commented it was one of the most remarkable examples of endurance he had ever seen in a courtroom. Meanwhile, the best hope Racehorse had of defending his client, Ellebracht Senior, was to shift as much of the blame as possible on to Carlton. Senior was not an unlikable man. He was the antithesis of Hollywood's image of a Texas rancher. He was more like a stern 19th patriarchal farmer. The old man loved to repair and invent things. After the trial he was sentenced to serve "shock" time in state prison. When his term was up, he stayed an extra day to fix a balky door.

Carlton on the other hand was slightly built, wan looking and about as threatening as the neighborhood newspaper boy. Racehorse did not command multimillion dollar fees for nothing and day after day he would hammer away at Carlton. He was the foreman, he ran the ranch, he did the hiring. It followed that he also did the torturing and killing. Right? If there was any mayhem on the ranch, Carlton was the one to know about it.

It was pure Racehorse, a bravo bit of courtroom action. Besides it certainly did not hurt Racehorse's case that Carlton's voice was clearly on the tapes. Scott was in a tough spot. He had to defend against attacks from the prosecution and from Racehorse. Then at the right moment he had to join forces with one or the other.

"The prosecution would pass me notes with questions they felt I should ask," he recalled. "Then Racehorse would slip me notes with questions he thought I should ask. I had a problem because I couldn't read Racehorse's handwriting. While I was trying to decipher one of his notes he would be whispering loudly behind me, 'Ask it! Come on, Scott. Ask it.'"

Eventually, the final arguments were made and the case went to the jury. The jury rendered its verdicts. The old man got ninety days "shock" time and seven years probation, Wesley Jr., got seventeen years and Carlton got fifteen years. Scott got the going court-appointed fee. Racehorse got the ranch.

It was a victory of sorts. Racehorse told reporters Scott was one of "the best damn defense lawyers in the state of Texas." No one published the quote. Instead, the TV trucks lowered their satellite dish antennas and motored away on Interstate Highway 10. Reporters turned their rented sedans back in at San Antonio International Airport and impatiently waited for the quickest flight out. Kerrville settled back to being a quiet pleasant place to live. Carlton went to prison.

Scott returned to practicing small town law. He hoped some more high-profile cases would come his way because of the exposure. Although the law had changed, Scott still held to the old custom of not advertising. Not much happened. After all, who thinks of calling a lawyer in Kerrville? In Houston or Dallas things might have been different.

Six years later Darwin walked into his office. Scott stands six foot three inches but carries himself such that his height is somehow not intimidating. His grey (he prefers to call it silver) hair and friendly manner reassured Darwin. Although Scott likes to pretend he is unsentimental and tough, in truth, he has a fundamental soft spot for people like Darwin.

Scott listened to Darwin's initial plea. Martin needed help. So, what would it take to retain Scott as Martin's lawyer? Scott wanted to hear the whole story first. Darwin began to recount in detail the events leading up to Martin's arrest.

"From the way he told the story," Scott recalled, "It sounded pretty straightforward. Martin was a witness to a killing. He had not taken part in the shooting. And, Martin had turned in the killers to the police. It sounded like Martin had a reasonable case, so I took it."

Scott said he needed a retainer and quoted a figure far more modest than Barrera's. There was no mention of titles to property. Darwin's brother took out a checkbook, filled in the amount, signed and handed it over. Scott Stehling was now Martin Sweeten's lawyer. He was about to be launched into one hell of a legal battle. Darwin was to get his money's worth and then some.

Scott put in a call to the county courthouse in Del Rio and confirmed the pretrial hearings would be in the District Court of Edwards County, 63rd Judicial District, the Honorable George M. Thurmond presiding. Scott felt a little uneasy, Judge Thurmond, a former prosecutor, was not exactly known for tender sentiments toward defense lawyers.

Scott next called Tom Lee to test the prosecutorial waters.

He figured the case looked pretty straightforward. Lee had his killers, thanks to Martin. He had statements, thanks to Martin. Martin had not pulled a trigger, had contacted law enforcement as quickly as possible, and, of the three, was the only one to show remorse. At the very worst, Martin might face a charge of conspiracy to commit murder.

The waters were dark and cold.

"We are going to the grand jury on this, Scott." Lee informed him.

"Okay. Can Martin make an appearance before them?" Scott

requested, seeking a lifeline. An appearance would have allowed him to show the grand jury proofs and arguments as to how Martin helped the lawmen and, therefore, Martin should not even be indicted. With a little luck and understanding Scott could perhaps end the case right there. Nip it in the bud good and proper. *Voila!* and Martin would be free.

"I don't think that will be necessary. We are going to present all three as capital murder indictments," Lee coolly announced.

Grand juries are creatures of the prosecution. DA's do not like defense attorneys clouding the issues with inconvenient questions of innocence. Giving defense attorneys access to the grand jury is rather like letting unruly, hungry children loose on a beautifully laid out buffet table. It makes a mess of a nice thing.

Scott called Darwin and told him the bad news. Oddly for Darwin it was a relief. His dream was coming true. Now the worst was known. Not only were his problems taking on shape and form but he had allies. The voice had given him heart and hope. Whatever came he could deal with it. Darwin now knew who was with him, who was against him. He knew, aside from his family and Scott and John Pannell, he was alone. Well, there was also the Lord, but Darwin would have to rely on his own resources and what the Good Lord provided. It was a prospect which did not daunt him. In short, Darwin had drawn the line and was ready to fight.

"Well, okay. Let's get on with it," was all he said in reply.

The next day Darwin called Scott and asked him to come to Camp Wood. Scott drove over that afternoon and was amazed. Darwin had more than a dozen people lined up at his furniture store ready to tell him what they knew. He sat there for hours listening to the whole story: Tommy's history of badness; Andy, the unknown drifter; the girlfriends' role; Martin and his precious car; various local theories, rumors and fantasies. Scott stayed well into the evening taking extensive notes.

From that day until the trials ended, Darwin never stopped. He searched for witnesses, for anyone who could add another piece of evidence. He was always ready to talk to anyone who might know a little more. Darwin gathered information from any and every source. He was like the Ancient Mariner in the famous poem stopping strangers and compelling them to hear his tale. Once a month he would drive over to Kerrville and personally bring a modest payment to Scott along with a full report. Once or twice a week he called Scott with more information: some of it useless, some of it vital.

Every day, every single day for the next year, Darwin did something to advance Martin's cause. He lobbied, he begged, he pleaded. He became the talk of Camp Wood and Barksdale. He drove some people nuts, but most were sympathetic. Even some of Edmund's relatives came to pity Darwin. The deputies got to know him well and would shake their heads in sympathy. But Darwin never stopped. Sympathy, hatred or pity, it did not matter. From the moment he rose in the morning until he laid down to sleep, he did something to help Martin. He knew what he wanted, and he was going to get it.

It worked. Darwin canvassed the county, asking for help. Letters on Martin's behalf flowed in to Scott's office. Businessmen, housewives, kids, grandmothers, grandpas, preachers all rose up in Martin's support. A few had possibly useful information, but most wrote touching letters of support.

One fifteen-year-old girl wrote: "My name is Traci. I am 15 years old. I have known Martin for about 3 and one half years. As long as I have known him, he has always been kind, sweet and respectful. I don't really think a kid of his standards could commit such a crime. If you only know the true Martin you would feel that way too."

A sixteen-year-old girl typed in a letter: "I do not believe Martin is capable of killing anyone, or helping to kill anyone. I believe he must have been in the wrong place at the wrong time. I saw Martin in jail on Tuesday, April 14. He was very remorseful about his involvement. He even said he wished he had wrecked his car and killed himself in the process. He told me he had been reading the Bible and was now closer to God.

"On the other hand, I believe Tommy Eiland is capable of killing someone. Tommy used to come over to my house all the time. On one occasion, about three years ago, Tommy placed his hands around my throat and casually told me he could break my neck if he wanted to. Of course, I thought he was just joking; however, it still gives me chills. My grandmother overheard this and was also concerned."

A couple wrote that: "as long as we have known Martin he has been a nice, well-mannered boy. Martin has visited our church several times and also has visited our son in our home on occasion. It is totally out of character for him to kill anyone."

A middle-aged man wrote: "If Martin did have a part in this crime, I can't help but believe he was a pawn, not a knight! Please understand that as a forty-one-year-old man, I would gladly change places with this boy to give him a chance to live his life."

A young boy wrote: "To Whom It May Concern, I think Martin Sweeten is inosent. He was very trusting. Martin would help anyone with anything. He would take anyone anywhere if they gave him gas money. He wasn't the fighting type . . ."

A young couple wrote that . . . "our assessment of Martin is he is incapable of murder. He is a quiet, unassuming boy, a dreamer who knowingly made no enemies. He is non-violent, as well as not malicious . . ."

Regrettably, the letters did very little to prove Martin innocent. All of the character references in the world would not get Martin out on bail. Scott and Darwin collected over 125 signatures from people in Real and Edwards counties in a formal petition to the court for bond. Considering the modest populations of these counties, just a few thousand residents, it was an impressive response. It was nice to know so many people cared and offered so much support, but, when the DA got an indictment for capital murder popular sentiment became a moot point. There is no bail for capital murder when the death penalty is sought. Martin remained in jail.

Always, no matter what was done to help Martin's case, there was ever the presence of the James family and their understandably furious grief. They wanted anybody directly involved in the murder of their beloved Edmund to face some tough justice. They would not accept any excuses like "these were just mixed up kids." The family was rich, powerful and tended to get their way. Blood had been shed, and blood was required.

Scott prepared for the first of three pretrial hearings. At the time he did not know where all of this would lead. He had no idea he would soon fight a desperate courtroom battle, far from the public eye, in a dusty West Texas town with the unlikely name of Ozona.

CHAPTER V

TEXAS V. TOMMY AND ANDY

ANDREW MILAM WENT TO TRIAL in January 1993 almost ten months after Edmund James was shot down. He was charged with capital murder in the course of committing robbery, burglary of a habitation and kidnapping in count one; murder with the intent to cause serious bodily injury in count two and criminal conspiracy to commit capital murder in count three. The Honorable George M. Thurmond presided with Thomas F. Lee representing the State of Texas in his office as District Attorney of Val Verde County, Texas. Roy Barrera, Sr. appeared for the state by consent of the court. Andrew, having been found indigent, was represented by court appointed counsel, Victor R. Garcia, attorney at law from Del Rio, Texas.

The attorneys for all of the defendants, including Scott, had met with Judge Thurmond in Rocksprings at a preliminary hearing the previous December. Judge Thurmond reluctantly expressed reservations about holding any trials in Edwards County. The publicity was too fierce. Thus, all the defendants filed motions requesting a change of venue which the court graciously granted. Judge Thurmond did not, however, actually sign any orders transferring the trials at that time.

The venue of the trials could be changed to any county within the judicial district or, if necessary for very good and sufficient reasons, to any adjoining judicial district. Attorneys and judges do not particularly like change of venue trials. It usually means a long stay in motels and eating road food. The attorneys have to set up field offices and do their homework on awkward motel furniture. It means big telephone bills, and, if an important piece of evidence or document is forgotten, the choice is either Federal Express or a long drive. Worse, lucrative legal work back home is neglected.

The next issue for the court was the possibility of severance. In the best of all possible worlds the state wanted to try all three defendants together. There was little doubt that Tommy Eiland was going to be convicted. A jury, having convicted Tommy, the obvious instigator, would be much more inclined to nail the other two for good measure. Tommy's evil was thick enough to fully coat Andy and Martin, one brush doing nicely for all.

Naturally, Scott badly wanted to sever Martin's trial from the other two. He also wanted Martin to be tried last. By the time Martin's case came to the court, tiny Edwards County just might put heat on the DA, Tom Lee, to save the money required for another capital murder trial. They might be more agreeable to a lesser charge. Meanwhile, observing the other trials would give Scott some much needed advantage. He was ready to put up a hard fight to gain those two objectives. Instead, he got his wishes without asking. He certainly got Martin's trial located as far away as possible.

Judge Thurmond, a former prosecutor himself, wanted to accommodate Tom Lee's wishes, but there was a big problem with one trial for all. Lee would have to use the defendants' own statements to convict them. If he read out Tommy's statement in court, it would unfairly prejudice the case against Andy and Martin. It would also raise uncomfortable questions of hearsay evidence. Using Tommy's and Andy's statements during the trial would double the load on Martin's case. There was no real solution except to sever the trials. The motions were made and granted. Tom Lee got to choose the order of the trials. He wanted to try Andy Milam first. Andy's attorney agreed. Tommy Eiland would go to trial in March of 1993 in Junction, Kimble

County, Texas. Martin's trial was tentatively set for May of 1993 in Kerrville, Kerr County, Texas.

Andy was tried in Del Rio, Tom Lee, and Thurmond's home ground. At the last minute, Judge Thurmond prepared and signed an order moving the trial. Del Rio is a quiet little border town, almost due west of San Antonio. A short walk through the courtroom's doors of polished wood and engraved glass and down the steps was the Rio Grande River and Mexico. In many ways Del Rio still has the rough edges which have characterized Texas border towns for years. Everything seems somewhat unfinished. It has not boomed like Laredo, having neither oil nor the glitzy shopping centers to attract Mexican middle class consumers.

Across the river is Ciudad Acuna, formerly Villa Acuna. The change of name from "village" to "city" reflected more of a hope than any reality. The town, with very few cosmetic alterations, could easily serve as the set for a Clint Eastwood western movie. A friend of Scott's who had not been there since 1968, crossed over for lunch.

"I don't believe it!" he exclaimed later over dinner. "The place hasn't changed a bit in twenty-five years. I swear, I saw the same people standing around on the same street corners."

A voice chimed in from a neighboring table and observed, "He probably saw the same dogs too."

In the quaint nineteenth century English of Texas courts, Andrew Milam and his attorney were commanded to rise the morning of the trial and Tom Lee read the allegations. After the reading, Judge Thurmond asked the defendant, "And to these allegations and each and all of same how does the defendant plead?"

"Not Guilty," Andrew replied.

"Thank you. You may have your seat, and members of the jury, the defendant's plea of 'not guilty' has been entered and is before you, and issue has been joined in this case," Judge Thurmond chanted the time-honored phrases.

It was not a long trial. The prosecution laid out the evidence meticulously. As expected, Andy's statement nailed him cold. It was so damning, so final, from the very first sentence.

"I, Andrew James Milam, Tommy Ray Eiland, and Martin David Sweeten started planning on Wednesday, April 8, 1992 to kill someone. Tommy came to my house and we were just joking around about killing somebody, and Tommy said we can kill Edmond *[sic]* James. Tommy said he owed Edmond $200, he borrowed to fix something he tore up at school. We decided we would kill him. Tommy thought up the idea and we went along with him. Martin and I said, 'let's do it.' We all three agreed to kill Edmond, no one was forced to do anything. We never discussed beating him up . . .

"Martin was going to go up to the door at the Edmond James residence and shine a flashlight in Edmond eyes and Tommy was going to shoot him. We agreed after he was dead Tommy and I would put on gloves and go into the house and look for money mostly. Edmond met us outside. We talked to him, Edmond, about going coon hunting. We were holding the rifles at this time. It was dark and the porch lights was on. I don't remember if Martin shined the light in Edmond's eyes or not. He had the flashlight. Tommy shot first, hitting somewhere in Edmond's face twice. Edmond started to fall down. I kinda freaked out and Tommy said shoot him. After Edmond was on the ground I shot him in the head and back six or seven times. Tommy didn't shoot anymore. Martin was just standing there watching. Tommy and I put on the gloves.

Then we went inside Edmond's house and started looking around. We carried the rifles with us into the house. I found a .357 magnum pistol in a night stand beside Edmond's bed. Me and Martin were together and Tommy was in another part of the house. I found a Seiko wrist watch on a table in Edmond's bedroom. I took it. I found some money in a closet with a window. The money was laying on the window sill. There was about $65 in cash and a bunch of change. I took the money. I told Tommy, let's go, and we went to the kitchen and I picked up a bottle of Vodka and Tommy picked a bottle of some kind of Whiskey and took it. Martin didn't take anything because he didn't have gloves on. We left for town.

"We got $10.00 worth of gas at the Get-N-Go. Then we went to Uvalde. We stopped at 19 mile crossing and opened the trunk and looked at the pistol. We didn't talk about much. We went on in to Uvalde and ate at What-A-Burger. We went to the movie, but there was only a few minutes left so we didn't go in. We cruised around and we stopped at my aunt's house. I visited with her and my cousin. Then we came back to Camp Wood and unloaded the guns at Tommy's house. I went to my house and went to bed. Tommy and Martin went to Tommy's and went to bed."

From the voluntary statement given by Andrew James Milam, completed at 1:15 A.M. on the 10th day of April 1992, Edwards County Sheriff's Office, Sheriff Don G. Letsinger and Deputy Jay Adams witnesses.

It was a tough case to defend. Garcia tried to attack the statement but got nowhere. The state's witnesses were prepared and certain of their positions:

> **Q: (by Mr. Garcia)** Deputy Adams, the statement that you give to any suspect or accused is — you are telling him that you have a right to talk to a lawyer and have him present with you while you are being questioned, is that correct?
> **A:** Yes, sir. It is.
> **Q:** Okay, No other questions of the witness, Your Honor.

Garcia scored some points during the trial but nothing which would have freed Andy. The statement was an impenetrable wall. At best Garcia knocked loose a few bricks. The State called eighteen witnesses. Patricia Butts was naturally sympathetic to Andy. The defense had been unable to shake any of them on cross-examination. Garcia could put Andy on the stand as a possible defense. There was a frightful risk in doing that with little to gain. Garcia knew Barrera would tear the boy to pieces and take his time about doing it. Garcia did what he could to limit the damage.

> **Mr. Garcia:** Your Honor, comes now the defendant Andrew Milam and makes a motion for directed verdict in reference to the indictment. The first one; there has been no evidence of a kidnapping. Therefore, we ask that, that count of the indictment, paragraph of the indictment be stricken.
> **The Court:** I'm going to sustain you.
> **Mr. Garcia:** Your Honor, we make our second point in reference to the assertion that the State has failed to prove a conspiracy. The only evidence which was brought was in reference to a confession introduced by Andrew Milam and there is no other evidence. The testimony, which brings about any agreement between Andrew

Miliam and Tommy Eiland and the confession, has not been corroborated whatsoever regarding the fruits of the crime. So I ask that, this part of the evidence also be stricken.

And we ask for a directed verdict also in reference to the burglary charge, Your Honor. The only testimony, which was from the evidence, was that it appears somebody was making a drink inside. That would lead to the conclusion, maybe, the boys were inside with permission. There is no evidence of any forced entry or any entry without consent of Edmund James. Also in reference to robbery, we feel, if anything, the evidence has shown a murder followed by theft, but not a robbery. We ask for a directed verdict.
The Court: Okay. The motion that the court direct the jury to return a verdict of not guilty, having been presented to the court when the State closed its case in chief and having been considered by the court, is hereby in all things respectfully overruled except as to count one — pardon me — yes, count one, paragraph three.

The court directed the jury to render a verdict of "not guilty" in regards to the charge of capital murder in the course of committing or attempting to commit kidnapping. However, the rest of the charges stood. That ended the Friday afternoon session. On Monday morning, Judge Thurmond charged the jury. This meant he gave them instructions about what they were to consider, what charges they were to rule on and procedures they were to follow. The jury retired to consider their verdict.

It did not take them long. They convicted Andy of count one of the indictment, capital murder in the course of committing burglary. They did not buy capital murder in the course of committing robbery which was interesting because it showed just how closely a panel of "ordinary" citizens listen to the complex legal arguments of trained attorneys.

The next day the court met for the penalty phase. The state asked for death by lethal injection. The defense plead that Andy was just a kid with a lousy upbringing who fell in with bad company. The jury was told, "you shall consider only the conduct and state of mind of this defendant in determining what your answers to the issues shall be . . . Issue No. 1: Is there a probability the defendant, Andrew Milam, would commit criminal acts of violence which would constitute a continuing threat to society? . . . Issue No. 2: Do you find from the evidence beyond a reasonable doubt that the defendant, Andrew Milam himself, actually caused the death of Edmund James, the deceased, on the occasion in question, or if he did not actually cause the deceased's death, that he intended to kill the deceased or another, or that he anticipated that a human life would be taken on such occasion? . . . Issue No. 3: Taking into consideration all of the evidence, including the circumstances of the offense, the defendant's character and background, and the personal moral culpability of the defendant, do you find there is sufficient mitigating circumstances to warrant a sentence of life imprisonment rather than a death sentence be imposed?"

It was an interesting arrangement of questions. If a jury became careless in their zeal to convict or even lazy and simply answered "yes" to all questions; then the "mitigating circumstance" phrase would be activated and the defendant's life would be spared. To send a defendant to his death, the jury would have to consciously and deliberately answer "yes, yes, no." The jury in Andrew Milam's case answered, "yes, yes, yes." Andy would live.

He received life imprisonment for the capital murder of Edmund James. As silly as it sounds, a life sentence for capital murder is different from a life sentence for mere murder. Andy will serve a minimum of thirty-five years before he can even be considered for parole. Andy will not earn credits for good behavior or good deeds which could be deducted from his sentence. He will serve hard time. Andy will be a fifty-three-year-old man when he becomes eligible for parole. The year will be 2027.

For taking Edmund's life, Andy gave up his youth, his young manhood and his early middle age. It will be a very different world Andy will confront when he leaves the Texas Department of Corrections — if he lives so long.

The sentence was not entirely what the James family wanted, but it would have to do. Anyway, the real culprit, Tommy Eiland, was about to come before the court. There was strategy in the timing of the trials. By trying Andy first, any weaknesses in the prosecution's case could be spotted and corrected without the danger of the main target going free on some technicality. Once Tommy and Andy were disposed of, Martin could be picked off at leisure with a doubly perfected case. Barrera and Tom Lee could live with Andy getting life, but they wanted Tommy strapped to a prison table and sweating out his last few moments staring at the tubes with big, scared eyes.

Darwin attended every day of Andy's trial. It meant getting up early and driving 100 miles each way on some so-so roads. Scott accompanied him for most of the trial unless some pressing matter prevented him. They would take notes on the testimony, check out the good and bad witnesses and generally look over the prosecution's case.

On March 9, 1993, Tommy Eiland's trial opened in Junction, Texas, on the change of venue motion. Again, Judge Thurmond signed the actual order changing the venue just before the trial began. Tommy was charged with the same list of offenses as Andy: capital murder committed in the course of burglary of a habitation, robbery and kidnapping; murder with intent to cause serious bodily injury and, finally, conspiracy to commit capital murder.

Junction sits along the banks of the Llano River which flows northeastward through the Edwards Plateau into the Colorado River. The town is about 120 miles from San Antonio, west along Interstate Highway 10. To get there a motorist must traverse the Hill Country. At Junction the highway drops down a long, high hill and gives a marvelous view of the Llano River valley. In the spring, it is a place of such beauty that it tempts the traveler to stop and settle down right there. It is where West Texas, as a cultural entity, begins.

Darwin wanted to attend each day of Tommy's trial, but Junction was a far piece from Camp Wood. He did not have the money for a motel room, much less living expenses. The trial would last for perhaps a week or more. While he was out there for the jury selection phase of the trial, that strange inspiration, which had guided him this far, struck. He looked through the local phone book for anyone he might know. He noticed a familiar name who just might be an old army buddy. Darwin had not seen the man for many years. He took a chance and called. It was his friend. Darwin got his lodgings for the course of the trial. It was typical of Darwin's uncanny, last minute, rabbit-out-of-the-hat tricks. Scott came out for the jury selection.

Tommy Eiland was defended by a court appointed lawyer from Del Rio, Texas, Richard F. Gutierrez, who was assisted by a local lawyer the judge appointed named Keaton Blackburn. Blackburn's father had been a well-known lawyer from Junction, and his uncle was a retired state district judge. Tommy's defense team immediately attacked the defendant's signed statement to the Edwards County deputies. The motion was overruled.

Tom Lee, District Attorney for Val Verde County, opened for the state by explaining the case and what the prosecution was going to prove to the jury. He told them who Edmund James was and who his alleged killers were:

". . . We'll show you in the evidence, however, that Edmund James was a real person, a person who was much loved by his family. We'll show you he was a man of approximately forty-four years of age. He was a very interesting man because he was the great-grandson of C. H. Guenther, the founder of the Pioneer Flour Mills in San Antonio. He was also the great-grandson of a man named John James who was one of the early Texas surveyors — in fact, he laid out the plats for San Antonio and Bandera and many of the surveys done in that area.

". . . Our evidence will show you, ladies and gentlemen, that Edmund James had a real passion for the land. He lived on that land. He much preferred to live in that country and to take care of that ranch, better than even San Antonio. He was a man who loved and cared for that land very much. Unfortunately, on April 8 of last year, our evidence will show you that his life came to a very tragic end.

"About a week prior to that, I believe you will see from the evidence, three young men — well, actually our defendant in this case, hatched a plan or began to conceive of an idea to go out and rob and murder Edmund James because he thought he had money. We'll show you from the evidence that on April 8th Tommy Eiland, the defendant in this case, a man named Martin Sweeten and another man by the name of Andrew Milam got together and started planning in earnest this idea about murdering and robbing and burglarizing Edmund James.

". . . I think you will see from the evidence that is exactly what happened. They followed through with the plan, and followed it to the minutest detail. We'll show you that they shot Edmund James approximately nine times. Tommy Eiland was the first one to shoot him, and then Andrew Milam shot him approximately eight times, and then Tommy Eiland shot him a last time, sort of a *coup de grace,* through the head.

"... We think when you hear this evidence you will agree this crime was committed, that it was capital murder and that it was committed in a cold, well-planned and calculative manner. It was a great, great tragedy. We think when you have heard this evidence you will find the defendant guilty of capital murder."

The evidence against Tommy was so overwhelming that a defense was almost impossible. Tommy was going down for the crime, no doubt about it. Besides, Tom Lee virtually told the jury that Tommy not only killed Edmund James but also had murdered a living bit of Texas history. The best Gutierrez could hope for was to somehow mitigate the natural outrage of sober citizens when confronted with such crimes.

The judge had ruled Tommy's statement as admissible into evidence. Gutierrez could still nudge the jury toward suspecting the police methods: "Ladies and Gentlemen of the jury . . . I want to ask you all to pay special attention to one thing. There is a written statement or confession which was signed by Tommy Eiland. I think it is probably the most important single piece of evidence in the trial. I ask you to pay special attention to the way it was obtained. The reason it is important, because I believe the court is going to tell you, at the end of this stage of the trial, that if you find from the evidence that prior to the giving of the alleged statement by the defendant the officers having him in custody questioned him persistently over a prolonged period of time without allowing him to sleep, drink or food; or if they refused to allow him to contact an attorney, then you will wholly disregard the alleged statement and not consider it for any purpose, nor will you then consider any evidence obtained as a result thereof.

In other words, if you don't think the statement was obtained under the proper procedures, you, under the law, are to disregard it. Now, it is a tough thing to do but you are going to get that instruction directly from the court."

Now Gutierrez knew very well there was not a chance in hell that a West Texas jury was going to cut Tommy Eiland loose because the cops were mean to him. Though folks in Kimble County Texas had never heard of Edmund James, the words "rancher" and "murder" put them in a hard mood. The possibility the deputies had not read Tommy his Miranda warnings at just the right time or had denied him a requested Pepsi Cola would not sway them one inch. Miranda warnings were considered in West Texas to be something better applied to drug dealers in New York. It made for nifty TV shows, but let the Yankees get all stirred up about it if they wanted to. The question here was simple, did the kid do it?

No, the defense would have to show some good and impressive reasons for killing Edmund before the jury would even consider a "not guilty" verdict. They would be fair, and they would listen intently. They would take their duty seriously but they were not a bunch of snotty, left-wing civil libertarians. The kid was not going to walk because his feelings had been hurt by law enforcement officers doing their duty.

Of course, the insuperable problem for the defense was that there were no good and impressive reasons for killing Edmund. It was demoralizing. This led Gutierrez to close his opening remarks with a virtual admission of defeat. "Once again, on behalf of Tommy Eiland, I thank you, and we're literally going to be dealing with his life here. I don't think I need to tell you to be attentive. I can tell by looking at your faces you are already. This isn't going to be an easy job, but I ask you to look at this open-minded. It is also not too early for you to start looking for possible mitigating circumstances. In the event, you do find Tommy guilty, we'll have a second stage, the punishment stage. At the punishment stage you can look at things you heard at the beginning, during the guilt stage. So, it is not too early to start looking for possible mitigating circumstances in the event you find yourselves so inclined. I am going to try to be brief during the trial. I'll try not to beat around the bush, and will try to focus on the issues. Thank you very much."

He might just as well have said, "Convict him, I know you are going to but let's talk afterwards." The prosecution obliged on the first part. They called twenty-one witnesses and then read Tommy's signed statement into the record as evidence. It would have been difficult for the jurors not to convict. Just to nail the case solidly shut, Barrera and Lee called Jennifer Noblett to testify about a conversation she had with Tommy a week before the murder.

Q: What did Tommy Eiland tell you?
A: Told me somebody was going to get killed, and he was going to do it.
Q: . . . Did you ask him who or why or what or anything of that nature?
A: I figured it was a bluff, and we were arguing, so I left.

That was not the full response the prosecution wanted. Barrera made Jennifer review her written statement to the deputies. He then asked her again:

Q: Have you had a chance to review it?
A: Yes.
Q: Now, with regard to the statement Tommy Ray Eiland made to you that somebody was going to get killed, and it's probably going to be me that does it, did he say who was going to get killed?
A: No.
Q: Did you ask him why he would want to kill anyone?
A: Well, Now that I think about, he did.
Q: All right. What was his response . . . ?
A: Very jokingly he said, money.
Q: Was he laughing when he said, money?
A: It was kind of a snicker, yeah.

The state next called Blanca Flores, the attractive and bright fifteen-year-old high school student from Camp Wood. Tommy had lived with her family for a few months, and he had dated her for a while. The day after the murder Tommy had approached Blanca during PE, or physical education class.

Q: . . . Did he talk to you about what he did the night before?
A: He talked to me.
Q: What did he tell you he did the night before?
A: He told me he had killed Edmund James, and he told me he had shot him.
Q: Did he tell where he had shot him?
A: Under his eye and in the head.

Finally the State called Jason White, the young man who gave Tommy rides to school. He said Tommy had told him the morning after the murder, "Edmund James would not wake up for a long, long time." But Jason, too, had to reread his statement to the sheriff to give the testimony the prosecution was looking for.

> **Q:** Now, let me ask you whether or not in connection with the taking of a — well, you tell me what items were taken as you now recall and as you — if you have refreshed your memory?
> **A:** The .357 magnum, a watch and $80.
> **Q:** Okay, did he describe the .357 magnum in any way other than just that?
> **A:** I believe it was chrome.
> **Q:** And a watch and about $80 —
> **A:** Uh-huh.
> **Q:** Did he mention what if anything they did or tried to do in the house?
> **A:** He mentioned they tried to get in the safe, but that they couldn't get into the safe.

Gutierrez cross-examined Jennifer by asking her address and then if Tommy had specified who was going to get killed. She said he had not specified. Gutierrez had no questions for Blanca Flores. He asked for Jason White's address. Scott had asked him to get the addresses so he could subpoena them for Martin's trial.

The prosecution then asked that Tommy's statement be admitted as evidence. The court granted the motion over Mr. Gutierrez's objections. Tom Lee read it to the jury.

Built into the word processing form Deputy Jay Adams used were three standard paragraphs in which Tommy acknowledged a peace officer was recording his statement, that the officer had administered the Miranda warning, that Tommy did not want a lawyer present and that this was a voluntary statement given without coercion.

"I, Tommy Ray Eiland, was sitting in school, third period on Monday April 6, 1992 and I got the idea of robbing Edmund James and taking his money. I used to work for him, and I knew he had a lot of money. Edmund has war games on weekends. War games are expensive, but Edmund lets people participate free. So I knew he had money if he could do this. I told Martin Sweeten on Monday or Tuesday, April 6 or 7th about my plan to hold Edmund at gunpoint and take his money. Martin said, 'Yeah, sure.'

"Martin and I went to Andrew Milam's house after school. I think we went to his bedroom and I told him the plan. I told him we would take a couple of guns and gloves and hold him up at gunpoint until he told us where the money was. I guessed he had a safe and we were going to hold him at gunpoint until he told us the combination. We took some duct tape so we could tie him up. I owed him some money and I was going to use that as an excuse to talk to him. On the way to Edmund's we made a vow of silence. We all agreed if any one of us talked the other two would kill him. We all agreed.

"We went to Edmund's during daylight hours and we talked to him about twenty minutes. We had the rifles in Martin's car (white Toyota). We told Edmund we wanted to sell him a couple of guns. We handed him the two rifles to look at, each rifle was loaded with a round in the chamber. Edmund looked at them and gave them back. Edmund said he didn't want to buy any .22 cal. rifles. Edmund told us to call him tomorrow and see if he had any work. We got in Martin's car and left.

"We went to a small cabin on Edmund's place. We were going to wait there until dark, but we decided to go on into town and try to make up an alibi. Martin said we should have shot him then. Andy said he didn't care. We kept asking Martin if he was going to freak out or anything. He told us if he freaked out just knock him out and put him in the car.

"We went back to Andrew's house and got some more .22 rounds. Then we went to the Get 'N Go, and I called Carolyn Hodge and told her we were going to go to a movie in Uvalde. Andrew was talking to Jennifer Noblett on the phone telling her the same thing. Martin didn't have anyone to talk to on the phone so when we got finished talking Martin said, 'Let's go.'

"We left to go back to Edmund's. On the way, I said we would take the guns and a flashlight. Martin would hold the flashlight. I was going to ask Edmund if we could go coon hunting. I was going to tell Edmund we had two guns and a flashlight. When I said flashlight, it was the signal for Martin to shine the light in his face and I was going to shoot him. Everything went according to plan.

"When I said 'flashlight' Martin hesitated and I thought he was backing out. Then he shined the light in his (Edmund's) face and I shot him once in the face and he dropped and Andrew started shooting him in the back and several times in the head and once in the ear. We weren't sure if he was dead or not. I put my gun in Martin's trunk and I grabbed two sets of gloves. Martin didn't have any gloves so he wouldn't touch anything. I felt his pocket (Edmund's) for his wallet but didn't find one. We opened the doors and everything so Martin wouldn't have to touch anything.

"We went inside the house. We started checking the house out for money and a safe. I had never been in his house before except when we went earlier to see if anyone besides Edmund was there. Andrew and Martin went into his bedroom and Andrew found a pistol in a night stand and some money on a window sill in a closet. There was $65 and a whole bunch of change. They said there was three hands full of change.

"I went upstairs when they said they had found the safe. We didn't try to open the safe because Martin said we were spending too much time and had better leave. We went downstairs to the kitchen and I got a bottle of Rum and Andrew got a bottle of Vodka. We got into Martin's car and left.

"We talked on the way to town. Andrew and I said *(sic)* I thought we would feel different. Martin looked like he had a queasy stomach. He looked kind'a sick. We went to the Get 'N Go and got $10 worth of gas, three Cokes and a pack of cigarettes. It was about 9:30 P.M. We went to Uvalde. We stopped at 19 mile crossing. We looked at the pistol. We went on to Uvalde. We went to the movies, but there was only ten minutes left so we didn't go inside. We went to What-A-Burger to eat. Andrew started driving after we ate and I fell asleep in the back of the car. I woke up just as we got to my house. I took the pistol and my rifle in my house and Martin stayed at my house and Andrew took the other rifle and went to his house.

This statement was completed at 3:15 A.M. on the 10th day of April, 1992."

The State rested.

Gutierrez moved for an instructed verdict of "not guilty" on all of the counts of the indictment "and particularly the counts alleging capital murder by way of kidnapping. We would also believe there has not been a sufficient showing of evidence of the submission of this or the conspiracy to commit murder either . . ."

Barrera argued the defendant had given testimony in his statement that "it was their intention to take him and to hold him until they caused him to reveal the location of his money" therefore they had "kidnapped" Edmund. That was a bit much for Judge Thurmond.

"Restraint means to restrict a person's movements without consent so as to interfere with his liberty by moving him from one place to another or by confining him. What is your evidence?" he asked.

Barrera answered that Tommy's statement was the evidence.

Again, the judge challenged him, "That's robbery if you are holding someone. It's aggravated robbery if you are holding someone at gunpoint, to take possession of property. Robbery and kidnapping are both offenses against a person, I believe, but there is a difference. You don't commit kidnapping every time you, to use the common vernacular, hold someone up. You are restraining them."

Barrera argued the very act of restraining someone until he revealed the location of his money was "if not an actual kidnapping, as such, it was an intended or proposed kidnapping. Then they planned robbing him, and or burglarizing his house by holding him — so I do think you have a combination of all three." Besides, he continued, the boys had tape and ropes which indicated they planned to hold Edmund by force.

Gutierrez disagreed, "Your Honor, we don't believe there has been any evidence of any overt act to commit kidnapping. Although it may have been planned and there may have been a conspiracy, there certainly was no overt act to restrain him. They never tried to restrain him at all once he was shot. When does robbery cease to be robbery and become kidnapping?"

Barrera continued to argue for kidnapping until Judge Thurmond brought up another problem. . . . "Now, what concerns me is: has the State proved habitation of the house in this case, that this house was a habitation? . . . It is so simple to ask a witness, was this building adapted for overnight accommodation of people? I don't recall one question being asked of any State witness about that."

It was an embarrassing omission, a first-year law school goof. Barrera pointed out that Judge Smart had gone into the house to turn off the TV and lights. He had testified that the place looked "lived in." Judge Thurmond was in a forgiving mood and replied, "But it's so easy to prove up by the magic words. Well, I shouldn't — you have had a lot on your mind. What about the defense?"

Gutierrez, taking the friendly cue from the judge, immediately moved for a directed verdict of "not guilty" on the charge of burglary of habitation. Judge Thurmond asked the attorneys to step back and ruled, "Okay. The defendant's motion for instructed verdict is, in all things, respectfully overruled. The defendant's exception is noted."

It was the judicial equivalent of a pie in the face. Judge Thurmond had, at least, granted a similar motion on the charge of burglary in Andy's case. Gutierrez was slightly bewildered, like a victim of a practical joke. Later Judge Thurmond reconsidered and dropped the charge of capital murder in the course of committing kidnapping.

The defense called Tommy's grandmother, Patsy Eiland. She had already testified earlier of her difficulties reaching authorities the night of Tommy's arrest. Now she had her notes from that night and could be more specific. Prior to 1:25 A.M. she had made six different telephone calls to the sheriff's office in Rocksprings. She was rebuffed each time. At 1:25 she got ahold of Jay Adams, "and he told me Tommy had signed a waiver, and at that time I became real upset because I said — I asked if Tommy even knew what a waiver was. Again I requested that he have a lawyer, and again I was denied to talk to Tommy."

Everyone felt sorry for her. She was a nice lady caught in a terrible dilemma. It was a version of everyone's contemporary nightmare. Your kid calls in the middle of the night saying he is charged with murder, or worse, a cop calls saying your kid has been murdered. The variations are endless while the pain and despair are predictable.

It was easy to sympathize with Patsy. She came from a generation when things like this did not happen to good people. Patsy came from a time when people were generally decent, living in a decent world. But it was obvious she loved her grandson and did all she could for him. Her testimony was moving but the fact remained Tommy had reached his maturity. He was no longer a troubled little boy. The defense rested. The judge's charge to the jury was similar to the one he used in Andy's case.

The jury convicted Tommy of capital murder.

However, like the jurors in Del Rio, the jurors could not bring themselves to take Tommy's life. He was sentenced to life imprisonment. And like Andy he will reenter society when one quarter of the twenty-first century has passed — if he lives that long. Prison is a tough place.

Martin's third and final preliminary hearing followed shortly after Tommy's conviction. It was held in Rocksprings at the Edwards County Courthouse, a sturdy, square stone building built in 1891. Its two stories were painted white to withstand summer's heat. The original jail, built separately on the courthouse grounds, now served as a men's privy and storage room. Thick layers of black paint covered the heavy window bars. Going to the restroom was a historical tour.

The hearing was held on the second floor of the courthouse. The creaking wooden floors and aged hardwood seats gave the place the feel of a one-room school. Judge Thurmond once again presided. Scott Stehling represented the defendant. Tom Lee appeared for the State of Texas. He announced the State would not be seeking the death penalty in Martin's case, although the charge would still be capital murder. Judge Thurmond told Scott that he had just won "a tremendous victory."

It did look like victory without battle on the surface. Although it removed the threat of death from over Martin's head, the change actually hurt the defense in many ways. Lee was not acting out of compassion. The simple truth was the State had no compelling evidence that Martin posed a "future danger" of repeating his alleged crime or a "continuing threat" to society. Those were the two key elements a jury had to consider in imposing the death penalty. And two juries in two separate counties had balked at giving out death penalties in this case. The prosecution was not anxious to be rebuffed a third time. The tactic this time was to anticipate and roll with the punch.

Scott had come armed with several motions. He first moved to have Martin declared indigent. Then he moved for the appointment of additional counsel to offset the prosecutorial services of Roy Barrera. Andy had the benefit of an appointed assistant counsel out in Junction. Judge Thurmond knew Blackburn's uncle and had granted the defense request readily. Now Thurmond acknowledged Martin as indigent, but denied Scott's motion for additional counsel. This was no longer a death penalty case, he reasoned and the defense did not need any extra help at state expense.

Scott moved for the provision of funds to pay a psychologist to examine Martin and Tommy. He moved for funds to pay a professional graphologist to examine notes Tommy and Andy had been passing in jail. The judge looked at Scott as if he were out of his mind and denied the motions. This was no longer a death penalty case. There was simply no need for such extravagances.

The defense moved for individual *voir dire* examinations of potential jurors as had been the case in Tommy's and Andy's trials. Thurmond denied the motion, again because this was no longer a death penalty trial. The potential jurors would be questioned en masse. The defense moved that since the death penalty had been dropped, the defendant be granted a personal recognizance bond and released from custody during the trial. To support the motion, Scott submitted the 125 signature petition requesting a PR bond for Martin. The judge denied the PR bond because this was still a capital murder trial and set bail at $100,000. That meant Darwin would either have to put up $100,000 worth of property or give a bondsman $10,000 to get his son out. Needless to say, Martin remained in jail.

The defense moved to suppress Martin's signed written statements. The motion was denied. The defense made a motion objecting to the firm of Nicholas and Barrera serving as assistant prosecutors as they had prior knowledge of the defendant's case. The motion was denied. The defense moved for a bench warrant requiring Tommy and Andy to be available to the court for possible testimony. The motion had to be withdrawn because they had filed appeals.

Thus the defense's "tremendous victory" served as the basis for denying most of Scott's initial motions.

The defense had originally moved, as had the other defense attorneys, for a change of venue. Judge Thurmond had indicated back in December that Martin's trial would probably be changed to Kerrville, but scheduling problems prevented a trial there. He then chose Fredericksburg in Gillespie County. As in the other two trials, he had not yet signed an order. Meanwhile, the defense decided to keep the case in Edwards County.

It was a bit risky, but Scott figured there were a couple of good reasons. First, the usual reaction of people in Barksdale/Camp Wood area when told of the murder was "I can believe Tommy did it, but Martin Sweeten? No way!" Since the population of Edwards County was less than 5,000 people, Scott thought Martin's reputation would offset the bad feelings over the murder of a "rancher." Secondly, the potential defense witnesses were mostly lower income people who could ill afford to leave work, travel many miles and perhaps stay overnight at a motel. With the trial in Rocksprings, everyone they needed would be nearby, and many could even stay home on standby.

The judge had not signed an order transferring the trial to Fredericksburg, so the defense merely withdrew the original motion for change of venue. It was a mildly curious tactic because it is usually the defense who wants to move the case to evade local hostility and prejudice. A prosecutor can ask for a change if the DA believes the local population might unduly favor the accused or there is a "lawless condition of the county." That was a phrase Lee, as an elected official, would rather avoid. A judge can order the change by ruling that the trial could not be fair. Judges rarely do it because they like the comforts of their own courtrooms.

Judge Thurmond ruled the trial would be moved due to local prejudice. The court issued an order moving the trial, and he signed a second order based on the original defense motion. Now there were two orders changing the venue. Officially, it appeared as if he were granting the defense motion as well as issuing his own order. It was another "tremendous victory" for the defense.

"Uh, oh and oops! This is not going to be an easy trial," was Scott's immediate assessment.

The defense had a couple of cards to play. There were problems with holding the trial in Fredericksburg. The town was preparing to closely follow another capital murder trial. A local man had been accused of killing his in-laws, a respected couple and long-time residents. He then kidnapped his estranged wife and their child. He held them hostage in a dramatic standoff until captured. Local feelings were running very high indeed. The trial had been moved to nearby Bandera County and was scheduled to start the same day as Martin's trial. Judge Thurmond would be holding Martin's trial in that super heated atmosphere. Tom Lee was probably licking his chops anticipating a meaty win. Scott doubted Thurmond would change the location just because of the other pending trial. He had to come up with another good reason for changing the venue again.

He had one in his pocket. A few days before the preliminary hearing an old friend of Scott's, Jon Wolfmueller, dropped by his office and plopped an excellent reason on to his desk. It was a newspaper article in the *San Antonio Express-News*.

When Judge Thurmond announced the trial location would be changed to Fredericksburg, Scott rose, "Your Honor —"

"Mr. Stehling, the court has ruled and will entertain no more arguments," came the curt reply.

"But Your Honor . . ."

"Mr. Stehling!"

"Please, Your Honor . . ."

"Mr. Stehling, do you understand courtroom procedure? The court has ruled!"

"Your Honor, if the court pleases, I have reason to believe that there would be serious problems with the location the court has chosen."

"What problems?"

Scott offered up the newspaper clipping from the San Antonio paper, "See for yourself, Your Honor."

Judge Thurmond read a few paragraphs and muttered, "This does seem to change things, uh, can't have this . . ."

The article was about a recent celebration in Fredericksburg. The whole of Gillespie County had joined in the festivities. There had been a street fair, picnic and speeches. Brightly colored bunting and decorations had adorned the town. It was a major county-wide frolic, all to honor an established Texas business which had its humble origins in Fredericksbug. Later it moved to San Antonio and greatness. The holiday was called Pioneer Flour Day; the company was Pioneer Flour Mills. It was the very company Edmund James' grandfather had founded and the present day family owned. It was the company upon whose board of directors Edmund had sat. Needless to say "it certainly did change things." The trial was swiftly moved ninety miles west to Ozona, Texas.

To travel two hundred miles west along IH 10 out from San

Antonio is to pass into a very different world. Ozona sits firmly in what is romantically called the Trans-Pecos region. It is the only town in a county larger than the state of Delaware. According to local legend, this is as far west as Davy Crockett got before he returned to San Antonio de Bexar to fight at the Alamo. It is hard to blame him for this is hard country, almost desert.

Ozona sits flatly on the high plains of the Edwards Plateau, directly south is Lake Amistad and Mexico. Northeast is San Angelo, and to the northwest is Midland-Odessa. Crockett County was legislated into existence during the general westward movement in post-Civil War Texas. In those days, the Texas legislature had a charming custom of creating large counties with no population. Thus, even today Crockett County boasts a population of less than 5,000.

The city of Ozona was founded in 1891 around the most valuable property asset in the county, a working water well. The origin of its name spawned many different stories. All agree, however, that somehow early promoters sought to invoke the notion of "fresh air." At that time, ozone was newly discovered and thought to be especially beneficial. As the town grew and prospered, ranchers built grand town homes around the courthouse. In 1925 oil was discovered, and the town boomed. Today, after the oil industry bust, it has settled back to a population of about 3,500. Ozona serves local ranchers and those oil fields still operating. It also tends the needs of motorists making the long reach west to El Paso, a weary 340 miles farther on.

The countryside is classified as semi-arid, which means it is only a few inches of annual rainfall away from desert. It is tough country, the topsoil being thin and alkaline. The limestone bedrock is only twenty inches or so below the surface. The natural flora is well-adapted for the climate — tough desert shrubs and the inevitable scrubby oaks. The sheriff likes to tell the story of a wanted fugitive from Oklahoma. He eluded the pursuit through a number of Oklahoma and Texas counties as he made for the border in a stolen truck. Crockett County officers took up the chase and ran him to ground south of Ozona. The young man wrecked the truck, jumped out and ran off into the bush. He had driven a couple of hundred miles without being caught but got less than 100 yards before collapsing. His feet were bloodied by thorns and sharp stones. He had been driving with his shoes off. The law officers easily apprehended him because they were wearing boots.

From IH 10 Ozona does not look like much. It is easy to zip by and dismiss the town. But just off of the highway is a lovely city park. It is shamelessly green and shaded. Large trees cover tables for resting or outdoor picnicking. A few months before Martin's trial, the citizens had a festival celebrating the city's founding. They put up various life-sized, wooden cutouts depicting a cowboy, gunfighter, dancehall girl and townsfolk. The effect was rather like advertisements for some television show about the "old west." Everybody liked them so much the cutouts stayed up after the celebration.

There is also a monument in the park with a plaque explaining just why the county was named for a Tennessee frontiersman. There is a portrait of Davy in stone and an inscription about his trek out here. The monument has his famous motto, "Be sure you're right, then go ahead" carved into its stone base.

Facing west, looking out over the park and set on a hill is the Crockett County Courthouse. It was built in 1902 out of the usual limestone. Designed by one Oscar Ruffini, it originally sported "faux clock spaces." It is a handsome and imposing building. A stairway leads to a stone porch which seems almost carved out of the limestone. Squat stone pillars guard the formal entrance. The grounds are well-kept and flowers bloom in the garden beds.

Next door, to the north, is the volunteer fire department equipped with a vintage engine and a huge siren to call the volunteers to action. Beyond the fire station is the sheriff's office and jail. Behind the courthouse, farther up the hill, are a few humble rental houses and an incongruous miniature golf course.

Around the park square are various small town businesses. To the east are imposing houses built during the various booms which marked the town's history. There is a dry waterway to the west which, during heavy rains, directs flash floods away from the central town. Back in the 1950s, one horrible day, floodwater over ran the banks and swept away the mayor as he fought for his town.

In short, Ozona is a pleasant town, almost an oasis. It is a tough and durable fixture of the Trans-Pecos area. It was here a jury chosen from among the good citizens of Crockett County would decide Martin's fate.

Scott and his assistants gathered in Ozona on the weekend of May 1, 1993. Scott chose the Circle Bar Motel as living quarters. It is a large service center for truckers, located a few miles east of the town. The Circle Bar has typical Best Western Motel rooms equipped with cable television and incredibly efficient air conditioners. The rooms are arranged around a covered swimming pool decorated in a "tropical" motif. The idea is apparently to invoke the Texas Gulf Coast in the middle of a desert, a sort of truck driver's heaven. The decor actually works in a goofy sort of way. The air is always heavy with moisture, a real luxury out there. A restaurant, combined with a shop featuring truckers' impediments such as boots, CB radios, sunglasses, radar detectors and gloves, serves the motel patrons. Next to the motel is a huge truck wash with giant bays, a filling station, mechanical repair service, and an antique car museum. The complex is surrounded by a flat featureless plain dominated by high radio antennas. Once there, it was easy to imagine what everyday life would be like at a Martian outpost.

The prosecution team and Judge Thurmond and court recorder, John Price stayed at a motel alongside IH 10 in Ozona proper. Martin stayed in the county jail.

Debbi Puckett is the County and District Clerk for Crockett County. A statuesque blonde with blue eyes, Debbi is friendly, hospitable and competent. She rules her office with a firm almost maternal hand. For reasons of her own, Debbi more or less adopted the defense team. She let them use a storeroom in the back of the county clerk's offices as unofficial headquarters. It was like having a bunch of actors or circus people come to town. Debbi found it all amusing. There, amid nineteenth century files, unused furniture and outmoded office equipment, Scott's assistants set up a support desk. Debbi allowed reasonable access to her copier and early morning doughnuts. All she ever asked in return was a running commentary on the trial.

Debbi had also given Scott an invaluable head start. The day before the trial was to begin, a Monday, Scott and his wife, Julia, had come into Debbi's office to examine the list of eligible jurors in the county. As they went down the names, Debbi and her staff gave them a thumbnail description of each potential juror. Actually, it was a lot of fun, an inside portrait of the county's residents laced with local irony. Dixon Mahon, a retired Crockett County district attorney, happened into the office. He had retired to Hunt, Texas, just a few miles from Kerrville, and Scott knew him well. Scott told him about the case. Dixon could not resist the fun and joined in the session.

"You don't want him," they would say of someone on the list. "His brother was a constable."

Scott would put a mark by the name and call out the next.

"You better skip her too," they would exclaim almost in unison.

"Why?" Scott would ask.

"She's not too bright," they would explain, then burst into laughter.

It was a very productive exercise. The next day the prosecution would confront a list of mere names; Scott, meanwhile, knew something of the people behind the names, their characters, idiosyncrasies and backgrounds.

Jury selection began Tuesday, May 4, 1993. The courtroom was on the second floor of the courthouse. It had the traditional high ceiling covered in wonderfully ornamented metal sheeting but sadly coated with thick white paint. There were large ceiling fans. The huge wood frame windows were sealed but allowed plenty of light.

There were fifteen or twenty rows of wooden seats for spectators. The attorneys for the defense and prosecution shared two wooden tables shoved together. Immediately to the left, as one faced the judge's dais was the witness chair. The twelve jurors would sit in two rows farther to the left side at right angles to the judge and attorneys. They, mercifully, had padded chairs. The courtroom was equipped with an amusingly inadequate sound system which looked like something someone's brother had left behind when he went away to college. The jury deliberation room was to the rear (or away from the judge's dais) and served double duty as a coffee and doughnut room in the mornings. There were high frame windows along two sides of the jury room. Behind the judge's dais was a rosette window which gave the place an almost religious quality. To each side of dais were two "robing rooms" in various states of suspended repair. Judge Thurmond and the prosecution expropriated one room for their coffee maker and doughnuts. The other room, just behind the jury seats remained unused.

All in all, it was a grand courtroom, invoking the pleasant memories and smells of old high school auditoriums. It was an excellent forum for a good old-fashioned trial, a nineteenth century forensic clash. The courtroom was delightful except for one horrible flaw. Sometime back, someone (best left unknown) had the bright idea of painting virtually everything a ghastly institutional green. The pale colored paint must have been on sale or war surplus because it had been laid on thickly and everywhere. Sanity had recently asserted itself and arrangements were in place for county jail inmates to scrape away the paint and restore the original fine woodwork. Unfortunately, crime rates were down in the county and the work was proceeding slowly because of too few inmates. By the time of the trial, the project was just getting underway. It was only barely possible to imagine how pleasant and satisfactory the finished effect would be.

The judge handed out an eight page questionnaire to prospective jurors which asked the usual questions: Do any of your family work for law enforcement? Have you ever been arrested? Have you or any of your family ever been convicted of a felony? It also asked some curious questions, such as: What magazines do you read? What are your favorite television shows? What bumper stickers do you have on your car? Naturally it was the odd ball questions which eventually revealed the most interesting insights.

Selecting a jury want list was at times fun, at times frustrating. The questionnaires provided useful information, some of it highly amusing, some touching, all of it highly confidential. The final decision was Scott's. He was open to suggestions and counsel from his defense team. He would listen to the arguments pro and con and considering appropriate advice. But, in the end the responsibility was his.

It is a heavy burden for the defense attorney. Despite the presumption of innocence and the due process of law, it is human nature to assume someone accused of capital murder must have done something terribly wrong. Jurors tend to sit themselves down clothed in unconscious presumptions of guilt despite their best intentions. The defense, in theory, need not prove anything for the burden of proof is upon the prosecution. But the prosecution has the "majesty" and the authority of the state on its side, and accusations are so easy to make. No, the real task belongs to the defense. Somehow, some way or other, the defense attorney must give each juror a reason, and a damn good one too, to render a verdict of "not guilty."

For a couple of weeks, Darwin had been worried about what kind of arrangements he could make to house his family during the trial. His daughter and her husband would be there along with their children. His brothers and other relatives would be coming. Everybody needed a place to stay. Darwin simply could not afford to keep everyone in motel rooms. He told everyone not to worry he would come up with something. Darwin began looking for lodgings. As late as the last week in April, he still had not found a place and was very worried.

Monday morning Darwin showed up calm and collected. He had found adequate living quarters. He was set up in a very modest rental house — directly behind the courthouse. When jurors retired to deliberate, they could easily look down from their east windows and see Darwin's grandchildren playing outside their temporary home.

The defense team began to look upon Darwin and his prayer groups with greater respect.

Chapter VI

He's Just Evil

Tommy and Andy escaped execution. However, it was not a spirited defense nor the mercy of the court which saved them. It was simply that two small town Texas juries were reluctant to condemn seventeen-year-old kids to death. The jurors had not yet been hardened by vicious big city crime. They still honored the old decencies. They just could not do it. Nonetheless, Tommy and Andy would serve at least thirty-five years in prison: no probation, no parole, no "good time" discounts. They would be on the verge of old age before such things could even be considered.

As Martin's trial was beginning, Andy was going through evaluation procedures at an intake unit of the Texas Department of Corrections. Tommy languished in the Rocksprings jail. He waited for someone to be released from the crowded Texas prison system to make room for him. The court transferred Martin from the Rocksprings jail to the Crockett County Jail in Ozona. It would be his home during the trial.

The trials of Tommy Eiland and Andy Milam had been, if anything, routine, their defense virtually a plea for mercy. It would be easy to turn and blame the court appointed attorneys. It is a thankless task. The money is only so-so and the facts marshalled against Tommy and Andy were overwhelming. Court appointed attorneys have tiny budgets to work with defending clients. They do not have the immense resources a DA can command: police investigative reports, testimony of trained lawmen, first crack at the murder scene, custody of evidence, state and FBI forensic resources, and all the expert witnesses tax money can buy. The list goes on. Andy's attorney might have put up a defense by blaming Tommy but he chose not to do so, perhaps because Andy's signed statement was too disheartening.

Their fate, nonetheless, was sealed. They would live in the feral world of hardened prisoners for the next three decades — a world of rape and violence and regimentation. When they came out again they would be very different men, broken and thoroughly accustomed to institutional life. The James family had their justice, not as harsh as they sought, but severe enough.

Now it was Martin's turn.

Trials are fun, or would be, if so much were not riding on the outcome such as money, freedom or even life itself. Trials are ritualistic ordeals of intellectual combat, complete with elaborate rules, ceremony and liturgy. High above the fray sits the presiding judge. He is clothed in the black robes of a medieval scholar. His office endows him with the majesty of more noble times. All who come before him must pay deference. He is treated as the living symbol and representative of the sovereign, in our system replaced by constitutional law. We no longer bow, but everyone must stand when he enters and leaves the courtroom. When he presides, none may cross the bar except those authorized to have business with the court. When he presides, all must ask permission to approach his person. None may speak when he presides except with his consent.

He is addressed in all cases as "Your Honor." His rulings within the courtroom are absolute. An attorney may register formal exception to his rulings, appeal to a higher authority or hold his peace. But for the time of the trial, the judge's rulings are final. If he wants the courtroom hot, it is made so; if cold, it is made so. To disobey, to show contempt, can mean instant imprisonment. The only people exempt from the judge's power are the jury. When they enter the jury room to deliberate, they are sovereign but usually do not know it. Jurors can not be punished for their judgments and decisions. They are sacrosanct, not to be touched by anyone, and above the law.

Into this ancient world, handed down by tradition from Medieval Europe and now recreated in lonely Ozona, Texas, came Martin Sweeten seeking justice. He would be charged by the time honored forms and rituals and be judged by a jury of his peers and the Honorable George Thurmond. Scott Stehling would stand between the court and Martin to defend the defendant, to answer the charges the State of Texas had lodged against this young man.

Scott's weekdays during the trial followed a predictable pattern. He rose early, took a walk, ate a simple breakfast then loaded his trial materials into his car. He would not take his assistants, but drove alone the five miles into town. Above all and before anything else, he wanted to be first to arrive in the courtroom, especially this courtroom. Usually the prosecution has the position nearest the jury. There is no particular rule about it, but that is the usual way. It is customary. In some modern courtrooms this arrangement is built in, so to speak, or formalized. But in Crockett County things were still old-fashioned. The two sides shared two old tables pushed together in front of the judge's dais.

By getting there early, Scott seated himself nearest the jury. He placed his files and notebooks on the table, pushed his file boxes underneath and generally made himself at home. If the judge noticed or felt so inclined he could "request" him to move. Scott bet that the judge and the prosecution would neither notice nor care. He further bet that if Judge Thurmond did not notice him the first day of the trial, he would probably not order Scott to move once underway.

Scott had good reasons to get the position nearest the jury. It has subtle advantages. Whoever is nearest the jury can influence the jurors in a thousand different ways. He can sigh quietly, make subtle facial expressions or even roll his eyes when the other side or a witness displeases him. It is a stage for a silent show directed at the jury, and the jurors notice such things. The awful truth is that jurors get bored during long trials. In most of Texas, they are not allowed to take notes so there is nothing to do but pay attention or look around. By the end of a long trial jurors have looked at everything and everyone in the courtroom many times. To take further advantage of that fact, Scott had a couple of things in mind.

He had two posters to be used as exhibits. He brought them each day and placed them alongside his desk. Everytime the jurors looked down during the trial they saw these posters and read the messages. They were like roadside billboards. Each day for, hours on end, the jurors were exposed to the messages. They probably read and looked at the posters hundreds of times during the trial without even consciously realizing it. Neither the judge nor the prosecution ever caught on to this ploy.

The first poster was a blow up of Martin's battered white Toyota. The idea was to keep the image of the car in the jury's mind because Scott pinned a number of arguments to it: that the only reason Martin was involved with this case was his pathetic habit of giving rides to buy popularity, that in doing so he was innocently sucked into Tommy and Andy's murderous scheme, and that he was finally forced by threats against his life to be present at Edmund's murder.

The second poster gave a new definition of the legal concept "reasonable doubt." Until 1991, Texas law had no formal definition. That year the Texas Court of Criminal Appeals adopted the federal wording. Each day of the trial the jurors looked down and saw in bold, clear type that the prosecution's case must provide "... **proof of such a convincing character that you would be willing to rely and act upon it, without hesitation, in the most important of your own affairs.**"

Scott had another minor but effective lawyerly trick. He made a visit to the gift center of the Pioneer Flour Mills in San Antonio. He bought an oversized coffee mug inscribed with a large company logo and the inscription "San Antonio River Mill Brand since 1851." Each day of the trial he set out the mug on his desk, carefully turning the cup so the logo faced the jury. The prosecution, not to mention the judge, never noticed this either.

"I did it to remind the jury just who was financing this impressive prosecution," he explained later.

For the death of Edmund James, Martin Sweeten was tried for the following offenses: **in count one:** for capital murder in the course of committing or attempting to commit robbery and for capital murder in the course of committing or attempting to commit burglary of a habitation; **in count two,** for murder with the intent to cause serious bodily injury; **in count three,** for criminal conspiracy to commit capital murder. The State had learned its lessons from Tommy's and Andy's trials. For one thing, Tom Lee decided not to seek the death penalty against Martin. If convicted he would get the same sentence as the others, a minimum of thirty-five years, no probation, no parole, no "good time."

There were good and sufficient reasons for not seeking the death penalty against Martin. None of them had anything to do with kind heartedness. As already mentioned, two juries had been reluctant to inflict the death penalty on the other defendants because of their youth. But just as importantly, the State had used the expert testimony of Dr. Richard Coons of Austin, Texas, to assert that Tommy and Andy posed a "continuing threat to society." He based this opinion on the facts that they had done the actual shooting and that they showed a complete lack of remorse for their actions. Therefore, in Dr. Coons expert opinion, Andy and Tommy were candidates for the death penalty. But Martin had shown plenty of demonstrable remorse, also he had not pulled a trigger (although the jury did not know it yet). To paint him with Dr. Coons's testimony would be virtually useless.

After the jury was seated, Martin's trial began May 4, 1993, in Ozona, Crockett County, Texas.

After each side made their opening statements, the first prosecution witness called to the stand was Edwards County Deputy Sheriff Jay Adams. He had been a deputy for seven years under Letsinger and risen to the rank of chief deputy. He obviously did his job well because after Letsinger was voted out of office, the new sheriff kept Adams on duty. Jay was a nice guy. He did not swagger with lawman's pride but rather spoke softly and with courtesy. He was friendly in his dealings with the defense, but maintained professional neutrality. Jay was not tall or particularly brawny. He had an average build with a slightly rounded face which made him look younger than his years. He and his Asian wife would make the long drive from Rocksprings to Ozona each day. She would bring a book and read in the car during boring testimony.

As he took the stand it had been almost a year ago to the day that Jay had arrived at the murder scene. Once there he took command as senior officer in charge. He had met Edmund once and identified the photographs of the body for the court. Tom Lee led him through routine questions designed to introduce the jury to the basic facts of the case, what procedures Jay had employed and a description of the ranch. Scott did not object until the State attempted to introduce more than one photograph of the body. The objection was overruled. Jay continued to testify. There was nothing particularly disturbing to the defense until Tom Lee asked Jay what happened while the photographs were being taken.

> **A:** A vehicle approached the scene, and a man started walking toward the scene. And I was – I went to meet him, and I was told Martin Sweeten was in the back of Deputy Wood's car.
> **Q:** Okay. Do you know who the man was that was walking toward you?
> **A:** It was Martin's dad, Darwin Sweeten.

Scott was taking notes by this time. This testimony went straight to a vital point. Both Darwin and Martin claimed that Darwin had admonished his son to seek legal counsel soon after meeting Jay and that Martin had been locked in the back seat of the patrol car. If Scott could get Jay to confirm this, he would bolster his planned motion to have Martin's subsequent statements ruled as inadmissible. There was fat chance Jay would oblige, but Scott could not let the testimony go unchallenged. The jury had to know the defense questioned the deputy's account. Meanwhile, he let Tom Lee set the groundwork.

> **Q:** Okay, did you tell Darwin Sweeten anything?
> **A:** He asked me – if he could speak with his son . . . I first conferred with Deputy Woods, and he told me Martin was not under arrest for anything, he was a witness in the case, and . . .
> **Q:** Okay. All right. Now, tell us what happened then as a result of this being said. What did you do?
> **A:** I went with Mr. Sweeten back to – just a hundred yards from the house.

At this point Tom Lee had Jay identify Martin.

Q: Did you notice if Darwin Sweeten, the man you spoke to, was in the courtroom before the trial began?
A: Yes, He was the gentleman sitting right over here wearing suspenders. We went back to Deputy Wood's car where Martin was sitting and –
Q: Did you observe Martin at that point?
A: Yes, I did.
Q: Was he under arrest?
A: No, he wasn't.
Q: Was he handcuffed?
A: No, sir.
Q: Was he locked in the car?
A: I don't remember exactly. He was in the back seat.

Lee continued asking if the doors were closed, if Martin had been searched, if he had been under guard? Jay answered "no" to them all.

Q: Okay. Tell us what happened then after you arrived at the car. You were standing with Darwin Sweeten, the father of the defendant?
A: They started talking.
Q: Were you standing there listening to Darwin Sweeten and Martin Sweeten talk?
A: No, sir.
Q: Was any other deputy standing there listening to them talk?
A: No, sir.
Q: Did you hear anything said between Darwin Sweeten and Martin Sweeten?
A: No, I didn't.

Jay testified about his activities that evening, about recovering Andy's .22, a filet knife and Edmund's watch. He testified about the chain of custody he maintained of the physical evidence. He told of watching Tommy and Andy being magistrated, on his return to Camp Wood to recover the other .22 rifle and Edmund's pistol found under Tommy's mattress. He told of returning to Rocksprings. He told of taking Tommy's statement after reading him his rights. He told of watching Sheriff Letsinger take Andy into his office to read him his rights and take his statement. He told of driving to Camp Wood the next day to retrieve the bottles of liquor where Mike Pannell and Martin had hidden them. Finally, he ran through the bottles' chain of custody. Tom Lee passed the witness to Scott for cross-examination.

Scott took Jay back a month ago, to a day when Jay had accompanied Scott, Darwin and Scott's investigator to the ranch. He used this testimony to give the jury a feel for the elaborate complex of houses, storerooms, workrooms and garage which made up the ranch "house."

It had been a strange experience to walk through a murdered man's home, though all traces of the crime had disappeared. The family had removed much of the valuable furniture, art and jewelry. There was only the bare outline of Edmund's life remaining. A heavy aura of death and tragedy lingered in every corner. One of Edmund's nephews acted as guide that day. The log cabin kitchen had a large dining room outfitted with a big screen TV, VCR and stereo sound system. Edmund had died near the back door.

Out the other side, the covered walkway led to the comfortable living quarters. To the left, children's outdoor gym equipment stood empty and forlorn in the side yard. The walk-in closet where Andy had picked up the cash was upstairs in Edmund's bedroom and still packed with clothes Edmund would never wear again. By his bed was the table where Andy had taken the watch. On the other side was another table where he found the pistol.

The storerooms filled with electronics, tools, games and paintball equipment stood outside. There was a shed with woodworking tools and machines; next to it was a well-stocked tool room. Everything was covered in dust. The last storeroom was where Edmund had his elaborate video arcade set up. Scott flipped on a switch and all of the games sprang to life. No one wanted to play. The three-car garage was filled with tools, sporting equipment, machines, motorcycles, scuba gear, and two trucks. It reminded the visitors of the last scene in the film "Citizen Kane," rooms filled with possessions no longer possessed.

It took hours for Scott to videotape and inspect the complex. The whole exercise had been spooky, sad and depressing all at once. Darwin had followed the group quietly on the inspection. Subdued and respectful he apologized to the nephew about the tragedy and his son's involvement. The apology was accepted but little more was said.

On the way out Darwin sat silently in the back seat. Scott let out a long sigh. It had been uncomfortable going through the house and Edmund's possessions, a necessary exercise but nonetheless disturbing. Scott said wistfully, to no one in particular, how he wished the judge would be called to other pressing duties instead of presiding over Martin's trial. Judge Thurmond had relentlessly ruled against the defense in Tommy and Andy's trial. He had put the heat on Scott during Martin's pretrial hearing. Scott knew the trial would be tough.

"I've been praying for the judge to get sick," Darwin suddenly offered from the back seat.

"Darwin, I'm surprised at you, a Christian gentleman, saying something like that," Scott's investigator responded. "Shouldn't you be praying that the judge will be fair and compassionate?"

"I tried that and it didn't work," Darwin dryly explained.

On the stand Scott had Jay describe that day's tour and used the occasion to introduce his photographs of the ranch buildings. It was a necessary exercise, but routine. At the same time he hoped to show the jury that this was no working ranch house, and that Edmund had lived a life very different from ordinary ranchers in Crockett County.

Scott gently moved Jay toward the important questions about Darwin's conversation with Martin. Who had been there when Jay arrived? Had the body been disturbed? Who covered it with a tarp? Why had the contents of Edmund's blue jeans been turned over to the family instead of retained as evidence? Where had Martin been when Jay arrived at the scene?

> **Q:** Now, I believe you testified you could not remember if the car doors were open or closed or if the doors were locked or not?
> **A:** I believe the door was closed, but the window was down.
> **Q:** Was Martin Sweeten free to leave at that point if he wanted to?
> **A:** No, he wasn't.

Scott backed off and shifted the questioning. When had Jay learned Martin was the third youth in the car and had driven the killers to the ranch? Jay did not remember, nor did Jay recall anyone explaining at that time how Martin came to be a witness.

Q: Do you recall Darwin Sweeten asking you if Martin needed a lawyer and your advising him that he did not?
A: I don't remember saying that.
Q: But at this time Martin was a witness and not a suspect, is that right?
A: That's right.
Q: In your testimony this morning you referred to Tommy and Andy as the "two other suspects." In addition to whom were they suspects?
A: Well, that was improperly worded.

Scott bored in. If Martin was not a suspect at the time, is that why he had not been magistrated along with Tommy and Andy? Is that why Jay had not read him his rights at the scene?

Q: Did you personally talk to Martin Sweeten out there at the scene?
A: I don't remember if I did.

So, according to his own testimony the officer in charge had not been informed of Martin's role in the murder, did not know why Martin was being held in a patrol car as a "witness," and had, therefore, not bothered to read him his rights. Under further questioning, Jay testified he did not know what Buck Pruitt said to Tommy or Andy to convince them to talk. Jay certainly had no recollection of Buck telling them Martin turned them in. Jay could not even remember the outline of Buck's conversations with Tommy and Andy. "I don't remember exactly," he said again and again.

Q: How did he convince them to talk?
A: I don't remember exactly.
Q: What do you remember exactly?
A: Just a conversation between the two of them.

Jay's memory did not improve. He did remember where Tommy and Andy lived, but did not know that Martin lived just up the road. Scott shifted the questioning to the times the various statements were given. Jay testified that Martin's first statement had begun at 11:55 P.M. and finished at 2:24 A.M., over two and a half hours. Andy's statement began at 12:44 A.M. and finished at 1:15 A.M., just thirty-one minutes. Tommy began his statement at

2:46 A.M. and finished at 3:15 A.M., just twenty-nine minutes. Martin's second statement began at 3:20 A.M. and he finished at 6:10 A.M., two hours and forty minutes. Martin had been interrogated for over five hours!

Jay remembered Darwin and Sue arriving at the Rocksprings Sheriffs Office. He also remembered John Pannell and his family arriving. He remembered Darwin asking if he could get Martin something to eat. But Jay remembered nothing about Darwin asking for a lawyer. Despite the fact the Rocksprings office is small, Jay could not even remember Darwin asking loudly to see his son.

> **Q:** Do you recall being in the room with Martin during his second statement?
> **A:** I don't remember exactly. I could have been.
> **Q:** Do you remember Martin Sweeten saying he wanted to stop the questioning and that he would like a lawyer?
> **A:** No, I don't remember that.

Jay could not remember anything the deputies said to Martin during questioning. He could not remember anything about "coming clean . . . telling the whole truth," nothing about telling Martin that Tommy and Andy had "implicated him." Jay did not remember Martin asking him to leave the room because Martin preferred to talk to his "pal" Deputy Sheriff Lowrie. Scott suddenly switched back to the evening Jay arrived at the ranch to take over the murder scene.

> **Q:** You testified this morning you could not remember if Martin could get out of the car, that you did not remember if the doors were open or not; but you do remember the windows were down?
> **A:** I don't remember exactly.

Scott opened the pretrial transcript to Jay's testimony. "You remember testifying during the pretrial that Martin was in the back seat. You testified that Martin was 'unable to get out of the car without someone else letting him out.' You testified the car doors were locked and Martin could not unlock it. Does this refresh your recollection?"

It did.

It had been a nifty day's work. Jay had not looked good on

the stand. He said way too many I-don't-remember's. Scott hoped he had scored a few points with the jury. It was pretty obvious the cops had been rather fast and loose with Miranda rights. They had really put the heat to Martin.

Once they got his first statement, they had used it to quickly pry open Tommy and Andy. Then the officers turned back around and used their statements to wring the last drops from Martin. They allowed Martin to dream on regarding the distant DA's affection for him. They certainly had not disabused him of his illusions about the seriousness of his situation. Finally, they had successfully run the old "good cop-bad cop" routine, the staple of a thousand TV shows. Martin had bought it all from his "pals."

All in all, it had been a nice opening cross-examination.

But Scott knew full well it would have no effect on the admissibility of Martin's statements. Judge Thurmond had ruled on that during the pretrials. The statements would stand. Nor would it likely move the jury very far. Twelve pragmatic West Texans were not going to free Martin just because some deputies had been casual about Miranda rules. Too many hardened criminals had escaped a term in prison because of legal technicalities. An Ozona jury was not going to let this kid off just because the cops were playing tough games. They needed a lot more to justify that.

In the evening after trial, Scott warned his assistants not to be too encouraged by these early skirmishes, "there are going to be days when we will think we have it made and there will be days when we think we have lost the case. That's the way long trials go. Get ready for it," he told them.

The next witness continued the theme of "magistration," Marjorie Merritt, Justice of the Peace of Edwards County, testified she read Martin his Miranda rights in her office on the morning of April 10, 1992. She also had been to the ranch to officially pronounce Edmund James as dead. On cross she produced the warrants and complaints against Martin, Andy, and Tommy. Scott waged a brief skirmish over the fact that Tommy and Andy had been charged with capital murder while Martin was charged with simply murder.

The State then called Dr. Odelle Deborah Zivot, an extraordinary woman. She had been an assistant medical examiner for Bexar County and had performed the autopsy of Edmund James.

She took the stand with an aura of authority, and no one could take their eyes from her. Her head was swathed in a bandage which swept down covering the left half of her face. The effect was bizarre and disturbing. Dr. Zivot was no longer with Bexar County because she had taken time off to fight a personal battle. She had brain cancer but it was now in remission. It had taken her left eye. She was a living example of almost unbelievable courage. She had a horrible deadly disease, yet still coolly performed autopsies and calmly reported the results in court.

She said Edmund had suffered ten gunshot wounds. Roy Barrera asked her to elaborate. Scott objected, "We object to the introduction of the autopsy report on the basis that it is already clear Mr. James died of gunshot wounds. It would be unfairly prejudicial under rule 403 to go into details, which are very gory, about all the different wounds in this case."

Rule 403 states that relevant evidence may be excluded if it is highly prejudicial, confuses the issue, misleads the jury or is a needless presentation of corroborating evidence. Scott argued that everyone conceded Edmund had been shot multiple times. Besides, the prosecution had already admitted photographs of the body, and given the jury a good long look at them. Why go into more details which could inflame the jury's sensibilities?

"Overruled," Judge Thurmond responded.

Barrera led Dr. Zivot on an intricate tour of Edmund's wounds, all ten of them: ". . . This is the entrance wound of gunshot wound number six. The entrance wound of gunshot wound number seven . . . Now, with regard to any other wounds, entrances or exits which may appear on that side of the body, the front side of the body this is the exit wound of gunshot wound number five. It was an actual exit. A hole where it poked through but the bullet was still within the fat subcutaneous tissue, and this darkened area was ecchymosis, or blood which had seeped through there . . .," she explained with a flat, professional voice.

Q: What is the significance of the stippling to be found on the face or the nose area of entrance wound number one?
A: This is characteristic of what is known as an intermediate range, the gun is held away from the body. It is not in contact with it, but it is far enough – still close enough, so that the powder grains expelled from the gun strike the body and cause these abrasions.

Barrera asked how far away the rifle had been. "Three to four inches away," she replied. He asked how many bullets had been recovered from the body. "Nine bullets were recovered," she replied. Barrera led her through the chain of custody of the bullets, then switched back to the injuries done by the shots, ". . . the bullet wounds which were inflicted upon the head of Edmund James, generally what was their trajectory from a standpoint of injury done and physical injury inflicted?"

"Okay," Dr. Zivot obliged. "In gunshot wound number one, which was the perforating — in other words, it entered and exited the body, it was of the bridge of the nose. It tracked through the right maxillary sinus and subcutaneous tissue which is mainly fat and muscle of the right lateral neck, and exited the right lateral neck. . . ."

Q: Was that in and of itself, from the injury inflicted, was it a fatal wound?
A: It could have been, yes.
Q: If left unattended?
A: Yes.

Scott tried again, ". . . I renew my objection. The testimony is cumulative, and it is highly prejudicial. It is uncontroverted that Mr. James died from a gunshot wound, and that he was shot."

The Court said, "Well, I think the State has to endeavor to prove cause of death in the indictment. Overruled."

Mr. Barrera asked the witness, "Your wound number two? . . ."

There was not much Scott could do as Dr. Zivot and Roy Barrera catalogued each entrance and exit wound, the patterns of powder tattooing on the body and location of slugs remaining in the body. At this point in the trial, for all the jury knew, Martin had been the shooter. That was one good reason the defense put up a fuss. Barrera was doing what a good prosecutor should do, letting the jury know just what the killers had done to Edmund in every possible detail. Even if the testimony eventually bored the jury, it pounded home the idea that Edmund's killers had no mercy. If it could bore the jury, it could also set small fires of outrage and disgust. There was only one target for that outrage in the courtroom, Martin Sweeten.

Scott kept a running objection. The court overruled him. Dr. Zivot's report, charts and fragments of bullets were admitted into evidence. On cross, Scott merely asked Dr. Zivot to confirm that the first shot was fired closest to the body, three to five inches from Edmund's face. She further confirmed that all of the other shots had been "distant entrance wounds." So far, the jury had not heard testimony or seen evidence about who had done what to whom. Scott wanted solid groundwork laid to point the finger straight at Tommy.

Neither Tommy nor Andy could be called to testify. Their statements to the police were inadmissible. They had appealed their convictions. Therefore, their persons and the documents related to their guilt were under seal and unobtainable. This did not make Martin's defense any easier.

The prosecution called Wayne Woods to the stand. He was no longer a deputy sheriff. In his fall from the brotherhood, he landed at a construction company in Barksdale. He was a little uncomfortable to be back on the witness stand. Woods recounted his actions on the evening of April 9: how he had been eating supper with friends when he got the call, how he raced to the James Ranch, how he approached the house with Buck and how he helped in the investigation.

His testimony was intense because he had known Edmund and considered him a friend. Woods even had been scuba diving on the ranch. That night he was the first to identify the body and the first to read Martin the Miranda warning. He said he had accompanied Martin to Rocksprings and been present during questioning. The next day he had gone back to the scene. It was Deputy Woods who had found the single .22 brass casing "approximately two feet from where Mr. James's body had been lying."

The evening of April 10, Woods and Jay Adams went to West Cooksey Road to recover the evidence Martin and Mike Pannell had hidden. "There was a half a gallon bottle of some type of rum and then a half a gallon bottle of Smirnoff vodka, I believe, along with a butcher knife, an ice pick, masking tape, some rope, and two sets of gloves."

On cross-examination some very odd facts emerged from Wood's testimony, reinforcing hints the scene had been tampered with:

Q: It was dark when you got there. It was — was it past dark? I mean, was it night when you got there?
A: It was still fairly light, but it was getting dark. Right at dusk.
Q: Okay. Were there lights on at the house? . . . You said the TV was still going?
A: Yes, sir.
Q: The front door was unlocked, is that correct?
A: The best I recall, yes, sir.
Q: Was it open?
A: No, sir, the door was closed.
Q: Okay, were the lights on inside the house?
A: None that I recall.
Q: Was there a light on, on the outside of the house?
A: Not that I recall.
Q: Is it possible it was on and you don't recall; or you just don't recall; or it wasn't; or –
A: It's possible, but I don't recall one. I know we turned the back light on when we left.
Q: The back light? What light are you talking about?
A: The little porch light on the back door.

Woods later testified he clearly remembered opening the screen door to the log-cabin kitchen but did not remember opening the wooden door. He was adamant there were no lights on in the kitchen. He remembered the TV was on. The whole business of the lights was significant only because it reinforced Martin's contention that he had not shined the flashlight into Edmund's eyes as Tommy had ordered. If the scene had been well-lighted, whether Martin shined the light or not would be of less importance. There was some testimony that the lights had been on, now there was testimony the lights had been off. There is nothing the defense loves more than confusing contradictory testimony from lawmen. Also, if Scott could show lights had been on but the officers found them off, then the possibility of tampering became greater. The more doubt there was, the better for the defense.

When he and Buck checked the outbuildings, Woods remembered all of the doors were closed. He did not mention the dogs. As they were checking the woodworking shop, Martin and Elton arrived. Woods questioned him and ". . . he gave us the names — Martin gave us the names . . . Tommy Eiland and Andy Milam."

Q: Were you advised how they got out to the ranch?
A: Martin stated he took them out there in his car.
Q: What else did Martin say?
A: That he did not participate in any shooting or anything.
Q: What about taking stuff out of the house, what did he say about that?
A: He stated he did not take anything; he was not involved other than he took them out there . . .
Q: Did he say anything about being shocked by the shooting?
A: No, sir.
Q: What was his composure like?
A: He seemed to be nervous.
Q: Well, was he shaking?
A: Not that I could tell.
Q: Why do you say he seemed to be nervous?
A: He just kept wanting to tell me what had taken place. You know, he kept saying, 'I want to tell you, I want to tell you.' That's why I read him his Miranda rights, because I didn't know what role he had really played in the shooting. . . .
Q: Did he tell you of being afraid?
A: Yes, sir.
Q: And he was afraid of law enforcement officers, is that what he told you?
A: No, sir, not that I know of.
Q: What did he tell you he was afraid of?
A: He was afraid – he told me he was afraid of Andy and Tommy.

Woods said Martin told him Tommy and Andy had threatened not only Martin's life but his family as well. Martin also told him Tommy had pointed the .357 at him on the way to Uvalde and that he was terrified. It was great stuff. Through Woods, Scott was planting the notion early in the trial that Martin had been forced into this mess. Later he would somehow have to convince the jury that Tommy had the charisma to control Martin and the ruthlessness to kill him. It was Martin's best defense, but it guaranteed absolutely nothing.

Scott moved on to Martin's arrival at the scene. Woods said he had told Martin to "just have a seat in my patrol car."

Q: All right. And what seat in your patrol car did you invite him to sit in?
A: I didn't invite him to sit in any of them. I said he could have a seat. He sat down in the back seat of my patrol car.

Q: Once he was in the back seat, he could not get out, could he?
A: No, sir.
Q: . . . The door won't open from the inside, will it?
A: No, sir, it wouldn't.

The point was made. Once Martin got into the car he was a virtual prisoner. He may have been called a "witness" but he was locked into the back of the car. He was under virtual arrest. Woods tried to keep the faith.

A: All I knew was that Martin was a witness.
Q: Just a witness? Do you have any idea how he happened to be out at the James residence to witness Mr. James' being shot?
A: No, sir.

On the way to Rocksprings, Woods read Martin his rights:

Q: Did he ask you why you were reading from the card when you read it to him?
A: Yes, sir.
Q: What did he say?
A: He asked me if he was under arrest.
Q: What did you tell him?
A: I told him at that time, no, as far as I knew, he was just a witness to a murder.

There was one other piece of unfinished business Woods could throw light upon:

Q: Where were the dogs?
A: They were in a video room.
Q: And were they in the video room when you got there?
A: Yes, sir.
Q: How do you know?
A: There was a noise coming from that room.

Scott shifted to the other mystery:

Q: You found a .22 shell casing?
A: Yes, sir.
Q: . . . How many shell casings did you find?
A: Just the one.
Q: Did you look for more?
A: Yes, sir, I did.

Q: It was obvious there were more wounds just from looking at Mr. James's body, is that right?
A: Yes, sir.
Q: What area did you search?
A: All around the trees, picnic area; approximately about a 30-foot area.
Q: Did you look carefully?
A: Yes, sir. I got down on my hands and knees.
Q: Did you think you missed nine other shell casings?
A: No, sir, no way.

It was late afternoon and it was enough for one day. Court adjourned until nine A.M. The jury rose and left the room. The Honorable Judge Thurmond rose as did all in the courtroom.

In the evening, back at the Best Western Truck Stop, there were restrained congratulations and a feeling of relief. Things were off to a reasonably good start. Scott wanted to keep things at a low key. He knew there could be real trouble ahead and told everyone to be ready. They reviewed the day over supper. One of Scott's assistants read back notes while everyone helped themselves to barbecued chicken and fresh salsa.

Scott had scored some points in the early skirmishes, but there was a long way to go. For one thing, the way Judge Thurmond was ruling at this early stage, there was little chance he was going to buy any arguments to throw out either or both of Martin's statements. It seemed as if all he had to say to Scott was, "Good morning" and "overruled."

Woods resumed the stand the next day. Things immediately veered in a very dangerous direction Scott wanted to avoid. Tom Lee asked Woods on redirect examination, "What type of evidence did you recover during the investigation?"

A: I recovered some items taken in a burglary.
Mr. Stehling: Your honor, this would be improper redirect. It would be a new matter.
The Court: Overruled.

Lee produced a box containing many items and asked they be introduced as evidence. The bailiff and Lee catalogued the items but did not take them out of the box. The jury could not see them. They were admitted into evidence and Lee continued the questioning.

Q: Can you describe what that is?
A: Some items I found in Andy Milam's room where he was staying, at Patricia Butts's residence.
Q: There are several individual items which are a part of this. Can you describe, just so the record will show what you are talking about, what these items are?
A: Two fire extinguishers, small tackle box, pair of binoculars, a pump which went to a rubber raft and also, I believe, there was an electric drill or cordless drill. And a pillowcase.

These were the pathetic fruits of the so-called burglaries Tommy, Andy, and Martin pulled on an empty building and a couple of hunting cabins. In and of itself, this box of near junk had nothing to do with the issue at hand, but it had profound implications. It was a doorway which led to some very dangerous evidence. At this early date, Scott wanted to avoid the issue at all costs. On cross-examination, he pulled each item out of the box as he questioned Woods:

Q: We have the pillowcase; you said you found two fire extinguishers . . . Were they in the pillowcase when you found them?
A: No, sir, they were just laying in the closet.
Q: You put them into the pillowcase?
A: Yes, sir.

As Woods confirmed each item, Scott stuffed it into the pillowcase in full view of the jury. Later, when Lee submitted a box of Tommy's clothing as evidence, Scott went through the same procedure, pulling each item out of the box to show the jury.

Q: This little jacket in it?
A: I believe it was.
Q: A little gray sweater?
A: I believe it was.
Q: A shirt?
A: That's correct?

On and on, Scott pulled out Tommy's pathetic worldly goods for all to see: green pants, blue jeans, grey pants, blue sweater, blue shirt, a pair of socks, another pair of socks, a card from his grandmother, a Mennen Speed Stick Deodorant, a bottle of Jergen's lotion . . .

Judge Thurmond had just about enough, "Are we going to go through each —"

"There are just about five more things, your honor," Scott offered.

"Let's go ahead then," Thurmond grumbled.

Scott later explained that he had two purposes in displaying the contents of both boxes, "Well, they admitted those boxes without clearly showing the jury what was in them. I wanted to take any mystery out of it. I did not want the jury to think there was some big deal in those boxes. Secondly, I wanted to get well away from the subject of burglaries."

The State called Buck Pruitt to the stand. He ran through his version of April 9, 1993. He told of how he organized the EMS crews and other personnel, how he and Woods approached the house, found the body and secured the scene. It sounded great, like a SWAT operation. The whole evening had gone like clockwork, no confusion, no mistakes. Buck was impressive, authoritative, confident. Buck had cop-speak down pat. It would be hard to shake him on cross-examination. Buck also dropped a little bomb in the middle of his testimony. He had recovered Edmund's .357 revolver, State's exhibit number 27, from underneath Tommy's mattress.

> **Q:** Is State's exhibit number 27 in the same condition now as it was the first time you recovered it?
> **A:** No, sir.
> **Q:** Is there anything different?
> **A:** Yes, sir. It is functional now.
> **Q:** Can you explain what you mean by that?
> **A:** This revolver, the cylinder was locked up when we recovered it.
> **Q:** Meaning it would not fire at that point.
> **A:** No, it would not function.

This testimony went straight to Martin's claim he was forced to accompany Tommy and Andy to Uvalde at gunpoint. Forced? By a weapon which could not fire? It was an issue which had to be addressed immediately on cross-examination. It was a small brush fire for the moment but had to be extinguished.

> **Mr. Stehling:** Deputy Pruitt, you said that concerning this pistol . . . that it was — that the cylinder was frozen, was locked-up?

A: Uh-huh.
Q: How did you determine that?
A: It wouldn't turn.
Q: Can you tell by looking at it?
A: I don't know. I suppose it would be hard.
Q: What was preventing it from turning?
A: I do not know.

For the next hour or so Scott took Buck back through Martin's detention and questioning, the arrest of Tommy and Andy, and when and where Miranda rights had been read. Buck answered in detail and professionally, but around his official demeanor seeped his contempt for the defense. With body language and tone of voice, Buck let the courtroom know he did not think very highly of defense attorneys, especially this one. There was not much Scott could do about it except let loose one good shot. In the midst of questioning Buck about Martin's statement, Scott suddenly asked:

Q: Did you take Martin Sweeten out of the Edwards County jail later on?
A: Sure, uh-huh.
Q: And did you contact me before you did it?
A: No.
Q: Okay.
A: I didn't take him out of the jail; I just talked to him in the jail.
Q: Well, did he leave with you from the jail?
A: No.
Q: Later on, to go to Uvalde?
A: Not with me.
Q: Who were you with?
A: (no audible response.)
Q: You met Martin and Mike Lowrie in Camp Wood, is that correct?
A: That's true.
Q: Deputy Lowrie?
A: Right.
Q: And where did you go from there?
A: Went to Uvalde.
Q: And what did you do in Uvalde?
A: Mike and Martin had decided they were going to go down there and Martin was going to show Mike some places where there was some illegal activity.

Q: What was the nature of the illegal activity?
A: Drug transactions.
Q: Did Martin say he had ever gotten any drugs there?
A: He was just basically relating what he had heard.

In other words, one fine day Lowrie and Buck had taken Martin out of jail in Rocksprings and transported him to Uvalde. There they used him to run down all of the local high school rumors about where to buy drugs. It was a stupid thing to do. Martin was represented by an attorney, and any such action by the deputies must be cleared with him. In any competent big city police force, Lowrie and Pruitt would have faced severe reprimands, and any evidence they obtained would have probably been useless. In the Edwards County Sheriff's Department the response was, "Gee, what's the problem?"

The whole issue made little difference to Martin's case, but Scott wanted Buck's explanation on the record. He also wanted to make him squirm in front of the jury. He did.

Buck was excused and left the courtroom.

After some brief testimony by Shane Holman, the game warden who arrested Andy, the State called Patricia Eileen Butts, "Jinks," to the stand. If ever there was a woman unprepossessing in her appearance, it had to be Jinks. She arrived in court wearing old shorts, a T-shirt and flip-flop thongs. As she flapped her way to the stand, her little pot belly swayed. Her voice was gravelly from too many cigarettes and her face prematurely aged. Jinks had made no effort to style her stringy blonde hair and had barely brushed it. She was hardly the stuff of courtroom drama, and yet, that was exactly what she would provide.

Roy Barrera questioned her. He knew she loved Andy like a son and was fond of Martin. He sternly cautioned her to, "answer the questions I ask you only. Don't volunteer anything because we need to keep within the area of questions which are asked and nothing else. Do you understand?"

"Yes, sir," she meekly replied.

Barrera ran her through some routine questioning: did she know Martin, did she know Tommy Eiland, Andy Milam, Jennifer Noblett, Carolyn Hodge, did she own a .22 caliber rifle, could she identify it, did she lend it to Andy on April 8, 1993, did she give a statement to the sheriff's deputies regarding the events of that day, did she agree to have her trailer searched? To each question she answered, "yes."

Jinks looked like a small girl on the stand. She was wary of Barrera, but determined to answer each question. She knew Barrera was no friend. Each time she tried to back away from his questions, Barrera would make her refer to the statement she had given a few days after the murder. He could not afford to bully her or even appear to as she looked so vulnerable on the stand. Yet, he had to be firm and keep her from straying too far from her original statement. It was a subtle struggle that ebbed and flowed all afternoon. At times Barrera seemed to be asking the questions through gritted teeth. Patricia would reluctantly answer, looking at him as if she were a doe ready to jump the nearest fence. It was a real test of the biblical promise that "the meek shall inherit the earth."

> **Q:** At or about that time or sometime thereafter did Martin Sweeten have occasion to come over to the house?
> **A:** I believe he did.
> **Q:** Would you take a look at your statement, see if it refreshes your memory as to whether he did or did not?
> **A:** Yes, he was there.
> **Q:** At what time did he arrive?
> **A:** About six P.M., is what I said?
> **Q:** About six P.M.?
> **A:** Yes, sir.
> **Q:** Okay, did they then have occasion to come into the house?
> **A:** Now, I'm not going to swear Martin came in that day because I don't remember him being in there, but I knew he was in there the day before.
> **Q:** Would you take a look at your statement, see if it refreshes your memory?
> **A:** I know what it says in the statement.
> **Q:** Please let me ask the question first and then give me your answer. Having looked at your statement does it refresh your memory as to what your impression was and your recollections at the time?
> **A:** Where I told -- in my statement here I told Mr. Lee, I said about Martin being in the house. I can't swear he was in the house that day because I knew he was in there one day, but not the special day all this took place.

Q: But at the time is it a fair statement that your recollection was Andy, Tommy, and Martin were all in the house?
A: Yes, they were in the house.

In the midst of these questions, Barrera suddenly lunged at Martin's fundamental contentions, that he never intended to become involved in murder, had no prior knowledge any such crime was seriously planned, and that he went to Edmund's ranch to ask for a job.

Q: What time did they leave your house?
A: It was after six o'clock.
Q: Would you look at your statement to see what your recollection of the events was on that date? Look up toward the top, in the interest of time.
A: That's what I'm looking at. What part of the time do you want?
Q: At the time they left in Martin's car, what time was it?
A: It says Martin Sweeten came over after six P.M., so I guess it was about seven, something like that when they left.
Q: Was your recollection . . . that they left at seven o'clock in Martin's car?
A: Yes, sir.
Q: Okay, and what did they tell you they were going to do?
A: Go coon hunting.
Q: Did Martin or anyone call to your attention that they were going someplace to look for a job?
A: Not especially, no. That day?
Q: Well, especially or otherwise, did anyone mention to you, Martin in particular, 'We are going to look for a job?'
A: I don't remember them saying anything about a job.

Scott opened his cross-examination with a bit of judicial judo:

Q: Mrs. Butts would you show me the – statement you have been reading from? It is marked State's Exhibit 64. Is this the one you have been reading from?
A: Yes, sir.
Mr. Stehling: We would like to offer State's Exhibit 64 into evidence.
Mr. Barrera: I don't know; I have no reaction to it, but –

Judge Thurmond ordered the two attorneys to approach the

bench. It was odd for the defense to ask for the state's evidence to be admitted as its evidence. Judge Thurmond knew exactly what Scott was after. So far, the jury did not know that Andy and Tommy had been convicted of killing Edmund, or that they had done the actual shooting. Jinks had made plenty of remarks in her statement which indirectly pointed to Tommy's guilt. The prosecution wanted to keep the spotlight on Martin despite the fact Tommy's name kept cropping up. (During the trial, it was mentioned as often as Martin's, if not more so.)

"The exhibit number 64, State's Exhibit is admitted," Judge Thurmond finally ruled.

> **Mr. Stehling:** Mrs. Butts would you read the last paragraph?
> **Mr. Barrera:** Just a minute. Hold it one second. This would be inadmissible and totally outside, if he goes into this as being an opinion being asked of this lady. It is wholly and totally improper. We didn't go in to that phase of it, that part. If the court doesn't have it and is at a disadvantage —

Judge Thurmond was taken aback by the intensity of Barrera's objections. The judge was not quite sure what was in the statement which would cause Barrera to almost sputter with annoyance.

"I have no idea –," he said almost bewildered.

"Would you please permit the court to see the statement. Mrs. Butts, show that to the court." Barrera asked the equally bemused Jinks.

Judge Thurmond looked it over and immediately spotted what pushed Barrera's buttons. But, there was no way to keep it out of testimony. The statement was already admitted into evidence.

"Objection, overruled," he said.

"Mrs. Butts go ahead and read the last paragraph," Scott requested.

> **A:** About Tommy?
> **Q:** Yes, ma'am.
> **A:** It says Tommy made a statement while he was in my house about a week before this happened that he wished his grandmother, grandfather, and father were dead, and I heard him say this. I told

him that is no way to talk about your relatives. Tommy said he did not care, he wanted to — I can't read that word.
Mr. Barrera: Inherit.
A: Yes, inherit a lot of money. Tommy said this two or three times on different occasions.

It was mildly incredible if not amusing. Roy Barrera had actually helped Jinks interpret a word in her statement after strenuously objecting to the statement's admission as evidence. It was hard to break old defense attorney habits.

Scott took Patricia back over her relationship with Andy. She said Andy had been fine, quiet and gentle until he met Tommy. She said she warned Andy about Tommy but to no avail. Meanwhile, Martin had begun to hang around with both boys.

Q: Would you describe Tommy Eiland as a strong-willed person.
A: Yes.
Q: How would you compare him, as far as being strong-willed, to Andy and Martin?
A: Well, I would compare Tommy as leader and Martin and Andy as followers.
Q: Did you know if the kids would ever use Martin because he had a car?
A: Yes, sir.
Q: How often would this happen?
A: I know Tommy did it quite often.
Q: Did you have an impression of whether or not Tommy actually liked Martin?
A: I don't know if Tommy liked anybody.
Mr. Barrera: Objection . . .

There was one more moment in Patricia's testimony. It was one of those unexpected moments which are impossible to fully describe. It was not so much what she said, but how. She was having problems speaking, her asthma was bothering her. As she testified, her voice would lower and become rougher. The day was dry, almost hot, a typical West Texas spring. Plenty of dust was in the air.

Scott was cross-examining her, and it was going well. Jinks was telling the story Scott wanted told. He had to establish somehow that Tommy had exceptional control over Andy and Martin.

It was vital to show that Tommy's powers went beyond those of a mere tough guy.

> **Q:** Were other kids – do you know whether or not other kids were scared of Tommy?
> **A:** I don't know but, – I can't say, but I know that he had a bad temper.
> **Q:** Had Tommy ever shown that around you?
> **A:** I seen him mad one time.
> **Q:** How did that affect you?
> **A:** Well, it kind of upset me. I mean, he didn't really do anything, but just watching him being mad was enough.
> **Q:** Was Tommy kind of a scary guy?
> **A:** Tommy was **evil** looking, if you want to put it bluntly.

A palpable chill went through the courtroom. Patricia had said "evil" in such a way that it almost invoked a presence. She seemed to shrink back into the witness stand. Later when people tried to recall precisely what she said, they inevitably remembered, "Tommy was evil . . ." This was an odd phenomena. It was not what she had said, but it was exactly what she meant.

Chapter VII

Hidden Serpents

IN THE MIDDLE EAST, even in Islamic countries, there are many oral tales about Jesus which have been passed down through the centuries. Pious Muslims recognize Jesus as a prophet and a wise man, a forerunner of Muhammad. No one is sure just how these stories originated for they are certainly non-canonical. In one story Jesus and his disciples were in a town early one morning, gathered around the main water well. Jesus was teaching his disciples about prophecy, and the disciples, like students everywhere, questioned their Master.

"Lord, we do not doubt you but we would beg to see a small demonstration of such powers," they requested.

They looked around and spotted a humble man setting out to cut a few days' worth of firewood. He carried a short axe and a pouch with a bit of lunch. "Master, tell us what awaits that man?" the disciples asked him.

Jesus beheld the man and said sadly, "He will not live out the day. His time in this world is over. He will die in the woods."

The disciples marvelled and watched as the man passed through the town's gates. After he was gone they returned to their task. All day they studied scriptures and listened to Jesus's teachings. As the sun began to set, a disciple gasped loudly. Through the gates walked the woodsman carrying a large bundle of cut wood. The disciples were horrified and looked at Jesus. They did not dare to confront him with what appeared to be a major failure of his divinely-given powers.

"You marvel that this man still lives?" Jesus asked. The disciples reluctantly nodded that they most certainly did.

"I tell you he was to die this very day. Yet, he shared his small bit of food with a starving man in the woods. The Lord took notice of his mercy and was merciful to him," Jesus explained.

There was not much the disciples could say without directly challenging the authority of their chosen Master. However, they could not disguise their doubts. Jesus took note. He walked over to the woodsman and commanded him to set down his burden. The man, bewildered, did so. Jesus asked him to cut the cords binding the bundle of wood. The man did so. Jesus chose a stout stick, handed it to the man and told him to spread the bundle. The man did so.

Out from the middle of the wood came a large, deadly serpent. Everyone gasped and jumped back as the serpent coiled, ready to strike. The woodsman looked with gratitude at Jesus, lifted his axe and slew the serpent. The chastened disciples wondered at the prophetic powers of their Master.

This is perhaps the best "snake in the woodpile" story around. Setting aside the main point of the parable, it graphically illustrates that an unseen peril is the most dangerous. Martin's "woodpile" was the second statement he gave to the cops. Curled up in there was one big ol' snake.

In his first statement Martin had told Letsinger and Lowrie that Tommy had broached the subject of getting a job from Edmund. Martin said they had been at Andy's house, "I talked to Tommy about getting a job with Don Jackmon. I told him Don would give me a job, but he wanted me to work during school hours. Tommy then told me about getting a job from Edmund James . . . Tommy came out of the house carrying two .22 rifles. I asked Tommy what the .22's were for. He told me he was going to trade the rifles to Edmund James because he owed James $200. So then we left . . . It was dark before we got there. We pulled up into the drive way, turned off my engine and headlights. James came to the door . . . He said he could give us jobs for five dollars an hour and we could start Friday.

"After the job part was settled, Tommy asked him if he could trade the guns he brought with him for some of the money he owed him. Mr. James said he would take a look . . . After he looked over the second gun, he handed it back to Tommy. Tommy said the second gun was Andy's. The first gun had the initials 'JP' something on the stock. Tommy said Andy owed him some money. That is why Andy's gun was up for sale. James was leaning up against the picnic table. When James looked away, Tommy lifted the rifle and shot James one or two times. He fell forward on his face. Tommy said 'get him Andy!'

"Andy shot him five or six times in the head and in the back. The flashlight I was holding was not on. Then Andy and Tommy started laughing. I stood there shocked. Tommy then told me I was an accomplice to murder and that *[sic]* had better cooperate or I would get in a lot of trouble . . ."

In Martin's second statement, however, the story changed: ". . . Everything in the first statement is true up to the point where we picked up the cat [at Carolyn Sue's home]. I talked to both Tommy and Andy about the job with Don Jackmon while we were at Andy's house. Tommy said we needed more money to go to the party in Mexico. It was a high school party with people from Camp Wood. Before all this, we had already done two burglaries, one at the Double D rental in Camp Wood . . . The second burglary was at Josh Cox's in Camp Wood Hills . . . all of Josh Cox's trailers we broke into were hunting cabins . . . At school, Tommy and I were joking around about killing someone. Tommy said, "I'm thinking about killing Edmund James." I just laughed because I thought he was kidding around. Tommy told me further on that when he asked to borrow some money, James just reached in his pocket and pulled out $200. Tommy then told me he knew where James's safe was and he knew how to break into safes. He said, 'All safes have hinges.'

 . . . I was going home when Tommy waved me over at his house. Tommy and Andy were there. They were talking about killing James. They were both psyched up about the whole possibility of killing him. I told Andy and Tommy, 'All I wanted to do is go and try to get a job from James.' After all, all we needed was money. We didn't need to kill anybody. . . ."

This was devastating stuff, and as soon as the prosecution could introduce it, Martin's case was going to be severely damaged. As part of the pretrial hearing, Judge Thurmond agreed to take Scott's motion to suppress the statements under advisement. At this point in the trial, the prosecution approached the end of its presentation. Still, the court had yet to admit the statements into evidence. They were exhibits only.

The second statement made it possible for the prosecution to argue that Martin knew Tommy was plotting murder, or at the very least, inclined toward it. The prosecution would further contend that Martin consented, knowing what was planned, to "go along." He willingly drove Tommy and Andy out to the ranch, watched the murder, and then drove them back to town. Finally, he waited almost a full day before reporting the crime. These actions, if true, could make Martin as guilty of felony capital murder as those who pulled the triggers. If nothing else they showed an "intent" to cooperate.

The very minute the prosecution got Martin's statements admitted as evidence, Scott's job would become more difficult by geometric factors. It was vital that Scott shaped the jury's perceptions of Martin and Tommy early in the case. Scott had to illustrate Tommy's uncanny ability to influence people and his swaggering boastfulness. The jury merely had to look at Martin to see the contrast. It was also vital to show them Martin's burning desire for acceptance which made him easy pickings for Tommy's deceptions. The threat from those statements was why Scott spent so much time attacking the deputies' methods in questioning Martin. There was little hope the statements would be thrown out, but the defense could plant serious doubts in the jurors' minds early and often. Scott believed in the rule that, "A trial is won or lost in the very beginning, not at the summation."

Scott gained many of his goals in the first few days of the trial through skillful cross-examination and with delightfully eccentric witnesses like Patricia. He used the prosecution's own witnesses to tell Martin's story, helped by a touch of prosecutorial overconfidence. Barrera and Lee had been through the same witnesses, the same testimony, the same evidence, and the same arguments in two trials. They had won two victories, albeit, not exactly resounding victories. Now they were ploughing through the same material again. They had the case down pat. Their presentation was almost routine. The edge was off. They certainly did believe in the justice of their case. It was, however, difficult to maintain the same level of passionate intensity the third time around.

The prosecution was laying out its case like traders spreading trade goods on a blanket. They simply could not believe their merchandise would be rejected. To them it was an open and shut case, a done deal. Scott could put on whatever clever little sideshow he wanted to because it was not going to affect the outcome. To the prosecution, Martin's trial was sort of a kick for the extra point in a game already three quarters won.

Once Martin's statements were introduced, there was an excellent chance the prosecution's hopes would be fully justified. The jurors might think Martin was the sweetest kid west of the Pecos, but they were bound by their oaths to the court to weigh matters of fact, not law. In other words, they must convict Martin if the facts warranted it despite their personal feelings. Most jurors do exactly that most times. Barrera and Lee firmly believed the facts were on their side.

The prosecution was nearing it's conclusion, and obviously Barrera was planning to introduce Martin's statements at the right time for maximum drama. He would conclude his case by hammering Martin's cell door closed, and the statements would be the nails. The wait for the blow to fall seemed endless to the defense. The State called John Paul Whipkey to testify about Tommy and the rifle and then called Scott James Petty, Edmund's twenty-six-year-old nephew, to identify Edmund's watch and .357 pistol.

The defense made a small advance when Petty testified he and Edmund fired the pistol on many occasions. This was the very pistol Buck claimed was inoperative and therefore no real threat to Martin in Tommy's hands.

Ronald Dodson, an expert witness from the Bexar County Medical Examiner's Office, took the stand for the state. His specialty was firearms and ballistics. He told which bullets found in Edmund's body came from which rifle and testified as to chain of custody.

When he finished, the trial was recessed for the weekend, to resume Monday morning at nine o'clock. Everyone released a sigh. Barrera and Lee walked around the bar to consult with various friends and relations of the James family. At the other side of the courtroom Darwin and Sue came in to comfort Martin. Sue was holding his hand almost desperately, while Martin was slightly embarrassed. He wanted the comfort, but he also wanted the three packs of cigarettes the deputies allowed Scott's assistants to pass him each day. He well knew his parents strongly disapproved, but it was a small point to argue in the middle of disaster.

Eventually the defense team split up, and headed back east along IH-10. Darwin and Sue retired with their grand kids and other children to the little house behind the courthouse to resume their prayer meetings and vigils. Barrera also drove back to San Antonio; he had a major law firm to tend to. Tom Lee and Judge Thurmond, each in his car, drove west to Del Rio. The ordinary agendas of small town life closed back over Ozona, a reassuring blanket of everyday-ness.

That weekend one of Scott's assistants had an odd experience. She was relaxing by watching a television drama. Toward the end of the story the TV cops informed one of the characters that "they could wrap up this situation quickly if you would just step into our office and sign a statement." She caught herself shouting at the TV screen, "Don't do it! Stupid!"

On Monday things changed. It was nearly mid-May in West Texas, and spring was for all purposes over and done with. Summer was impending with its unbearable heat. Every day of spring out there is precious. The cool mornings, the pleasant evenings, are so short lived. Summer pounces early usually by the middle of May. The beginning of June just confirms what everyone has long known, summer is king despite the calendar. Already the weather was oppressive. Local brush dried up, and the huge fire alarm siren shrieked daily warnings to the volunteer firemen. At odd moments the siren would blast forth. For two or three minutes, everything in the courtroom would halt, frozen in place by the overwhelming noise. Mere doors, windows or stone walls could not keep back the awful shriek.

The final battle over Martin's statements was about to begin. Scott had little hope of keeping them out. Judge Thurmond still had to rule formally on their admissibility, but there was little doubt he would admit them. So, Scott would continue to try to damage their credibility. He would have to wound them, to rip and tear until the statements were tattered and questionable in the eyes of the jury.

The looming statements presented another problem. If they were admitted, Scott would have to put Martin on the stand. It could be very dangerous. Many jurors and the public think a defendant who is innocent should not be afraid to testify – never mind the fifth amendment. If innocent, take the stand. However, innocent people can be inarticulate in front of a crowd, innocent people can become flustered, and innocent people can look very guilty when cross-examined by an expert.

Unanswered, the statements were deadly. Martin might as well step into the prison cell and toss away the key. But, putting Martin on the stand meant subjecting him to a Roy Barrera cross-examination. There was something of a contest among the defense team members to come up with the most horrifying similes to describe that moment: rabbit v. rattlesnake, Thumper v. Godzilla, lamb v. eagle, Hundai v. Mercedes Benz, etc.

The State opened Monday morning by calling John Michael Pannell III, Martin's best friend. Barrera steered him through familiar ground. Mike said he helped Martin hide the incriminating "stuff in the trunk" at a cattleguard. Mike was not exactly articulate on the stand, and Barrera pounced every time Mike stumbled:

> **Q:** You were afraid?
> **A:** Yes, sir.
> **Q:** What were you afraid of?
> **A:** That Andy and Tommy had said something and somehow made it look like I was involved and Martin was involved and were the two who did it.
> **Q:** I'm sorry I didn't quite hear you.
> **A:** Martin and I were afraid from the story Martin had told me that Tommy and Andy would go to the police and somehow involve me in this.
> **Q:** So at that time, Martin Sweeten was afraid that Tommy and/or Andy would go to the police?
> **Mr. Stehling:** Object to leading the witness.
> **Q:** Is that what you said?
> **A:** He was afraid of being killed, and he was thinking . . . I was the

one that was mainly thinking, what if they go to the police and say . . . well, because I always hung around them, and said somehow I was involved.

Q: Now, you made the statement that you all were afraid that Andy or Tommy would go to the police and get you all involved, is that what you said?

Mr. Stehling: Object as to leading.

A: Yes, sir.

The Court: Okay. All right.

Q: Having this conversation, then obviously you all went to the cattle guard for the purpose of doing what?

A: We had no purpose in going to the cattle guard. We just stopped, and we were stopped and we were at a cattle guard.

Mike told the court of hiding State's Exhibits 35 to 40: a bottle of liquor, gloves, an ice pick, a length of rope, and a roll of duct tape. Barrera wanted to know who decided what to take out of Martin's trunk to hide. Mike said, "Neither of us. We just cleaned out the trunk."

Scott used his cross-examination to bring out once again Martin's vulnerability to Tommy's power. Mike told of Martin's motorcycle accident and how it "had messed him up pretty bad."

Q: Did it set him back in school any?

A: A little ways.

Q: Did Martin have many friends?

A: No, sir.

Q: Why not?

Mr. Barrera: This would be a conclusion, it would appear to me, if it please the court.

The Court (after consultation at the bench): Overrule the objection.

Q: You say Martin didn't have a whole lot of friends. Why?

A: The only time people ever hung around him is if they needed something.

Q: Like what?

A: Rides, borrowed video games, money.

Q: Okay, would Martin try to please people?

A: Yes, sir.

Q: Who all would get rides from Martin?

A: Just about everybody . . . Anybody who wanted one or told him to give them one.

Q: Did you ever see him turn anybody down?
A: No, sir.

Scott now asked Mike questions directly bearing on Martin's capacity for violence. Did Martin like to hunt deer? "No." Did Martin kill deer or kill anything on the hunts? "No, he did not like to. He thought it was cruel."

Q: Do you like Tommy Eiland?
A: Not really.
Q: What was he, Tommy Eiland, like?
A: Just real dominant over people.
Q: What do you mean by that?
A: I mean he just kind of played people . . . He would get them to do what he wanted them to, and, you know, just use them.
Q: Would Tommy threaten people?
A: Freshmen.
Q: Did you ever see Tommy Eiland fight?
A: Yes, sir.
Q: Was he a good fighter?
A: He was real rough.
Q: Was he a fair fighter?
A: No, sir.
Q: Was he mean?
A: Yes, sir.
Q: Did he hurt animals?
A: Yes sir . . . I saw him chop a cat one time with a machete.
Q: Did he kill it?
A: He just kind of let it bleed to death.
Q: Did he say anything about it?
A: He just kind of laughed.

Why Tom Lee and Roy Barrera did not at least try to object to this whole line of questioning is something of a mystery. Why did they allow Scott to persist in bolstering the argument that Tommy was the bad guy and Martin just a dupe? Tommy was not on trial, his statements to the police were inadmissible. They could have, at least, argued that Tommy's treatment of animals was totally irrelevant to Mike's direct testimony. It was odd, but every time Scott would veer off and extract testimony about Tommy, the prosecution said nothing.

One explanation advanced was that this was strategy. By all means, let Scott flail away at the absent Tommy. No one disagreed that Tommy and Andy pulled the triggers. The central point of the prosecution's case was that Martin drove the killers to the ranch, knowing full well they planned to kill Edmund. Martin passed up plenty of easy opportunities to "escape" and sound the alarm. Martin drove them to Uvalde, even spent the night with Tommy. In fact, Martin did nothing until the next day, and then only to save his own skin by beating Tommy and Andy to the punch.

Martin may be of a weak character, but it did not alter the fact he consented and participated in the murder. So why not let Scott savage Tommy all he wished? It simply did not matter. When the case was finally presented to the jury, the questions they must answer would be the same. Did Martin know beforehand? Did Martin consent? It did not matter one whit if Tommy was the Woolly Booger Bear himself. If the jury answered yes, then Martin was guilty.

Mike continued to testify. He said he had been bitten by a stray dog a few weeks before the murder. He had to undergo extensive treatment for rabies. During that time Martin began to hang around with Tommy. Mike told of working for Edmund a couple of times. He said he knew Tommy had worked there off and on for over four years, but Mike worked alongside Tommy on the ranch only once. Mike remembered the day after the murder. He remembered Martin was real "jittery" at school. Yes, he saw Tommy following Martin everywhere during the day. Mike said Martin eventually came to his house and told him of the murder. He recounted hiding the loot, returning to the house and telling his father of the murder. Mike said they tried to contact three law enforcement officers but finally went to Elton.

Scott was edging toward the opening salvo of the battle over the statements and the behavior of the cops that night. It had to come eventually, and it was going to be a running battle.

Q: What did Elton say when he got there?
A: He said something about placing him (Martin) in protective custody.
Q: Protective custody?
A: Yes, sir.

Q: Did Elton read him his rights?
A: No, sir.

Mike recalled the anxious ride with his father, mother, Darwin and Sue to Rocksprings. He told of the hours waiting for some kind of information about Martin and the drama of Andy and Tommy arriving in custody. He said Darwin was upset and demanding to see Martin.

Barrera came back for redirect examination with a vengeance. He asked Mike if he knew about the burglaries Tommy, Andy, and Martin had committed. "No, sir." Had Martin mentioned to Mike that on the day before the murder he and Tommy had talked about killing Edmund? "No, sir." Had Martin told him Tommy and Martin had discussed where Edmund kept his safe? "No, sir." Did Martin tell Mike that he, Tommy and Andy stopped at the Get 'N Go after the murder so Martin could call his father? "No, sir." Did Martin tell Mike whether he had shone the flashlight into Edmund's eyes, as he and Tommy had planned? "No, sir."

Barrera kept up a barrage of questions. He used Mike's testimony to show the jury Martin had a clear choice of his actions. He chose to give the killers a ride. He chose to hang around with Tommy. He wanted to go to the party in Mexico. Surprisingly, Martin had never told Mike, in so many words, that he was afraid of Tommy or that Tommy forced Martin to keep company with him.

Before the prosecution rested, there was some more housekeeping to do. They called former Edwards County Sheriff's Deputy Mike Lowrie to the stand. He went back over his actions at the murder scene. He told of the initial criminal investigation, securing the scene, searching the house and grounds. At one point he described the ranch as a "dude ranch . . . it was set up like a dude ranch . . . it was in motel, hotel style, fashion . . . everything was neat and in order, as if it had been waiting for somebody to come in." The defense was grateful.

Lowrie went over his preliminary examination of the body, and its disposition to Raymond Nelson for transportation to Bexar County Medical Examiner's Office. They closed down the crime scene for the evening:

Q: Did you do anything else at the scene following that point?
A: Well, Chief Deputy Jay Adams and I both secured the area. We

marked it as a crime scene, and had some of the neighbors watch over it.
Q: Then what happened?
A: Then we went to the sheriff's office to take statements . . . The sheriff's office is north of the location, this crime scene, and is approximately fifteen to twenty miles north.

Lowrie then described his arrival at the Edwards County sheriff's office at about ten P.M. He claimed he witnessed the reading of the Miranda warning to Martin Sweeten by Sheriff Letsinger:

Q: Did you notice Martin Sweeten's reaction or response as those rights were read to him?
A: Yes.
Q: What was it?
A: It was that he wanted to talk.
Q: Okay.
A: He wanted to get this thing out in the open, whatever it was at the moment.
Q: Did he have any questions of any sort that you remember him asking?
A: No, I don't.
Q: When Sheriff Letsinger read the information of rights off of the form, form fifty-six, what happened?
A: Martin waved his rights.

Lowrie described taking Martin's first statement:

A: I asked him to tell me the story and I put everything he said into a word processor. At the end of the statement I asked him if he wanted to omit, add, or change anything in the statement. If he did, I made the appropriate changes, and then I printed the statement out on a regular statement form. Then I placed it in front of him and had him read it, and told him if he still wanted to change anything that we would make the changes.
Q: Did he indicate to you he wanted to change anything?
A: He made a few minor changes as far as I remember. I made those changes, and then he went ahead and signed the statement.
Q: How long did it take you to complete this statement or to take down the information and transfer it on to a written statement?
A: It was about two or three hours. It was a three-page statement.
Q: Why did it take so long?

A: Well he wanted to go into it in detail, I mean, I'm not there to make him or tell him to cut it short or make it long or anything like this. This has to be in his words.

After taking Martin's statement, Lowrie said he let Darwin and Sue visit with Martin while he consulted with Adams about what Tommy and Andy had to say. They agreed the statements were inconsistent. He said he went back into the room and waited for Martin's parents to leave. Lowrie claimed neither Darwin nor Sue said anything to him. Once they were out of the room, Jay Adams came in and talked with Martin. Lowrie then informed Martin that they did not believe his first statement and "the best thing to do was come out with the truth regardless of the consequences."

Q: How did Martin respond?
A: Very favorably. He agreed, and he says — he said what he told me in the first statement was not all the truth. He wanted to tell me again.
Q: What happened next?
A: I said, 'Do you want any coffee? Because I sure do.' And, he said, 'Sure.' I said, 'Do you want anything to eat? Because I'm hungry.' And, he goes, 'No.' So I went and I got us both some coffee and we sat down and he told me the second story, which is on the second statement, taken in that same night.

Lowrie swore upon his oath Martin gave the statements of his own free will, that Martin had not been threatened, that he had not been offered promises of special treatment, that water, food or sleep had not been withheld and that no force had been used to extract the statements. When Martin signed the second statement, Lowrie arrested him for murder and sent him to be booked into the Edwards County jail. Lowrie refreshed himself and then drove to San Antonio to be present at Edmund's autopsy.

Lowrie testified as to the chain of custody of various state's exhibits and ended his direct testimony with an account of his own detailed grid search for shell casings a few days after the murder. He found none.

Scott opened his cross-examination with a few questions designed to undermine the natural and reflexive deference juries tend to extend lawmen. Lowrie, no longer a deputy, now worked for a plumbing company. Before he got that job, he ran a small cafe. The unspoken message to the jury was, "See, he is just like you. He's not ten feet tall. And, just like us he can fudge the truth. Watch."

First, Scott had to make a small point for possible future reference:

> **Q:** Who all was there at the ranch when you got there?
> **A:** Wayne and Buck and the EMS crew.
> **Q:** How many people were in the EMS crew?
> **A:** I don't remember.
> **Q:** Anybody else?
> **A:** I believe there was a neighboring rancher there — you have got to understand this — like any situation, any emergency situation, when something happens, people seem to come from all around, and if it is a small community or sparsely populated like in this case everybody comes out of the woodwork to help each other, so there were people from all around.

In other words, there had been far more people at the murder scene than anyone previously indicated. So many, in fact, Lowrie could not be sure just who was there or the actual number of spectators. He even found it necessary to begin rudimentary crowd control.

> **Q:** What other people, who were not law enforcement people, were out there?
> **A:** I couldn't – I can't tell you. When I arrived on the scene, my mind completely focused on the scene and doing my job.
> **Q:** Well, when you say people came out of the woodwork, I have an image of a whole lot of people out there. I'm just trying to get an idea of what you observed.
> **A:** I observed the deputies, Wayne Woods and Buck Pruitt, I observed the EMS crew, I observed some of the local ranchers, as far as I remember, some of the local ranchers to that ranch, and, of course, the county judge was there and Raymond Nelson was there, later the funeral home director.
> **Q:** Anyone else?
> **A:** I'm sure there was other people there when I went through, but I went through the crowd and I went up to the crime scene — the crowd was the people that were down below the hills and some up

there near the body, which was the EMS crew which was checking out the body. I went to the crime scene and I did my job.
Q: Can you estimate for the jury — when you say you went through the crowd, can you estimate for the jury how many people you are talking about?
A: Total, I would say, if I would have to estimate it would have to be about as few as six and as many as fifteen.
Q: And these people you are talking about were not law enforcement or EMS people?
A: Some were, some were not . . .
Q: Do you recall Martin Sweeten being there?
A: I recall someone sitting in a car, but I did not know it to be Martin Sweeten at the time . . . at the time, it was brought to my attention by somebody somewhere that he was a witness.
Q: A witness? Was it brought to your attention what he had witnessed?
A: No.
Q: Did you ever talk to the witness, Martin Sweeten, out there at Cedar Creek Ranch?
A: No, I didn't.
Q: Okay. You went through the crowd, went up to where the body was, and what did you do at that point?
A: I had everybody not connected with the criminal investigation get away from the crime scene and stay back . . .

It was fascinating testimony, ripe with implications. Buck had characterized the initial investigation as some sort of SWAT team exercise, rigorous with military precision. Now, Lowrie suddenly admitted there had been a dozen people, or even more, at the scene who were not law enforcement or EMS personnel. Moreover, he wasn't sure exactly who they were, or for that matter, how many there actually were. Better yet, at some point these unidentified people had unrestricted access to the body.

Lowrie described his version of the initial search of Edmund's house and ranch buildings. Scott raised the mystery of the locked dogs:

A: Some of the areas were locked. Some of the rooms in that area you are talking about were locked. One of them, one of the rooms there did contain barking dogs. We left them where they were.
Q: So you did not go into the room?
A: No.

> **Q:** Did you ask Wayne Woods if he had looked in the room to see what was in there?
> **A:** No. It was my understanding that when he got there the dogs were already locked in the room — And he did not open the door. He said he was warned that these were biting dogs, so we made it a point not to open the door.

Lowrie's characterization of the two labs as "biting dogs" brought an involuntary ironic laugh from the James family members in the audience. Would that they had been ferocious guard dogs, perhaps Edmund would still be alive. The mystery remained however: who had locked them up?

Scott took Lowrie back over his search for the shell casings which, as it turned out, had been the second intensive search. Lowrie implied that the large number of people at the scene that night may have driven the casings into the ground. If so they were probably beyond recovery. It was an unlikely, but possible answer.

It was time to make a run at the statements. Scott asked Lowrie to go back over the drive from the murder scene to Edwards County Jail. Lowrie said he did not hear much of Sheriff Letsinger's conversation with Martin because he was concentrating on making a sketch of the crime scene. When they arrived at the sheriff's office, Lowrie continued to work on the sketch.

> **Q:** Okay, after you drew this sketch then did Martin show you where everybody was on the sketch?
> **A:** Yes, he did.
> **Q:** At what point did the sheriff read Martin his Miranda warnings?
> **A:** As soon as he decided it was necessary.
> **Q:** How long had you been there drawing the sketch before you heard the Miranda warnings read?
> **A:** I had probably been there about twenty minutes, just a guess. It has been a year ago. It's hard to keep all the details exact.
> **Q:** So Martin had been talking to the sheriff at least the twenty minutes you were there before he gave the Miranda warnings?
> **A:** I did not say – at least – I said approximately twenty minutes had elapsed.

Lowrie kept backtracking as Scott drilled him regarding the length of Martin's interrogation sessions. The former deputy said he took over the transcription of Martin's statements from the sheriff and transferred all of the typewritten material to his computer. He threw away all of the typewritten pages. Scott asked again about the length of time they had spent with Martin compared to the other two suspects. Lowrie confirmed the timing: two hours and twenty-nine minutes on the first statement as opposed to thirty-one minutes for Andy and twenty-nine minutes for Tommy and then another two hours and thirty-one minutes for Martin's second statement.

Scott switched to questioning the methods the deputies employed to keep Martin talking. Lowrie claimed he had had a "rapport" with Martin and, "I made sure he understood, I was not going to be a threat to him."

> **Q:** You talked to him about – that some people go to prison, some people get probation, some people go to this "boot camp," this new thing they have. You talked to him about that didn't you?
> **A:** Yeah, he asked me what the penalty was, and I said, "I don't have any idea, but, you know, of all the choices in the world there is this – there is boot camp, there is prison, there is probation. Who knows? It is all up to the judge."
> **Q:** You said, some guys go to this boot camp, that it is a new thing they have now. You said that, did you not?
> **A:** Yes, sir.
> **Q:** What was the point in telling him that?
> **A:** He wanted to know what the penalty was. And, I told him, "I don't know what the penalty would be. However, there are these choices in the criminal justice system in Texas."
> **Q:** Did you mention to him other options were death by lethal injection or life imprisonment?
> **A:** I don't remember, and I –
> **Q:** Sir?
> **A:** I don't remember and I don't think I did.
> **Q:** What did you say about the District Attorney?
> **A:** Okay, I'm getting to that. He was coming on with all of this stuff and I said, "Well, I'll tell this to the District Attorney. He can't make you any promises. I can't make you any promises." Martin – at first he wanted to make some kind of deal. I'm sure he picked (that notion) up from somebody as some kind of idea. I told him there couldn't be any deals. I couldn't make any deals. The District Attorney couldn't make any deals, but I would tell him what he (Martin) said.
> **Q:** Did you ever mention anything to him that, although, of course,

you couldn't make any deals, that the District Attorney in this district was very cooperative?
A: I might have.

Lowrie denied repeatedly he had heard Darwin tell Martin to stop talking and ask for a lawyer. Lowrie claimed he heard none of the conversation between father and son. At some point in taking the second statement Lowrie said he placed Martin formally under arrest for murder. Scott was pushing him hard, and Lowrie began to get confused.

> **A:** Martin Sweeten asked me if there was a possibility of him going home with his parents. At that time, I told Martin I probably — I just didn't know.
> **Q:** Obviously before you told him he was under arrest for murder?
> **A:** No, not obviously.
> **Q:** Was it?
> **A:** I don't recollect.
> **Q:** All right. Now, before you took the second statement, Martin Sweeten told you, did he not, that he had talked to his dad, and his dad had told him he needed a lawyer and shouldn't talk any more?
> **A:** No.
> **Q:** What did he tell you?
> **A:** He said, "My parents advised me that I should remain silent."
> **Q:** You don't recall anything about a lawyer.
> **A:** He never said anything about a lawyer.
> **Q:** What specifically did he say about remaining silent?
> **A:** He said, as far as I can remember, and I quote, "My parents advised me that I should remain silent." End quote.
> **Q:** And at that point you stopped questioning him, right?
> **A:** No.
> **Q:** No?
> **A:** I said, "Well, that's too bad, because I wanted to ask you a few more questions about what went on."
> **Q:** So you initiated the further conversation, after he said that, is that correct?
> **A:** What is "initiating the first conversation after that?" His statement? What exactly is "initiating the conversation?"
> **Q:** You asked the next question — he said, "my parents advised me" — "My parents advised me I shouldn't talk any more" or "I should remain silent" and you said, "Well, then," you said, "Well, that's too bad, because I wanted to ask you some more questions." Is that right?

A: I did say that, yes, but it was not a question.

Time was running out, nearly a week had gone by and the trial was still in the prosecution phase. The jury was getting restless. They could stand only so much haggling about police procedures. It was a fine line between clearly showing that the law enforcement officers had used questionable tactics, and boring the jurors into a glassy-eyed stupor. Scott had two more points to make with this witness:

Q: What's this about (Martin) not wanting to talk to Jay? Is that Jay Adams?
A: Yes. True, he did not want to talk to Jay.
Q: Why did he want to talk to you and not to Jay?
A: I suppose — I can only assume and speculate on this, that in some way, form or fashion, that he visualized Jay as some sort of threat.
Q: Had Jay done anything in your presence so that Martin would "visualize" Jay as some sort of threat, as opposed to you being a threat?
A: I can visualize it as a degree of threat from the viewpoint of looking at Martin's character, as opposed to Jay's character?
Q: What did Jay do? What did Jay say, so that Martin would see it that way?
A: Jay came in and pointed his finger at Martin and said, "If you respect that man . . ." Jay came into the room and he was talking to Martin, and he said, "If you respect that man over there . . ." He was referring to me. "You will tell the truth."
Q: What did Jay say?
A: I don't remember.
Q: Do you remember if he said anything more?
A: I'm sure he did, but I do remember those words.
Q: What is your best recollection as to what else he said?
A: I'm sorry, I just can't remember. The only thing I remember is what I just told you. I'm sure he said something, and I'm sure if you have got something to tell me it will remind me, but, at the moment, I really don't remember exactly what he said.

Lowrie was almost pleading. He had been testifying for what seemed like hours. An edge of desperation entered his voice. He had just about had it. After all he was no longer a deputy, all of this happened over a year ago and the kid was obviously guilty. Enough was enough.

Q: Was Martin still visibly upset?
A: At what time period, when he was talking to me during the interview?
Q: Right.
A: He appeared mildly nervous on the first interview, on the first statement, and at ease on the second statement.
Q: Okay, when you say he appeared nervous on the first statement, what visual symptoms did you observe?
Mr. Lee: Your honor, once again Mr. Stehling is mischaracterizing and saying he was nervous instead of mildly nervous.
The Court: Well, overruled. Go ahead. What outer manifestations of nervousness or mild nervousness did you observe on the part of Martin Sweeten?
A: Martin shakes. He has, I'm speculating, some sort of nervous condition. When he gets nervous, he visibly, physically shakes.
Q: And that's — you observed that during the first statement?
A: Yes.
Q: For the full two hours and twenty-nine minutes, did you observe that?
A: No, not the two hours and twenty-nine minutes — is it the first statement or the second?
Q: First statement.
A: Not for the whole time, no.
Q: When did he stop shaking?
A: I don't know. Sometime during the process, when he became comfortable with me.
Q: Was it after you established your unique rapport with him that you testified about earlier?
A: Yes.
Q: You later took Martin out of the jail and went to Uvalde with him?
A: Yes.
Q: Did you call me first to ask me about that?
A: No.
Q: Did you —
A: I wasn't aware you were the attorney, I don't think.
Q: Did you know Martin had an attorney at this point?
A: I don't recall whether he had a lawyer at that point, no.
Q: How long was this – was this some three weeks or so after he was arrested?
A: That's about right.
Q: Where did you take him?

A: I took him – which time?
Q: How many times did you take him out of jail?
A: He was taken out twice.
Q: Did you call me either time?
A: No.

Scott made Lowrie explain thoroughly the whole sorry operation. The first trip had Martin Sweeten, under indictment for capital murder, directing Lowrie to various locations in Camp Wood where drugs were supposedly for sale. Martin was just repeating school yard rumors, but the deputies lapped it up. They were not exactly in solid with local students. The trip was such a hit with the lawmen, they decided to take him out to Uvalde. They cruised around until Martin, still eager to please, recognized a street. He would point to a house and repeat stories he had heard. The deputies knew Martin himself never bought drugs at these places. He just knew the latest schoolboy stories.

Lowrie's testimony conjured up a ludicrous portrait of rural police work. Scott enjoyed the exercise and although it was not a lethal blow to the state's case and had nothing directly to do with the admissibility of the statements, Lowrie squirmed.

However, the story did call into question the overall competence of the deputies and their methods. Lowrie's testimony might plant the right seeds of doubt in the jurors' minds. If they decided to convict Martin they might agreeably lean toward a lesser charge because of those doubts. This supposed the judge even allowed the jurors the choice of convicting the defendant on lesser charges. If he did, the behavior of the deputies just might tip the balance. Scott knew the possibility of Martin walking out of the courtroom a free young man was dim. Juries tended to convict. Just the fact Martin was even present at the murder scene worked against him, never mind why he was there.

Each day representatives of the James family and their friends filled the seating directly behind the prosecution's table, and directly in front of the judge. They were like a Greek chorus of doom. Well-dressed and determined, they were a constant reminder of Edmund's unjust murder. Their presence was a constant demand for justice. At the end of each day's session and during breaks, they would confer with Barrera for a constant assessment of the day's proceedings. In the evenings, they would retire to a motel in town, the same motel where the judge and prosecution stayed. Some returned to San Antonio to follow pressing business, others arrived to take their place. They never let up, never relaxed. They remained silently stoic during horrific testimony. They kept to themselves, but they dominated the courtroom.

Darwin's family were a poor showing next to them. They huddled far back in the pews behind the defense table but near the back wall. They dressed in blue jeans and simple cotton frocks. They were also silent, but could not keep the anxiety off their faces. Darwin, the leader of the clan, was not there. He was going to testify and therefore could not enter the courtroom. He had spent almost a year talking, begging and finagling his son's defense. He had been everywhere, talked to everyone, making a virtual pest of himself. Whereas before he had bombarded Scott with daily questions and plans, now that the trial was underway he was almost shy. He sat quietly outside in the hall, alongside Sue, sometimes holding one of his half-naked grand kids, and waited. In the evenings, he and the family would hold their prayer meetings at the simple rental house directly below the jury room.

The State called former Edward's County Sheriff Donald G. Letsinger. A big man, Letsinger carried himself with easy authority. He took the stand as if it were his own. Letsinger's authoritative demeanor was tainted with arrogance. Being a sheriff affects some men that way. It brings forth a meaner, colder side of their nature. In others, it encourages a disinterested tolerance for human failings. The difference is usually accounted for by a well-developed sense of humor. Letsinger seemed humorless and slightly bitter.

He told, yet again, of that evening in the sheriff's office. Letsinger said he read Martin his Miranda warnings soon after first encountering him in the sheriff's office.

> **A:** I informed Mr. Sweeten we needed to get a statement of what he knew of the events and circumstances. I asked him to give me an oral statement, but before I let him give me the statement, I had him sign or read him his rights, and he signed a waiver of those rights.
>
> **Q: (Mr. Lee)** Can you tell us why you had Martin Sweeten – or why

you advised him of his rights before any statement was taken of any sort?
A: Even though he was supposedly or allegedly just a witness to this incident, Deputy Woods had already told me some things which made me believe it would be better if Mr. Sweeten was informed of his rights before we started taking any statement.

Letsinger said he had Martin date and sign the waiver. Martin agreed to tell his story and Letsinger listened. He then ordered Deputy Lowrie to take Martin's formal written statement. He had not taken down the written statement himself because he had two other suspects coming in to be processed. Letsinger identified State's Exhibit 57 as Martin's first signed statement.

Q: Did anybody request to see Martin Sweeten at that time or at any time during the time these statements were being taken?
A: When Martin Sweeten first came to the office, when Mr. Woods first brought him in and he was in my office and I was taking an oral statement from him, at that time, his father came in and was going to bust right in my office. I had to send him back down to the waiting room. That's the only person that came in and wanted to — I guess that was a form of a request. It wasn't actually a request. He was demanding to come in.

Letsinger identified State's Exhibit 58 as the second statement Martin signed that evening. He testified that no force was used or promises made to compel Martin to sign; Martin was not deprived of food, water or sleep. The prosecution passed the witness.

Q: (Mr. Stehling) Sheriff Letsinger, where are you working now?
A: Amistad Area Narcotics Task Force.
Q: Did you resign from your position as sheriff?
A: No, I was not reelected.
Q: And you worked for the narcotics task force every since?
A: I started the day — the next day, didn't lose a day's work.

This opening exchange characterized the rest of the cross-examination. Scott would take a run at Letsinger to bring him down a peg, and Letsinger would snarl back, barely containing his contempt. Scott tried to probe more deeply into Letsinger's first encounter with Martin. He used some of the former sheriff's testimony at Tommy Eiland's trial to show that Letsinger considered Martin a culprit from the beginning. Letsinger had been merely leading Martin on:

> **Q:** The two other boys, Tommy Eiland and Andrew Milam, they were magistrated by a justice of the peace before they gave their statements, is that right?
> **A:** They were magistrated in Real County, yes.
> **Q:** And Martin was magistrated when?
> **A:** On the 10th.
> **Q:** At what time?
> **A:** Of April, it's on the magistrate's warning.
> **Q:** I show you what is marked as Defendant's Exhibit 78 and ask you if you can recognize it?
> **A:** This is the magistrate's warning used by the Justice of the Peace Marjorie Merritt of Edwards County. It is a form she uses consistently in her office.
> **Q:** Does that form she uses consistently reflect what time Martin Sweeten was magistrated?
> **A:** Says 11:20 A.M., on April 10, 1992.
> **Q:** And this was when in relation to taking Martin's statements?
> **A:** It was five hours after he signed his second statement.
> **Q:** Thank you. This oral interview you did with Martin Sweeten, did you tell him he was under arrest?
> **A:** No.
> **Q:** Did you tell him he was a suspect?
> **A:** You know, I may have told him that.

All morning they went back and forth, even breaking out into full-scale arguments. Judge Thurmond had to intervene. They even argued about how far the lobby was from Letsinger's office:

> **Q:** What did you do with Darwin Sweeten?
> **A:** I had him wait in the lobby.
> **Q:** And where is the lobby relative to your office?
> **A:** Half way down the building.
> **Q:** How far is that?
> **A:** From here to Deputy Adams.
> **Q:** What did you say?
> **The Court:** We had the same statement in the record earlier. Can we agree what "that" is, the distance, for the record?
> **Mr. Stehling:** Estimate how far it is?
> **The Court:** Can we agree what "it" is between the sheriff and —

The Witness: 40 feet?
The Court: Can we –
Mr. Stehling: I agree with that.
The Court: Okay. That's appeared twice in the record.

Throughout the rest of the cross-examination, Scott tried to shake and challenge Letsinger's handling of the case. In reply, Letsinger twisted and turned, prevaricated and asserted. He could barely contain his fury. He angrily claimed he had not placed Martin under arrest, one of his deputies did it. But had he not ordered it? It was possible he had. Then Scott turned back to his favorite secondary subject, the adventure of the deputies and Martin in Uvalde. It really galled him that the cops had been so blatant and arrogant as to pull his client out of his cell without even a "gee, do you mind" to his attorney. Now he had the man responsible on the stand.

Q: Did you give permission for Martin Sweeten to be taken to – to be taken out of jail after he was arrested?
A: This is a hard question to answer. It requires some explanation. I did give permission, but I did not give permission in the way it was handled.
Q: In what way did you give permission?
A: I discussed with Deputy Lowrie that we might take your client in this case back to the crime scene, and have him go over step by step and then – and also there was an investigation related to Real County, had to do with narcotics. The deputy sheriff in Real County was wanting to know if there could be some help done on it. What I actually told Deputy Lowrie was that we could probably work it out. He took it to mean, okay, to go right ahead. As a result of that, it resulted in me calling you immediately after I found out what happened . . .
Q: Are you sure you called me about it?
A: You don't recall me calling you?
Q: I recall Darwin Sweeten calling me.
A: I called you. I spoke to you. I believe your words were, I have advised my client to cooperate fully with you.

It was a remarkable performance, Letsinger had never called Scott. Even if he had, Scott Stehling would never have let his client just hop into a car with Buck Pruitt and Lowrie for a jaunt to Uvalde. What is more, as a good defense attorney, Scott would never have allowed such an expedition without some sort of *quid pro quo,* something in return.

Letsinger's quote about "I believe your words were, I have advised my client . . . etc." was the boldest bluffery of the whole trial. Letsinger was daring Scott to call him a liar in open court, knowing full well he could not. Letsinger was willing to risk his reputation, his testimony under oath, to make the defense look foolish. It was time to pass the witness. After some routine redirect questions from Tom Lee, Letsinger stepped down, looked around and went back to his new job chasing dope dealers along the Mexican border.

The last bit of prosecution business before the defense began was to recall Jay Adams to the stand. He reconfirmed Letsinger's testimony about taking of Martin's statements. Scott cross-examined with a few questions. The judge dismissed the jury until 1: 30 P.M. while he and the attorneys took up the matter of Martin's statements and other exhibits proposed as evidence.

When the jury returned, the State's Exhibits numbers 57 and 58, Martin's signed statements, were admitted into evidence and read to the jury. The prosecution rested.

Chapter VIII

The Defense

MARTIN'S FORMAL DEFENSE was to begin with a flourish. Scott would call Darwin Sweeten to the stand. Suddenly Barrera Jr. swept into the courtroom accompanied by an associate and took a seat up front. Barrera explained to Scott he had a speech to give that evening and needed to get back to San Antonio. After thinking a moment, Scott concluded that starting with Roy Barrera, Jr. would also be a nifty opener.

Roy Jr. was a contrast to his father. Dressed in a dark blue suit, he was handsome and commanding as he took the stand. He appeared almost aristocratic. He was former state district judge and a former candidate for Texas Attorney General, in short, a highly successful attorney with bright political prospects. His manner warned that here was no pushover witness. Behind his friendly, almost jovial entrance, lurked very real annoyance that he had been required to drive 200 miles merely to testify in a dusty, backwater town. A small town lawyer compelling a Roy Barrera, Jr. to testify was a small town lawyer looking for trouble.

In fairness, Barrera Jr. was defending the honor of the family practice. He could hardly be expected to say on the stand, "Gee, you're right we should have recused *(sic)* ourselves from representing the James family in this matter."

Scott jumped right in. He knew he had only one shot to make his point:

> **Q:** Do you have a recollection of the events of April 10th of last year, of receiving a phone call concerning Martin Sweeten?
> **A:** Yes, I do.
> **Q:** Do you have any notes or phone records or logs or anything that you brought with you concerning those events?
> **A:** No sir, I do not.
> **Q:** Did you have any?
> **A:** I did not look, to tell you the truth. I did not know you wanted any phone logs.
> **Q:** Did the subpoena *duces tecum* make reference to these matters?
> **A:** I was asked to be here to testify, but I was never given a copy of a subpoena.
> **Q:** Let me refresh your recollection. Could I see the court's file? I did ask through a letter, initially delivered to you by your father, that you are to come here to testify. Do you recall that?
> **A:** I was asked by my father — uh, he received a subpoena for me to be here and to testify and asked me if I would. I said, of course, and so I am here.
> **Q:** Let me show you the court's file. It reflects your father, yourself and Robert Barrera, who is your brother, right?
> **A:** He is.
> **Q:** And it has — this is a subpoena?
> **A:** It is.
> **Q:** It says, "see attached" for the attachment, and it lists, does it not, a request to bring all notes and memorandum, telephone logs, billing records, other records of any nature concerning communications by you or taken by you or others concerning communications concerning the representation or possible representation of the defendant Martin Sweeten. It does reflect that?
> **A:** Yes, it does.
> **Q:** Now, this indicates the subpoena was served on all three of you by Mr. Barrera's secretary, Sylvia. Does it not?
> **A:** Well, it bears her signature.
> **Q:** And it indicates it was served when and at what time?
> **A:** 4-27-93, 9 o'clock.
> **Q:** But she was mistaken when she filled that out, as far as having shown you, is that — or served you with that?

A: Well, you would have to ask her.
Q: You never were served a subpoena?
A: No, sir.

Barrera Jr. put on one slick performance. He casually tossed the whole question back into the defense's lap. Scott could not very well charge Barrera with intentionally refusing to honor the subpoena. First, Barrera Jr. presented himself to the court at the proper time. Secondly, he explained, in effect, that it was his father's secretary's fault. Thirdly, he contended, he never actually, physically received the subpoena, although it had been served in good faith. However, he honored the subpoena by appearing before the court. His demeanor was sincere and respectful. He made an impressive witness. The real message was quite different and not so pleasant. He delivered the message with a charming smile.

There was nothing Scott could do about this, short of asking the judge to halt the trial while Barrera Senior's secretary in San Antonio drove 200 miles to testify. Anybody else, say a businessman, who tried this kind of thing would have been stomped by the judge into the dry Ozona soil. It was time to soldier on. As things stood, Barrera Jr.'s account of his conversations with Darwin would be from memory, so any discrepancies would be his word against Darwin's. Memory is a fragile thing. Barrera did remember taking a call from "someone named Sweeten."

Q: What was the nature of the communication?
A: Basically he said his son was in jail, and he wanted to hire an attorney, possibly our firm, specifically my father, to get his son out of jail.
Q: What did you advise Mr. Sweeten?
A: I advised him that he would have to come to the office and retain us.
Q: Did he ask you to check and see what you could find out about why his son was in jail?
A: I believe he did.
Q: What steps did you take in that regard?
A: I recall calling the sheriff . . . He told me Sweeten was being held, I believe, without bond, but it could change. I believe he said something about looking for the District Attorney.
Q: Did you find out any other information from the sheriff regarding the nature of the charges or accusations against Martin Sweeten?
A: Murder.

Q: Any of the details.
A: Not that I recall.
Q: Is it possible you were given more details but you don't recall them?
A: It's very possible.

Barrera Jr. testified he asked Darwin for a retainer of between ten and fifteen thousand dollars. He said Darwin called him a number of times, and he called Darwin several times. Barrera took no notes of these conversations. Barrera admitted he may have indicated to the sheriff that his firm might eventually represent Martin. He said the sheriff may have told him Martin was involved in a murder, but to a lesser degree than the other two suspects. But the witness, a prominent attorney, contended these recollections were uncertain because they were from telephone conversations held a year ago — and he kept no notes.

The prosecution had no questions of Mr. Barrera.

Darwin Sweeten took the stand. He was born in Uvalde, Texas, December 12, 1941. He went to school, but only got as far as the eighth grade. He married Wilma Sue Barker and had two children, Martin and Mary Ellen. For most of his adult life he has been, "an auto mechanic. I have worked in the oil field some. I have done just a little bit of everything, carpentry work. I used to run a bargain barn there in Camp Wood selling used stuff, clothes and just all kinds of used stuff, appliances and so on."

At the present time Darwin was still doing "a little bit of everything. I do plumbing, electrical, just whatever comes along. In Camp Wood you have got to do more than one thing to make a living. If you just throw shingles and say I do this, forget it, you are out of luck. You have got to do four, five, six or seven things to make a living."

Scott showed him a piece of paper. Darwin identified it as Martin's high school diploma. "Well, Martin has — he lacked just a little bit of graduating when he got arrested, and due to me helping and the Sheriff's Department and the school system and the State of Texas, the work I did, calling different ones, we got his high school diploma for him. He finished it. Had to take the books back and forth between school and jail for him."

Q: I show you what is marked as Defendant's Exhibit 104. What is that?

A: That's a Nueces Canyon High School diploma, and that is what we obtained.
Q: You can't show it to the jury yet, Mr. Sweeten.
A: Can't show it yet? I'm proud of it. Sorry.

What volumes this testimony spoke about Darwin and Martin. The seeds of Martin's rebellion were so obvious. In his litany of the struggles to gain Martin's high school diploma, Darwin indirectly referred to Martin own efforts to gain the diploma. Martin had, after all, studied and worked to earn it. It was the sort of thing, which, no doubt, left Martin frustrated, but well hidden behind a passive exterior. Ironically, Darwin was really proud of the diploma. It was his in a way.

Darwin meant no harm, nor did he mean to embarrass Martin. He could work wonders arranging Martin's defense, or his high school diploma, or a car for school. He had a marvelous capacity "to make things happen." Darwin could focus his will and apply it to achieve astonishing things. What he seemed to miss or appreciate were the more subtle effects of his actions. It was both his strength and weakness. Darwin soldiered on through victories and defeats with a singleness of purpose that was awesome and frightening.

He told his story to the court, as he had told it at the preliminary hearings. He had told it again and again to Scott and to many others. This time it really counted. This was for keeps. It was also the last time he would have to tell it.

He told of getting Martin the car, the instrument of his son's peril, "I got it for him about two years before this incident happened, something like that, maybe two and a half years. Martin had a bad motorcycle accident, and it was part of his rehabilitation, to get him going again. He had been in a full body cast for almost a full year. He was riding a motorcycle, ran out in front of a car and was hit. It broke his hip, his pelvic bone, his right leg, his ankle and tore half the ball of his foot off.

"Then he was in a wheelchair for — gosh, seems like probably six or seven months, and after that when he got able to walk I gave him the car. I told him, 'Martin when you show me you can get out of the wheelchair and work the pedals on the car you can have it.'"

Q: Once he was able to drive the car, would he take everybody in it?

> **A:** Yes, sir, that's one of the problems we had. He – anybody who wanted to go anywhere, he wanted to take them because he loved to drive. If they put gas in the car or if he had gas in it he was ready to go.
> **Q:** Now, and in that respect, would you, when you felt it necessary, punish Martin with the car?
> **A:** Yes, sir. There were several incidents when I felt like Martin was too old to whup or anything like that, so the way I would punish him was take the car away from him. Sometimes I would do it sort of sly. I'm a good mechanic. I would go out and disable the car where it would stop out on the roadway and I would let it sit a while until his attitude changed and I would fix it.

Martin reacted to this with visible astonishment. There was a low titter of amusement in the court room. Scott loved it. Martin at that moment became a real person to the jurors, the kid next door in a running adolescent battle with his sly father. It meant he was no longer just "the defendant," a cipher or abstraction. It also was one of those moments which seem to mark intangible turning points. Throughout the trial, Martin had been slowly emerging from his apparent passive state. People began to notice this. He was taking notes and conferring with Scott. He even suggested questions which Scott incorporated into his cross-examinations. Martin's whole demeanor had changed. It was as if he awakened. He was at least trying to take up some of the burden of his defense and it showed. He was more alert, more engaged.

Scott decided, with Darwin on the stand, it was time to dispose of some of the state's sinister, if unexplained, evidence:

> **Q:** The State had introduced some exhibits, some rope, duct tape and an ice pick. Did you ever use these items?
> **A:** Yes, sir. I used them when we would go on parking lot striping jobs. Martin would drive his car because I took the big one-ton truck and a trailer, and we would use Martin's car for going around the parking lot, to pick up the cones and string.
> **Q:** Did you ever use tape or rope or an ice pick in your work?
> **A:** Yes, sir. That's the way we get those nice straight lines. You take an ice pick and stick it into the blacktop; then you tie a string to it and paint right down it – and you use rope for marking off the area you don't want people driving on. You use the tape to tape off all the light posts so you don't get yellow paint on them.

Q: Did you keep this stuff in Martin's car?
A: Yes, sir.

Scott asked Darwin to recount his version of the events leading up to the murder. Darwin was eager to do so, but a little too eager. He kept wandering off the point. Tom Lee objected repeatedly. Judge Thurmond kept admonishing Darwin to "just answer questions." Darwin would meekly agree but then eagerly return to explaining, throwing in hearsay and unrequested conclusions. It tested Barrera's patience, not to mention, Judge Thurmond's. Nonetheless Darwin effectively conveyed the message he wanted told about his son.

Q: Have you ever seen Martin be mean to people or animals?
A: No, sir. Martin has never been mean, never had no trouble with Martin fighting. Other kids jumped him. You know, kids would up and jump on him and beat him up, but Martin never fought back. Until he had the accident, he had the fastest legs in the county.
Q: Did Martin ever go hunting?
A: No, sir. Martin doesn't shoot animals. Out there at the Pannell's, they go rabbit hunting at night, and fox hunting and different things. They couldn't get Martin to. In fact, during hunting season they took him, you know, to the deer blind and he wouldn't shoot the deer. He said the deer was too pretty to shoot, and after that they had to let Martin do the driving.

Darwin testified that on the night of the murder Martin had called him asking permission to spend the night with Tommy Eiland. It was the only time Martin ever spent the night with Tommy. It struck him as odd at the time. There was something else unusual about this call. Martin said they had been coon hunting, and his leg was hurting so he did not feel like driving home. Darwin did not realize that the boys were staying just down the road at the Whipkey trailer. He thought they were out at another ranch beyond Barksdale, so he told Martin, okay.

Q: When you got back there what did you see?
A: I didn't see too much. Martin was — I seen the sheriff's car parked back down a way and Martin was setting in the back seat.
Q: Do you know if Martin was able to get out?
A: No, sir, he was not able to get out of the car. I walked up to see

the sheriff, see what was happening and let him know who was there, so he would know what was going on.
Q: Who did you talk to?
A: I talked to Jay Adams. I told him who I was, told him I was Darwin Sweeten, and, of course, he didn't know me and I didn't know him. But, I found out he knew my brothers. He was real upset when he first started out but —
Mr. Barrera: Excuse me, unless these conversations were in the presence of the defendant, we object.
Q: Just what did you say?
A: I introduced myself and he said —
Q: No, I'm sorry, you are going to have to say only what you said.
A: All right. Okay. I told him I was Johnny Sweeten's brother and that they was my brothers and Sharon Pannell was down there and my wife was down there at the car talking to Martin, and he said, okay.
Q: No, just what did you say, skip what he said.
A: That's hard to do. I asked him if I didn't need to get a lawyer for my son, and he said, no, sir you don't need a lawyer.
Mr. Barrera: If it please the court . . .

Darwin finally got the idea and left out Jay's portion of the conversation. He affirmed the defense assertion that Martin had been denied legal representation until after lengthy questioning. He said the deputies had manipulated Martin's desperate urge to cooperate to deny him Miranda rights. It was an argument which might fly quite well in Berkeley, California, circa 1975, but not in Crockett County, Texas. At best, Scott could use this sort of testimony to cull a little sympathy. If he could gather a little bit here and a little bit there, some from this and that incident, like money in the bank, it might eventually pay off. The cumulative effect might sway the jury toward convicting Martin on a lesser charge. The only hope of an acquittal was still putting Martin on the stand. Meanwhile Scott questioned Darwin about his recollections of that night at the murder scene. He focused on the time Martin was seated in the sheriff's car:

Q: Was any of this conversation you had with Jay Adams, was it after you all got down to where Martin was present?
A: Some of it was, yes, sir.
Q: After you got down to where Martin could hear, what did Jay say to you?

A: He said Martin did not need a lawyer, that he was a – being held as a witness in protective custody.
Q: Did he say from whom he was being protected?
A: From Tommy Eiland and Andy Milam.
Q: Were other people talking to Martin in your presence?
A: My wife, Sharon and little Michael, John or Michael – whatever you call him, Pannell, were talking to him.
Q: Did you hear the conversation?
A: I could hear parts of it. My wife was just trying to calm Martin down. He was so nervous, just told him -- you know, don't worry, we're here with you, whatever; we tried to find out what had happened and calm him down some.
Q: Why did Martin need calming down?
A: He was shaking all over, just like a leaf, like it was cold, and he just looked give out, just so tired he could hardly go, he looked like – I never seen him that way before.
Q: Did Martin tell whether he thought he was a suspect?
A: No, Martin — he thought he was a witness. The whole time he thought he was a witness.
Q: Did he say anything about being scared of Tommy or Andy?
A: Yes, sir, definitely. In fact, he said to me, "If they don't catch Tommy Eiland or Andy, you and mom don't go home tonight, because if they don't kill me, they said they would kill you."
Q: Did you have anymore conversation with Martin that evening out at the ranch?
A: If I did I don't remember.
Q: Do you remember if you said anything to Martin at the Cedar Creek Ranch about getting a lawyer?
A: Yes, I do. I told Martin to keep his mouth — not to say anything more until I got him a lawyer, and he told me not to worry because he was a witness. He was on the DA's side.

Scott now asked Darwin about his confrontation with Sheriff Donnie Letsinger. It was a useful bit of theater. The jury had seen Letsinger and could compare his bulk to Darwin's five-foot six-inch frame.

A: So I told him who I was. I told him, I said, "I'm Darwin Sweeten, Martin Sweeten's daddy. I brought him this hamburger and Coke, some Pepto-Bismol and I would like to give it to him." He said, "Okay," took it and sat it down or something. I don't remember exactly, but anyway, he took it from us and then I said, "Doesn't

Martin need a lawyer for . . ." No, I said, "Don't I have the right to get Martin a lawyer to sit in there while you guys are questioning him?"

Mr. Barrera: Excuse me. Again, we interpose the objection that whatever conversations were had outside the presence of the defendant are hearsay and not admissible.

The Court: Well, you can say what you asked, what you recollect asking, Mr. Sweeten.

Q: Where was Martin when you were talking to Donnie Letsinger at that point?

A: He was in Donnie Letsinger's office.

Q: How far were you from the office?

A: I was just outside the office door, no more, no further.

Q: Was the door open?

A: Yes, sir.

Q: All right, you said what?

A: I asked him, I said, "Don't I have the right to get Martin a lawyer, or at least sit in there while you all are questioning him?"

Q: And what did he say?

A: He said, "No." He said Martin — he looks at me and says, "Martin is eighteen years old, isn't he?" And I says, "Yes, sir." And he says, "You have no rights." He says, "Go up front and sit down before I lock you up."

Darwin testified that much later the sheriff finally allowed him, Sue, and Mike Pannell to see Martin for a few minutes. One of the first things Darwin told Martin was to keep his mouth shut and let him get a lawyer. Martin said he was "just a witness" and was "on the DA's side."

"I said, 'Son don't believe a thing they tell you, because the DA isn't on anybody's side.' And he said to me, 'Dad, they have been talking back and forth to the DA on the telephone since I've been up here.' And I said, 'Martin, how do you know this?' And he said, 'Well, they said they had.'"

After Letsinger told them the visit was up, Darwin asked if Martin were charged with anything. The sheriff told them flatly there were no charges yet. It was around four A.M. and as they left the office to return to Camp Wood, Letsinger called them back. They waited for thirty minutes until the sheriff decided to hold Martin.

The next morning, a Friday, Darwin learned that Martin was

in big trouble. He called Roy Barrera's office and told his story, Barrera Jr. told him to wait for a call back in an hour or so. There was no call back.

"I called him several times that day because he never did get back with me, kept waiting for his dad to get out of a meeting of some kind. I think it was Monday morning before I found out what it would take for a retainer fee and what they wanted to do and everything . . . He told me what Martin was arrested for and that the bail was going to cost me $5,000 cash to get him out and he recommended that I do that on top of his retainer fee . . . that would be $20,000 he wanted, cash money."

Q: How much did you have in the bank then?
A: I didn't have anything in the bank . . .
Q: When was a meeting with Mr. Barrera Sr. and you set?
A: It was set up for either Monday morning or Tuesday morning. He said to call him Monday morning and he would let me know . . .
Q: When did you next see Martin?
A: I seen him later on Friday.
Q: Where did you see him?
A: In the jail for fifteen minutes.
Q: What did you say?
A: I told him that I had gotten him in touch with a lawyer or was trying to hire him a lawyer. I told him the lawyer said he was under arrest for conspiracy of murder and for him not to say anything else to anybody.
Q: What did Martin say?
A: He told me, "Dad, I'm not under arrest . . . I'm held as an — I am being held in protective custody. You have nothing to worry about. I don't need a lawyer. You are wasting your money."
Q: What did you say to Martin?
A: I said, "Martin, the lawyer has done talked to the sheriff, and you are under arrest for conspiracy of murder; believe it or not, you are, son." He said, "I can't be. I just talked to them not long ago." And I said, " Well, you better shut your mouth."
Q: What did you say next?
A: I told him — I know, I told him if I couldn't afford a lawyer he was going to have to tell them to get a court-appointed lawyer, but I was going to try to get this lawyer . . . I would see if this lawyer would take my house for payment or if he would take a part payment. Martin says, "Dad, I don't want you to do it. I don't need a lawyer."

Q: What did you say next?
A: I can't think of it, Scott . . .

Darwin said he spent the next few days trying to sell his house, collect some old debts and borrow as much as he could from his brothers. Meanwhile, he and Sue had to get sedatives from a doctor in order to sleep at night. He spoke with Martin on Monday. Incredibly, after three days in jail, Martin still believed he was in "protective custody," and was insisting he "did not need a lawyer."

On the following Tuesday, Roy Barrera, Sr. finally called Darwin and asked if he could get the money together. Darwin said he could not, but he had retained another lawyer to take his case. Barrera wished him luck and said he would be taking the case for the other side. Scott passed the witness.

Barrera Sr. came out swinging on cross-examination. This was personal. Darwin admitted he had only spoken with Barrera Sr. once, Tuesday, and by then he had already hired Scott. He admitted Barrera told him that he was not "pressing you but simply wanted to determine what your position was, since the family of the deceased had communicated with us and wanted me to represent them . . ." Darwin admitted his brother had failed to call Barrera on the appointed day. Darwin also admitted Barrera told him up front that " the family of the deceased had communicated with us through one of my other sons, and I wanted to make sure of your position because we were committed to you . . ."

Darwin conceded there had been no guards on Martin at the ranch and he had been allowed to warn Martin he needed a lawyer. Barrera pulled other admissions out of Darwin: Yes, Martin was eighteen and legally an adult. Yes, Martin earned his own money. Yes, Martin did make his own decisions about his future. Darwin also admitted he was hard of hearing in both ears and therefore he tended to speak loudly:

Q: Were you insisting on seeing your son and on the rights you believe you had?
A: Well, yes.
Q: Did the sheriff, at the time, tell you that your son was eighteen?
A: That is correct.
Q: Did the sheriff tell you to wait outside and when he was ready he would call you?

A: In a very nasty way, yes.
Q: At the time, you were insisting you had the right to talk to your son or to get him a lawyer?
A: Yes, I thought I had the right to be in there with him or to get him a lawyer in there.
Q: Was it at that time the sheriff told you, if you did not go out there and wait until he called you, and just wait there and be quiet or he would put you in jail? Did he tell you that?
A: Yes, sir.
Q: Now, the sheriff having told you this, however you may have been impressed with this conversation, did you at that time go to the phone and call your brothers or any lawyer for assistance?
A: At that time of the morning I didn't figure there was any sense trying to call anybody.
Q: Why did you figure that?
A: Well, I never heard of calling a lawyer at midnight.
Q: Didn't you think there was an emergency?
A: Sir, in all of my dealings with lawyers, you get them from 9 to 5.
Q: All right. And so you were going to wait until 9 to 5. Did you try to call a lawyer regardless?
A: I don't follow you.
Q: Under those circumstances, regardless of when you think you can call lawyers, did you, at least, try to call a lawyer?
A: No, sir. I did not know any lawyers to call.
Q: Did you ask anyone about what lawyer you might call?
A: Yes, sir. I asked John Pannell.
Q: And what did he say?
A: He gave me your name.

The jury and much of the audience were quietly snickering and barely restraining outright laughter. That was the remarkable thing about Darwin. Just when it appeared he was on the ropes, really struggling, he would snap out of it with some innocent remark, completely devoid of guile, which would leave those around him almost speechless.

Barrera did not back off. He grilled Darwin about his ignorance of legal considerations involved in a capital murder charge and his ignorance of what it costs to defend against the charge, especially if there is a change of venue. Barrera exposed Darwin's ignorance of how long such trials take. Of course, Roy Barrera was really defending himself. Then he rounded on the fateful telephone call Martin had made from the Get 'N Go:

Q: I'm satisfied your son is and has been a good son, as you have told us.
A: That is correct.
Q: I want to know if your son has ever told you an untruth?
A: Very seldom.
Q: On this particular evening at or about ten or 10:15 P.M., when he may have called, did your son tell you what he and these other boys had just been into?
A: No, sir. He did not say anything about anything like that.
Q: Did he tell you, "Dad, I have been a witness to a murder."?
A: No, sir.
Q: Did he tell you, "Dad, I need your help. Call the sheriff's office. I have problems."?
A: No, sir.
Q: Did your son tell you, "Dad, I am being forced to go over and sleep at a fellow's house who held a gun to my head. I need your help."?
A: He only told me what I told you here a little while ago, sir.

Barrera pounded away at Martin's credibility. Martin had passed up a perfectly reasonable chance to get away. Darwin's son had told quite a few whoppers that night, and he had not asked anyone to intervene. Then Barrera spun the questioning around. He returned to Sheriff Letsinger's behavior. This is basic cross-examination technique. Change the subject abruptly so as to confuse the witness. However, this time it was a minor mistake. Darwin was too unpredictable in his responses.

Q: After you say he had interviewed your son and talked to him and after he told you, to come in and visit with him, and you all were getting ready to leave, and the sheriff then goes out, reaches you at your car, says, "Just a minute, hang around, I may let him go." Did the sheriff tell you that?
A: Yes, sir.
Q: Did the sheriff then tell you, "I'm going to lock him up."?
A: Yes, the sheriff said I — can I say what the sheriff said or not?
Q: Well, I asked for it, and if there is no objection, tell us.
A: The sheriff said due to political reasons.
Q: Due to what?
A: Political reasons. People might think bad of him if he just let Martin go home now. He was going to take him over to the jail and lock him up. We could probably come up and get him in the morning.

Q: Have you ever used those words, "political reasons," before today?
A: I may not have, it is not my usual way of talking, but he did say that.

Barrera quickly and wisely switched to items found among Martin's possessions which may have been fruits of burglaries. One was a blanket, the other a cheap black and white TV. Darwin recalled giving them to the sheriff. Then Barrera could not resist having one more go at Darwin about his failure to call a lawyer at five A.M. It was not a good idea. Asking Darwin questions just encouraged him.

Q: You said you talked to Judge Smart there at the scene or at the jail?
A: At the sheriff's office, yes, sir.
Q: Do you know Judge Smart?
A: Never met him before. He knew John Pannell, and between the two of them they got me settled down after Sheriff Letsinger got me so mad.
Q: You were very angry?
A: Let's put it this way, I hadn't been so angry since I left the army.
Q: Did you ask the judge to appoint a lawyer for your son that night since you could not wake one up other than after nine A.M.?
A: He said he couldn't.
Q: He could not?
A: He could not help me. I asked him if he could help me get a lawyer, and he said he couldn't.
Q: Did you ask him about a district judge or anyone who could appoint his son a lawyer. I mean, your son a lawyer?
A: No, sir. I didn't know anything about district judges at the time.
Q: Well, the judge was there. Did you ask him, "Can my son have a lawyer appointed for him by the court?"
A: Well, I knew he could have. I mean, I watch enough television to know that.
Q: Okay. Did you tell him, "I want a lawyer appointed for my son right now?"
A: I told him I needed a lawyer appointed for my son right now, and he said I didn't need one at this point.
Q: So apparently everybody was assuring you that you did not need a lawyer for your son, including your son?
A: Yes, sir.

It was astonishing. Darwin, with his disarming, rural candor, had innocently maneuvered Barrera into succinctly stating the very point which Scott had been arguing for months before the court. Everyone in authority most certainly had been assuring Darwin that he did not need a lawyer for his son, including his son.

Barrera passed the witness. Darwin was excused and stepped down. Since his testimony was finished, he was exempt from the Rule. The Rule forbids potential witnesses from being present in the courtroom during other testimony. So, for the first time Darwin Sweeten was allowed to remain in the courtroom during the trial of his son.

The defense called Roy Barrera, Sr. to the stand and waded right in:

> **Q:** Other than these cases, these three cases we're involved with now, have you assisted a District Attorney as a prosecutor since you left the DA's office? (Barrera was a Bexar County prosecutor from 1951 to 1957.)
> **A:** Well, yes, but sometimes not necessarily in the trial of a case. Sometimes a family hires a lawyer on the outside to keep them posted, to keep them up to date, to explain to them the nuances of the law and what is going on . . .
> **Q:** Have you assisted a District Attorney in the trial of an actual case other than this — these cases since you left the DA's office?
> **A:** Not that I recall. I sat second one time, and, of course, all of these matters are subject to the District Attorney and what he permits a private lawyer to do. I have sat second in a case in which I kept my mouth shut, which is hard to do, and just sat there and aided and abetted insofar as the law and all that, but I didn't actually participate in the prosecution *per se*.
> **Q:** I see.
> **A:** These are very rare, yes, they are.

Scott intended to show the jury Barrera was a committed passionate defense attorney, lured over to the other side by the wealth and power of the James family. It was a bit unfair because few attorneys would turn down such a request and sizable retainer. However, Barrera was a big gun and a formidable opponent anything Scott could do to decrease his credibility helped. Scott asked him about the telephone calls from Darwin and the retainer and the timing of his office's contacts with Darwin. This was a fight to the finish, and, regardless of any mutual admiration, Barrera and Scott were opponents. It was also fun because lawyers hate to discuss fees openly.

Barrera defended his actions. Darwin's communications had been vague and no firm deal had been made. He had not committed to the James family cause until it was clear Darwin had another attorney. Finally, he had no direct communications with Darwin until the last telephone call. Until that moment, all arrangements were made through his sons, ". . . it has been my experience sometimes people call, they inquire about a lawyer. They inquire, they want to tell you all about the case, and then have you tell them what the fee is going to be. Sometimes it disqualifies you or taints you if there is more than one defendant, and they tell you secrets or privileged communications. It prevents you from representing him if they decide not to use you . . .

"If you have already had privileged conversations with one defendant you are disqualified from representing the other one, so generally my practice is don't get involved in the fine points of a case; go to the newspapers, to whatever is public information to try to get informed – don't get into privileged communications until such time as you know for sure you have been retained."

Scott had argued long and hard before Judge Thurmond, through three pretrial hearings and now at trial, that Barrera should not be prosecuting this case. His communications with Darwin "tainted" him. Thurmond always overruled his objections. For one thing, Barrera had already successfully prosecuted Tommy and Andy. To admit Scott's arguments now would throw doubt on those cases. Barrera's participation on the prosecution team was a done deal. Scott knew it, but it never hurts to let the jury in on the action. Nor did it hurt to let them see the prosecution discomforted.

He turned to the documents he had subpoenaed, which Roy Jr. had "neglected" to bring. Scott managed to wring an apology from his opponent. Barrera said there were no telephone records because most of the calls were from Darwin to Barrera's office. The initial contacts were so vague that no one had kept notes, and such initial notes were only kept for a week or so then they were discarded. Scott passed the witness. It had been fun, but it was time to get back to more germane matters.

Wayne Milburn Caldwell, the principal of Nueces Canyon High School for four years, took the stand. He testified he knew both Tommy Eiland and Martin Sweeten. As Scott tried to elicit his opinions of both, Barrera objected at each question. The questions were not relevant and too general. The judge sustained the objection. Another question and again the prosecution objected, again sustained by the court. Scott was stumbling and seemed at a loss. All he could get out of Caldwell was that Tommy Eiland was a leader and that Martin was a peaceful and law-abiding character.

Helen Adair was the high school secretary. She knew both Tommy and Martin. She said both were respectful to her. Tommy had even visited her son at their home on a couple of occasions. It was testimony going nowhere and Scott retreated. Barrera got her to admit she had never forbidden her son to associate with Tommy Eiland.

Doug Adair took the stand. He knew both Tommy and Martin. He had worked out on Edmund's ranch often, and played paintball war there. He said he had seen guns around Edmund's house. His testimony did little to advance Martin's cause. Scott passed the witness. Barrera managed to draw some blood on cross-examination. Doug admitted he had gone to the Double D Rental building in Camp Wood with Martin. In fact, they had gone there at night, after hours. He had also been there with Tommy.

> **Q:** Did you and Tommy take anything from there?
> **Mr. Stehling:** I think the witness should be warned that he has a fifth amendment right he should exercise, not to testify against himself as to any possible crime.
> **Mr. Barrera:** I will withdraw the question for the moment.
> **A:** The guy who worked there had the key to get in, so we went in and shot some pool.
> **Q:** Are you on probation?
> **A:** Yes, sir.
> **Q:** For what?
> **A:** Burglary of a habitation.

This was more dangerous testimony than it appeared on the surface. It tied Martin, by implication, back into the burglaries. It was a subject to avoid for now. The possibility of committing burglary was something Martin admitted he discussed with Tommy and Andy. He did it before they set out for Edmund's ranch. If the jury began to focus on this material then they might start believing Martin knew there was a probability Tommy and Andy would do violence to Edmund.

Unconvincing a jury was tough, and the task at hand was hard enough. Barrera had deftly led the jury right to the brink, the central question of Martin's guilt. Martin's defense was on a razor's edge of belief. This was an early warning. The defense's case could collapse quickly before anyone realized it – before anyone could stop it.

Scott was using up witnesses faster than expected, and it presented a minor problem in logistics. Most of the defense witnesses were from Camp Wood, over a hundred miles away from Ozona. As an accommodation, the defense team tried to avoid having them come to court and not be called that day. It was tricky scheduling and a mistake could be dangerous. If the defense ran through a day's worth of witnesses in a morning, it meant a major scramble in the afternoon.

Scott called Bobby Hatley who had been the school counselor for many years. He was a robust, compact man in his late middle age. He made a terrific witness, conveying charm, humor and authority all at once. He had told some fascinating Tommy Eiland stories during the preliminary interviews with Scott.

> **A:** I took some students to the Gary Job Corps, and Tommy Eiland was one of those students. We went over and looked through the Gary Job Corps.
> **Q:** Do you recall when it was?
> **A:** I think it was about ten days . . . before the incident of Edmund James's death.
> **Q:** Did you see Tommy interact with the Job Corps personnel?
> **A:** It was pretty interesting as the counselors of the Corps showed us one program. We went to many different programs they offered there that day. As we went into certain areas where job training was occurring, they would ask our students to intermingle with students there. I observed Tommy as he would approach the other students.
> **Q:** Was Tommy adept at dealing with other students?
> **A:** He was aggressive . . . If there were a conversation going on

among the students, he would immediately go to where the action seemed to be . . .

Hatley described Tommy's accounts of surviving on the street by caging money from friends and neighbors. Hatley said he counseled Tommy about his post graduation plans. He explained Tommy had faced a very real crisis of making a living.

Q: Would you describe Tommy as a leader or a follower.
A: He was definitely a leader.
Q: What do you mean?
A: When he wanted to do something – I mean, he always had transportation when he did not own a car. He got – he was able to do anything he wanted by his interactions with other students and even adults. He had a certain amount of charisma and when he requested, let's do this, a lot of people followed him.
Q: Was this pretty consistently the case?
A: I think it was developing more and more from the time I first knew Tommy until he left school.
Q: What about Martin Sweeten, was he – how would you describe him as far as being a leader or follower?
A: Martin never demonstrated to me those kinds of leadership skills at all.
Q: Would you call Martin a follower, someone Tommy would cause to do things?
Mr. Lee: Your honor, we are going to object as to the way Mr. Stehling asked the question. The issue is leadership or following, and he's going beyond that reputation.
The Court: Just state what your observations were . . . we will leave it at there.
A: Tommy was definitely a dominant personality.

Scott was back to scoring points, but it was definitely time to get out. He passed the witness. On cross, Barrera asked if Hatley thought Martin was stupid or simple minded? No, he did not. Had Tommy ever been expelled? No, he had not. When he characterized Tommy as aggressive, did he mean hostile or "pushy" rather like a "big man on campus." Hatley said he meant the latter.

"He was less than bashful?" Barrera asked.

"Less than bashful." Hatley replied thoughtfully.

Hatley had been a blessing. The defense was back on track and Scott was confident and in control. He applied classic defense tactics, run the questions right to the edge of what was allowable, stick a toe over the line until the inevitable objections sounded, then back off and come at it from a different angle. The message he was giving the jury at every opportunity was that Tommy was the charismatic leader who commanded, who dominated, who got what he want through fear and intimidation. Those around him just followed.

If the jury accepted those premises, then Scott could take the next step and lead them to the very heart of the defense's case, lack of intent. The jury must come to believe that Martin Sweeten, despite his pathetic submission to Tommy's lurid appeal, that Martin, who puked at the sight of a slain deer, never had any intention of killing Edmund or participating even indirectly in his murder. If the jury believed this, then acquittal was possible.

Scott called Wilma Sue Sweeten to testify. It was pretty basic stuff. After all, she was Martin's mother and a shy woman. She told her family's history from her marriage in 1965 in Gallup, New Mexico, to Martin's birth. She said the family suffered through hard times but survived. They were not particularly religious or rigorous about attending church, "We got out of the habit of going to church on a regular basis with all of us working and in school – but we still had our belief in God and our faith in God and we still had our religious preferences."

Q: Did Martin go to church too?
A: Yes, sir, he's gone to church even without us.
Q: Where would that be?
A: He's gone to the Baptist church in Barksdale and in Camp Wood, and he's also gone to the Full Trinity Gospel Church in Camp Wood.
Q: I show you what are marked as Defendant's Exhibits 113, 114, and 115, and ask if you can identify what those are?
A: The first two are diplomas from Bible study courses he finished, that Martin finished.
The Court: Don't go into the contents of the exhibits, ma'am.
Q: Just – can you tell what they are?
A: Yes, sir.
Mr. Barrera: We object. They are immaterial. They solve no issue in this case. Do not –
The Court: Sustained.

Scott had been lucky to get as far as he did. It was blatant pandering to the Bible Belt instincts of West Texans. Out there, even folks who merely roll over in bed on Sunday morning tend to hold those who turn out for the Sabbath in high regard. Out there, people who never got past "In the beginning . . ." still look upon Bible study diplomas as an admirable accomplishment. Even if the jurors were fully aware of Scott's shameless lobbying, their bone deep breeding would compel them to score a point for Martin.

Scott had to put Sue on the stand. For one thing, he could again go over the deputies' behavior. Secondly, he could not very well have Martin's father testify while his mother remained silent. After all, if a boy's mother won't testify for him, he surely must be a sorry case indeed. Sue confirmed Darwin's testimony with a few small variations:

Q: When you got to the ranch what did you see?
A: We saw Martin. He was sitting in the back of one of the police cars, and Darwin opened the door and Martin stepped out and we started talking to him.
Q: Could you tell if Martin could get out by himself.
A: He was not able to get out by himself.
Q: Are you sure it was Darwin who opened the door, or could it have been Sharon?
A: It was Darwin.
Q: What happened next?
A: We talked to him for a few minutes, and he told us what he had seen and how he had — just wanted to report it and get it — he just wanted someone to know it had happened.
Q: Did Darwin leave to go meet the officers?
A: One of the officers came down and talked with me.
Q: Do you know who it was?
A: Jay Adams.
Q: Okay was Martin around when Jay talked to you?
A: Yes, sir.
Q: Do you remember if Darwin asked Jay Adams anything about whether Martin needed a lawyer?
A: Yes, sir. He did ask Mr. Adams if we needed a lawyer, and Mr. Adams said, no, he didn't. He said Martin was a witness and they just needed him for questioning as to what happened.

Sue clearly remembered visiting with Martin in the sheriff's office in Rocksprings, "I told Martin he should not say anything else until we get him a lawyer, and Darwin told him the same thing. We all did, we told him to just wait until we got a lawyer."

Scott questioned her about the rest of the evening, their contacts with Barrera's law firm and their attempts to raise money. Sue answered calmly. Scott passed the witness.

Barrera was polite and almost courtly but he pounded away on what Martin had not told his parents:

Q: Did he tell you who had done the shooting?
A: Yes, sir. He did.
Q: Did he tell you how they got out there?
A: He just said he had driven them out there.
Q: Did he mention to you anything about a safe at the ranch?
A: No, sir. He did not.
Q: Did he tell you anything about needing money for a party in Mexico?
A: No, sir. He did not.
Q: Did he tell you about having obtained a flashlight?
A: No, sir. He did not.
Q: Did he say anything about having taped the soles of their shoes so they wouldn't leave tracks?
Mr. Stehling: Your Honor, I object to his asking all of these questions which answer "no, he did not." I request – as I have done that he just ask what the defendant did say.
The Court: Well, we'll just do like we did with you; ask, "do you recollect if he said this?" Let's go on.
Q: Did he tell you anything about Tommy having planned an alibi with regard to the movies?
A: No, sir.
Q: Did he tell you about anyone putting a rifle or gun to his head?
A: Not at that time, no, sir.

Sue was excused and stepped down from the stand.

Every trial has its own timing. The trial participants can sense when the midpoint passes and the end is approaching. It was obvious Martin's trial was nearly over. A day or two at the most and it would be finished. Scott decided to put Martin on the stand as the last witness.

Chapter IX

The Girlfriends

MARTIN FACED A TERRIBLE RISK. Scott would probably have to ask him to take the stand and testify. At that moment much of the weight of his defense would drop on his shoulders. Martin trusted Scott and was ready, but he was shy and awkward. He spent his time during the trial listening, formulating questions he wanted Scott to ask and drawing shields with legends like "Freedom" and "Innocent" on them. Martin had growing self-confidence. He was not the same young man he had been that night a year ago in Edmund's yard. It was doubtful a Tommy Eiland could have swayed him now.

However, a Barrera cross-examination was a very serious proposition, perhaps a test beyond Martin's capabilities. Drawn shields of "Freedom" would provide little protection. Barrera would tear him up. There was really no choice for both sides. They were too committed.

Scott called The Reverend Homer Stevens to the stand. The good reverend's testimony was of some value. Through him Scott established that Martin went to church on his own without his family. It was testimony that could not hurt Martin's cause. Anyway the defense had to play for time. The witness scheduling was not working and there was danger of Scott being left shy a couple of witnesses. Judge Thurmond would not be happy with an empty witness chair next to him. Behind the scenes there was a scramble of telephone calls for new arrangements.

Reverend Stevens knew Martin and had ministered to him at the church.

He also knew Tommy Eiland who had once come to him. Tommy led a group of kids who were playing with an Ouija board. Claiming he was afraid of what was coming through, Tommy had sought spiritual guidance.

Judge Thurmond gave Scott a reproving look; this was not going to be allowed to go much further. Scott sighed and said, "I guess I need to approach the bench."

After the conference, he passed the witness. Barrera said, with a hint of sympathy in his voice for the defense, "We have nothing to ask. Thank you Reverend." So much for Ouija boards and Satan.

The defense called Daniel Waters to the stand. He was a Canyon Boy through and through. Tough and confident, Daniel was the kind of kid who worked continually on his car. His hair was stringy and his fingernails still showed the black from sump oil. He and Tommy had been running buddies for a long time. Daniel described their nighttime forays, looking for something to do.

Q: Were you with Tommy when he would kill things?
A: Yes, sir.
Q: What kind of things?
A: Cats.
Q: How many times do you remember?
A: Just twice.
Q: Do you remember how he killed them?
A: One with a rock and one with a knife.
Q: The one with a knife, how did he kill it?
A: He stabbed it.

The prosecution had no questions. Mary Esquell took the stand. She was a substitute teacher at the high school and knew Tommy too well. Her daughter was Carolyn Sue Hodge, the object of Tommy's consuming passion.

Q: How did you know him through your daughter?
A: He called all the time. He would show up at the house until I threatened him with — if he came back I would call the law and have a restraining order put on him.
Q: Did he come back?
A: Once when I wasn't there.
Q: Why did you not want him around your daughter?
A: That is hard to explain. He would threaten any boy that talked to her.
Mr. Barrera: We object to that as hearsay.
The Witness: It is not hearsay.
The Court: Just a minute, Mrs. Esquell. Did you yourself hear Eiland make these threats?
The Witness: Once I got on the extension.
The Court: You can testify if there is no objection about what you observed and what you heard by way of a threat.
A: I got on the extension to tell him — I knew when it was late at night and the phone rang, I just figured it was Tommy. I picked up and I overheard him tell her that if he couldn't have her nobody could, and that he would kill anybody that ever touched her. I told him that if he ever called again, I would have a restraining order put on him. Immediately it was, yes ma'am, you know he would be real polite. When we had the store he would come in and just stare at me because he knew I disliked him. One day he came in with a machete, and I said, Tommy get out of this store now.
Mr. Barrera: This is all hearsay, Your Honor. Judge, we object to it.
The Witness: No, sir, it is not hearsay.
The Court: I'll overrule on hearsay. This isn't being admitted for the truth of what it is asserted to be.
Mr. Stehling: Just presence and observation?
The Court: For what was communicated. Overruled.
Q: Okay. He came into the store with a machete and what?
A: I told him to get out and that he knew better than to bring something like that into the store. He said, "I'm not going to kill anybody in here." I told him to get out or I was going to call the law . . . To my knowledge he never came back.
Q: Did he continue to call your daughter?
A: Yes, he did.

On cross-examination a different picture emerged:

Q: . . . you had a problem about how to keep your daughter away from Tommy?

A: No, sir, it was — what I should have done was forbid her to be around Jennifer Noblett. Then I think it would have stopped, but she and Jennifer had been best friends.
Q: Were you aware that she was seeing Tommy on the sly for about three months?
A: Yes, sir.

Mary Esquell said she knew about the visit Tommy, Jennifer, and Martin had made the afternoon of the murder to Carolyn's house. She knew about the call from Tommy that night at nine P.M. apparently to set up an alibi. Barrera switched suddenly to a grimmer topic.

Q: Were you aware that your daughter, this young lady, Jennifer, Tommy, and Andy had entered into a suicide pact?
A: Yes.
Q: And that they agreed among the four of them that if anything happened to one of them the others would commit suicide?
A: Yes.
Q: Did your daughter run away with Tommy on or about the 22nd day of January, 1992?
A: Not with just Tommy.
Q: How long was she gone?
A: Overnight.

This was juicy stuff, and the prosecution had just opened a major opportunity. Scott, on redirect examination, snapped it up. It would do nicely to illustrate a central point vital to Martin's defense:

Q: The suicide pact, whose idea was it?
A: Tommy's
Q: And what was the pact?
A: I was so upset when she told me. It was that if something happened to one the others would kill themselves. Carolyn Sue was very, very upset. She had no intention of agreeing to this, but she told me she was scared of not going along with it at the time. Then there was always something when it came to Tommy Eiland. I don't know. Always something.
Q: She was scared of what, not going along with it?
A: Of what Tommy might do. For a long time I worried about her mental state, because of Tommy Eiland. It was like he had some kind of hold on her. He was just bad and I think a lot of kids were

intimidated by Tommy Eiland. My daughter has had nightmares. I found out a lot of things later. I mean, I never liked him. I didn't want him around the house, or calling. After he was arrested and behind bars, Carolyn Sue started telling me a lot of things. I became very angry with my daughter. If I had known more I think I could have stepped in and done something, no matter how severe. I knew it was bad but I didn't know the degree.

After some brief recross-examination, Mary was excused and her daughter Carolyn Sue was called to testify. She approached the stand shyly. Carolyn Sue was hardly a femme fatale. Instead she was petite and a little countrified. She appeared as if she should be queen of the local 4-H club rather than a player in Tommy's dark drama.

Q: How would you hear from Tommy Eiland?
A: He was constantly around. I couldn't get rid of him. If I were to see anybody, he would threaten them, major league threaten them. He was constantly calling me about two or three o'clock in the morning.
Q: Would you tell him to stop calling you?
A: Yes, sir.
Q: Would you tell him to stop threatening your boyfriends?
A: Yes, sir.
Q: Was it just your boyfriends he threatened?
A: No, he threatened my brother.
Q: Were you afraid of Tommy Eiland?
A: Very much so.
The Court: Don't lead, counsel.
Q: Why were you afraid?
A: Because I couldn't get away from him. I mean, every time I turned around – I would try hanging around with other people and he would threaten me.
Q: Did that affect your friendships?
A: Yes, it did.
Q: Who all were in your group?
A: Me and Jennifer, Tommy, and Andy.
Q: Did Martin Sweeten run around with you all?
A: No, sir.

Carolyn said she agreed to the suicide pact because Tommy was quite capable of hurting her:

Q: What made you think he might do something to you?
A: Just the way he reacted. If I didn't do what he wanted he got very angry. He would grab me real hard, or hit the walls. He burned my arm with a cigarette.
Q: Can you still see that injury?
A: Yes, sir.
Q: Would you show the jury?
(Witness did as requested.)
Q: What had you done when he burned your arm with the cigarette?
A: I had done nothing.
Q: Did Tommy hurt animals?
A: Yes. He did. He was obsessed with killing things. He loved to read about the Mafia a lot. Tommy did terrible things to cats. He would spin them around because he liked to hear their bones break. He would hang them upside down and come back the next day to see blood coming out of their sockets. He would shoot them with bows and arrows through the tails and then the stomach and then the head.
Q: What about in a car?
A: He loved to hit things. If he saw a rabbit in the other lane he would go hit it. If he saw a deer he wanted to hit it. It did not matter what it was, he just wanted to hit it.
Q: What about setting fires?
A: He liked to set fire to things. I never saw him, but he talked about it. He said he liked to set fires.
Q: To what things?
A: To anything. Didn't matter what it was.

Again it was odd Carolyn was virtually admitting that the testimony about fires was total hearsay. She had never personally seen Tommy do any such thing, yet the prosecution just let it slide by. For that matter, no one bothered asking Carolyn if she had actually seen Tommy torture cats. She had not. For the defense, this was gold because it allowed Scott to point the finger of guilt directly at Tommy. It reinforced the defense's contention that Tommy's "charisma" was chillingly effective, that he could make people do what he wanted. What is more he was a sadist, a vicious killer in the making. The more the jury could be given reasons to believe in Tommy's powers, the more reason they would have to show mercy to Martin. The poor cats of Camp Wood would have not died in vain.

Carolyn testified that she only knew Martin casually from school, that she never saw him associate closely with Tommy except once, the day after the murder:

Q: Did you see Martin the next day?
A: Yes, sir.
Q: Was that at school?
A: Yes, sir.
Q: Did you notice how Martin was acting?
A: Tommy was following him around like a lost puppy. I mean, Martin couldn't go anywhere that Tommy wasn't there.
Q: Was this all during school?
A: Yes.
Q: Did Martin seem upset or nervous?
A: Yes, he did. He didn't like Tommy following him around. He was real jittery – that was about it.
Q: How was Tommy acting, other than following Martin around?
A: Fine. He was laughing and carrying on like he was having a good time.
Q: Was Tommy a leader or a follower?
A: He was a leader.
Q: What do you mean by that?
A: Everybody was scared of him. I mean, they basically did what he said. I mean, he threatened everybody.

Barrera moved to attack Carolyn Sue's assertion that she had been intimidated by Tommy:

Q: Your mother told you, don't see him anymore?
A: Yes.
Q: She had threatened to put a restraining order on him, is that correct?
A: Yes.
Q: Did you continue to see him?
A: I had no choice. I couldn't get away from him.
Q: The question is, did you continue to see him?
A: Yes.
Q: You have told this jury that you dated him for about two or three weeks, is that correct?
A: Yes, sir.
Q: Would it be closer to three months that you saw him on the sly?
A: I didn't see him for that long on the sly. We were friends. I saw him for about two or three weeks, and I told him I only wanted to be friends with him.

Q: Did you date Tommy Eiland for about three months on the sly?
A: No, it was about three weeks.

Barrera continued to question Carolyn's resolve to obey her mother and avoid Tommy. In a statement given to the deputies shortly after the murder Carolyn had said she had visited Andy's house on April 9 but left because she felt "unwanted."

Q: All right, "unwanted" by whom?
A: Tommy and Andy.
Q: Isn't the same Tommy who was obsessed with you?
A: Yes.
Q: And wanted you so badly that he was threatening to kill anybody who even talked to you?
A: Yes.
Q: And you felt unwanted by him, and so you left?
A: They were acting very strangely.
Q: No. Did you leave because you felt unwanted?
A: Yes.
Q: After you left, did you and Jennifer, in Jennifer's car, happen to pass Tommy and Andy walking along the street
A: I don't remember.
Q: If you told Officer Jay Adams that you wanted to pick them up, that you went to pick them up, would it have been true?
A: Yes.
Q: This Tommy, who was obsessed with you and infatuated with you and wouldn't leave you alone, who was threatening to kill people over you, did he accept your invitation to get in the car with you and Jennifer? Or did he just keep going?
A: I don't remember.
Q: If you told Officer Jay Adams –
A: If I told him –
Q: – that they just kept walking . . .
The Court: Let him ask his questions. Don't interrupt.
Q: If you told Officer Jay Adams they just kept walking, would it have been the truth?
A: Yes.
Q: If you didn't want Tommy around you for all of the many reasons you have told this court and this jury, why would you then – and your friend Jennifer, why would you agree with her to stop and pick them up?
A: Well, at the time we were hanging around with them, and like I said before, I could not get away from him.

> **Q:** But you were away from him. They were on the street and you were in the car. You stopped to pick them up. Is that getting away from them?
> **A:** (No audible response.)
> **Q:** Did you try to pick them up?
> **A:** Yes, we did.
> **Q:** Did you tell Officer Jay Adams that Tommy had an obsession with you for about four years and you had dated him on the sly for three months?
> **A:** I don't remember telling him that. I told him I had dated Tommy on the sly but I didn't say how long.
> **Q:** So, if he put it down, are you suggesting he just decided three months was a good period?
> **A:** No. That's not what I'm saying.
> **Q:** Is it possible you told him three months?
> **A:** I might have.
> **Q:** Did you date Tommy for three months?
> **A:** I did not date him for three months. I dated him for three weeks.
> **Q:** Did you tell Officer Adams that since the murder you did not want to see or talk to Tommy anymore?
> **A:** Yes, sir. I did.
> **Q:** All right. Then obviously before the murder happened you did want to see him and you did want to talk to him, didn't you?
> **A:** I had no choice. I had to. I never said I wanted to see him.

Barrera next turned to Carolyn's involvement in the "suicide" pact. Carolyn explained she had felt pressured into agreeing to it. He asked her about the jaunt to the Texas Gulf Coast with Terri, Jason, Jennifer, and Tommy. Why had she gone? Carolyn said she was "pressured" into it. She had "no choice." Barrera directed Carolyn's attention back to her statement she gave shortly after the murder. She read it over.

> **Q:** Having refreshed your memory, as far as the statement which you gave to Officer Adams, tell the jury if in this statement, this entire statement which you gave, if you any time mentioned that Tommy had threatened you into doing something?
> **A:** No. I didn't.
> **Q:** Did you, in this statement, tell Officer Adams any time that you did anything because you were scared to death of Tommy Eiland?
> **A:** No, sir.

Barrera moved in to close the trap. Tommy had been in jail

and no threat to Carolyn Sue when she gave the statement. Why had she not mentioned her fears? Carolyn's eyes teared up:

> **Q:** Did you receive a letter from Tommy on April, 14 after he was in jail?
> **A:** Yes. Sir.
> **Q:** In that letter did he tell you that if anyone hurt you he would get someone to hurt them?
> **A:** Yes. Sir.
> **Q:** Did he tell you that without you he had nothing to live for?
> **A:** Yes. Sir.

Barrera went back to the suicide pact, and asked Carolyn why she had not told Deputy Adams when she made her statement that Tommy had forced her into the pact? She replied she had been afraid of Tommy. She still did what she thought Tommy wanted her to do.

> **Q:** Okay, but now he is in jail.
> **A:** I know that.
> **Q:** Now you don't have to do it anymore.
> **A:** I know.
> **Q:** So, why don't you have to do it anymore?
> **A:** I don't have to see him. He is not there to watch my every move and to threaten people I'm with.
> **Q:** He is no longer an immediate threat to you.
> **A:** Right.
> **Q:** Why did you not tell Officer Adams all of these truths which you have told us today? You were no longer afraid of Tommy since he was in jail then too,
> **A:** I am still afraid of Tommy since he has been in jail. He is just not as big of a threat to me.
> **Q:** Is that why you did not tell Officer Adams the truth?
> **A:** I don't know why I did not tell him.

Scott had to step in for some quick repair work.

> **Q:** Why do you say Tommy is still a threat to you?
> **A:** Because he still threatens me.
> **Q:** How?
> **A:** Through the people he writes to, and telling me he has people watching me, and if they do anything to me he will have them hurt because he has good connections.

Q: How were Tommy and Andy acting strangely on April 9?
A: They had a knife. We asked them where they got it. They didn't say where. They kept throwing it at our feet. Everything we said was funny to them. They acted as if they wanted to tell us something but they didn't.
Q: And this is what you meant when you said they did not want you around?
A: Yes.
Q: Was that the first time that Tommy ever acted like he did not want you around?
A: Yes.
Q: Was that the first time Tommy ever refused a ride?
A: Yes.

Carolyn Sue left the stand in tears, somewhat humiliated and somewhat mollified at the same time. She was also relieved. She had testified at the other two trials and in a couple of pretrial hearings. She had made and signed a statement to the deputies. She had been interviewed, questioned and compelled to testify. She was sick of the whole thing. This was the last time she would be compelled by the legal system to tell her story. She and her mother left the courtroom and did not look back.

Barrera had tried, under difficult circumstances, to show that Tommy was no superman with occult powers. It was tough cross-examining a petite almost childlike young woman who was constantly on the verge of weeping. All it took was one false move, one too harsh of a question and the jury's sympathies could instantly shift. He would become Barrera the Bully.

He had used Carolyn to show that she and Martin and the others had chosen Tommy's company. They were not dragooned into his friendship. Barrera was saying to the jury that Tommy's charisma was no big mystery. Tommy was the biggest, baddest guy in school. Some like that quality and chose to follow him. It was an effective point, one which contained a lot of truth.

After a brief conference at the bench, Judge Thurmond recessed the trial until nine A.M. the next day, Thursday, May 13, 1993. It was to be the last day of the testimony.

By now there was a lot of tension in the courtroom. The James family studiously ignored everyone. They were like a fierce and noble tribe in hostile territory. They concentrated exclusively on Barrera, Lee, and the Judge. During breaks a social and psychological wall separated the two sides every bit as forbidding as the old Berlin Wall. Some of the deputies had become less friendly toward the defense staff. Their once ironic smiles had changed to curt frowns. The bailiff, named Harvey, a wizened little man was becoming downright hostile.

There was one sterling exception, Crockett County Sheriff Jim Wilson. If there is ever a *Gentlemen's Quarterly* magazine for sheriffs, he should be on the cover. Everyday he appeared in the courtroom dressed in sharply creased western wear. His unscuffed boots polished to a pleasing shine, his white shirts gleamed. His western trousers were always freshly dry cleaned and pressed. He wore an immaculate gun belt of elegantly tooled leather without an unsightly mark on it. The holster encased a handsome pearl-handled .45 automatic. He was like an old time western movie actor ready for the set.

The amazing thing was that his manners matched his appearance. He was friendly, polite and respectful, but above all, totally professional. He was scrupulously fair toward Martin and his family. He even allowed them to pass Martin a few packs of cigarettes each day, after careful examination of course, without a lengthy bureaucratic hassle. At the beginning and end of the trial he would patiently wait while Martin visited with family members. Sheriff Wilson took the constitutional presumption of innocence seriously. He said his rule was, "Play fair with me and I'll play fair with you." Each day of the trial he scrupulously kept his word.

Thursday morning Scott arrived early as usual. He made sure the poster spelling out the new legal definition of reasonable doubt was along side his desk and readable by the jury. He made sure the enlargement of Martin's car was also in place. He turned his coffee cup so the logo faced the jury. He went over his notes one more time.

Today would be the day Martin took the stand. Scott did not want to do it; no defense attorney does. If it worked, Scott would be a hero. If it failed, Martin went to prison, Scott would get some heavy peer disapproval and a load of personal guilt. It was a grave risk. To come this far only to watch the case explode was every lawyer's nightmare. Scott had hoped for Barrera to make a mistake during Carolyn's cross-examination. If he had, Scott might have been able to introduce a couple of nifty surprises. Barrera had not obliged.

The defense led off with a character witness named Billy Bernard, a building contractor. Martin had worked for him on a summertime construction job in San Antonio. He said Martin was an excellent worker, and he would be glad to have him as a full time employee. The next witness for the defense was Elton Baxter, the Real County constable in Camp Wood. He said he knew all of the defendants in the case. Elton was, of course, the first law enforcement officer told of the killing.

Q: How were you first notified?
A: John Pannell and his wife Sharon came up to my house, must have been between, say, four P.M. and six o'clock. I'm not sure what the time was, and they said, "Elton, we've got a problem; we need to talk to you, a bad problem." I said, "Okay, you all come on to the house." And they came in and told me that Martin had told them that Tommy and the other boy had killed a man. I said, "What are you talking about?" And he told me then and he said, "I'm afraid they are going to come down there and kill Martin, because I heard rumors they are going to."
Q: What did you do?
A: I radioed the deputy sheriff in Camp Wood, Buck Pruitt, about it, and I went down there and picked up Martin for his own safety. I picked him up at John Pannell's seven or eight miles out from Camp Wood.
Q: Can you tell what Martin was like when you got there?
A: He was real calm; never gave me no problem or nothing.
Q: Did he seem like he was scared?
Mr. Barrera: Excuse me. We are going to object to counsel leading his witness. This is his witness, he can't put words into his mouth.
The Court: Let's not ask leading questions of our own witnesses.
Q: Could you tell the jury whether he was scared?
A: Yes, sir, he was scared. I could tell.
Q: How could you tell?
A: Well, just the way he acted and what he told me coming in.
Q: What did he tell you?
A: He told me that Tommy and this other boy wanted him to take them out to the ranch, and he said he didn't want to do it but he finally – they kept aggravating him about it, and he finally said I'll take you all out there. I believe he told me that Tommy and the

other boy were supposed to go coon hunting. He told me he went out there, drove up in front of the house with Tommy and the other boy in back, and Tommy said, "Let's do it." And Martin said, "What are you going to do?" He said, "We're going to shoot that guy; we're going to kill him. That's what I came out here to do." And Martin told me he jumped out of the car and said, "I don't want no part of killing anybody." And he said Tommy came running around the front of the car with the gun pointed at him, said, "If you run, I'm going to shoot you." Martin said, "What could I do? I got back into the car."

This was not the same account Martin later gave authorities. It could be it was the way Elton remembered the conversation. It could also be argued Martin, in his excitement, gave an encapsulated, foreshortened version of the events to Elton. It could also be a self-serving version. It did not matter much at the time because he gave a full detailed account to the deputies later that night. Elton described taking Martin back out to the ranch and leaving him at the bottom of the hill. "We didn't want to let him see where the body was laying."

It was confusing at the scene; there were a lot of people there. Scott asked Elton who they were. "There was a bunch of them, but I couldn't tell you if they was law enforcement or not," he replied. Scott passed the witness.

Barrera went back to the one really sore point in Elton's direct testimony. At the Pannell's home Elton had begun to question Martin.

Q: At that time you said that he told you what happened?
A: Yes, sir, when we started in.
Q: That he was really calm, gave you no trouble?
A: Didn't give me no trouble.
Q: Aside from his telling you he was really scared, how did you decide whether he was?
A: Well, just the way he acted and everything.
Q: How did he act?
A: Well, he kind of acted like he was shy, you know, didn't talk too much, and then he was talking to me a little bit.
Q: Acted kind of shy?
A: Yes.
Q: You said he was real calm when he was talking to you, was he?
A: Yes, sir. He was pretty calm about it.

Q: Did he tell you he was real scared?
A: No, sir. He didn't.
Q: How did you determine that?
A: Just his actions and everything. When we brought him out of the car he kind of acted like the other boys might try to get him.
Q: No, excuse me. At the time that you were talking to him at the Pannell home, what did you see that led you to believe he was really scared?
A: . . . Just the way he looked at me and everything.
Q: How did he look at you?
A: He just kind of glanced at me, and he never did talk too much about it for a while to anyone. I could tell maybe he was probably being a little scared about it.
Q: And from that, from the fact he was quiet, bashful and he kind of glanced at you, you got the impression from that, that he was real scared that these other boys were going to hurt him?
A: Yes, sir.

Barrera went on to shred Elton's recollections of Martin's account of the murder. It was rather sad. It was Barrera's job but poor old Elton just could not stand up to such professional questioning. He had already backed off of his assessment of Martin's state of mind, ". . . maybe he was probably being a little scared about it." Barrera went over Elton's account line by line. His questions were loaded with irony.

Q: Did Martin say anything about stealing anything from the house?
A: No, sir.
Q: By some chance, did he mention anything about a safe –
A: No, sir.
Q: – in the house?
A: No, sir. He never mentioned nothing to me about it.
Q: Did he mention anything about an alibi?
A: No, sir.
Q: Did he mention anything about a flashlight?
A: No, sir.
Q: And shining a flashlight in somebody's eyes?

Elton got confused and thought Barrera was asking about the lighting conditions at the ranch when he arrived. It took Barrera a minute or so to bring him back to the question.

Q: . . . Did he say anything to you about a plan to shine a light in –

A: No, sir.
Q: – in Mr. James's eyes?
A: No, sir. He didn't mention it.
Q: Did he by some chance mention to you anything about having taped the soles of his shoes?
A: No, sir.
Q: Did he mention anything about some stolen merchandise hidden in a cattleguard?
A: No, sir.
Q: Did he mention anything to you about having said to the other boys, "If you were going to shoot him, I wish you had done it then?"
A: No, sir. He never –

It was classic cross-examination and good clean prosecutorial fun. Barrera knew full well Martin had mentioned none of those things to Elton. He just had to pound the embarrassing omissions home to the jury. Elton was a convenient vehicle. Barrera kept him on the stand for a few minutes longer getting in a few more licks. Elton admitted Martin had not said anything about Tommy pointing a .357 at him. Nor had he mentioned anything about Andy pointing a .22 rifle at his head.

Scott repaired the damage as best he could. He returned to Elton's testimony about the back door light. Elton had said it was bright and illuminated the scene. But other deputies had said the scene was dark. There were two lights at Edmund's door, one was a small bulb light and the other more powerful pullout light. Elton was excused.

The defense called Judge Neville Smart, the county judge for Edwards County. He gave his recollections of that night. He had pronounced Edmund to be dead and identified him. Two neighbors of Edmund's had confirmed the identification. Judge Smart had helped Deputy Lowrie turn off the lights and appliances in the house and secured the door. He did not recall any outside lights burning. Back in Rocksprings later, he recalled nothing about helping to calm Darwin or the subject of lawyers coming up. All he remembered was saying hello to Darwin. He had not been asked to magistrate although he was clearly available to do so. The other two boys had been magistrated in Leakey when they arrived there within an hour of their arrest. After a brief cross-examination he was excused.

Scott had Jennifer Noblett scheduled next. Afterwards he wanted to call Blanca Flores, Tommy's ex-girlfriend to testify. Blanca was ready to testify that Tommy had virtually exonerated Martin the day after the murder. Tommy had told her during school about the murder and further told her bluntly that Martin had not known ahead of time what was planned. Tommy had just used Martin and was bragging about it to Blanca. It was great stuff. It was hearsay. It was inadmissible.

Barrera asked for a conference in the judge's chambers. He knew what Blanca would say. He had heard her testimony at Tommy's trial. Since he thought Jennifer might say something similar, he wanted to put a stop to it now. During Tommy's trial Blanca's testimony had been admissible because it was a direct conversation she had with the defendant. Martin had not been present so at his trial her testimony was hearsay. Scott would have to come up with very convincing arguments to have it admitted. Judge Thurmond said he would take any arguments under advisement out of hearing of the jury during the lunch break. Meanwhile Jennifer Noblett could take the stand and testify within limits.

Jennifer told the court that she had been going to college in Beeville but had moved back to a town near Camp Wood. She recounted her high school friendships with Tommy, Andy, and Carolyn Sue. She knew Martin but "we never really went anywhere with him." As Scott questioned her about her relationship with the others, Barrera was ready with objections the instant the questions veered into forbidden territory.

Q: Have you ever heard of Tommy talking of killing anybody?
A: Yeah.
Q: Who was that?
A: Well, he would just threaten, saying somebody – one time he threatened, said somebody was going to get killed, and he was going to do it and – when he would just get mad at people.
Mr. Barrera: Just one second. Your Honor, this – unless the predicate is laid that this defendant was present, all of this is hearsay, and we hate to keep popping up and down objecting, but it is hearsay.
The Court: Overruled, but let's not get into specific acts.
Q: Did you hear – would you hear him talking about killing more than one person?
A: Not really.
Q: Did you have a cousin in Beeville or —

The Court: Again, I don't want to get into specific instances, counsel. I'll permit this line of questioning showing what type of person he was.

Scott continued to explore Jennifer's relations with Tommy. Then, she dropped a bit of pure gold:

Q: Did Tommy have a problem with your brother visiting you?
A: Yes. He was very jealous of my brother because of his relationship with Carolyn Sue.
Q: Were there any threats made?
A: Yes. Just —
Q: When Tommy talked about killing people did you believe him?
A: No, he just liked to threaten.
Q: He had never to your knowledge actually killed anyone?
A: No, not to my knowledge.
Q: How often would he threaten?
A: Well, he was very threatening. That's just the way he was. I don't know how often he did it.
Q: Was he threatening physically; I mean, threatening physical things or –
A: Yes.
Q: Would he threaten death?
A: Yeah, he was just trying to be intimidating to people.
Q: Okay.
The Court: Let's not lead.
Q: Why didn't you believe him?
A: Tommy was all talk.
Q: Did Tommy have the ability to make people do things they did not want to do?
A: Yes.
Q: What do you mean by that?
A: He would just scare you into doing things you didn't really want to do.
Q: How would he do that?
A: Just — he had this psychological thing. He would just keep talking to you until you thought you had to do it.
Q: Do you know whether or not Carolyn was afraid of him?
A: Not to my knowledge.
Q: What about you?
A: No.
Q: Did Tommy ever make you do anything you didn't want to do?
A: Yes.

Q: Things you did not want to do a lot?
A: All the time.
The Court: Let's stop leading, counsel. I've told you twice already. Stop leading the witness.
Q: What kinds of things?
A: Places I did not want to go, sexual activity, that kind of thing.
Q: Was Martin ever that kind of way, like Tommy?
A: Martin was never anything like Tommy.

It was a further sign of the tension which had been steadily building. A couple of days before, during the testimony of a prosecution witness, the judge had suddenly jumped up from his chair and adjusted the prosecution's exhibit poster. It had been one of those "What the hell?" moments for the defense. All Scott could do was look thoughtfully at the floor and hope the jury got it.

Now, things were getting testy. Normally a judge would wait for the other side to object before chiding an attorney for "leading" the witness. It was the common practice. Barrera was not shy about objecting. Yet, he had not even lifted an eyebrow. Clearly, the judge was just plain annoyed with the defense. Of course, Judge Thurmond was in a tough spot. Every time he looked up from his papers he look straight into three or four rows of determined James family members, assorted relatives and friends.

Everyone just wanted to get this thing over with. Even Harvey, the wizened bailiff, himself originally from Del Rio, was picking up the cues. He had been a model of disinterest and formal politeness. Now, he began to snap at defense witnesses waiting in the hall downstairs — ordering them about and chastising them for the smallest "infractions." It was bizarre. A small, nut brown little man dressed in a mustard yellow uniform had suddenly become a gnome from hell.

Scott continued to examine Jennifer, and each time he would take a run at the core of what he wanted out of her testimony, Barrera would object. It was hearsay, both knew it, but Scott's goal was to get close enough for the jury to get the idea. Tommy dominated people. Tommy could make kids do what he wanted. Martin was weak. Tommy had merely used Martin during the murder. Martin had not known beforehand what was going to happen.

When Scott got to the suicide pact, Barrera objected. The judge sustained the objection. When the questioning got to the great runaway adventure and Jennifer began to tell about Tommy's prowess at shoplifting, Barrera objected. The court sustained the objection. Scott passed the witness.

Barrera attacked Tommy's alleged hold over Jennifer and Carolyn:

> **Q:** Ms. Noblett, these things Tommy made you do, did you do them because you were afraid of him or because you were in love with him?
> **A:** It was mostly intimidation.
> **Q:** Well, how so?
> **A:** I was always afraid to make him mad. I would do things so that he wouldn't get mad at me.
> **Q:** What would happen?
> **A:** He would make threats.
> **Q:** Did he ever hurt you?
> **A:** Not physically but emotionally.
> **Q:** Did he ever strike you?
> **A:** No.
> **Q:** Never hurt you?
> **A:** No.
> **Q:** Andy, did he ever hit you?
> **A:** No.
> **Q:** Carolyn was in love with Tommy, wasn't she?
> **A:** Yes.
> **Q:** And she dated Tommy on the sly?
> **A:** Yes.
> **Q:** And, her mother did not want her hanging around with Tommy?
> **A:** Yes.
> **Q:** But she went ahead and did it anyway?
> **A:** Yes.
> **Q:** You were aware her mother did not want her visiting with Tommy?
> **A:** Yes, but we were always there anyway. My family didn't want me with him either.
> **Q:** But you went anyhow?
> **A:** Yes.
> **Q:** Because you were so afraid of him or because you loved him?
> **A:** Because –
> **Q:** Or thought you did?
> **A:** I thought we were a family. We were like a family, all four of us.

Barrera continued to question Jennifer about the events before and after the murder, and he would slip in questions about Martin. Seemingly innocent questions, harmless questions until he was ready to play one of his trump cards. It was a dilly.

> **Q:** Did you have occasion to visit Martin Sweeten in jail on Sunday?
> **A:** I'm sure I did.
> **Q:** I'm asking about what he may have said about himself. Did Martin Sweeten tell you that none of them were forced to do it?

Jennifer balked. She could not remember. She was not sure. Barrera confronted her with a signed statement she had given to the deputies, State's Exhibit No. 68. He showed her signature at the bottom. He virtually rubbed her nose in it. Jennifer kept balking and evading but eventually admitted she had signed it.

> **Q:** Having looked at the statement, did you tell – did Martin tell you then "none of us were forced to do it?"
> **A:** Yes. But they had tried to back out of it.
> **Q:** They had tried to back out of it, but none of them were forced to do it?
> **A:** Yes, that's what it says.

Scott tried to limit the damage but there was little he could do. On redirect examination, Jennifer said she did not remember Martin telling her anything specific. She said she had not carefully read over the statement before signing it. It was time to get Jennifer off the stand and quickly move on to something else.

Barrera had hurt Martin's case badly, perhaps fatally. The jury might love Martin like a son and still convict him because of that admission. It was amazing how quickly a trial could turn on a defendant, how just a few words could bring down a carefully constructed case. It was not as if victory had been in the bag up to this point. Martin's signed statements were damaging and a major obstacle. Scott was fairly confident that he had at least thrown some doubt on the statements by showing the deputies' questionable tactics. Nonetheless, Martin's case simply could not afford any more unexpected blows. Martin would have to take the stand and convince the jury of his innocence.

Meanwhile there was Will Baker, another Canyon Boy. He had been a drinking buddy with Tommy and Andy. His most important testimony was to confirm that Martin had appeared sick and depressed at school the day after the murder. He had also noticed that Tommy had seemed to follow Martin around that day. Barrera tried to shake him, but Will was certain they had been together all day because "you usually don't see them together."

Will was what most would call a good old country boy, but he had his pride. He did not like being cross-examined one bit. Barrera was tough and questioned him closely. When Will was finally excused he walked out of the courthouse, wiped his forehead, put on his cowboy hat and said to no one in particular, "Damn! That Mexican lawyer really worked me over. If I'd known I was going to be treated like that I wouldn't 've come."

Judge Thurmond recessed the court for lunch. The attorneys remained behind to argue out the admissibility of testimony from Jennifer, Blanca Flores, and Jason White regarding remarks Tommy had made to them. Since the remarks were not made by, or in the presence of the defendant the prosecution wanted them excluded.

Scott argued that the statements should be exempted from the hearsay rule because the alleged conspiracy to commit murder also included an ongoing conspiracy of silence. Barrera and Tom Lee naturally disagreed. They said the conspiracy to commit murder was over when Edmund James had been killed.

Judge Thurmond asked what the witnesses would say. Scott told him Jennifer would take the stand again and testify that Tommy had told her, before the murder, he was planning to kill Edmund James. She had not believed him. Jason White would testify that Tommy had bragged to him about the murder the next day. Blanca Flores would testify that Tommy had told her Martin had not known what was planned and had tagged along to ask for a job. Scott argued that the testimony of these three witness came under several exceptions to the rules regarding hearsay and were therefore admissible. Blanca's testimony, for example, was based on a written statement she had given to the deputies. It was therefore a "record of a regularly conducted activity" and a "public record."

The rest of the defense's arguments centered around the definition of "conspiracy" and just when the conspiracy in question began and when it ended. The defense contended that the conspiracy went beyond merely an agreement to murder Edmund James, leaving open the question of Martin's alleged involvement. The conspiracy extended to Tommy's efforts to keep Martin quiet so that it also included the day after the murder. The State said they would allow Jennifer's testimony regarding Tommy's threat to murder Edmund James. It had been made four or five days before the deadly trip to the ranch. Barrera wanted to get in Jennifer's testimony that Tommy had told her the reason for the murder was to steal Edmund's money.

Judge Thurmond did not accept the defense's arguments. Any testimony about remarks made out of Martin's presence regarding his complicity would not be admissible. Scott asked for and got a bill of exceptions to the judge's ruling. This would provide a basis for any appeal to higher courts. Judge Thurmond said the overriding fact in the matter was that Tommy's statements were made out of the presence of the defendant and therefore hearsay. Such testimony was inadmissible, period. It was time for lunch.

Blanca took the stand after lunch. She said she had been Tommy's girlfriend and, even after they broke up, she remained friendly toward him. Tommy had been nice to her. He never threatened or bullied her. Blanca told the court she knew Martin only casually from school. She had noticed that Martin was "nervous" during school the day after the murder, "real nervous, like he was tensed about something." She also noticed that Tommy kept "looking at Martin kind of funny" during the school day. This was all Scott could ask her in accordance with the judge's ruling. Barrera declined to cross-examine.

The defense called Jeff Pannell next. Jeff is John's younger son; Michael, Martin's best friend, is his older brother. Jeff had ridden home with Martin after school the day after the murder. Martin wanted to go out to Jeff's house and find Michael. Jeff testified that Martin seemed nervous. Before they headed for Jeff's house they stopped at the ubiquitous Get 'N Go. Jeff went in for a can of snuff and when he came out "Tommy and Angela Crawford were in the car." Tommy had some errands to run and, as usual, everyone obliged him. Jeff said they drove to Tommy's trailer, then back to the high school and then back to Camp Wood. Jeff said while Tommy was in the car Martin was "still shaken up. I figured it was just a girl turned him down or something." Jeff said he and Martin then went on to the Pannell residence in Uvalde County. Under questioning, Jeff said he did not hear the conversation between Martin, Mike, and his father John. The last he saw of Martin was Elton Baxter taking him away.

> **Q:** What was Elton driving when he came out there?
> **A:** His cop car.
> **Q:** Did you notice if he had his lights on or not?
> **A:** He did.
> **Q:** By his lights do you mean his headlights?
> **A:** His red and blue lights . . . on top.

After a perfunctory cross-examination, Scott scored a small point on redirect:

> **Q:** While Tommy was still with you all, did you talk about going to the movies?
> **A:** He mentioned something about how he went to the movies the night before and he wanted Martin to take him to the movies that night.
> **Q:** Take him to the movies where?
> **A:** In Uvalde.
> **Q:** When did he want Martin to take him to the movies in Uvalde?
> **A:** Something like five o'clock.
> **Q:** What did Martin say or do?
> **A:** He did not want to take him.
> **Q:** What did he say?
> **A:** He just said he was sick.

Once again Barrera helped the defense in a minor way by continuing this line of questioning when he picked up the cross-examination. It is a risk every lawyer runs. Even the most innocent questions can backfire.

> **Q:** Did Tommy say anything after Martin told him he was sick?
> **A:** He said, "You are not sick. You can take me anyway." He said, "Pick me up at Camp Wood at five o'clock and we will go to the movies."
> **Q:** All right. Did Martin go?
> **A:** No. Martin went to my house.

This, of course, bolstered Martin's contention that he was

terrified of Tommy and was certain he would not return from the trip to the movies. Jeff was excused and his father, John Pannell took the stand.

If one were pressed to describe John Pannell, the easiest way is to say he looks remarkably like the country-western singer Buck Owens. John is almost an archetype extrovert. Even in the midst of crisis he exudes a self-confidence that borders on arrogance. This could have led him to become a self-important bore, but his sense of irony and humor saved him from that fate. He also has an almost psychic ability to relate to teenagers.

Scott was in a bind. He had hoped somehow to get in some vital testimony from Blanca and Jennifer. They both said Tommy had told them that Martin did not know ahead of time what was planned. He told them Martin was in effect, a dupe. This would have been wonderfully exculpatory evidence. It might have vindicated and freed Martin. It was still inadmissible. Their evidence was pure hearsay. Scott had been hoping his arguments would sway the judge or that the prosecution would make some mistake which would allow him to present the testimony for the jury to consider. There had been no such luck. The case was turning against Martin.

Time was running out. Scott had planned to put John Pannell on the stand the next day, but by mid-morning it was obvious the defense needed John that afternoon. Scott hated to wind the defense up without the girls testifying, but there was little choice. Martin would have to take the stand in the late afternoon.

John was in the field delivering gas when the call came. He had waited for this moment for over a year. He came home, picked up Sharon and Jeff and drove to Ozona arriving in the middle of the lunch break. He found Scott, and they took a walk to talk about his testimony. John knew something which he had told no one until this moment. For over a year, he had held his peace not even telling Darwin. Now John Pannell told Scott in the deep privacy of this interview. John knew something that would go a long way toward clearing Martin.

The bad new was that John's testimony would be ruled as pure hearsay. The judge would never allow it on direct testimony. Judge Thurmond was watching Scott like a cat before a mouse hole. One false move and he would jump all over the defense.

That was why he kept admonishing Scott not to lead witnesses although the prosecution rarely objected. Judge Thurmond knew that much of the defense's best testimony was hearsay, and he was not going to allow it in his courtroom. The good news was that neither Barrera or Judge Thurmond knew what John knew. He had never said a word about it.

If Scott could somehow slip John's testimony in, he would feel much better about putting Martin on the stand. John's testimony would give Martin some cushion, some room to stumble or retreat before the onslaught of Barrera's cross-examination. But how to get the testimony admitted? There was only one answer. If the defense could not get it admitted on direct testimony, then it must be admitted on cross.

How to do that was the next problem. Scott had one sneaky lawyer's trick which might do the job. During his interview John had used a phrase a couple of times that immediately grabbed Scott's attention. If it worked on Scott, it would surely work the same magic on Barrera. Any prosecutor worth his salt would snap at it hungrily. If Scott could get John to repeat it on the stand, and if Barrera took the bait . . .

Chapter X

The End

JOHN PANNELL TOOK THE STAND with almost casual confidence. He lounged in the chair. Judge Thurmond stared at John and immediately bristled with annoyance. John said he had known Martin for years. Martin and his son, Michael, were best friends. There was a tone, a sense about John's testimony. It had a quality of anticipation that sharpened the atmosphere in the courtroom. Barrera sensed that something was up and began to more closely monitor the testimony.

> **Q:** Do you remember if Martin had ever been seriously injured?
> **A:** Had a motorcycle accident.
> **Q:** Okay. Did he recover from it?
> **A:** Not completely. He had a bad limp. He can't run, you know, still.
> **Q:** Have you noticed whether it affects his self-confidence?
> **A:** Tremendously. No self-confidence. He was in too long recuperating.
> **Q:** Is that true since the accident?
> **Mr. Barrera:** We object to that as leading.
> **The Court:** Overruled.
> **A:** Martin has never been confident a lot. He has always been small; but then that is how small kids are.

Mr. Barrera: We object to this as nonresponsive. We ask that the witness be asked to answer the questions and not go off on some narrative.
The Court: Overruled.
Q: Has this lack of self-confidence continued?
A: More so after the accident. I mean, it is like someone in a wheelchair. How confident can they be? Martin was in a wheelchair a long, long time.
Q: Did you all take Martin with you when you went hunting?
A: Martin did not like to go hunting. He would go, but he did not like to kill things.
Mr. Barrera: Again, we object as nonresponsive.
The Court: Try to be as direct as you can. You can explain your answer. There is more than a yes or no sometimes, but try to stay within the subject.
Q: What was it like when Martin would go hunting? What would Martin do?
A: Martin would stay back and cover his eyes if you shot something. He didn't like to hunt. He was real timid and didn't — that's the way he was.
Q: Would Martin help you clean the deer or whatever was killed?
A: Not unless you wanted him to puke all over you. He was real funny about things like that.
Q: Did you ever talk with him about why he was that way?
A: No. I never did get into it with him. Some people believe in different things than I do, and that's their belief.

Scott questioned John about Martin and his little car. John said Martin would give rides to anyone to gain favor or friendship with them. John attributed it to the blow to his confidence the motorcycle accident inflicted.

Q: Was Martin a leader or follower?
A: A follower, completely. It is like back to his accident. He hasn't — I don't know if it is initiative or what, but he is not sure of himself at all. He is real unsure, to the point you want to pity him or slap him and say "look, you need to do this or that." That's Martin. Great kid, but —
Q: Have you ever observed people talk Martin into things?
A: My boys, when they wanted something, yeah, or they wanted him to take them someplace or this or that. Even if Martin was tired and didn't want to go, it didn't take long and they would talk him into it. There were always girls at the house. When they needed a

ride someplace, even if it was to Uvalde forty miles away, Martin would take them.

Scott moved on to the night John came home to find Martin and his son waiting. John earns his living by selling propane gas to ranchers and small businesses, so he never arrives home at a certain time each day. That evening he pulled into his driveway shortly after 5:00 P.M. Martin and Michael asked him to step into his bedroom. Martin began to tell John about the murder. The minute Martin mentioned Tommy Eiland, it did not take mental gymnastics on John's part to figure out something bad had happened. Martin finished his story and John said he asked Martin what he wanted to do. Tell the cops, Martin replied, but he was afraid of Buck. John also did not hold the local law enforcement in particularly high regard. He had heard too many stories from his rancher customers.

Martin was afraid of Tommy and Andy. "I had to sleep with that murdering bastard last night," Martin had said. John testified that he particularly remembered that remark because Martin rarely used strong language. By now John was "shook up." He said he had his wife dial the telephone number of a Texas Ranger friend.

"I kept asking Martin, you know, repeatedly what he wanted to do, because I don't know if I would have turned him in or not," John told the court. "I'm not that keen on it. Too many – I've seen too many murders in Real County which have never been solved."

They finally had to settle on Elton. Martin was adamant that he wanted to talk to the cops, John said. Martin said he was supposed to take Tommy and Andy to Uvalde. He said, 'They are going to kill me down there. I know too much.'

Q: Where did you find Constable Baxter?
A: At his house.
Q: What did you tell him?
A: Everything, start to finish.
Q: What happened next?
A: He kind of went silly on me. I don't know.
Mr. Barrera: He went what, sir?
A: Silly.
Q: What does that mean to you?

A: Well, he kind of got all excited and jumping up and down. He called the EMS and all that stuff. I just said, well, I'll be down at the house. Elton stopped in the middle of town and stopped at the store and told them first. Of course, that's hearsay, but –
Q: Did he have his lights on?
A: Oh, yeah, he had to run his lights all the way down to the house, sure.
Q: Were you at the house when he got there?
A: Yeah, it kind of made me mad when he drove up blaring and — you know, with people in Nueces Canyon —
Mr. Barrera: We object to his going on and on to a dissertation.
The Court: Listen to the question asked; were his lights on when he drove up?
Q: You said he was blaring, what does that mean?
A: I mean he was hauling it. It's a caliche road. You can see dust for two miles.

After Elton picked up Martin, John, his wife Sharon, and Michael followed. They found Darwin and Sue standing forlornly in the park. John's wife and Michael took Darwin and Sue out to the ranch. John stayed behind to close up Darwin's store. Later they all drove up to Rocksprings.

Thus, began the vigil at the sheriff's office. John said they were there throughout the night. John said they were not allowed to see Martin until around four A.M. He remembered comforting Martin telling him that the sheriff was going to let him go home, so be patient and all would be well.

Q: Do you remember what Martin was saying?
A: We went in there to see and Martin told me, said, — I told him everything was going to be all right, I think they are probably going to let you go home. And he said, "I think they are trying to railroad me."
Q: Did he say why?
A: I asked him, how so. He said, "I don't know, they are acting so strange." I think those were the words he used.
Q: How long did you talk with him?
A: Me and my wife were probably in there about three minutes maybe. We walked out before Darwin and Sue did.
Q: Okay, did you try to tell the law what happened?
A: Sure.
Q: Who did you talk to?

A: I talked to the sheriff.
Q: Where?
A: I talked to him in the front office, and then I had to sign a statement. They asked me if I would.

This was it, the moment Scott had been waiting for. If only John would oblige and use the phrase, then truly all would be well:

Q: And when you signed that statement did you write it out yourself?
A: Yes, I did.
Q: And do you know if Michael also signed a statement?
A: He did the next day.
Q: Okay, what about your wife Sharon?
A: They did not ask her for one, and she didn't.
Q: Did you talk to them before you wrote it out?
A: Well, I talked to the sheriff, and anyway, they told me it was just a formality.
Q: Did you see those other boys when they came in?
A: Yes, I did.
Q: When did they come in?
A: It seems like it was around one o'clock. May have been later. I kind of lost track of time.
Q: What did Martin look like when you saw him?
A: He looked bad, real bad.
Q: Was he physically showing any signs of emotion?
A: Yes, all over. He was — he broke down when he was talking to me, talking about Mr. James, how — what they did to him. He said it was the horriblest thing he had ever seen in his life. I think I told him to straighten up.

Scott had to pass the witness. John had not used the phrase for which Scott was looking. He would have to try again on redirect. Barrera zeroed in on the fact Martin had not gone to his own father but waited for John. Barrera got John to admit Martin had an opportunity that morning to go to his father and tell the story, but he had gone to school instead.

A: I don't think they had that kind of relationship.
Q: His father and he did not have that kind of relationship?
A: I don't know that.
Q: Well, you know the Sweetens don't you?

A: I know them.
Q: Why do you think they didn't have that kind of relationship in which he could go tell his father, look what those fellows did?
A: I don't know. Kids get a certain age and they are not – they love their parents but they are not close.
Q: They want to do their own thing?
A: No. I don't think that. I don't know. There is a generation gap here.
Q: They are not inclined to follow the advice of their parents?
A: I don't think that's it. I think they are maybe afraid to tell their parents when they can tell an outsider.

It was a sharp exchange. John was answering Barrera's questions almost arrogantly. He was lounging back in the witness chair one arm slung over the back. It was obvious he did not like Barrera and the feeling was just as mutual. The judge was already well annoyed with John Pannell.

Barrera got on to the fact that Martin had been living off and on with the Pannells. In fact, for quite a while Martin had abandoned his father's house. It meant Martin was not so timid after all. He had defied his father. As Barrera pushed him, John would casually slouch back in the chair and almost toss off answers. He would make faces, roll his eyes. He was pushing it to the limit. He was right on the edge of contempt. The questions and answers took on a nastier tone. Everyone in the courtroom was glued to the performance.

Barrera picked at the details. Martin had not told John everything, had he?

Q: Did you hear Martin tell the constable that when he got to the ranch and they said they were going to kill this fellow, that Tommy got out of the car, ran around the front, pointed the gun at him and said, if you run we'll shoot you?
A: No. I did not hear that.
Q: You didn't hear that at all?
A: No. The only thing the constable said besides, "Come on, Martin. Let's go," was, "I knew this was going to happen." Because he said Tommy's stepmother said he pulled a gun on her the other day. Elton said, "I knew he was going to kill someone."
The Court: Why don't you be responsive to the questions, Mr. Pannell?
A: I thought I was.

Q: The constable said this?
A: That's what he said.
Q: You did make a statement with regard to allegedly what happened out there, did you not?
A: Yes, sir.
Q: Did you tell Mr. D. W. Woods or O. W. Woods any of these things about threats to the — to Martin by these fellows?
A: I haven't read the statement yet. I was going to tell everything in the statement, but I made it real, real brief.

That was the phrase Scott had been waiting for, "I made it real, real brief." If Barrera would bite, Scott knew what was coming next.

"Was there some reason for making it brief?" Barrera asked, nibbling at the line.

"Yes, sir, they — there was," John replied.

"What was the reason?" Barrera asked, smoothly taking the bait.

"The other deputy was in the other room with Andy, and I was writing a statement there. I heard him ask Andy if Martin had anything to do with it. And Andy said, 'Hell, no! Martin went crazy when we shot the man.'"

John related all of this with an innocent look on his face. He had waited over a year, keeping his own counsel, to say this in open court. He had even told Darwin a few nights after Martin's arrest, that he was not going to tell him everything he knew.

"You put me on the stand and I'll save your son," John had promised Darwin.

Scott could not have elicited John's testimony on direct examination. It was the purest sort of hearsay, but it was admissible on cross-examination. Barrera was almost in shock.

"So that is why you made your statement real brief," he asked weakly.

"That's it," John replied in a cocky, almost insulting, manner.

"He said Martin did not know anything about it?" Barrera repeated, not believing what John was saying.

There was something odd in the atmosphere of the courtroom. It was dead quiet. The spectators were strangely silent. At the same time, it was as if an uproar were breaking out, as if everyone were yelling, talking, and shouting all at once. There was an atmosphere of confusion and tumult, yet without sound or motion. It was as if the whole trial had just turned upside down and all the papers and exhibits had spilled out across the floor. Time seemed to freeze.

Judge Thurmond was furious.

Great twitches of anger rippled across his face. His body shivered. He had to grasp the bench to gather himself. The one thing he had forbidden, the very thing he had demanded not to happen had just occurred. Hearsay had been done. Not just any hearsay testimony, this was gross hearsay, outrageous hearsay — but admissible hearsay.

"Why don't you just wait until a question is asked before you blurt something out?" he demanded of John in a voice constricted with fury.

"Okay," John agreeably replied.

Barrera continued to cross-examine him. He was too much of a professional to let that moment stop him or throw him off for too long. Like any good lawyer he soldiered on, hoping to recoup his losses later, hoping to divert the jury's attention to other matters.

John admitted that Martin was not so timid or pliable that he did not know right from wrong:

> **Q:** Do you think that if someone told him let's go out there and kill this man and rob him; he's got a safe and we can take his property; do you think he would let somebody talk him into that?
> **A:** No, Martin would have hid under the bed somewhere.
> **Q:** Do you think that on his own, he would have been capable of burglary?
> **A:** No.
> **Q:** Do you think somebody could talk him in to taping the underside of his shoes so he wouldn't leave tracks at a house that was about to be burgled?
> **A:** No. I don't know. I mean, I don't know.
> **Q:** Do you think if he knew — if someone said to him, we're going to go out there and kill this fellow, we're psyched up about it and we want to go out there and kill him and take his property because he's got money, and we know where the safe is and we want you to take us there, do you think he would do that?
> **A:** No.
> **Q:** He wouldn't be a follower to that extent, would he, sir?

A: No, sir.

Barrera bored in, a lot of John's cockiness dissolved under some intense, if not, withering cross-examination:

Q: Now, as I understand you, you said Martin told you after the shooting and after this man had been shot several times in the back and was on the ground, that he thought it was some kind of joke, because they played war games out there he was confused?
A: Yeah, he said it hit him wrong just for an instant and then he saw the blood and he knew then.
Q: He saw blood, you're telling me?
A: Well, I don't think he used the word blood. I don't even remember now. It may have been blood.
Q: What else did he say?
A: He said it was the goriest thing he had ever seen, or the goriest thing that ever happened to him, something like that.

John began to backpedal and even prevaricate under Barrera's withering questions. It was not a good performance and went some way toward damaging his credibility. John admitted that he did not hold the local law enforcement personnel in high regard. He admitted he may not have heard all of Martin's conversations with Elton at his home because he had gone to the bathroom. He admitted upon being confronted with his signed statement that he had not informed the deputies about Martin's contention that Tommy had threatened him all night with a pistol.

Q: Did you tell the deputy that this defendant had told you he had had a rifle pointed at him at any time?
A: Yes, I believe I did.
Q: Would you find it for me in your statement, please?
A: I don't think I wrote it down in the statement.
Q: Did you tell him that?
A: I believe I did, yeah.
Q: You believe you did but you are not sure?
A: Well, I'm not sure about Mr. Woods. I think I was talking to Mr. Letsinger.
Q: It doesn't make any difference what you told anyone verbally, you didn't write it down in your handwriting at the time they asked you to give them the statement?
A: Yeah, this is my handwriting.

Q: That's right. You didn't say in your handwriting that the defendant told you that a rifle had been pointed at his head?
A: No, I was --
Q: You didn't tell them that, did you?
A: No, I was going to get into it but I didn't because like I said before, I heard the other boy stating what he said and then — in the next room.
Q: That's what caused you not to do it?
A: Sure.
Q: That's what caused you not to tell him about the pistol also?
A: I suppose so.

Barrera had drawn some blood. It takes a special kind of person to hold up under the onslaught of a really good cross-examiner. A cocky attitude and jaunty answers are meat for the monster. Barrera worked him over for a while longer, finding contradictions here and evasions there. He ran John through a list of things Martin had not told him, things Martin had conveniently left out. By the time Barrera let him go, John was chastened. It was hard to tell if Barrera had succeeded in demolishing his credibility before the jury.

Scott moved in to bind up the wounds:

Q: Mr. Pannell. What was it you overheard that caused you to stop writing that statement?
A: Andy, I don't even know his last name, was in the next room where I was making my statement. The sheriff's office is an old hospital. The walls are made out of tile or something. Andy was telling about the murder. I was catching parts of the conversation while I was writing. He was telling about the details . . . I heard whoever was in there questioning him, ask, did Martin know what was going on. Andy said, "No." He said, "He didn't know what we was going to do." And, he said he freaked out or flipped out or something when we did it. That is what he said.
Q: Did you hear anything about Andy's willingness?
Mr. Barrera: We're going to object to counsel leading him. First of all, this is his witness and he's calling for hearsay. Now, he made this statement before, but for him to further develop any of this by leading questions suggesting about what he heard is improper.
The Court: I think Mr. Stehling agrees with you. He is nodding his head up and down.
Q: What else did you hear Andy say?

A: Just about the murder. He said something about a security light coming on, then he said that Tommy had shot the man. What he was saying was what Martin had told me. So, I had no reason to doubt Martin's word, because he was corroborating what Martin had already told me. So, I made the statement real, real brief because I figured this was not going to take very damn long. You know, I said Martin is going to be coming home because this is it. The next thing I knew he is charged with capital murder.

After a few more questions about Martin's character Scott passed the witness back to Barrera for more cross-examination:

Q: Mr. Pannell, do you know this gentleman over here to my right, and for the record that is Mr. Jay Adams. Do you know him?
A: Yes, sir.
Q: Did you see him in the room with this fellow you heard talking and you heard say these things?
A: Yes, sir.
Q: Was he in the room taking that statement?
A: Yes, sir.
Q: Okay.

When Barrera finished, John stepped down. Judge Thurmond called for a fifteen minute recess. Scott called Darwin over to the defense side of the table for a hasty conference with Martin. If Martin were going to testify on his own behalf, now was the time.

Judge Thurmond reconvened the court and nodded toward Scott.

"The defense rests," he announced.

That evening was busy back at the Best Western Hotel and Truck Stop. After a hasty meal, Scott dispatched one of his assistants to pick up Judge Thurmond's Charge of the Court. This lists the instructions a judge gives to the jury regarding the charges against the defendant and the principles of law involved. The prosecution and the defense are given copies beforehand and allowed to make motions for changes in the wording. The district attorney, Tom Lee in this case, would read and explain the charge as part of his final summation to the jury.

It is an important document. In it, the judge frames the argument, condenses the case for and against the defendant and limits what the jury can consider. Lately there has been a movement afoot which challenges this long held practice. It contends that the power of the jury has slowly been eroded. That in the early days of the Republic, juries could also decide matters of law.

The principle is called jury nullification. It means a jury could decide a law was a bad law and refuse to convict. Many northern juries in the 1850s did just that with cases involving the Fugitive Slave Act. This principle asserts a jury is sovereign and even supersedes the legislature. Jury nullification was well recognized by the founding fathers and even U.S. Supreme Court Chief Justice Oliver Wendell Holmes. It has never been repealed or legislated against.

However, in 1897 the Supreme Court ruled that judges need not tell jurors about these powers. Today most judges go one step further. They extract an oath from each juror that they will limit themselves to deciding matters of fact only, and "are bound to receive the law from the court which is given to them and they must be governed by it."

Most jurors do not understand just what they are actually swearing to or the oath's implications. They just figure it is some ritual associated with jury duty. The oath is one of the best kept secrets in jurisprudence. Any attorney who attempts to tell jurors about the power of nullification during a trial is usually subject to immediate charges of contempt.

In a way, Scott was going to have to ask the jury to indulge in a bit of nullification. Of course, he would do it without openly asking them. Martin had virtually convicted himself when he signed his second statement. Although he claimed he thought Tommy was joking when he spoke about killing Edmund James, it was a slender thread to support a "not guilty" verdict.

John's testimony helped; no doubt about it. Jennifer and Carolyn Sue's testimonies helped because they had confirmed no one took Tommy's threats seriously. But, were these testimonies enough for reasonable doubt?

The jurors could easily say among themselves, "Is this kid stupid or what? He must have known something was up. After all, they had decided to commit a felony and burglarize the place if Mr. James was not there. Tommy clearly told Martin what he planned to do. Martin said so in his own statement. Martin had to know murder or violence was, at least, a possibility. Andy had claimed Martin told them to 'knock him out' if he did not play his part properly. And, for that matter, when they went back the second time, Martin voluntarily put tape on his shoes. We like this kid. We feel real sorry for him but he is guilty under the law."

The jury had other options and could convict Martin of lesser charges as outlined in Judge Thurmond's Preliminary Instructions which ran as follows:

> 1. Under the instructions in this charge you are to first consider if the Defendant is guilty of the charge in Count 1, Paragraph 1 of the indictment wherein he is charged with capital murder in the course of attempting to commit and committing robbery. And consider, if he is guilty of the charge in Count 1, Paragraph 2 of the indictment wherein he is charged with capital murder in the course of attempting to commit and committing burglary of a habitation . . .
> 2. If you have acquitted the Defendant of capital murder as charged in Count 1 of the indictment, then you will next consider if the Defendant is guilty of the lesser included offense of murder with intent to cause death.
> 3. The charge . . . of murder with intent to cause serious bodily injury is withdrawn . . .
> 4. If you have acquitted the Defendant of capital murder, and of the included offense of murder with intent to cause death. You will consider if the Defendant is guilty of the charge in Count 3 of the indictment, criminal conspiracy to commit the offense of capital murder . . .

The Charge of the Court continued with a series of definitions. For example, under Texas law, ". . . a person commits the offense of murder when he intentionally causes the death of an individual. He commits capital murder when such person intentionally commits the murder in the course of committing or attempting to commit robbery or burglary of a habitation."

If, from the evidence, the jury found beyond a reasonable doubt, that Martin voluntarily entered a conspiracy with Tommy and Andy to rob Edmund James or burglarize his habitation, and, in the course of either of these felonies when Tommy and Andy shot Edmund, that Martin voluntarily aided or acted with them, or if the jury found that the shooting of Edmund "should have been anticipated by the Defendant," then the jury "will" find Martin guilty of capital murder as charged.

The charge instructed the jury that in order to convict Martin they would have to conclude the trio were not only engaged in a felony, but also that Tommy and Andy "intended to kill Edmund James when he was shot." If that were so and Martin knew it beforehand, then he was guilty also. The mere presence of Martin at the scene is not enough to convict him.

If the jury came to believe beyond a reasonable doubt that Martin intended "to promote or assist the commission of the offense of murder . . . of Edmund James" and that he "voluntarily did aid and assist Tommy Eiland and/or Andrew Milam in the commission of said offense" or "that the Defendant Martin Sweeten did then and there use a flashlight and position Edmund James to be so shot by Tommy Eiland and/or Andrew Milam . . . then you will find the Defendant Martin Sweeten guilty of murder with intent to cause death and not capital murder."

In case the jury decided beyond a reasonable doubt that Martin was guilty of neither capital murder or murder with intent to cause death, or had a reasonable doubt thereof, then they must resolve the doubt in the Defendant's favor and convict him of the lesser offense.

Finally, the jury had to decide if Martin had entered a criminal conspiracy with Tommy and Andy: "A person commits the offense of criminal conspiracy if, with intent that a felony be committed, he agrees with one or more persons that they or one or more of them engage in a conduct that would constitute the offense, and he or one or more of them performs an overt act in the pursuance of the agreement."

The affirmative defense to the charge of conspiracy to commit capital murder is that Martin was "compelled to do so by the threat of imminent death or serious bodily injury to himself or another . . ." However the burden of proof for such a defense is, by law, on the defendant. This is a reversal of the usual presumption of innocence. He must prove it by a preponderance of the evidence, which means "the greater weight and degree of the credible evidence in the case."

These are just excerpts of the entire charge to the jury. The entire document consists of instructions and legal definitions written in legalese English. The jury is merely handed copies of the charge and must figure out the implications on their own. The usual practice is for the judge to offer as little verbal assistance as possible. This is supposed to prevent the judge from influencing the jurors' decisions. In paractice, jurors have to pick their way through complicated instructions, sometimes with minimal understanding.

On Friday morning, May 14, 1993, in the District Court of Crockett County, Texas, 112th Judicial District, Thomas Lee began his summation of the case to the jury. Lee would be followed by Scott Stehling for the Defendant and finally Roy Barrera, Sr. would address the jury for the prosecution. In Texas the last word is given to the state.

Tom Lee laid out the task of the jury according to the Charge of the Court. The jury is the finder of fact. It must weigh the credibility of the evidence, a difficult task even in the clearest of cases. The jury must decide which facts are important and which are unimportant. It must decide which rules of evidence apply in this case. It must weigh the two types of evidence presented in this case, testimonial and demonstrative. The jury must follow every item and instruction found in the charge.

Lee pointed out that if Martin Sweeten was merely present at the scene of the murder, that would not constitute guilt. If Martin had aided the killers or even attempted to aid them in the commission of the crime, that was a different story. Had Martin been in a culpable mental state when he was there? Did he participate knowingly, recklessly and with intent? Had he assisted Tommy and Andy, promoted the crime, and helped plan it?

The jury had to "plug in" the law to the facts as they believed them to be in this case. The jury had to consider the charge of capital murder first. The rest would follow naturally from that decision. Martin could claim duress as a positive defense to the charges against him. However, if the jury found he had knowingly placed himself in a dangerous situation, then he could not claim duress.

Finally the jury should consider the testimony given by witnesses for the state: witnesses that a crime had occurred, witnesses as to the crime scene, the expert witnesses' testimonies on the physical evidence, and the witnesses who had pieced together or linked the evidence of events. Finally, the jury should consider the defendant's own formal statements. These elements would help the jury to decide the central question: What was Martin David Sweeten's role in the murder of Edmund James?

Scott rose to present the summation for the defense. He began with his "Rumpole of the Bailey" speech praising the jury system, and invoking our ancient rights outlined in the Magna Carta.

"It is the best chance any citizen has to be sure his rights are protected," he reminded them.

He went on to praise the citizens of Crockett County and a jury with "a real rancher, a housewife, a gas plant operator, an insurance agent, a mechanic, a retailer . . . a perfect cross section of the county. Somehow, you twelve have been brought together in order to find the truth of this case. How can a jury take in all of the details? The collective consciousness of all twelve of you will remember everything you have heard during this trial.

"Martin has spent 401 days in jail," he continued. "It is time to evaluate the evidence and apply the law. The charge runs thirteen pages, which is a lot of legal language. But in fact there are just three charges the State is trying to prove by evidence beyond a reasonable doubt. First, let's consider the charge of murder, the one different from capital murder. I mean murder with intent to cause death . . . You know from the evidence Martin did not help anyone kill Edmund James. Martin was the guy who thought deer were too pretty to shoot and would cover his eyes when one was shot. This charge, a lesser and included charge, is not open to you based on the evidence and testimony."

In a similar vein, Scott attacked the charge of conspiracy to commit capital murder. Finally, he turned to the charge of capital murder. To convict Martin, the jurors would have to believe that all three agreed to burglarize and rob Edmund James -- that they had conspired together.

Scott argued it was not so, "They never agreed to go out and rob and harm him at the same time."

The only evidence of burglary was evidence from previous burglaries. Martin's first statement, which Scott told the jury was in some respects the most truthful, said Martin went along to "get a job." He reminded them this was what Martin had told Deputy

Adams. He reminded the jury of John Pannell's dramatic testimony in which Andy himself had said Martin had not known what was planned.

"Let's say," Scott continued, "that the second statement was voluntary, given without pressure or persuasion. Let's give it all the credit in the world. Even there, Martin said he thought Tommy was joking about killing somebody. Martin said he just wanted to get a job from Edmund James. Having gotten a job, he convinced the others to leave. It was only then the others forced Martin to go back with them. So if it were a conspiracy to do anything, it was a conspiracy to get jobs, not to burglarize . . ."

Scott reminded the jurors of the defense's photographs of the ranch. There was plenty to burglarize there. It was a "teenager's dream" with rooms, storerooms and a garage filled with portable goodies. Yet all these boys took was a few dollars, two bottles of liquor, a pistol and a watch. Some burglars, some plan.

He took the jurors back to Patricia Butt's testimony regarding the night before the murder when the trio allegedly burglarized some shacks. She had given them her .22 rifle that evening. No one had been killed that night, so it was perfectly reasonable for Martin to suspect nothing when he saw Tommy with a rifle on the night of the murder.

Patricia testified she had heard Tommy threaten to kill his mother, father, and grandmother. She did not believe him. Carolyn Sue's mother testified she had heard Tommy threaten to "kill anyone" who came near Carolyn Sue. She did not believe him. Carolyn Sue and Jennifer Noblett had heard similar threats from Tommy. They did not believe him. How is it that these people, who knew Tommy far more intimately than Martin, did not believe him, yet Martin is held criminally responsible for disregarding Tommy's boastful threats?

"This was Tommy's deal," Scott explained. "He set it up. Tommy had charisma — it worked on adults as well as with kids. Tommy was sick. Tommy was a killer. He went out there with the intention of killing someone, not to burglarize. He just used Martin . . ."

Scott returned to his favorite theme, the statements and the police methods involved. Martin's first statement was remarkably like Andrew Milam's statement. That is because it was closest to the truth. In any interrogation, certain procedures must be followed. They were not in this case. At the ranch, Jay Adams dissuades Martin and his father from getting a lawyer by calling Martin a "witness" under protective custody. Time and again Martin is told he doesn't need a lawyer.

Later in the sheriff's office, deputies told Martin he would probably be sent to "boot camp" or that he probably would get "probation." They interrogated Martin for much longer than the other two. They kept him awake all night. They told Martin he was "working for the DA." They did not magistrate Martin until the next day at eleven A.M. Yet, Judge Neville Smart was right there the night before, right at hand. After giving his second statement, in the wee hours of the morning, Martin was told "by the way, you are under arrest for murder."

"I think you can easily evaluate the testimony of Mike Lowrie, Jay Adams, and Don Letsinger for yourselves," Scott told the jury. " Isn't it funny that about four A.M. Don Letsinger said to Martin and his family 'Hold on a minute, Martin may be able to go home?' Letsinger testified to us that, 'I was fixing to let him go.' The others were charged with capital murder, and the sheriff told us, 'I thought about letting him go.' And, 'thought I might let Martin go home by that time . . .'

"Isn't that funny, ladies and gentlemen. Remember 'reasonable doubt.' Remember the sheriff telling Darwin and his family, 'I think I'll let you take him home, now.' Who had reasonable doubts then?"

Scott added one more appeal to down home sensibilities. He quoted the famous motto attributed to Davy Crockett and carved on the memorial in the park outside : "Be sure you are right, then go ahead." The great frontiersman knew all about jury nullification. He thanked the jury and sat down.

Roy Barrera rose to finish for the prosecution. He conducted an entirely proper summation. He went over each point of the defenses's case. Like a scientist investigating an unknown phenomena, he held each assertion up for the jury's inspection. He displayed for all to see the weaknesses of Martin's case. He proposed alternate, darker explanations of the facts. He presented "what really happened." He did all of these things but in a particularly brilliant fashion. He told it as a story. He was like a beloved grandfather or favorite uncle telling a thrilling, enthralling story. He wove magic. Everyone in the courtroom was riveted. It was pure genius, a marvellous performance.

As he reached for each fact, each assertion, he would weave it into the story. He made them live. Each part of the story fitted neatly and rationally. Each fact took its place on Barrera's stage, bowed and played its role. It was devastating. As Barrera went on, the defense's case began to look pale and contrived.

Barrera reached the climax, his account of the murder. Everyone in the courtroom was fascinated. Everyone was avidly following the story. Then — the fire siren next door shrieked an alarm. No one could hear a word as the massive siren wiped out any possibility of speech. Like a popped balloon Barrera's magic story burst and was gone. Everyone sat numbed as the siren screeched on and on. It seemed like forever.

The siren finally wound down. Barrera patiently began to retell the story, to rebuild the momentum, to recast the spell. The siren shrieked on again. When silence was restored, Barrera returned to his story. The siren blasted on again.

Three times the siren interrupted Barrera's summation. Of course, there was a perfectly reasonable explanation. Major grass fires had broken out in the county. The weather had been dry for weeks, and fires were becoming a serious problem. The volunteer firemen had to be summoned. But the defense knew the real reason. Darwin's prayer groups had struck.

It was early afternoon when the judge turned the case over to the jury. There had been no lunch break, so everyone wandered out with food in mind. Some headed for restaurants, but the James clan gathered around a picnic table on the south side of the park. Darwin's clan took a table at the northern end.

It was a simple lunch: sandwiches, potato salad, soft drinks, and some store bought cookies. Before the eating began, Darwin had everyone, including Scott and Julia, join hands for a prayer. His teenaged cousin, Diane, led them. She was great. She could have held her own with any slick television evangelist. Invoking the Lord and his mercy, asking for forgiveness and reconciliation, Diane exhorted the faithful. It was a down-home, Pentecostal, Bible-believing, faith-affirming, Yahoo! dunk-me-in-the-river prayer. Afterwards there were no long faces at the table. Every one of the Sweeten clan believed Martin was going to be let free. Well, almost everyone. One of Darwin's brothers voiced his doubt in a quiet voice to one of Scott's assistants who, in turn, quietly agreed it would be a close run thing.

The crowd began to disperse. Plans were made for the evening. Scott's wife, Julia, and his parents had come out to hear his summation and perhaps the verdict. Friends of Scott's assistants had driven out. Everyone had to know how it would end.

The jury could easily be out until late that evening or tomorrow. No one wanted a quick verdict. That would have been too scary. It usually meant all or nothing. The clock showed well after three o'clock. Darwin fell into an intense conversation with a spectator about the value of old Studebaker automobiles. The bailiff stepped out of the courthouse and announced the jury was back. They had deliberated for almost three hours, not very long for a capital murder charge.

When the courtroom settled, Judge Thurmond gavelled the trial to order. He called for the jury. He sternly warned the defense and the audience that he would tolerate no loud demonstrations of emotion when the verdict was read. There would be no cries of despair.

"Have you reached a verdict," he asked the foreman, a young rancher.

"Yes, your honor."

Judge Thurmond asked the foreman to hand the bailiff the verdict sheet. The bailiff took the form and handed it up to Judge Thurmond. He read it quickly and sent it back to the foreman.

"What is your verdict?" he asked tersely.

"Not guilty. Not guilty on all counts, Your Honor."

The trial of Martin Sweeten was over.

"The defendant is acquitted of all charges and released from custody. The jury is excused, with the thanks of the court."

After 401 days of imprisonment Martin was free. He rose from the desk, smiled and embraced his mother and father. He walked down the center aisle of the courtroom, his sister and her children followed. He descended the creaky stairway, and walked across the street into the deeply green park.

Epilogue

A FEW MINUTES AFTER THE TRIAL, Martin left Ozona. He went to stay with relatives in an undisclosed location out of the state. He eventually returned to Camp Wood to work with his father. His goal was still to raise enough money to get into nursing school. He never attained that goal. He lived in West Texas for a while working for a major retail chain. Martin recently moved to East Texas and is engaged to be married.

Darwin and Sue continue to live in Camp Wood. Darwin works at several enterprises to make his living. Sue is still a nurse caring for the elderly. Darwin sold the little white Toyota as quickly as possible.

Patricia Butts still lives in her old house trailer. Blanca Flores has married her son James. Her granddaughter recently had a baby and Patricia devotes her full time caring for the child. The added expense forced her to cancel her telephone service.

Jennifer and Carolyn Sue attend college. Elton Baxter is still constable of Camp Wood, Real County. Buck Pruitt left law enforcement, married and is now a rancher.

John Pannell still lives near Camp Wood. His younger son

Jeff, lives at home. He is now in his last year of high school. John says he rarely sees Darwin.

"It's okay. It is like when you owe someone a debt that can never be repaid. What can you say?" he explained. John also says he never crosses the line into Edwards County.

Tommy Eiland is presently held in the Ferguson Unit of the Texas Department of Corrections in Midway, Texas. He is taking a typing course. There is no projected release date on his record, and he will not be eligible for a parole hearing until March 8, 2027. Andy is in the McConnell unit in Beeville, Texas. It is a new prison built on an old Air Force base. His also has no projected release date and is not eligible for a parole hearing until March 8, 2027.

Edmund's family and friends still grieve his untimely and unnecessary death. He is remembered and loved. People still talk about the case. Some decry the Texas judicial system. Most people involved in the case are glad Tommy and Andy are in jail.

Scott Stehling continues to practice law in Kerrville, Texas. He still has the coffee cup from Pioneer Flour Mills on his desk. Once a month Darwin faithfully comes by his office to pay on his account. Martin's case was Scott's first capital murder trial.

Everyone paid a terrible price for the murder and the subsequent trials. The effects linger. The ripples of evil still travel out but now are smaller and weaker. Someone made an observation about the lighter side saying, "Well, at least the cats of Camp Wood are happier now."

The mysteries of the two dogs and the shell casings were solved but only unofficially. After the trial, a witness came to Scott and on condition of anonymity told him what had happened.

"The answer is really simple," he said. "This is a small town. When something like murder happens everyone wants to get in on the act. Everyone heads for the crime scene. There were a whole bunch of people out there at the ranch that night — more than the deputies will admit to. They were all over the place, including where James's body was. Everyone wanted a look, you see. When the cops got through out there, they just turned off the lights and left. They did not bother leaving a guard at the scene.

"Well, people, being what they are, had been picking up souvenirs. Those shell casings are probably in desk drawers or glove boxes all over the county. People are like that around here," he continued. "I remember when one rancher blew his brains out, committed suicide. One ol' boy around here was out at the scene and picked up a piece of this fella's skull. He carried it around for a year, pulling it out every time he got drunk or wanted to show off. Finally everyone got sick of it and made him bury it. That's what happened here. While all of those cops were off chasing Tommy or questioning Martin, people were picking up those shells. They put them in their pockets and went home. They probably haul them out every once and a while hold them up to the light and say, 'Looky here . . .'"

"It is the same story with the dogs," he explained. "As I understand it some kindhearted neighbor got there either just before or just after the cops did. They called the dogs over and locked them up in the storeroom to keep them safe and out of the way. It was just a neighborly act. You know. The cops just don't want to admit that there was a bunch of people out there interfering with the crime scene and all. It makes them look bad."

The day after the trial ended, a group of Scott's assistants were having lunch in Ozona. At the table next to them were some jurors who told them that it had taken them three hours to figure out how to render "not guilty" verdicts and still abide by Judge Thurmond's instructions. The jurors asked them to deliver a message to Martin.

"Tell him to do something useful with his life," they said.

After the jury announced the verdict and the judge dismissed the defendant, Roy Barrera turned to Scott, held out his hand and said, "You did a great job confusing the jury."

Scott just smiled and shook hands.

The James Ranch houses. In the foreground is the dining and kitchen house, Edmund was shot as he stood by the table at center right.

The Sweeten family: in front Darwin and Sue with Martin in the middle.

Tom Lee, District Attorney for Val Verde County Texas.

Roy Barrera, Judge George M. Thurmond, and Scott Stehling on the steps of the Crockett County Courthouse.

The Crockett County Courthouse as viewed from the town's park.

The view of the surrounding countryside from the balcony of the Best Western Motel.

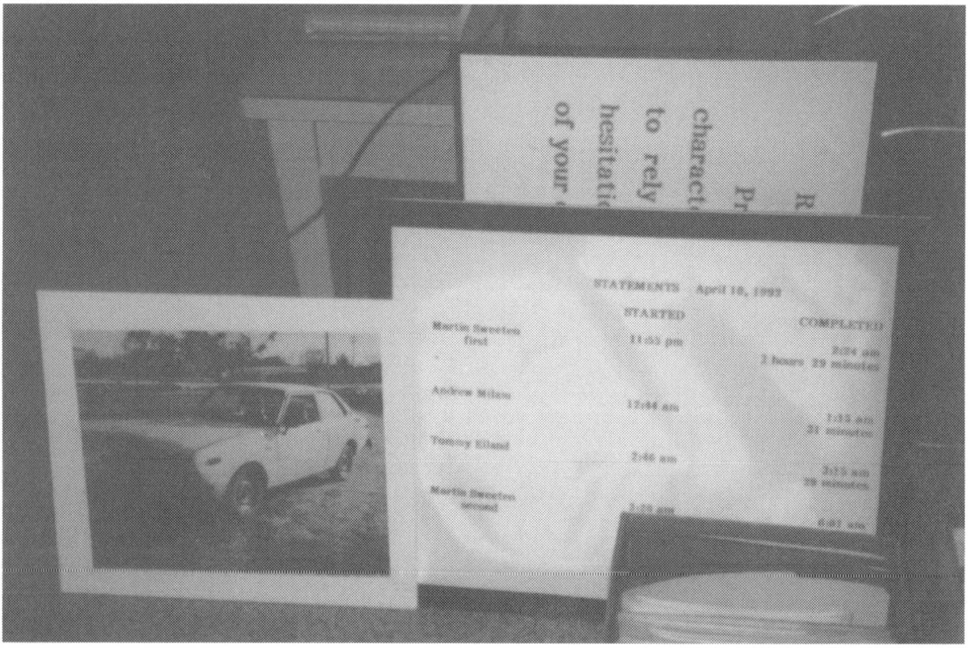

The defense's exhibits.

APPENDIX

These statements are reproduced with the original mistakes and mis-spellings.

Martin David Sweeten's first statement, dated 4/9/92 and given at the Edwards County Sheriff's Office. The statement commenced at 2355 P.M. Don G. Letsinger and Mike Lowrie were the peace officers taking the statement.

On April 8th, 1992, around 4: 00 P.M., I was driving home. As I drove by Tommy Eiland's house, he waited for me to stop. I stopped at his house. Jenifer Noblet was there, as well as Andrew Milam. Jeneifer wanted me to get her kitten from Carolyn Hodges. I didn't have enough gas, so Tommy Eiland and I went to my house. Tommy and I went inside the house. We waited for my dad to get back from Camp Wood, which took approximately 30 minutes.

When he got back, I asked for some gas money. After he gave me five dollars, we went back to the trailer park. I stopped at Andy's house. I then picked up Jenifer Noblet. Andy stayed at this house while Jenifer, Tommy and I went to town and got some gas. From there we went to Carolyn Hodges house and picked up the cat. We stayed there for about an hour. No body was there except for Carolyn. We left the house and went back to Andy's. Jenifer left for her house. I talked to Tommy about getting a job with Don Jackmon. I told him that Don would give me a job, but he wanted me to work during school hours. Tommy then told me about getting a job from Edmond James.

We stayed at Andy's house and talked for a while. Tommy then went over to his house to change his clothes. I stayed in Andy's house. Andy's and Tommy's house were next to each other. I walked over to my car. Tommy came out of his house and went to Andy's house to see if he was ready. When they came out, Tommy came out of the house carrying 2 - .22 cal. rifles. I asked Tommy what the .22's were for. He told me that he was going to trade the rifles to Edmond James because he owed James $200. So then we left.

It was right before dark. I drove everyone in my car. On the way out there we saw a deer. They wanted me to hit the deer with the car. I turned around but could not find the deer. I then turned around and went back toward Edmond James. It was dark before we got there. We pulled up to the drive way, turned off my engine and headlights. James came to the door. He walked outside when we got out of the car. I grabbed the flashlight and all of us walked up to each other outside of the house.

We were talking to him about a job. He said he could give us a job for five dollars an hour and we would start Friday. After the job part was settled, Tommy asked him if he could trade the guns he brought with him for some of the money he owed him. Mr. James said he would take a look at the guns. So Tommy walked over to the car and got the guns. He gave them both to Mr. James.

James said he had no use for the guns. He handed one of them back to Tommy. After he looked over he second gun, he handed it back to Tommy. Tommy said the second gun was Andy's. The first gun had the initials 'JP' something on the stock. Tommy said that Andy owed him some money. That is why Andy's gun was up for sale. James was leaning up against the picnic table. When James looked away, Tommy lifted the rifle and shot James one or two times. He fell forward on his face.

Tommy said, "Get him, Andy."

Andy shot him five or six times in the head and in the back. The flashlight I was holding was not on. Then Andy and Tommy started laughing. I stood there shocked. Tommy then told me that I was an accomplice to murder and that had better cooperate or I would get into a lot of trouble. He went to my car and got his jacket and brought out two pairs of gloves. He then gave one pair to Andy. While Andy put on his gloves, Tommy held on to the rifle. When Andy put them on, Tommy then put on his gloves and Andy held his rifle in his hands.

Tommy said, "Let's go into the house."

I'm trying to cooperate with them because I was scared. We went into the house and one of them stayed with me at all times. We went into the same door that James came out of. Tommy told me to go with Andy to the other house that had an upstairs. Andy found some money on a window shelf of the upstairs. He then told me to open up my jacket, mostly change. I remember 3 twenty dollar bills. Andy found a .357 pistol on a shelf next to the bed. We then went out. Andy and

Tommy went back inside the house part where James came out from and took two bottles of alcohol.

We went to my car. Tommy took the keys out of the ignition and opened the trunk. He put his rifle in the trunk. Andy got in the car with his rifle. Tommy got into the car with the .357. He handed the keys to me. We left and went to Camp Wood. On the way to Camp Wood, they kept reminding me that they were not scared to kill somebody.

Tommy said that they needed an alibi. Andy seemed scared of being caught. Tommy planned that the alibi was that that all of us were going to be at the movies in Uvalde. We went to the Get and go and put ten dollars in my car.They bought a few things at the store and went to the phone. I talked to my dad on the phone and Tommy was talking to Carolyn. Andy was filling up the car. Both mentioned on the way that they would kill anybody that talked.

We stopped at 19 mile and Andy put the rifle in the trunk. Then the pistol was put in the trunk. We then went to the movie theater in Uvalde. The movie was over by the time we got there. We then went to Whataburger. We cruised Uvalde. Dan Caldwel saw me in Uvalde. Andy drove us home to Tommy's house in Camp Wood. I stayed the night at Tommy's house. the next day we all went to school. Tommy stayed very close to me at school. I asked Jeff Pannell to ride home with me so I could get away from Tommy.

I finally got the situation where I took Jeff Pannell home by our selves. When we got to his house, I wanted to talked John Pannell, Jeff Pannell's older brother and me are best friends. I told John and his girlfriend April about the incident. John told me that I needed to get rid of the things in my trunk. All that was in my trunk was the gloves and alcohol. We stashed them at some cattle guard that I don't remember where. April Guerra is John's girlfriend and was with us. We took her back to her house after we stashed the goods. We then went to John's house and told his dad. He then got a hold of Alton Baxter. Alton came and got me at John's. MDS.

This three page statement was completed at 0244 A.M., the 10th day of April 1992 with O. W. Woods and Don G. Letsinger as witnesses.

* * * * * * *

Martin David Sweeten's second statement, dated 4/10/92 and given at Edwards County Sheriff's Office. The statement commenced at 0320 A.M. Mike Lowrie and Don Letsinger were the peace officers taking the statement.

This statement is a revision of the first statement given of the first, three page statement, on 4-9-92, 11:55 hrs. Everything in the first statement is true up to the point where we picked up the cat. I talked to both Tommy and Andy about the job with Don Jackmon while we were at Andy's house. Tommy said we needed more money to go to the party in Mexico. It was a high school party with people from Camp Wood.

Before all this, we had already done two burglaries, one at the Double D rental in Camp Wood. We took a TV, a briefcase (that was dumped in the river), a homemade baseball club and a tape case. The TV is in my room. The tape case is either in the trunk of my car or with the other items from the murder at the cattle guard. The second burglary was at Josh Cox's in Camp Wood Hills. We took 2 blankets. One is in my room, on my bed. The other blanket is at Tommy Eilands house. It is a plad type with mainly red. Along with the things that we put in the blankets were a pair of binoculars, 2 fire extinguishers, an inflatable raft with pump . . . a black flashlight, a machety, a cordless screwdriver and drill, canned goods (food), an ice pick and a butcher knife. All of those things are stored in Andy's closet in pillow cases. All of Josh Cox's trailers that we broke into were hunting cabins.

At school, Tommy and I were joking around about killing Edmond James. Tommy said, "I'm thinking about killing Edmond James." I just laughed because I thought that he was kidding around. Tommy told me further on, that when he asked to borrow some money, James just reached in his pocket and pulled out $200. Tommy then told me that he knew where James's safe was and he knew how to break into safes. He said, "All safes have hinges."

Later after school, I went to talk to Don Jackmon about the job. After our talk, I was going home when Tommy waved me over at his house. Tommy and Andy were there. They were talking about killing James. They were both psyched up about the whole possibility of killing him. I told Tommy and Andy, "All I wanted to do is go and try to get a job from James." After all all we needed was money. We didn't need to kill anybody. Andy got some .22 shells from Jinks and Tommy got his gun from John Paul with John Paul's permission and without John's parents. The other gun came from Jinks. Andy told her that we were going to go coon hunting.

Tommy said, "Let's do it if we are going to do it."

We ended up going to Edmond James's place. One the way out there we passed a blue van that was parked on the road. The time was about 6:00 or 7:00 P.M. It was not close to dark and the sun had not began to set. We discussed several different plans on the way out there. When we arrived at James', we talked to him about the job and he said he would give it to us. During this time we were talking and standing around around the car. Tommy asked Mr. James if he would take the .22s for some of the money that he owed him. He handed both the guns to James.

James said he had no use for the guns and handed them back to Tommy. Tommy handed one of the guns to Andy. He tells James that Andy owes him money. That was the reason that the gun was up for grabs. They all talked for a while. Tommy and Andy were holding the guns, pointed toward James but not in a threatening manor. I saw Andy take his gun off safety. I tried to keep the situation down. I walked around to the driver's side of the car, opened the door and said, "Come on guys, Lets go."

I was scared that they both were going to do it and I was trying to leave. Andy and Tommy both got in the car and we left. On the way out they went gun crazy. Andy was sitting in the back seat and pointed his rifle at my head. Tommy grabbed the wheel and I asked why. He told me just in case that Andy killed me. On the way out Cedar Road, Tommy told me to pull over at this deserted house. He told me that we would wait there until dark, and when dark came we would go back and kill him.

I said, "If you were going to kill him, I wished you would have done it then."

I actually had no intention of killing him or even coming back. Tommy said, "No, lets turn around and kill him now. "

Andy said, "Lets wait until dark, I don't feel right killing someone on broad daylight."

Tommy wanted me to go and cut doughnuts in a nearby field so James would come out and they could shoot him. I refused. Tommy then said that him and Andy would go up to James's house when it got dark and shoot James. He wanted me to then drive up to the house when I heard the shots and pick them up. We took off and headed toward town. I told them we needed and alibi and our plan was to call people and inform them that we were going to the movies in Uvalde.

We road hunted on the way out Cedar Creek road. Tommy did shoot and wound one deer. we went into town and made our phone calls. During this time I was looking for a chance to get out of the situation. We taped up the bottom of our shoes so we wouldn't leave any foot prints. Then we went back to James's.

I keep two flashlights and two pars of gloves on the floorboard from the burglaries that we had done. Our plan was for me to blind James with the flashlight while Tommy and Andy shot him. When we pulled up to the house, I cut off the engine and turned off the lights.

We got out and met James at the picnic table. My cue was when Tommy mentioned "flashlight." I was supposed to turn it on and blind James. We were asking him to about hunting coons that night. James was going to let us go. When my cue came, I didn't turn on the flashlight. Later on I turned on the flashlight toward the ground, so not to blind James. I could tell by the look that Tommy had, he was going to go through with the plan.

I started slowly easing off toward the car. When I was right behind Tommy, James glanced away and Tommy shot him in the head. I think twice. James fell straight down on his face. James was leaning up against the picnic table when the shots began. I stood there shocked. Tommy told me to cut his throat and handed me his knife. I told him no and Tommy backed off. Everything that we took is included in the first statement with the exception of the watch in James's bedroom. It was a Seiko. Everything following the incident is accurately stated in the first statement.

This three page statement was completed at 0601 A.M., the 10th day of April 1992 with Don G. Letsinger and Jay Adams as witnesses.